❂ ❂ ❂ ❂ ❂ ❂ ❂

The exciting saga of The Dreaming Dark begun in *The City of Towers* continues as the heroes embark on a desperate adventure to save one of their own. Their one hope for salvation lies across the Thunder Sea on the dark continent of Xen'drik . . .

. . . The Shattered Land!

# THE
# DREAMING DARK

Book 1
## CITY OF TOWERS

Book 2
## THE SHATTERED LAND

Book 3
## THE GATES OF NIGHT
December 2006

EBERRON

# THE SHATTERED LAND

## THE
## DREAMING DARK
### BOOK 2

## KEITH BAKER

Wizards
OF THE COAST
™

# THE SHATTERED LAND

Cover art by Mark Zug
First Printing: February 2006
Library of Congress Catalog Card Number: 2004116924

9 8 7 6 5 4 3 2 1

ISBN-10: 0-7869-3821-8
ISBN-13: 978-0-7869-3821-6
620-95014740-001-EN

U.S., CANADA,                          EUROPEAN HEADQUARTERS
ASIA, PACIFIC, & LATIN AMERICA                     Hasbro UK Ltd
Wizards of the Coast, Inc                           Caswell Way
P.O. Box 707                           Newport, Gwent NP9 0YH
Renton, WA 98057-0707                            GREAT BRITAIN
+1-800-324-6496                   Save this address for your records.

Visit our web site at www.wizards.com

# DEDICATION

*To everyone who has
helped to make the dream
of Eberron into reality.*

*And to Patricia Baker,
who has helped me to shape
my stories and dreams since
the day I was born.*

*—KB*

**D**aine dove across the makeshift barricade, but the enemy was right behind him. He caught a glimpse of the warforged soldier as it hurtled over the wall; in the firelight it was a nightmare of steel and sharp edges. Even as it landed, it lashed out with an elongated forearm covered with razor-sharp spikes.

Daine could barely remember the start of the battle. It might have been hours since the army of steel soldiers came bursting out of the night, tearing into the Cyran camp. The troop had been taken by surprise, and the butchery was all too fresh in Daine's mind. It was this memory that gave him the strength to keep fighting, to overcome exhaustion and the pain of a dozen cuts and bruises. The reason for the attack was a mystery—and Daine wasn't going to let the rest of his troop fall to this unknown foe.

Exhausted as he was, Daine had a lifetime of training to fall back on. The warforged was just a shadow in the darkness, and Daine let the image fall away. As the spiked limb flew toward his head, he remembered his days on the drilling fields in Metrol, duel after duel after duel. He could hear his grandfather barking instructions as he spun toward his foe and lashed out with his longsword, blocking the warforged's clublike arm with all the force he could muster. *Strength versus strength, speed versus speed.* His forearm ached from the impact, but he forced himself to move. *Close the distance, use the space!* Pushing forward and twisting his blade, Daine held the 'forged's arm in place as he stepped in close and thrust with his dagger. The adamantine blade slid into the gap in the 'forged's armor where a human would keep his stomach, and Daine smiled as he cut through leathery cords and felt something shatter.

This triumph was short lived. *Don't expect one blow to end every fight*, his grandfather whispered in his mind . . . too late. Pain lanced through his thigh, and he caught a glimpse of bloody spikes bristling on his enemy's knee. Gritting his teeth, Daine stepped back into his guard position. His left leg burned when he shifted his weight onto it, but the 'forged was staggering as well; Daine's blow had struck true.

The two wounded soldiers studied each other, waiting for an opening.

"You don't have to do this," Daine said. "Lay down your . . . arms, and you might live out the night."

The warforged said nothing. For all Daine knew, it couldn't speak. It was an unusual design, blackened metal studded with long spikes and sharp blades. Blue fire burned in its crystal eyes. It watched Daine and slowly stepped to the right.

Daine grimaced. It might be silent, but it wasn't stupid; it wanted to force Daine to move on his wounded leg until the pain wore him down.

"Who are you fighting for?" he said. "What do they gain from your death?"

Silence. It continued the slow circle.

In truth, Daine hadn't expected the soldier to surrender. Warforged were remarkably loyal to their causes; they were built for battle and knew no other life. But the conversation had served its purpose.

"It's yours, Lei."

Distracted by Daine's words, the warforged hadn't heard the woman approach. She rose up from behind a mound of rubble, a glittering crossbow in her hands. The warforged staggered as a bolt smashed into its back, and its eye-crystals flared with light.

Even as the bolt struck, Daine was flying forward in a swift lunge. He cried out with pain as his foot hit the ground, but his blade slammed into the gap in his enemy's stomach. The warforged collapsed, an inert mass of metal and wood, and Daine fell to one knee.

Lei walked out from behind the rubble. Her coppery hair gleamed in the firelight, and the golden studs on her leather vest gleamed with the same faint radiance that surrounded her crossbow. She knelt by the fallen warforged, examining its body.

"I'm fine," Daine said. "Thanks for asking."

She looked up from the 'forged. Soot and dirt blackened her face, and her eyes were distant; the battle was clearly taking its toll. "Sorry. I . . . these warforged . . ." She gestured vaguely at the fallen soldier. "This doesn't make any sense."

"A lot of things don't make sense. Look, Pierce was taking the longer route back here, but as soon as he returns—"

"He's already back."

*Warforged.* "Fine. Get him, Jholeg, Jani, and Krazhal, and bring them to me."

"Understood." Lei's eyes were back on the warforged. "What's going on?"

"Get the others. I only want to explain this once, and now . . . I've got to see a halfling about this leg."

Daine braced himself against the wall and stood up. The moons were hidden by clouds of black smoke, and the smell of blood and fire filled the air. Out in the valley, the wreckage of the fallen airship still burned amidst the ruined tents. Corpses were intertwined with shattered warforged, but no movement could be seen in the flickering firelight. Glancing around, he saw a few of his soldiers reinforcing the barricade and tending to the injured. Krazhal, the siege engineer, was standing over another warforged, hammering relentlessly on his fallen foe. His eyes were wild, and he struck again and again, heedless of the fact that his victim was already in pieces.

⊙ ⊙ ⊙ ◉ ⊙ ⊙ ⊙

They'd lost most of their supplies in the initial attack, but Jode had done the best he could, assembling a makeshift infirmary in the midst of the camp. Lei arrived with Pierce and the other three soldiers while the halfling healer was examining Daine's leg.

"You're lucky your opponent had such poor aim," Jode said, studying the wound. Daine was wearing a coat of chainmail over leather, but the spikes had punched through both layers to leave a bloody gouge in the thigh. "There may yet be little Daines frolicking on the battlefields of the future."

Daine shook his head. Humor might be Jode's way of dealing with the horror, but it wasn't his. "Just deal with it."

The halfling placed his tiny hand over the wound, and the intricate blue pattern traced across his bald head burst into light. When he lifted his hand, the gash had mended, leaving a dark bruise. "Good enough?"

"It'll have to do." Daine stood, flexing the muscle. Satisfied, he turned to the knot of people who'd come at his call. "None of this makes any sense. Leagues from any settlement, in one of the least hospitable regions of the ridge—this may be contested land, but it holds no strategic value. This should have been a safe path to the gap garrison, yet here we are. Lei, what have you found?"

"I examined the bodies that you recovered, and . . . I'm not sure what to say. They're warforged, certainly, but they don't have the markings of the house, let alone the symbols of any national allegiance."

"Someone else is making 'forged, then?" Krazhal said. The dwarf tugged on one of the remaining tufts of his unruly brown beard; most of it had been singed away in the course of his duties.

Lei shook her head. "That's impossible. Only an heir of House Cannith can activate a creation forge, and only the forges can produce true warforged. Although . . ."

"What?"

"They're so different from one another. We must have seen a hundred different designs—I'm not sure I saw two soldiers that looked alike. The warforged were designed to serve specific roles in battle. There's no need for this level of variation, and the forges were designed to facilitate mass production. Making so many unique designs—it would require a tremendous amount of work and resources. I don't know who could do it—or why they would."

Daine nodded. "House Cannith marks every 'forged it

makes. These are unmarked. It's an enemy that shouldn't exist in a place with no need for an army. You don't send a raiding party in a region with nothing to raid, leaving one simple answer."

"They're guards?" Jode ventured

"That's right. No reason for anyone to be out here—which makes it a great place to set up shop. Pierce and I scouted the field, and there is a tunnel entrance not far from where we set up camp. Pierce?"

Pierce was the only Cyran warforged left in Daine's unit. Over six and a half feet in height, he was a shadow formed from dark mithral and black leather. His voice was like running water, slow and deep. "I located four guard posts, equidistant from the entrance. Two guards per post. Magical weaponry seems likely, but nothing was brought to bear against our forces, so range would be limited."

"We've got less than a third of our troop, but we inflicted heavy losses on our enemy, and the fact that they haven't come out to finish us off suggests that they're stretched to their limits. They've hurt us—now they want us to go away."

"We'd be fools not to!" Krazhal said.

"I think not. We're taking that base."

"Launch an attack? *Are you out of your mind?*"

"*Dolurrh!*" Daine swore, glaring down at Krazhal. "We're soldiers of Cyre! We are all that stands between the innocent and destruction! We've discovered an unknown and deadly enemy in the very borders of our land. We're days from the nearest garrison—and who knows what horrors this place could spawn in that time. We are the shield of Cyre, and we *shall* protect our kingdom! Is that understood?"

Krazhal scowled, but eventually nodded, staring down at his feet.

"Good! Jholeg, you're heading to Casalon, quick as you can. There's a good chance we won't survive this, and the queen needs to know of it."

The goblin scout shrugged. "Yao'lhesh, but wouldn't Pierce be a better choice? He can travel night and day."

"We'll need his skill with the bow. Pierce, you and the bulk of the troops will be protecting Lei."

"Oh?" Lei said. "What will I be doing?"

"Preparing a siege staff, one capable of striking that base from the middle of the valley outside the range of their weapons."

"We don't have a siege staff!"

"You know that: they don't. Make it look good, that's all that matters—they can't take the chance that it's real."

"Ah!" Krazhal said. "So they need to be sending their remnants out and then in you go."

"In *we* go, Krazhal. With Saerath gone, I'll be needing you to get through any barriers."

"Joyous news, that."

"Jode, Krazhal, Donal, Kesht, and I will make up the inside team. The rest of you, keep 'em busy. You're in command, Jani. If you need to retreat, head west up the slopes. If we survive, we'll meet you at the Dorn Peak by tomorrow evening. If not, I want you heading for Casalon at first light. Understood?"

Faces were grim, but this was not the first time they'd faced death together. Jani nodded.

"These metal bastards killed our friends, and who knows how many more will die if we don't put an end to it now. If we die, we die for Cyre. *Soldiers! Destiny awaits!*"

❀ ❀ ❀ ❀ ❀ ❀ ❀

Across the valley, a warforged soldier observed an increase in activity at the Cyran redoubt. It tapped the shoulder of its companion, a tiny scout covered with intricate silver tracery. The scout studied the enemy soldiers, nodded, and scampered out of the concealed post, racing down the tunnel and into the darkness. The masters would know what to do.

# CHAPTER I

**D**aine," Jode said, his voice low and urgent.

Daine's head was pounding, and his left cheek burned; he could feel the slash running from cheekbone to chin. He opened his eyes and tried to make sense of his surroundings. The tunnel was made of worked stone, covered with mold and dirt. A shallow stream of foul water was flowing past his boots. A sewer? Pale light came from behind him, casting long shadows across the approaching insects.

Tens of thousands of insects.

It was a living carpet of vermin—an army of beetles and centipedes that stretched out beyond the pool of light. They moved forward in eerie unison, as if guided by a single thought.

A strong hand gripped Daine's shoulder and slammed him up against the wall, and the tunnel was filled with flame. Daine closed his eyes as the terrible heat scorched his skin, but the fires did not consume him. When he opened his eyes, the tunnel was filled with steaming sewage and the charred husks of the insect horde.

Cold fury filled Daine's heart. His dagger was already in his hand, and as he turned he brought it up to the throat of his unknown assailant. The face was a familiar one: Pierce was standing just behind him, studying him through crystal eyes.

"Dorn's teeth, Pierce! What is this?"

"Daine!"

He turned toward the voice. A slender figure shone in the

7

darkness, a woman wearing a coat of stars. As she stepped forward, he recognized Lei. She held her darkwood staff in one hand, and the golden rivets embedded in her green leather vest glowed with a cold light, the only source of illumination in the tunnel. She put her hand on his cheek, tears glittering in her green eyes.

"Do you know where we are?"

Her touch brought a flood of memories—the horrors of the Mourning, the long journey across Breland, Jode's frail form lying on a mountain of corpses. He recoiled and fell to his knees, retching into the filthy water. Finally he reached up to touch his cheek: the pain was gone, and he ran his fingers over the long scar that had graced his face since the night of the Mourning.

"Daine. Do you know where we are?"

"Sharn. Under Sharn. The sewers beneath High Walls." He rose to his feet. "*Flame!* It happened again?"

"Yes," Lei said. "You told me to stay between you and Pierce and to hold the fire until you gave the order, but when we finally saw the creatures—you just froze." She let her hand slip to his shoulder, and Daine covered it with his own. "What did you see?"

Daine ground his teeth together. This was the fifth blackout in the last ten days, and they were coming ever more frequently. "Keldan Ridge. Again."

"Was there anything new?"

Daine nodded. "Planning an assault on the base Pierce and I discovered. Split forces, regrouping at Dorn Peak if it fell apart."

"Which, apparently, it did."

"Yeah."

Almost three years had passed since they'd found themselves on the Dorn plateau just beyond the sinister mists of the Mournland. Until now, the events of that night had been a complete mystery; none of them could remember after the third wave of the warforged assault. Now those memories were finally coming back—but why, and at what cost? Daine's head still throbbed, and he could barely hold his sword steady; his nerves were frayed to the breaking point, and his restless nights were filled with nightmares.

Daine had always believed that he could handle any problem on his own. As a child of House Deneith, he had been taught to fight his own battles, to stand against any foe. As a captain, he had to keep his own council—to make decisions that could determine the fates of hundreds, but how could he fight his own mind and memories? He squeezed Lei's hand, finding unexpected comfort from her touch.

"Lei—"

"*Danger!*" Pierce's voice rang throughout the tunnel.

Lei spun toward the sound, tearing her hand free and gripping her black staff. Daine raised his sword, cursing inside. *Don't expect one blow to end every fight.*

Moments ago the floor had been covered with the charred remnants of a million insects. Now a new host had arisen from the old, a river of gleaming chitin and quivering antenna rising up from the ashes. The creatures clustered together in a dense, unnatural mass—in the dim light the swarm seemed to have the shape of a dark fist. Pierce was prepared for danger, and he lashed out with his flail as the mass approached him. An instant later the swarm was upon him, and he vanished in the depths of the living cloud.

There was no time to waste. Individually, the insects might be harmless, but a thousand beetles acting in unison could chew through the leather and fibrous cords that lay beneath Pierce's armor plates. Daine had seen the flail pass through the swarm; it was clear that steel would not win this battle, and even if Lei had the energy to produce another flame blast, Pierce would be caught in the burst. Daine swung his sword toward Lei.

"I need fire. Quickly."

Lei had anticipated the request and was already rummaging through her many pouches. She produced a pinch of powdered volcanic glass and a vial of dark oil; she sprinkled these on Daine's blade, her features tight with concentration. Within seconds the blade was wreathed in magical flame, shedding flickering light across the sewer tunnel.

Daine sprinted toward the dark mass surrounding his friend. He was still dizzy; the blackouts always affected his balance, and this was the worst yet, but there was no time to surrender to pain. As he closed on the cloud of buzzing beetles, he kept his blade spinning before him, creating a brilliant wall of flame. Dozens of insects fell to the flaming blade.

Then the horde engulfed him.

The world went dark, lost in a buzzing cloud of insect wings. Centipedes were crawling up his legs, wriggling beneath chainmail and cloth in search of flesh. Flies were swarming about his face. Daine closed his eyes and covered his mouth and nose with his left hand, continuing to spin his blade from side to side. He ground his teeth, ignoring the pain of a hundred stings and bites. As moments passed, the cloud of insects began to thin, and he pulled his hand away from his face to crush the creatures that had crawled beneath his armor. Opening his eyes, he saw that Lei had joined the fray. The upper end of her staff was shrouded in flame, and she was staying on the fringes of the swarm, thrusting the flaming brand into the mass of vermin. A moment later Pierce burst out of the heart of the horde, crushing insects by the handful.

Daine held his ground, lashing out against the diminishing horde. "Pierce, are you hurt?"

"No."

Over the last few months, Pierce had been growing increasingly taciturn. He'd never been especially talkative; he was built to serve as scout and sniper, and silence was in his nature. Still, Daine felt that there was a change—that his warforged friend was retreating into his own mind—but this was hardly the time to explore feelings.

"See if you've got anything in your pack that you can use to make fire."

"Understood."

The next few minutes were a horrible blur, the smell of burning chitin blending with the buzzing of dying insects, but the vermin were no match for the flame, and eventually the last of the insects fell or fled. This time Daine was taking no chances, and they crushed and burnt every last shell. He knelt in the carpet of ash and searched for any signs of movement, but minutes passed and no new insects emerged.

"Lei?"

The artificer produced a small crystal half-sphere from a pouch—a device she'd crafted to sense the presence of magical energies. "There's nothing here, Daine. Whatever power regenerated these creatures earlier, we seem to have broken it. Greykell should be pleased."

Daine stood up, brushing crushed bugs from his byrnie. "Great. That and a crown will buy me a cup of tal."

Lei looked at him. "I seem to recall that helping the people of High Walls was your idea."

"Doesn't mean it was a good one."

Pierce plucked his flail from the ashes. Perhaps he was ignoring the conversation; perhaps he simply had nothing to add. Either way, he kept his silence as they began the long walk back to the surface.

❂ ❂ ❂ ❂ ❂ ❂ ❂

There was little conversation as the group made their way through the sewers. Daine knew that Lei wanted to hear about the blackout, but he didn't feel like talking. Every vision took a toll on his body and spirit. His head was still pounding, and he was exhausted. The memories were far worse than the physical pain: The smell of the battlefield, the sight of friends' corpses scattered across the battlefield, the fear that he might make the wrong decision and lead the rest of his soldiers to their deaths. These visions seized his mind with a terrible strength, blotting out all other thoughts. When he awoke, all recent memories—everything since the war—were pushed away by the horrors of Keldan Ridge. If it continued to get worse, would he lose his memory for good, or might he be trapped in his memories of the past, forced to relive the battle over and over again?

At the same time, he couldn't deny his curiosity. None of them could remember that night. Until four days ago, Daine had completely forgotten the discovery of the warforged base. As frightening as the visions were, there was a part of him that yearned to know more—to finally unlock the secrets of that night, the last night before the Mourning destroyed his homeland.

Eventually the trio emerged onto the streets of High Walls. Once this district had served as a prison camp, housing foreigners and others Breland considered a threat to the security of Sharn. Now that the Treaty of Thronehold had brought an end to the Last War, relations between the people of the Five Nations were a little less strained, but while a Sharn guard might treat a Cyran refugee or Karrn merchant with less suspicion than he would have a year ago, the psychological wounds of a century of war wouldn't vanish overnight, and prejudice still ran deep. High Walls was no longer a prison, but it remained a ghetto. The majority of the inhabitants were refugees from Cyre, people who had lost almost everything in the Mourning. Some were struggling to make a new life in the City of Towers, and these tradesfolk and laborers provided the services that kept the district on its feet. Many refugees were simply looking for a place to waste away, pining for their fallen nation. The other inhabitants were a motley assortment, bound together by misery: beggars, cripples, orphans, and others unwanted in the more prosperous regions of the city. The walls were cracked, cobblestones were missing from the streets, and it rained as often as not. It was depressing, and it could be dangerous, but it was home.

Daine and his companions lived in an old inn. When they'd taken possession, the building had been a shambles; it had served as a home for generations of squatters, and Daine had seen battlefields with less damage. Lei had surprised them all. It was a trivial matter for her cleansing magics to dispel the layers of dirt and excrement covering the walls and floors. Lei was also a fair carpenter, a skill left over from her early training in the schools of the House of Making. Over the last few months she had produced new furniture and acquired a few squares of painted cloth to decorate the common room. Lei had set up a workshop in the wine cellar, and Pierce and Daine even had enough space for combat drills, if they pushed aside the tables. It wasn't a palace by any means, but there was more than enough space for the three of them, and on a rainy night it was comforting to sit by the large hearth.

Tonight Daine went straight up to his room. He shut the heavy door and laid the wooden bar across it then quickly stripped off his armor. While he'd crushed the life from the insects, the remnants of centipedes and beetles were scattered throughout his clothing and mashed against his skin, and a hot bath and fresh clothes were definitely called for. As he stripped off his belt and breeches, he paused, looking at his belt pouch. A memory returned—Jode's voice, calling out and waking him from his stupor. Daine reached into the pouch and pulled out a small bundle of black leather. Carefully, he untied the cord and unwrapped the package, revealing a tiny crystal bottle filled with a luminous blue liquid. He slowly ran a finger across the lead seal, tracing the complex dragonmark embedded on the top.

"Jode?" he whispered.

"There are many things you should be concerned about, but ghosts are not one of them." It was a woman's voice, low and warm—certainly not Lei.

Daine's sword was hanging on the handle of the door, and the door was still barred.

# CHAPTER 2

BRELAND
SHARN
*Lharvion 11, 997 YK*

Daine rolled across the bed, snatching his breeches as he hit the worn mattress. He came up with his back to the wall and quickly covered himself.

The woman was standing in the far corner of the room, half-hidden in the dim light of the evening. She was wrapped in a dark cloak that clung to her slender frame like a shadow, and a deep hood concealed her face. Daine couldn't see any weapons, but in a world of wizards and sorcerers an unarmed man could be the deadliest enemy of all, and Daine crouched, preparing to leap for his sword.

Before he could move, the woman spoke again. Her words were soft but clear; though she was across the room, it seemed as though she was whispering into his ear.

"I have no intention of harming you, Daine. You wouldn't be here today if you hadn't sought my help." Slowly, she freed her hands from her cloak and pulled back her hood. A flood of inky black surrounded perfect features that could have been sculpted from marble, but it was the eyes that he remembered: slightly too large, with just a hint of an elven slant. Her irises were emerald pools that a man could get lost in, and they seemed to draw all the light in the room. "I do hope you remember."

If she was disturbed by Daine's state of undress, she didn't show it. Perhaps that was what pushed him over the edge. Tearing his eyes away from her, Daine walked over to the door and pulled his sword from its sheath, continuing to shield himself with his breeches.

"Lakashtai. I owe you. I'm not one to forget a debt, but let's get something straight. If you want to talk to me, you can knock on the front door like everyone else. You can wait in the common room, but I've had it with surprises. If you've got something to say, I want it now. No riddles or mysteries."

The hint of a smile played about her lips. "My apologies, Daine. I know that it was rude to invade your privacy in this way, but I assumed that this situation called for discretion."

"I'm still not hearing an explanation."

For all his frustration, Daine found it hard to hold onto his anger. Lakashtai's voice was rough music, with a slight accent that was impossible to place; though he'd only seen her once before, Daine felt as if he'd heard that voice as a child. He felt like a fool for raising a weapon against an unarmed woman—worse yet, one who had saved his life.

"You've been having visions, haven't you?"

Daine paused in the midst of returning his sword to its sheath. "What do you know about that?"

"They pose a threat, and I intend to deal with it."

"I don't remember asking for help this time."

"Did I say you had a choice?" Lakashtai's eyes seemed to glow in the darkness.

"It's my mind."

He wasn't sure why he was arguing. The visions had nearly gotten him killed, and they seemed to be getting worse. He found he had a morbid desire to know more about that night—and a strange reluctance to let the kalashtar woman touch his thoughts.

"For now. That could change."

"I haven't seen a crazy changeling in my dreams lately."

Daine turned away for a moment, just long enough to pull on his breeches, but even as he tightened the drawstring he felt a hand on his shoulder, warm breath against his neck. All his training demanded that he react, spin around, push her away, but he found that he simply couldn't move. Her scent was intoxicating, filled with strange spices and hints of unknown lands. Now she was whispering directly into his ear—or were her words entirely in his mind?

"I am sorry, Daine, but it's time to sleep."

And he did.

❂ ❂ ❂ ❂ ❂ ❂ ❂

Daine looked down from the barricade, staring into the Keldan valley. The light of the burning skyship cast long shadows across the bodies of humans and warforged. From the safety of the ridge they looked like broken toys, scattered across the floor by an angry child. There was no sign of enemy activity—no reason to wait. It was time to launch the attack.

Only—something was wrong. It was too quiet. Where were the sounds of his soldiers sharpening blades, praying to the Sovereigns, and going through the dozens of other preparations for battle? He looked back toward the camp, and the answer became clear.

He was alone.

When he'd last seen it, there had been three dozen soldiers clustered around the salvaged tents. Now the campsite was empty, and the only movement was the rustling of torn cloth in time with the faint night wind. Daine slowly drew his sword, only to discover another unpleasant surprise. Instead of Deneith steel, the blade was now formed from glass; one solid blow and it would shatter into a dozen fragments.

As he stared at the fragile blade, memories slowly began to slip into place. The Mourning. Sharn. His uninvited guest.

"Lakashtai!" Daine looked up at the night sky. "What is this? What do you want with me?"

*This is not my doing.*

The voice was right behind him. Daine whirled toward the sound, blade raised. The glass sword might shatter against steel, but it could still pierce soft flesh.

No one was there.

*I did not bring you here, Daine. Your thoughts are under siege, and this is the moment your enemies seek.*

"What enemies?"

*The answer lies here, hidden in your dreams. Search the battlefield, and you will find your foe.*

Daine scowled. "You break into my home, drag me into my

dreams, and now you're telling me what to do. What happens if I don't go along with your plan? What if I just stay here?"

*Feel free. Stay here as long as you like, because you aren't going to wake up until I let you.*

"I see. Fine. I'll play your little game, but I should warn you—after all this is done, you'd best be gone when I wake up."

*There is more to this than you know, Daine. Far more than your mind is at risk. I cannot be bound by your pride.*

Daine moved through the empty camp, prodding at blankets and bundles of arrows with his glass sword. He studied the pallet where Jode had set up the infirmary, and he could still see spots of his own blood staining the moldy cloth. For a moment, he thought he saw the halfling out of the corner of his eye—but the phantom vanished when he turned, if it had ever existed.

"There's nothing here," he said to himself as much as to Lakashtai.

*This is your refuge. It is not the site of the battle.*

"You could have told me that before."

*This is your battle, not mine. I can only observe.*

Cursing meddling kalashtar, Daine walked to the barricade wall and hoisted himself over it. Instinct kept him close to the shadows; perhaps there was something to this hidden enemy after all.

The battlefield was eerily familiar, every detail exactly as he remembered it. He stepped over the bodies of fallen soldiers and shattered warforged, looking for any signs of life, but the field was just as cold as the campsite and far too silent. Even the flames made no sound. As he approached the burning wreckage of the airship, there was no crackle of flame, no aura of heat. If anything, he felt a slight chill, a shivering cold that seemed to pass through leather and cloth. Then he saw it: a dark blot stretched beyond the ruined vessel. From a distance, it had seemed to be the shadow of the shattered ship, but as he moved closer, he could see that it was nothing so natural. It looked like a pit of glittering tar, but he could see that the surface was in constant motion—not bubbling, but shifting, tiny tendrils rising up and collapsing back into the darkness. He moved slowly toward the pool. With every step, the chill increased.

"You've come too late." The voice was distant, as though cast onto the wind. It was female, low, and despite the distortion he could hear the predatory satisfaction. "We have claimed this place, and this is only the beginning."

A figure stepped out from behind the burning wreckage, moving forward into the light. Her cloak was woven of pure shadow, and green eyes gleamed beneath the deep hood.

"Lakashtai?" Daine said. He raised his crystal blade into guard position, warily waiting for the woman to make her next move.

The stranger laughed, musical notes scattered across the dark wind. "Not quite, but you might say that we're sisters." She tossed back her head, and her hood fell back from her face. Like Lakashtai, her delicate features had an inhuman perfection, as if crafted by an artist who sought beauty with no sense of realism or compassion, but her skin was even paler than that of Lakashtai. Her hair was pure white, bound into a thick braid and wound about her neck; it seemed to glow with an inner light. "I am Tashana, little Daine, and your mind is mine to do with as I will."

"We'll see about that."

She wasn't armed, but her confidence suggested unseen powers, and Daine wasn't about to take chances. He walked forward slowly, ready to launch into a swift lunge as soon as he was close enough. Glass or not, he should be able to pierce her skin.

"So we shall."

The pale woman raised a hand. Tendrils of shadow rose from the pool and twined around her arm. The darkness flowed along her skin, and in seconds she was encased in a shield of shadows.

Daine shivered. There was something deeply wrong with this situation, and he felt the fear that only comes in a nightmare—the certain knowledge that as bad as things were, they could get even worse in the blink of an eye, with no limits on what terrors could appear. He fought the urge to turn and flee, running back to the safety of the camp, but he forced himself to seize hold of his emotions, to quiet his fears and hold his ground. If this was only a dream, nothing could truly harm him here.

"It's not *only* a dream."

Even as she spoke, the mists surrounding the woman rippled and reformed, creating a monstrous silhouette. Two muscular arms were tipped with massive pincers, and a dozen smaller tendrils writhed around the headless torso. There were no clear legs on the shadowform, just a long, powerful tail tipped with a fearsome stinger.

Daine had seen worse sights in the Mournland, but the lingering fears remained. Though he tried to silence his doubts, he could feel his heart racing.

*I'm dreaming. None of this is real, not even my fear.*

He brought his blade into the fourth guard position, presenting his right side and placing the point between him and the creature. Pushing away his doubts, he studied the monster. As disturbing as it was, it was a thing of mist and shadow; he could almost see the woman within. *It's a trick, some sort of magic—a disguise, nothing more.*

"Allow me to prove otherwise."

The shadowbeast charged forward. A huge pincer lanced out to crush Daine's head, but he slid to one knee, dropping beneath the blow as he slashed up with his sword.

It was a perfect stroke and would have crippled a creature of flesh and blood, but this was like striking the wind, and the blade passed through the dark form with no effect whatsoever. For a moment, Daine let his guard drop. *It's just a shadow, after all.* Then the creature caught him with a backhanded blow. The pincer slammed into his chest with the force of a sledgehammer, throwing him backwards and onto the ground. He rolled to the side just in time to keep the dark stinger from piercing his heart; instead it caught the edge of his chest, tugging against his chainmail.

Rising to his feet, he did his best to dodge the lashing claws. For a few moments he spun around the monstrosity, backing away and fighting to stay a step ahead of the dark horror. *It can hit me. I can't hurt it.* A memory was lingering on the edge of his thoughts, and even as he ducked beneath another blow, it came to him: Pierce's flail passing harmlessly through the insect swarm. Perhaps physical force wasn't the answer. Heat might not hurt this thing, but light just might.

As the creature swung at him again, Daine stepped to the side and dove forward, rolling beneath the blow and toward the wreckage of the stormship. Dropping his useless sword, he grabbed a chunk of burning wood from the ground.

He flung the spar with all of his might, aiming directly at the creature's chest—right where he guessed the woman's head would be, if she was in fact within the shadowy form. Even as the makeshift torch left his hand, the dark shape shifted, becoming ever more solid; for a moment, the mist became pure obsidian, thick and hard as stone. The wood shattered into a thousand sparks.

The beast shook with laughter, even as it resumed its shadowy state. "You can't win this, Daine," she said, her voice a howling wind. "You cannot begin to comprehend my power. I am the darkness."

"Scary. Scarier if you were just a little bit faster." Despite his bravado, Daine was still fighting the fear that clenched at his stomach and cried in the back of his mind.

"My physical strength is the least of your worries. There are greater weapons at my disposal."

She raised her massive arms, and the ground around Daine erupted in motion. Across the battlefield, corpses were moving: maimed human and broken warforged, all of the fallen were rising to their feet, forming a living wall around Daine.

"Now would be a really good time to wake up," Daine muttered.

He set his back against the keel of the stormship and grabbed another broken spar. He could see familiar faces among the shuffling masses: Lynna carried the morningstar that had shattered her chest, and Cadrian staggered forward despite his broken face. Daine took his guard position and prepared for the first onslaught . . .

And then came the light.

A brilliant luminescence flowed over the field, and the lurching corpses paused to shield their eyes—even those with no eyes left to shield. A glowing figure stepped out of the wreckage next to Daine, a woman wrapped in a hooded cloak that shone with the brilliance of the sun.

"Let him go, Tashana." It was Lakashtai.

Laughter. "You're a fool to come here, child of Kashtai—as great a fool as your ancient mother. We claim this man and his dreams. Leave now, and you can earn a few more days of life."

"He will not stand alone."

The nimbus of light surrounding Lakashtai intensified, and the shadowy figure seemed to wilt in the glow. But even as the monster cringed, tendrils rose from the dark pool, flooding into the beast and restoring its strength. In moments, it was even larger then before—and the aura of light was beginning to fade.

"Then fall together."

A vast wave of darkness rippled forward from the shadowy figure. It slammed into Daine, enveloping him in cold and silence, and he knew no more.

# CHAPTER 3

Lei was working on a wand.

She had a gift for weaving enchantments, creating magical tools to serve the needs of the moment, but these magical infusions were temporary, and the power would quickly fade if it wasn't used. Binding a permanent enchantment into an object was a more difficult task, and one that could take days. The wand itself was a short stick of livewood—an unusual form of lumber that still held the spark of life even after it was severed from its tree. Lei was weaving a healing enchantment, and the livewood was ideally suited to holding this power. For the last few days she had been preparing the wand, bathing it in a series of alchemical liquids and planting the initial paths into the wood. Now it was time to bind it all together. Holding her hands over the livewood, she reached out with her mind. The world receded until all her senses were focused on the wand and the patterns of mystical energy around it. Slowly, painstakingly, she began to pull at these glittering threads, weaving a web of power that would let her channel the lifeforce of the living wood to heal the wounds of another.

It was a difficult task. The slightest slip in concentration could cause the entire pattern to collapse, ruining days of work, yet Lei found that she was never as relaxed as when she was binding the forces of magic. Challenging as it was, it was clean and logical, and it was as natural to her as breathing. Her daily life, on the other hand, was chaotic and painful. Over the last few

22

years, she'd seen battlefield horrors she'd never forget. She'd lost her parents, her home, and her birthright—everything that had given her life meaning. She'd lost the man who was to be her husband, though it wasn't a match she'd asked for. Pierce and Daine were all she had left, and Daine . . . When she'd served with him in the war, things were simple. She was the heir to a dragonmark house, and despite his rank, he was just a soldier. A friend, certainly—but once the war was over, they would never see each other again. There was no point in thinking of anything beyond friendship; they belonged to different worlds, but now . . .

Something was wrong.

She pulled back from her trance and looked around. The old wine cellar was just as it had been a moment ago. The crystals were properly aligned on the table, and the silverwax candles were all alight.

"Dasei, what just happened?"

Dasei was Lei's assistant. She was a homunculus—a magical construct given a semblance of life by Lei's talents. While similar in principle to the warforged, the little wooden woman was not fully sentient. She could follow instructions, and her skills were invaluable when Daine's crazy jobs took Lei from her work; enchanting was delicate work, and it was not something that could be left unattended. Despite her mystical talents, the homunculus lacked initiative or free will. She was a tool, not a person.

Dasei could not speak, but she could send her simple thoughts directly to Lei's mind. *Nothing changed. Paths prepared.*

Lei frowned. She couldn't explain the feeling. There was a feeling in the back of her mind, a thought she couldn't quite catch hold of. Something had just happened, something bad, and if it wasn't related to her work . . .

"Finish this binding. I'll be back in a moment." Lei had named the little creature after one of her more annoying cousins, and she always took a certain satisfaction in ordering the homunculus about.

*Understood.* Dasei climbed up onto the table and sat next to the wand, stabilizing the magical energies Lei had been working with.

Lei picked up her staff and made her way up the rickety stairs. The staff was formed of darkwood, jet black and stronger than oak. One end was carved in the image of a beautiful elf maiden, with long hair winding around the shaft. The staff was a gift from her deranged Uncle Jura and a mysterious sphinx. Considerable magical powers were bound within the wood, but Lei had been unable to determine the extent of its abilities or how to activate them. She was beginning to think that the staff itself was intelligent—that it was aware of its surroundings and acted only when it suited its own unknown goals. While she still had her doubts about the staff, it had served her well so far. Beyond its unknown powers, it was a strong and sturdy weapon, and it had saved her life on more than one occasion.

The stairway brought Lei out into the kitchen. She paused and listened intently. Though the initial chill had passed, the sense of unease was still with her—a lurking dread that she couldn't explain. At first she heard nothing, but then she caught the faintest rustle, the barest sound of movement. She slowly moved toward the door, staff at the ready. When she was a child, her parents had arranged for her to be trained in the arts of stealth; her father had been determined to educate her in a broad range of skills, and while it had been a hard life, she silently thanked him for it now. Crouching low, she let one eye slide beyond the doorframe, peering into the large common room that lay beyond. A large humanoid figure was standing in the shadows by the fireplace, a flat object in one hand. As she watched, he reached up and made an adjustment, and the rustling came again.

It was Pierce, reading a book. He looked up as Lei entered the room. With a glance, he took in the staff in her hands and the tension in her walk.

"What is wrong?" he said, setting his book on the nearest table.

Lei studied the room, searching for anything out of the ordinary. "I don't know. Nerves, probably. Daine's upstairs?" She felt like a fool, but the inexplicable feeling lingered at the back of her mind.

"I believe so. Do you require assistance?" He already had a

hand on the haft of his flail. Born to war, Pierce was quick to react to any possible threat.

"No, no . . . I'm sure it's nothing. I'll just go and check on him."

Pierce released his flail and retrieved his book, a history of the kings of Galifar. If he'd been human, he would have shrugged. "As you wish."

Lei sighed as she made her way up the stairs. She considered Pierce to be one of her closest friends, but somehow . . . things hadn't been the same between them these past few months. When they'd first arrived in Sharn, Lei had been forced to fight Pierce and had almost destroyed him. She still had nightmares of that moment, of shredding his lifeforce with her touch; while he didn't seem to harbor any ill will toward her, she still felt the guilt. There was something further—a dream she'd had in the wake of the battle. The memories were vague, but her parents had been there, with a handful of warforged—including Pierce. Was it a true vision of the past or pure delirium? The dream had left her with a strange sense of dread, of a terrible secret just out of reach. She knew she should ask Pierce about it, but somehow she couldn't; it was as if the secret refused to be let loose.

Daine's door was shut, and she rapped on it with her staff. "Daine?"

No answer.

She knocked again, louder. "Daine? Are you sleeping?"

She waited for the acerbic *not now* that would typically follow such a question, but she received only silence. Frowning, she tried the door. It was barred.

"Daine! Answer me!" She struck the door again. No response.

She closed her eyes and drew on the reserves of mystical energy bound within her green and gold jerkin. She visualized this power flowing into her right glove and quickly wove the glittering strands to form a charm of opening. Studying the door, she struck it with her hand; there was a brilliant flash and the door sprung open, the wooden bar clattering to the floor.

Daine was lying just inside the door, naked save for his breeches. The first thing Lei noticed was his awkward position; he'd fallen unexpectedly and hard. She dropped to her knees and put a hand on his back. His skin was still warm, and she could feel his breathing. She opened her mouth to call for Pierce, but then she saw the other body. Sprawled across the floor in the center of the room, this stranger was completely hidden beneath a dark hooded cloak. For a moment, Lei froze. She opened her mouth to call for Pierce—and a hand grasped her throat.

Lei had been trained in defense, but her eyes were on the intruder. The action was a blur; she was thrown off-balance, then an iron vise caught her neck and slammed her into the ground. A knee came down against her chest, driving the air from her lungs. As she struggled to draw breath, the face of her attacker came into focus: Daine, no sign of recognition in his wild eyes. She gasped, trying to speak, but she couldn't form the words.

"Daine." The voice was cool and clear, even over the sound of her beating heart. "Let it go. Come back from the darkness."

There was a woman standing over Daine, a blurred phantom wrapped in the night. She placed a pale hand on the side of his head, and slowly the pressure eased on Lei's neck. The madness faded from Daine's eyes, and they focused on Lei's face.

Recognition washed over him, and he leapt up, backing away from her. He gazed down at his hands, as if he didn't know whom they belonged to. Lei drew a deep, ragged breath.

The stranger was standing over her, green eyes glittering in the darkness. She held out her hand. "Get up, Lei," she said, holding out her hand. "I'm afraid this nightmare is just beginning."

# CHAPTER 4

BRELAND
SHARN
*Lharvion 11, 997 YK*

The darkness slammed into Daine like a wave of tar—thick and fluid, yet charged with a terrible chill. He was thrown back off his feet, and in that instant it was all around him. The physical pressure built with every passing second, but the mental agony was far worse. He could feel the shadows seeping into his mind, slowly sinking into his thoughts and melting them away. Emotion, will, all was dissolving in the cold. A few more moments and there would be nothing left—an empty shell suspended in the dark.

*No.*

This would not happen. This was *his* mind—his battleground. Struggling against the darkness, he summoned his strongest memories, his deepest pains: his father's face in the great hall of the Blademark, shame and rage warring in his expression; his first view of the Mournland, of the sweeping ruin that was once his home; a gnome woman's laughter in a candlelit room; Jode's shattered body sprawled across a pile of corpses; and Lei—the first time he'd seen her, the sun bringing out the fire in her coppery hair. Her hand was against his cheek earlier that night. Binding joy and pain into a single bright force, he threw this raw emotion against the encompassing dark, and the cold shadows retreated before the light. Even as the chill began to fade, he was consumed by fire. The faces he'd conjured wouldn't go away, and now these phantoms of the past clutched at his mind. The mad artificer Kharizal d'Cannith

27

and the changeling Monan howled with laughter, while Naelan of Valenar spun his bloody scimitar into a shield of razored steel. Teral ir'Soras stepped out of the shadows, wearing armor formed of raw flesh and muscle. Daine thrust his way through the phantoms and seized Teral by the throat, slamming the treacherous counselor to the ground, but even as he tightened his grip, his victim's features flowed away, and now it was Lei who lay beneath him. Horrified, he released her and staggered back. With every second the mental cacophony increased. The mocking calls of his enemies and the cries of dying friends tore into his mind, crushing all thought.

*Daine. Come back from the darkness.*

It was a command. A brilliant light flowed down from above, shattering the shadows. He was back in his room at the inn with no name. Every muscle ached, and he fell back against the wall, slowly sinking to the floor.

Voices called to him. *Daine.* A radiant figure knelt before him, and at her touch confusion and pain were swept away.

Lei and Lakashtai pulled him to his feet, each of the women holding one of his hands. He didn't know the kalashtar woman well enough to read her expressions, but Lei's face was full of fear.

"I'm . . . I'm fine," he said, mustering as much strength as he could. Surprisingly, the words were almost true; his strength was swiftly returning, and he actually felt better than he had all day.

"Not nearly." Lakashtai had set aside her bantering manner, and her flickering smile had vanished. Her eyes were cold; her mouth a tight line. "Tashana. It would be her."

Lei whirled to face the kalashtar. *"What is going on?"*

Lakashtai's eyes flashed, and Lei took an involuntary step back. "A great evil has touched the mind of your friend, and I can't allow it to spread any further." She looked at Daine, and glittering green energy flowed around her hand. "I am sorry it has to end like this."

"Move and you will share his end." Pierce was standing in the doorway. His bow was in his hands, and an arrowhead of black steel was leveled at her heart.

For the briefest instant, Lakashtai's eyes flickered toward

Pierce. That moment was all that was needed. Daine latched onto her wrist with one hand, gripping her elbow with the other. Even as he moved, Lei brought her darkwood staff around in a low arc, sweeping Lakashtai's legs out from under her. Daine knelt to keep his grip on her arm, and Lei put the point of her staff against the kalashtar's throat.

"Thanks, Lei."

She nodded.

The verdant energy faded from Lakashtai's hand, but her face was a serene mask. "I bear no malice toward you, Daine. You may not believe it, but I saved your life a few moments ago, for the second time."

"What was that? A healing touch?"

"In a manner of speaking."

She glanced at her pinioned hand, and raised her delicate eyebrows. Daine took a deep breath and released her arm, moving back to stand by Pierce. "Try speaking more plainly."

"The fears that brought me here were proven true. Your mind is under siege, and it is a battle that can only end with your death."

Was there the slightest trace of pity in her eyes?

"I cannot allow my enemies to break you, but I lack the power to drive them from your mind. I can only hold them off, as I did moments ago, but I can offer you a quick and painless end."

Lei prodded Lakashtai's neck with her staff. "*Your* enemies? You're responsible for this?"

"Lei . . ." Lakashtai looked up at the angry young woman. "Your fury is misplaced, and your weapons are unnecessary. Allow me to stand, so we may discuss this as equals; you know that I would do the same for you, were our positions reversed."

That's true, Daine thought. Lei was frowning slightly, but she raised her staff and took a step back. Pierce lowered his bow and returned the arrow to his quiver.

Lakashtai stood up and straightened her cloak. "Better." She glanced at Lei. "My enemies are the enemies of all. I do not know what they want from Daine's mind, but the fact that they seek it is all that I need to know. This sacrifice is a tragedy, but we must serve the greater good."

Daine found himself nodding; strange as it was, it seemed to make sense. After all, who was he to stand in the way of the greater good?

"There has to be another way."

Lei's words pulled Daine out of his fog. What had he been thinking? He stared at Lakashtai suspiciously, but she showed no signs of guilt.

"I don't know what's going on here, but you said that you held it off—that you saved his life. If you could do it once, why can't you do it again?"

"I shielded our spirits from the attack, and were I to remain by Daine's side, I could continue to hold it at bay, but I cannot remain with him forever; I have my own duties to attend to. There is no power that can drive the darkness from his mind. There are only two options: swift death or an inexorable descent into insanity."

"Well, at least I've got options," Daine said.

"I don't accept that!" Lei's knuckles were white against the dark wood of her staff. "I don't know you, and I'll be damned to Dolurrh before you touch my friend. If I learned one thing as a child, it's that there are always solutions—you just have to find them."

"I take no pleasure in this, Lei—"

"*You don't know me.*"

Lakashtai met Lei's gaze, and this time it was the kalashtar who looked away. "You don't understand what you are dealing with. This is the source of every nightmare. Its power is beyond comprehension, and no—" She broke off abruptly, her brow furrowed in concentration.

"What?" Daine and Lei said together. Pierce watched silently.

"Yes . . ." she said, as if speaking to herself. "I had forgotten . . . but it might be possible."

Daine could see that Lei was preparing for another blow with her staff, and he put a hand on her shoulder. "Many things are possible," he said. "Can you be more specific?"

Lakashtai glanced back at him, and the intensity of her gaze sent a shiver down his spine. "I have booked passage to Storm-reach. I am leaving in a few hours. You will travel with me."

"Oh, I think not," Lei said.

Daine tightened his grip on her shoulder. "Lei—"

"No. *Stormreach?* That's *Xen'drik*, Daine. Across the Thunder Sea? Barren wastes filled with savage giants and creatures we've never even dreamt of?" Lei shrugged off his restraining hand and took a step toward the kalashtar woman. "First you try to kill him, and now you want him to take a little trip to Xen'drik? If you think I'm letting Daine out of my sight, you're insane."

Lakashtai shrugged, a surprisingly human gesture. Her voice had regained its cool composure. "Then join us. I never wanted him dead, Lei. I simply saw no alternative."

"And now?"

"A slim chance, to be certain, but if there is hope, it lies in the shattered land."

"You just happen to be going there. Why is that?"

"A fortunate coincidence, and one I have no time to explain." Lakashtai took a step toward Daine, and Pierce and Lei leveled their weapons; she glanced at them with the faintest trace of exasperation in her luminous eyes. "Daine, nothing in this land can save you. I know not why the darkness seeks your memories, but I must oppose them. Xen'drik is your only chance, and at the least I can shield you from further harm for the duration of the journey."

Daine pondered. Lei and Pierce remained at the ready.

"You sought my help before, Daine. I saved your life then, and I will do it again if I can."

Lei glanced at Daine, puzzled.

It seemed insane, but Lakashtai had helped him before. Although she had been planning to kill him a moment earlier, he found that he believed her. "Fine. I'll do it."

Lei glared at him. "Not alone."

"I won't be alone." He nodded at Lakashtai. "That's the point."

"You know what I mean. You're not going without me."

"I don't recall giving you a choice." It had been a long day and a strange evening, and while Daine wasn't angry at Lei, it felt good to have some sort of outlet for his anger and frustration.

*"She* did," Lei snapped.

"I'm not asking, Lei. You've already been through too much.

We've all heard the stories, and you're not risking your life on my account."

"On *your* account? Did it ever occur to you that I might *prefer* risking my life in Xen'drik to living in this . . . this dungheap? My parents were exploring Xen'drik before you were born, Daine. Perhaps I want to go there for *myself*."

"Do you?"

For a moment Daine thought she was going to hit him. Then she turned and strode out of the room, slamming the door behind her.

Lakashtai was the first to speak. She seemed unaffected by the outburst, and her voice was as calm and confident as ever. "I cannot say where our travels will take us, Daine, but Xen'drik is a land of many dangers. If your friends—" she glanced over at Pierce, who had been still and silent as a statue throughout the exchange— "would accompany you, I would not be so quick to dismiss them."

"Did I ask you?" Anger and guilt mingled in his gut.

"I have never needed your permission to speak my mind." There was no heat to her words—it was a simple statement of fact. "I have preparations to make, and I'm sure you do as well. Pack for a long journey, and be at the Greenman Pier by the sixth bell. The ship is the *Kraken's Wake* . . . I'll tell the captain to expect multiple guests." She pulled up her hood and stepped into the hall. Pierce followed her; apparently the warforged had no intention of leaving her unwatched.

A minute later Daine heard the sound of the front door. Sighing, he pulled on his shirt and considered what to pack.

# CHAPTER 5

BRELAND
SHARN
*Lharvion 11, 997 YK*

**P**ierce kept an arrow on the string as he followed Lakashtai down the hallway. He'd met this woman once before, but the circumstances had been unusual. The war had been a simpler time, when friends and enemies were clearly defined. Lakashtai—he didn't know where she belonged.

They made their way down the stairs and into the common room in silence. Lei was nowhere to be seen, and Pierce concluded that she had returned to the cellar workshop. At the door, Lakashtai turned to look at him.

"Are you going to ask your question, or shall I go?" She wore her usual ghostly smile, eyes hidden in the shadows of the hood.

"What question would that be?"

"Why I'm here. Why I'd try to kill Daine or offer to help him. Why you should trust me."

"Why ask, if I will not believe the answers?"

She laughed. "I see this city has already made its mark on you, Pierce. Very well, but whatever you choose to think about me—I believe that Daine needs you. I hope you will join us."

"That is his choice."

"No. You choose your own path, but I think you already know that, don't you?"

Smiling, she opened the door and walked out into the street. Pierce watched her disappear into the crowd, then slowly released the bowstring and shut the door.

Daine was stuffing some clothing in a backpack when Pierce returned. "I will be traveling with you to Xen'drik, and I believe that you owe Lei an apology."

"No, and not likely."

"Why?"

Daine looked up from his work. A year ago, Pierce never would have questioned an order. He was warforged, and Daine was his commander; it was in his nature to obey the chain of command. There was no time for debate on the battlefield.

"Why do you not want our company?" Pierce said.

"I told Lei. This is going to be dangerous. I don't have any choice here, but there's no reason for you to take the chance."

"When we had escaped the battle at Keldan Ridge, you led us back into Cyre. We could have started the journey toward Sharn immediately, but you chose to take us back through the mists. Why?"

"I thought there'd be survivors."

"You placed our lives at risk then; why won't you do it now?"

"Do you think I'm proud of that decision?" Daine slammed his hand down on the chain byrnie spread across the table. "I went looking for survivors, and what came of it? Another four people lost their lives, soldiers who went into that horror on *my* orders. I brought us to Sharn, and Jode . . . " He took a deep breath. "No one else is going to die for me."

"So you intend to die instead?"

Daine turned back to the clothes. "I'm dying anyway. I doubt there's anything that woman can do about it. At least you won't have to watch."

"Your chances of survival will be increased if I am by your side, and we will both be safer if Lei accompanies us. The last year alone has shown this to be true."

"This isn't a discussion. It's an order."

There it was again. Part of Pierce wanted to nod, to walk out of the room and leave Daine to his work. His commander had made a decision, but now . . . "No, it's not."

"What?" Daine looked up, exasperated.

"It is not an order, because I am not a soldier. I believe that I am a friend, and that makes us equals."

"Pierce—"

"Am I mistaken? Are we your friends, or are we simple soldiers?"

Daine closed his eyes and rubbed his forehead. "Pierce . . . of course you're my friends. You're the only friends I have left."

"And if it were Lei? If Lei said that she planned to return to Cyre in the company of a dangerous stranger—you would let her leave us behind?"

"Lei never was a soldier. She'd need our help."

A memory emerged—Lei fighting a minotaur with her bare hands, while Pierce and Daine stood and watched, but Pierce already knew what tactics were required to win this battle. "If she ordered you?"

"She can't give me orders. She's . . ."

"Your friend?"

Daine shook his head, striking the table again. "*Flame*, Pierce! Why can't you just let this go?"

Pierce stepped forward and put his hand on Daine's shoulder. Daine froze—Pierce had never made such a gesture before. Pierce looked down at him. "Because I will not let you go, any more than you would leave Lei. This is our choice—not yours. I will not stand by and watch you die."

Moments passed, as Daine and Pierce stood in silence. Finally Daine nodded. "I guess I'd better go down and talk to Lei."

"I will accompany you."

"Oh, I don't think that's necessary."

"I told you—I will not stand by and watch you die."

Daine looked up at his friend, and a smile slowly spread across his face.

CHAPTER 6

BRELAND
SHARN
*Lharvion 11, 997 YK*

The Dagger River flows through a deep canyon. As it runs south toward the coastline and the Thunder Sea, it meets up with two tributaries running east and west; the humans who first settled the region called this the Hilt. The city of Sharn was built on the top of the canyon wall hundreds of feet above the vast river, but the river trade was far too valuable for the city to pass up, so Cliffside was born: a community carved into the wall of the canyon itself. A web of stairways and bridges criss-crossed the stone face, and the wall was studded with the facades of buildings that stretched deep into the rock beyond.

A steady stream of skycoaches passed between the docks of the Dagger and the city far above, occasionally pausing at one of the Cliffside inns or brothels. These flying boats were an indulgence for those with silver to spare; for Daine, paying for a skycoach was as sensible as throwing a few sovereigns off the edge of a tower. Daine preferred to use the lifts—levitating platforms that slowly made their way from the tops of the towers to the bottom and back again. Travelers might have to wait a little while before one would arrive, but the lifts were free, safe, and reliable.

Usually.

"Oh, *this* is a good omen," Daine said. "Eight months in Sharn, and this is the first time I've ever heard of a lift needing to be repaired. What could go wrong with a lift, anyway?"

Lei said nothing. A light rain was sweeping through the

canyon, and Lei had her oilskin cloak wrapped tightly around her body. Her silence was a beacon warning of her foul mood; Lei rarely passed up a chance to talk about anything magical. She had accepted Daine's apology, but she'd barely spoken to him since then. Pierce was walking ahead of them, carving a safe path through the throngs of people clustered on the Cliffside bridges. Merchants called out to them as they passed, and beggars cajoled and pleaded, flaunting the wounds that they had supposedly suffered during the Last War. Daine knew that Jode would have known the difference between the true cripples and the fakes, but he saw only misery. The thought of Jode's face brought a wave of loneliness.

"Lei," he said. "You're angry. I get it, but what's the point of coming if we're not even going to talk?"

He reached and put his hand on her shoulder, and she turned to look at him. Without saying a word, she thrust the tip of her staff directly at his face. Instinct took over; he threw himself to the side, and the staff narrowly missed his neck. Even as he opened his mouth, he heard a loud cry followed by choking gasps. A tall, emaciated changeling was kneeling on the bridge behind him, gagging and clutching his throat; a small knife had fallen from his hand.

"Someone needs to watch out for you," Lei said. She didn't smile as she offered him a hand up. "Around here, watch your purse."

❀ ❀ ❀ ❀ ❀ ❀ ❀

The incident on the bridge helped to cool Lei's anger, and by the time they had reached the docks on the Dagger's edge she had dropped the wall of silence.

"Why haven't we been here before?" Daine said, stepping over a pile of what appeared to be ogre dung. He could see a few of the massive creatures unloading crates from a nearby cargo ship; apparently they weren't very particular when it came to hygiene. "It's got all the comforts of High Walls, not to mention a thief in every crowd and fresh shit in the streets." He studied a pair of merchants who were haggling with their fists. "I wonder how much one of those little caves on the cliffs costs."

"I came down here a time or two during my guild training,"

Lei said absently, studying the ships.

This wasn't much of a surprise, considering that it was Lei who'd known the directions to Greenman Pier, but all the same Daine wondered what business a young Lei might have in such a dingy neighborhood. "Why was that, exactly?"

"Oh, combat training."

Daine glanced at her, but her face was a picture of distracted innocence. "You couldn't do that at the enclave?"

"My instructor said it wasn't the same if you learned under controlled conditions. Though I don't know . . . looking back on it, perhaps he was just trying to get rid of me."

"Yeah . . . perhaps."

Pierce paused, and Daine almost walked into him. Pierce pointed toward the river. "I believe that is our ship."

Greenman Pier was, surprisingly enough, green. Daine couldn't make out the names of the vessels docked there, but Pierce's eyes were far sharper than his. The ship Pierce had chosen was a small boat, its hull stained black and silver. The sails were black, and the kraken's arms of House Lyrandar were emblazoned on the main sail.

"There's a wind spirit bound to the sail," Lei said thoughtfully. "See how it's rippling slightly, but none of the others are? Should make for a swift voyage, even if it's not as fast as an airship or a larger elemental galleon." She pondered the ship for a moment, and just as Daine was about to start walking she spoke again. "Who is she?"

"Lakashtai?" It had to come up sooner or later. "We met her at the King of Fire months ago, during that whole business with Teral and the brainsucker. She bought us drinks. Remember?"

Lei rolled her eyes. "Of course. She bought us drinks, and eight months later, she shows up and threatens to kill you, and on that basis you're about to jump on a boat with her? She said you sought *her* out."

"Oh, *that*. Well. Yeah."

"I don't like this. I don't like *her*. How do you know anything she says is true?"

"I don't, Lei. All I can tell you is that I trust her. I had a problem when we first came to Sharn, and she helped me with it. You don't have to come."

"Don't start that again." Lei looked back at the boat. "It's just . . . did you ask for her help this time?"

"No," Daine admitted. "She just showed up."

"How did she even know you were having problems?"

"Because I am the cause of them?" The voice was right behind then.

Daine and Lei spun around. There was Lakashtai, a back-pack slung over a shoulder and her cloak draped across one pale arm. She was wearing dark blue breeches tucked into tall boots of black leather and a sleeveless shirt with the same indigo hue. A wide black belt was wrapped around her waist, dark leather laced with an intricate, mazelike pattern of silver lines. Her only other adornment was a silver pendant bearing a large green crystal. The stone was exactly the same shade as her eyes, and it too seemed to glow in the shadows. Seeing their expressions, she laughed musically.

"Will you stop DOING that?" Daine said. His sword was already in his hand—he'd drawn it as he was turning.

She nodded solemnly. "There was no door to knock on."

"Some people just make noise. It works wonders." Daine studied the kalashtar woman. "Lei has a point though—how *did* you know I was in trouble?"

"You told me."

"No, I didn't."

"Oh, but you did." She pointed at his belt, and Lei blanched. "When I helped you before, I left a crystal for you. It's in your pouch right now."

Daine reached into the pouch and produced the sliver of emerald crystal. He did have the vaguest memory of picking it up after she'd helped him fight off the changeling that had been attacking his mind, but since then he'd completely forgotten about it. "This?"

"Yes. Think of it as a sort of alarm. I wanted to be certain that your treatment had been successful. If anyone tampers with your thoughts," she tapped the green stone of her pendant, "I can feel it. I should have found you sooner, but distance is a factor and I've been far from Sharn."

Daine looked down at the shard, a little disturbed that the thing could actually peer into his mind. He tossed it to

Lakashtai. "Great. Now we're all here, you can have it back."

She shook her head and tossed it back to him, and he instinctively caught it. "Keep it," she said. "Now more than ever, you are in need of protection. I do not know what lies ahead of us, and I must know if your status changes."

He didn't like it, but it made sense, and Daine slipped the stone back into the purse.

"Now," Lakashtai said, "our ship awaits. Pardon the pressure, but I think it would be best if we were to leave swiftly."

She walked toward the pier. Her posture was straight, every step precisely measured. Just like her appearance, there was something about her that wasn't quite right—something just a little too perfect.

Lei and Daine exchanged glances, but Daine couldn't think of anything to say, so they followed.

❂ ❂ ❂ ◉ ❂ ❂ ❂

"Why are you going to Xen'drik, anyway?" Lei asked as they walked down the green pier.

There were a few other ships moored at the docks, but few signs of people; the sun had set, and Daine imagined that most of the sailors were at Cliffside taverns. Even looking at their ship, he didn't see any movement in the rigging or people on deck.

"I am afraid that is not my secret to tell," Lakashtai said.

"Oh?"

"You have finally emerged from your last war, Lei. My people have a struggle of their own, and it is far from over."

"For you, it ends here." A figure leapt down from the deck of the Lyrandar vessel—a lithe figure in a long, dark cloak. Her face was hidden by her hood, but Daine could see the glow of green eyes, and he remembered that voice. Catching Lei's eye, he glanced down at his hands, placing his right index finger on his left thumb. She blinked slowly, her hand dropping down to her belt. Pierce had also seen the motion—*prepare to engage, supernatural threat.*

"Tashana." Lakashtai stepped forward, raising her hands before her. There was surprise in her voice—was there even a touch of fear?

"Must we go through these useless motions of battle?" the other woman said.

Though she appeared to be unarmed, she had the menacing aura of a predator, a tiger waiting to unsheathe her claws. She stepped forward and passed into the pool of light from a hanging lantern—and in that moment Daine caught a clear glimpse of her pale features and the white braid wrapped around her throat. There was no question—it was the woman from his dream.

Sword and dagger were in his hand in an instant. Pierce's arrow flew to his bowstring, and Lei pulled a short wand of polished densewood from her belt, but as Daine took his first step toward the stranger, he met her gaze—and a wave of rippling force spread out toward him. It was just the vaguest distortion in the air, the shimmer of heat in the desert. When it struck him, there was no heat. There was no sensation at all. All feeling, all thought seemed to recede, and he hardly noticed when his hands fell to his sides. Though he couldn't turn his head to look at Pierce and Lei, the sound of bow, staff, and wand striking the ground told him they were as powerless as he was.

Whatever the force was, Lakashtai had evaded it. The kalashtar woman brought up her hand in a sweeping arc, and Daine saw that it was glittering with light; as it passed across her torso, every sparkle became a jagged shard of green crystal flying toward the foe. Tashana howled with rage and pain as the storm of glass slammed into her, but she was still standing when the burst had passed.

"How many of you do I have to kill?"

Tashana ripped away the shreds of her cloak, and darkness boiled out from beneath. Oily mist surrounded her, forming the ghostly outline of the terrible creature he'd seen in his vision. The few sailors on the docks scattered, a few pausing at a safe distance to watch the spectacle; none showed any interest in getting involved or summoning the watch.

It was more like a dance than a battle. Lakashtai moved with unnatural grace, as if she knew every move her enemy was going to make; she would duck or spin just far enough to avoid Tashana's shadowy claws. Her expression was one of calm determination. As impressive as her efforts were,

Lakashtai had no time to counterattack; her every thought was on defense, and it was clear that her skills would not protect her forever; the next pass left her with a long gash along her forearm, darkness parting flesh as a blade cuts grass.

The sight of blood against the pale skin gave Daine new resolve. He was weak and numb, but it was nothing compared to the horror he'd fought just hours before, and that memory was fresh in his mind. Reaching within, he called on that same energy—anger, sorrow, anything he could *feel*—and threw that fury against the dull weight that seemed to hang across his muscles. Feeling returned, a slow throbbing as if his entire body was being jabbed with needles. Ignoring the pain, he dropped to one knee and snatched up his weapons.

Even as he broke free from the paralysis, the shadowy creature finally caught up with Lakashtai. A powerful backhanded blow threw her down against the boards of the pier. Her enemy raised a massive claw high in the air to deal the final blow.

Daine flung his dagger, and the blade cut through the monstrous silhouette to pierce the uplraised hand within. Tashana howled, pulling the dagger from her and flinging it aside. He was charging forward even as she turned to face him.

There was no time to think, and Daine let his instincts take over. Her claws were long, but his blade was longer. He took full advantage of that reach, pouncing in with a quick thrust and then darting back before she could strike. As Daine fell into the rhythm of the battle, he began to grow more confident; in time, he was sure that he could wear her down.

Presently, Tashana stopped trying to hit Daine. She matched his movements, and they slowly circled one another. "You're a fool to stand with her," Tashana said. Her voice was distorted by the shadows, inhumanly deep and slow.

"Just doing what comes naturally," Daine said.

Something was bothering him—after a moment he realized what it was. Tashana's dark shroud was shifting, twisting into a new shape. What did it mean? What was she doing?

"Then learn the price of your folly." The mist faded completely, and Daine froze in horror.

The figure beneath the darkness was not Tashana—it was Lei. Blood was streaming from her maimed hand and a dozen small wounds. Her eyes rolled up in her head and she fell to the ground. Without thinking, he dropped his sword and ran toward her.

There was a terrible cry of pain, and in that instant Lei was gone. The dark figure was there again, right in front of him, but now two white-feathered arrows were protruding from her chest. A moment later the cry faded away—and so did Tashana.

Turning around, Daine saw Pierce, his great bow in his hands. Behind him, Lei—uninjured—moaned and rubbed her head.

"What happened?" she said, gingerly kneeling to pick up her fallen weapons.

"I don't know," Daine replied. He looked over at Lakashtai, who lay crumpled against a wooden pylon. "But I think we'd better find out."

# CHAPTER 7

BRELAND
SHARN
*Lharvion 11, 997 YK*

"P ierce, check the ship," Daine said. There were no signs of movement on the deck of the *Kraken's Wake*, no sounds beside the rhythmic motion of the water. "It'd be just our luck if she killed the crew."

Pierce nodded and moved cautiously up the gangplank.

"Lei, with me," Daine knelt beside Lakashtai and studied the fallen kalashtar. Her shoulder wound was deep, but there wasn't much blood—and she was still breathing. "Do what you can."

Lei produced a small rod of green wood and slowly passed it over Lakashtai's shoulder. The wand began to glow with a pale light, and the injured flesh began to knit together.

"Well, I'm certainly feeling better about this trip. Do you suppose she's got more friends like that?"

"I've seen that woman before, Lei. Tashana."

Lei's eyes narrowed. "You're full of surprises today. Any other women I should know about?"

"It's not like that. I saw her in my . . . dream, I guess it was, when Lakashtai was in my mind. I think she's the one responsible for what's been happening to me."

"Lakashtai," Lei said distastefully. "I get tongue-tied just saying it. Can't we call her 'La'?"

Lakashtai opened her eyes, looking straight at Lei. Startled, Lei cried out and dropped the wand.

"It is the name of my soul," Lakashtai said calmly, as if she

44

was talking over a cup of Tal and not lying on a blood-stained pier. "La is only a part of who I am. It is my bond to Kashtai that makes me complete."

Lei snatched up her wand and glared at Daine. "Sure. It was only a suggestion."

Lakashtai was on her feet before Daine could even hold out a hand to help her. "Where is Tashana?"

"She's gone." Daine showed her the bloody tip of his sword. "I landed a few blows, then Pierce hit her dead center with two arrows, and she just faded away."

"If she was the one causing Daine's problems, does that mean this is all over?" Lei asked.

Lakashtai studied the pier. "The arrows that struck her . . . they disappeared as well."

"Yes."

"Then you did not destroy her. She can move through space in the blink of an eye—she must have teleported away. You did well to defeat her, but we must be gone from here. Others may soon arrive."

Lei grabbed Lakashtai's arm. "Wait. Others? When you invited us to come on your little trip, you said you could help Daine—you didn't say anything about being hunted by shadowy killers."

"Lei—" Daine began.

"Tashana came for Daine," Lakashtai said. Her eyes burned with emerald fire, and Lei released her arm and took a step back. "She sought to kill me so I could not protect him."

"Really?" Lei said, rubbing her hand. "Why's she so interested in Daine, anyway?"

"This is not the time for this conversation. We must embark on our journey."

As if on cue, Pierce appeared at the railing of the ship. "The crew appears to be alive but unconscious," he called down to them. "There is no indication of any hostile presence on board."

Lakashtai strode up the gangplank. Lei and Daine exchanged glances, and Daine shrugged. Lei picked up her fallen staff, and they followed her onto the ship.

The crew of the *Kraken's Wake* were sleeping. A handful of sailors were sprawled across the deck. Lakashtai knelt beside a young man with a hint of elven blood in his fine features; he wore the uniform of a Lyrandar ship's captain, a long black coat with blue and silver trim.

"Tashana's work," she said, touching his forehead. "Trapping their spirits in the world of dreams. We were lucky—she must have expended much of her energy to accomplish this."

"So she's usually even scarier? Great. That's reassuring."

Lakashtai closed her eyes for a moment, and the captain moaned. "Captain Helais. Return to us. Your dreaming is done."

The man slowly sat up. "Lady . . . Lakashtai?" He looked across the deck. "What's . . . What happened?"

"No harm has come to you or your crew, but we must leave swiftly, before the villain who did this returns. I shall see to the rest of your crew."

"This one's already waking up," Lei said, kneeling next to a large, balding man with pockmarked skin. Lakashtai looked over, and Daine saw a trace of surprise pass across her usually serene features.

"That is . . . good. Let us check on the others."

Daine helped the captain to his feet as Lei, Lakashtai, and Pierce disappeared below decks. "I'm Daine, and my companions are Pierce and Lei. We're joining Lakashtai on this voyage—I hope that she made the necessary arrangements."

The man nodded. "She's bought the services of the entire boat, so she can bring whoever she wants, friend. I'm Helais Lyrandar." He turned to the groggy crewman standing about. "Look alive, you lot! Check the sails, and stow the gangplank. Dulan, go see what happened to Fin."

Sailors scattered across the decks, rubbing their heads and laughing. Daine followed the captain as he headed up to the wheel.

"Have you made this run before?" the captain asked Daine as he checked the wheel and studied the deck.

"No—my only time on the water was on the rivers."

"Military transports, or merchant barges?"

"Military, during the war."

"Who did you fight for?" The new voice was a loud rasp, a whetstone against granite—and a distinctly Brelish accent. It was the burly man woken by Lei; he wore a leather vest, and an iron-bound cudgel was hanging from his broad belt. One of his eyes was clouded over, and scars around the lid suggested violence was the cause. "I see Cyran markings on your warforged." His hostility was unmistakable.

"He's not *my* warforged," Daine said. The recent treaty that officially put an end to the last war had declared the warforged to be free beings, with all the rights of other citizens of the Five Nations. "As for whom I fought for—" His sword was out in an instant, and the point flashed before the sailor's eyes. Daine held it for a moment, then spun the blade and reversed the grip, revealing the eye-in-sun sigil of House Deneith on the pommel. "I went where my skills were most needed."

"*Lon!*" the captain said. "I've told you before, if you're going to serve on my ship, you leave your nation behind. This is a vessel of House Lyrandar, not Breland, not Cyre. Your war is over; let it lie."

The giant nodded, his gaze still fixed on the Deneith emblem. Muttering an apology, he made his way back across the deck. Daine grinned and returned his blade to its sheath.

"I must apologize for my crew, Master Daine," Helais said once Lon was out of earshot. "The markless are still bound by their petty national rivalries. It's good to have a member of the Blademark aboard; piracy is a rare occurrence on the route I have planned, but there are always dangers on and below the seas."

Daine nodded. It wasn't entirely a lie—he was simply letting them draw their own conclusions. He had been born into House Deneith. The blade was his birthright, handed down from his grandfather. He had trained and served with the Blademark, and in the end, he had gone where his skills were most needed: the Queen's Guard of Cyre. The mercenaries of House Deneith were forbidden to choose sides in a conflict. As Helais said, the houses were supposed to be above national rivalries. A soldier of the Blademark went where the gold was—fighting for Cyre one day and Breland the next, but Daine had a fatal flaw: he cared about Cyre. He was born in that land, and the soldiers dying on the battlefield were his childhood friends. It had taken some time; as a young man, he'd been full of house pride, just as Helais was. While serving the house, he'd done things he wasn't proud of—things that still haunted his memories—and in the end he'd come to see that he needed to believe that he was serving a cause greater than gold. But the heirs of Deneith had a well-earned reputation for skill in battle, and Daine wasn't above using that to his advantage.

"Well, it's been a long day, and I'm sure you don't need me in your way," Daine said. "Where do I bunk?"

"We're a cargo ship, mainly," Helais said. "We've only got one stateroom, so you'll be sharing. Otherwise, we've got a few extra berths in the crew room."

"It's no problem for me," Daine said. He and Lei had slept in ditches and trenches during the war—he assumed they could share a cabin.

"Good then. It's just below decks, door on your left. We'll ring the bell for dinner, and by then we'll be on our way to the Thunder Sea."

Daine nodded and turned away. He made his way below decks, hoping to find a warm bed and dreamless sleep.

CHAPTER 8

BRELAND
THE
DAGGER RIVER
Lharvion 11, 997 YK

**D**aine lay on a hard bunk in the small cabin, his mind slowly drifting in and out of sleep. Vague images drifted through his mind. A memory of Jode passed across his thoughts, and he found himself following, seeking one more moment of conversation with his friend, even if it was only in his imagination. A vision slowly resolved around him. Night. The sounds of sword and steel in the distant background. A warforged corpse lay on the ground; Jode was kneeling next to the fallen foe, studying the shattered body. Krazhal stood over him, looking down.

"Captain?" the dwarf growled. "How long do we wait? You can hear the battle above, and here we stand studying—"

Daine silenced him with a glare and a sharp gesture. "What have you found, Jode?" he whispered.

"Well, Captain, I'm a healer, not a spectacularly gifted House Cannith artificer standing less than a mile away from our current location—"

"Jode!"

The halfling smiled disarmingly. "I did manage to extract this from the arm of our little friend." He held up a small platinum cylinder etched with arcane symbols. "I can't decipher all of these signs, but I think it's a key."

Daine nodded, taking the cylinder. "Good work. Krazhal, keep that blast disk ready, but if the Flame is with us this day, we won't need it." He caught Kesht's eye with a sharp gesture;

pointing to Kesht and Donal, he gave the signal for them to move deeper into the tunnel.

"And when has the Flame been with us?" Krazhal grumbled as he slowly began to follow in the path of the scouts.

"The Flame is always with us," Daine said. "Look for the Light and listen for the Voice. We'll see this through, old friend."

The words were ritual, but they felt empty even to him. Two years ago he'd had confidence in the Silver Flame, in the force that brought strength to the righteous and defended the innocent. These days, that faith was harder and harder to find. Every massacred village, every tale of atrocity from across Khorvaire, even Thrane itself—when he went to sleep at night, it was becoming increasingly difficult to say his prayers without biting his tongue, but his troops needed his faith, even if it was failing him inside.

Indeed, the faintest smile crossed Krazhal's lips, the first of the night. "Aye," he said. "Aye, I do believe we will, sir."

Blades drawn, Daine stepped into the tunnel, moving as quietly as he could. He could see the glint of Donal's hammer in the darkness ahead, and slid along the wall in the scout's wake.

There was a flash of brilliant white light, a sunburst spilling blinding radiance over the field. Daine's last thought was that this was wrong . . . that this hadn't happened.

❀ ❀ ❀ ❀ ❀ ❀ ❀

"Fool!" Lakashtai was standing over him, her eyes burning like emerald coals. "After all you've faced today, you would give yourself to dreams so easily?"

The room slowly came into focus. Lakashtai stood by the bunk, and Daine could *feel* her concern as if it was a physical force pressing against his thoughts. Pierce and Lei were standing to either side of her—Lei, worried and weary, Pierce as impassive as ever.

"Hnh—What?" he said, trying to make sense of her words.

"Your dreams are the path our enemies use to enter your mind. With Tashana in hiding—it is best that you do not dream for now."

Lei snorted, and Daine pushed himself up into a sitting position. "Oh, is it?" he said. His thoughts were still muddy. "Just . . . stop, just like that?"

Lakashtai nodded, as if this was a perfectly ordinary request. "I must be present when you are going to sleep. I can divert your spirit, and keep the gateway closed. As long as I am here, I can shield you from this foe and protect you from the attacks you have been suffering . . . at least, for a time."

"That's enough," Lei said, her voice cold. "I've had it with all of this mysterious nonsense. This isn't the first time Daine's ever been asleep. If his head was going to rot away, why didn't it happen yesterday? All I see is you showing up, threatening Daine, and then this other creature joining the fight . . . A woman who looked rather remarkably like you, looking back on things. Why don't you tell us exactly what's going on?"

"Daine has been at risk these last few nights. You have been losing consciousness during waking hours. When did this first occur?"

"Four days ago," Daine said.

"This is when they first found your dreams. With each night, the bond grows stronger, and if you let them into your dreams, they can track us . . . and then all will be lost."

*"Them,"* Lei said. "What 'them?' "

"Il-Lashtavar," Lakashtai said quietly. "The darkness that dreams."

"Oh, well, that makes everything clear. Why didn't you just say so in the first place?" Lei said.

Lakashtai looked at her, and as before the intensity of the kalashtar's gaze silenced Lei. "We do not speak of this to those we do not know. This is our war: the battle of the kalashtar, the struggle we were born to. You and all those creatures who dream when the night comes—I would spare you from knowing of the horrors that await you."

There was no trace of a smile on her lips, and though her voice was music, it was a cold and chilling tune. For a moment, no one spoke. Then Pierce's voice filled the room, deep and calm.

"You may have chosen this battle, but we have been drawn into it, and a soldier who cannot identify his foe—one who knows nothing of the nature of the battlefield—cannot expect to triumph."

Daine nodded. "I can't avoid making mistakes unless I know what I'm fighting, and damn it, it's my mind!"

Lakashtai studied each of them, then turned and walked toward the far corner of the room. When she looked back at them, the light had faded from her eyes.

"You are correct, of course," she said softly. "I cannot say what lies ahead of us, and you must be prepared. Please, Lei, be seated. This will be a long tale, and I know that you have had a trying day."

Lei glanced at Daine, and he gave her a slight nod. Grumbling, she sat on the bunk next to him. Pierce stepped back away from Lakashtai, creating as much space as possible in the small room.

Lakashtai turned to face them. Despite her torn clothing, despite the dried blood on her skin, she carried herself with the dignity of a queen. Her beauty was breathtaking, but it was the cold beauty of a marble statue—human perfection, yet fundamentally unnatural.

"I am kalashtar, born of two worlds. Over a thousand years ago, my ancestor bound her bloodline to the spirit Kashtai, and I am a child of that union. Kashtai moves within me. Her memories come to me as dreams, and at times her voice whispers in the silence of my mind. As long as at least one of my sisters is alive, Kashtai will survive—and as long as she lives, she will fight il-Lashtavar.

"While I can tell you of this struggle, it is far better if you see it for yourselves. Relax. Let your thoughts wander. Open your minds, and let me show you the nightmare that lies within."

Her voice was soft and lulling. She continued to speak, but her words seemed to blur together in a warm, relaxing song. Eventually Daine closed his eyes and dropped into another world.

❋ ❋ ❋ ❋ ❋ ❋ ❋

A glowing halo lay before him, a wreath of light hanging in a field of utter darkness. As he studied it, he saw that it was composed of glittering particles. There must have been billions, yet somehow he could see each and every one; his eyes were unnaturally sharp, and though each particle was no larger than a grain of sand, with every passing second they became clearer.

Where was he? He tried to turn his head and found that he couldn't. It was then that he realized he had no body. He could sense his surroundings, yet there was no *he* there; he simply *knew* what was around him. *It's like a dream,* he thought.

*It is a dream.* It was Lakashtai's voice—or her thoughts. *But it is more than that. It is all dreams. Every point of light is a dreamer, drawn from the waking world into this realm of Dal Quor.*

Daine struggled to grasp the concept. *So this is . . . another world?*

*Your sages would call it another plane of existence. It is a shadow of the material world, a place that exists in the minds and souls of all living things. It is always there, always a part of you, but it is when you sleep that you open up that gateway, forming your own world in Dal Quor—the fortress of your dreams.*

*You're saying that when I see Lei in my dreams, it's really Lei,* Daine thought.

*No. You create your own dreams, shaping them from memories, hopes, fears. As does Lei. You are two different points of light, two different worlds, each as deep and rich as Eberron itself.*

Daine pondered. *What does this have to do with us? Or this Tashana?*

*Dal Quor is a mutable realm, a place where thought becomes reality, but the mortal spirit only has the strength to shape its outermost regions. Those lights that you see are the distant edges of the region of dreams. Look deeper.*

Daine directed his attention toward the ring of lights. At first he saw nothing beyond the glittering halo. Then he realized . . . the darkness within the circle of lights was deeper than the void that surrounded it. Both were jet black, but the darkness within—it was more than just empty shadow. There was something there . . . a presence.

*Look closer.*

Then he was falling toward the shadow, the ring of lights becoming larger and larger with each passing second. He now saw that each glittering speck, though they had seemed like grains of sand, *were* the size of worlds—that he'd been watching from an almost unimaginable distance. He began to see details within the central darkness. Textures. Shapes. A vast landscape stretching out around him. A river of tar flowed through a wasteland of jagged black marble. An orchard of skeletal darkwood trees swayed to a ghostly breeze. Tendrils of dark smoke crawled along the surface, as if driven by a conscious mind, then it all changed. The marble plain dissolved into a desert of black sand, and the trees were consumed by flames that seemed to draw in the darkness instead of releasing any light. Faces emerged from the surface of the desert, visages of sand twisted in silent screams. Daine tried to look away, but he couldn't; he had no eyes to close.

*This is the heart of Dal Quor. It is a living thing, though not in a way we understand the word. It is a spiritual force that dwarfs worlds, a hungry god that yearns to devour the hopes and dreams of all mortals. It is the cradle of nightmares, and it lurks just beyond your dreams, just beyond the edge of your mind. This is il-Lashtavar.*

*So this is what's been attacking my mind,* Daine thought.

*Not exactly. Il-Lashtavar is the source of all darkness. It is the force that shapes Dal Quor, but it is too vast, too alien, to focus on your mind directly; it is a whirlwind, and you are a mere mote of dust. So it spawned children to do its bidding. Look again.*

The dark desert rose up in a massive sandstorm. The sand turned to mist, which drifted away, revealing a citadel of black glass. Shapes were swarming around the tower, and as before, Daine's vision grew closer and closer. The creatures were strange, impossible things—beings that could not exist in any rational world. A maelstrom of eyes and wings drifted by, equal parts human, insect, and avian. A circle of cloaked figures were engaged in conversation, but as Daine drifted closer, he realized that each creature was actually formed from a mass of fleshy tendrils, woven together in a crude approximation of human form.

*These are the children of this dream. They are darkness incarnate—the worst aspects of the mortal mind made manifest. Fury, fear, the lust for power or pleasure. Every dark impulse lives among the quori. They are immortal, and their minds are beyond your understanding. They are pure, driven, unburdened by empathy or personal ambition. They exist to serve the Dreaming Dark, and that is all that they do.*

*Even amid this darkness, there have been a few who have found a path to light. These rebellious spirits sought to incite the others against il-Lashtavar, to find a way to transform this world. There in the circle, two of these agents of change are pleading their case, but it is a futile cause. They are the aberrations, and no amount of reason will persuade the others.*

A host of horrors emerged from the citadel, charging toward the unearthly council. There were creatures formed of dark fire, swirling clouds of raw emotion, and far stranger things. Daine spotted a serpentine creature in the mass, eyes and cilia running along its length. Two oversized arms extended from its headless torso, tipped with massive claws; a vicious stinger lay at the end of its long tail.

*Tashana,* Daine thought.

*No, but one of her siblings. A tsucora, a spirit of terror that feeds off of mortal fear.*

Suddenly Daine found himself in the midst of the circle. Suddenly he *was* the speaker, trying to show the others that there was a cycle to existence, that the transition from darkness to light should be embraced, not feared. The shadowy figures said nothing. The army of terrors spread around the circle, the venomous clouds drifting overhead.

*You are flawed. Embrace the gift of destruction, so your soul can be reforged in the depths and brought back to il-Lashtavar.*

The storm descended, and claw, tentacle, and raw hatred tore into his soul.

❋ ❋ ❋ ❋ ❋ ❋ ❋

Daine's eyes flew open. His breath came in gasps, and he could still feel icy tendrils of shadow sinking into his mind. Lei was pale, and she closed her eyes and slumped against the wall.

"This is what my ancestors faced," Lakashtai said. "Those who sought the light were hunted down and destroyed, absorbed back into the core of il-Lashtavar. They were hopelessly outnumbered, and fighting was useless; those killed would simply be reborn. The only hope was flight, so they fled into mortal dreams, searching for some form of sanctuary. The forces of the dark hunted them through the borderlands, through the dreams of elf and dragon. When all hope seemed lost, their leader stumbled into the dreams of a human monk from the land of Adar, a place that offered sanctuary to those in need. Together, monk and quori found a way for the spirits to abandon their physical forms—to leave Dal Quor forever and find refuge within mortal lines, so the first kalashtar was born. Kashtai lives in me and in my sisters, and should I have a daughter, Kashtai will guide her as well."

Pierce seemed the least affected by the experience. "None of this explains the woman who attacked us or why she was interested in Daine."

"Kashtai only touches my soul; she is spread throughout my lineage. Tashana—she *is* a dark spirit, utterly dominating the mortal vessel bred to hold her. The Dreaming Dark has agents spread across this world, and destroying the kalashtar is but one of their goals. In time, they hope to dominate the waking world as they do Dal Quor—to create a stagnant world where nothing ever changes, where there is no light to threaten the darkness."

Daine massaged his forehead. "Yeah, and we all know I'm the key to conquering the world."

Lakashtai did not smile. "I do not know what it is the darkness wants from you, Daine. Some secret has been locked within your mind. These memories are from the night before the Mourning, are they not? That alone should give you pause. Perhaps the secret of that terrible power is hidden within you."

"Why me? Why now? Jode was with me; he must have seen everything I saw."

"You have seen Dal Quor—the billions of dreams that swirl around the edges. Most likely, some spirit stumbled into your dreams recently and saw some hint of what was contained within. By that time, Jode was already dead."

"I suppose," Daine said. He thought about the blue vial hidden in his pouch.

"Whatever mystery is hidden in your mind, il-Lashtavar cannot be allowed to claim it, and I will do whatever is necessary to prevent it."

"That's reassuring," Lei said. "It seems to me that if it wasn't for Daine, your innards would be decorating the docks of Sharn."

Daine glared at her, but Lakashtai seemed unruffled.

"Tashana is a powerful warrior, and her presence is a sign of the importance of the secret within Daine's dreams. We are stronger together than apart, and all that strength will be required if we are to survive the days ahead."

Daine yawned. "Well, now you've got me scared to close my eyes, but I don't know how much longer I can keep them open. So you said you can do something that will allow me to sleep safely?"

"For now, yes, and you as well, Lei; they may not have found your dreams yet, but they may try to find Daine through you; we must be cautious."

Lei shrugged. "Are you going to tuck me in, too? Or make a cold fire candle for me? I've always been afraid of the dark."

"Then there may be hope for you yet," Lakashtai said, as she lowered the shutter on the lamp, filling the room with shadows.

**P**ierce emerged on the deck of the *Kraken's Wake*. The ship was entering the waters of the Thunder Sea, and the coast of Breland was falling behind and disappearing into the night. Pierce had never seen an ocean before, and he was fascinated by the scope of it—water stretching across the horizon, as far as the eye could see. To the southwest, occasional flashes of light suggested the presence of one of the storms the region was known for, but for now the waters were calm. Pierce gazed down along the side of the ship, watching the prow cut through the water. He could sense the spray and the moisture against his skin, and as he often did, he tried to analyze these feelings, to justify them. He had no nerves, and his "skin" was steel and mithral, so how was it that he could *feel* the drops of moisture rolling down his arm?

Most warforged had been created with the capacity to read so that they could convey messages and read maps and instructions. In the past, the warforged had no time for leisure pursuits, but recently Pierce had taken to reading while the others were asleep. He was particularly intrigued by the subject of spirit binding, and the creation of the warforged, though he could find little reliable information on either subject. Much about the warforged was a mystery—either secret knowledge hidden away in the vaults of House Cannith or simply unknown. From what Pierce had learned so far, the process leading to the creation of the warforged was as much luck and chance as it was skill. House Cannith had produced magical constructs for many centuries. These golems were powerful creatures; they had the strength of stone or steel and felt neither pain nor emotion, but they lacked true awareness; they could follow simple instructions but could not adapt to unexpected situations, display initiative, or learn from their experiences. When Galifar collapsed into civil war, Cannith artificers sought to improve their golems, to produce sentient constructs with enough intelligence to employ strategy on the battlefield—tireless soldiers that could be sent into enemy territory with only general instructions, who could devise their own plans based on the tactical situation. The early stages of the project met with limited success. The warforged titans were living siege engines, and possessed a basic intelligence and self-awareness—but this was little better than that of a human child. A generation later, an artificer named Aaren d'Cannith led the team that made the critical breakthough, creating a truly sentient soldier with the skills of an elite warrior. Somehow Aaren's soldiers had gained more than just human intelligence. They could feel pain. They could smell, and even taste, despite the fact that they could not eat, and they possessed the capacity for emotion. An ideal soldier should be able to ignore pain and act without being influenced by emotion, but somehow, these things were magically bound to the warforged sentience: with the ability to think came the power to feel.

While the artificers could not remove emotion entirely, House Cannith at least worked to suppress it. Every aspect of the warforged consciousness that could be shaped was directed toward its chosen path, and the warforged were given minimal information about anything besides their purpose. A warforged soldier didn't need to know the reason for the battle: all that mattered was that he was built to fight it, and for as long as there was war, that was enough.

Now the war was over. The treaty that had secured the peace had also freed the warforged, recognizing their rights as sentient beings, not just weapons of war.

What did freedom mean for the warforged?

Pierce turned away from the horizon to study the ship. Beyond the sail that billowed even on this windless night, there was little to distinguish the *Kraken's Wake* from a mundane vessel. A tall, muscular human was minding the ropes, and as he looked at Pierce there was an unmistakable charge of hostility. Pierce instantly evaluated the threat presented by the sailor. Size and build were taken into consideration, along with the cudgel hanging from the man's belt and the leather jerkin he was wearing. Scars surrounded his filmy left eye, and Pierce had already considered ways to take advantage of this handicap in close combat. It took only a second for Pierce to decide that the man presented little threat to him—and that despite his apparent hostility, he lacked the resolve to act on his aggression.

If Pierce had lungs, he might have sighed. Cyre had fallen, but war was still the essence of his existence; forged to serve as scout and skirmisher, it was an effort for him to walk in the daylight without clinging to the shadows. Slowly, he was exploring other paths of thought, other aspects of life, but it was only in battle that he felt truly alive. Even now, despite his evaluation, part of him hoped this Brelish sailor would attack him so that for a few minutes, he could feel the satisfaction that came from serving his true purpose.

This was the paradox of freedom. Compared to humans, there was little that warforged needed. The warforged could feel physical sensations, but they did not feel physical pleasure in the same way as organic creatures. They did not eat or sleep and were immune to all but the harshest weather conditions, making shelter an option as opposed to a necessity. Few felt any need to amass possessions beyond their weapons or the tools they required to fulfill their function. For a human, freedom meant the opportunity to do whatever he wanted, but for the typical warforged, what he wanted was to perform the function he was made for.

A memory surfaced in Pierce's mind—a slender, cloaked warforged, its skin plated in dark blue enamel, its voice that of a human female. He had only met her for a few moments, but he'd never forgotten the encounter. She'd sought to recruit him, hinting that somewhere a group of warforged was building a new future for his kind. He'd turned her down, choosing to remain with his three friends, but ever since that night, he'd wondered what would have happened if he'd gone with her. Recently, he had been reading a history of Galifar and was amazed by what one human had accomplished. The warforged had no history to look back to, but what future lay ahead? Was there a warforged Galifar, waiting to be built?

There was no wind, but the main sail billowed and fluttered, and Pierce turned to study it. The kraken-and-lightning emblem of House Lyrandar gleamed in the darkness. It had been charged with cold fire, and set amid the black sail as it was, it would seem to be floating in mid-air to any approaching vessels. The wind was the result of an elemental bound into the fabric—a spirit of the air that could generate a pinpoint gale just behind the sail. Studying the rippling sail, Pierce wondered about the life of the bound spirit. Was it conscious, aware of its surroundings? Most of the books Pierce had found claimed that elementals were simple creatures and that binding them was no different than domesticating horses. Pierce couldn't help but wonder: Was the sail a prison for the spirit, or was it doing what it loved most—was the wind its one joy in life? Looking at the sail and imagining the spirit trapped within, Pierce didn't know whether to feel pity . . . or envy.

# CHAPTER 10

## THE THUNDER SEA
*Lharvion 14, 997 YK*

**D**ie!" Lei cried. She spun forward, and her staff was an arc of darkwood flying toward Daine's head. It was a blow that could shatter a skull—but only if it connected. As Lei moved forward, Daine ducked. In that instant, Lei knew her mistake, but it was too late. Her momentum carried her forward, and before she recovered her balance the tip of Daine's sword was at her belly. She gasped and dropped to one knee as the staff slipped from her grasp. For a moment she managed to hold herself upright.

"Why?" she whispered and then fell to the ground.

"That's what I'd like to know." Daine poked her in the stomach. He'd wound a strip of thick leather around the tip of his blade, but it was still enough to make her wince. "If I kill you one more time, I think Dolurrh will run out of space."

Someone else might have dismissed it as a joke, but Lei had known Daine long enough to recognize the edge in his voice. "What do you care? I thought we were just playing."

They were on the deck of the *Kraken's Wake*. It was midday, but the sun was hidden behind a blanket of dark clouds. Beyond one memorable storm, the voyage had been unremarkable, and the novelty of being out on the open sea had worn off after a few days of choppy water and nausea. When the day brought a pause in the rain and a period of relative calm, Daine had suggested that they go to the deck to practice, but it seemed that they had different ideas as to what this meant.

"You need to thrust more and stop with the wild swings. Use your reach. This isn't a time for games." Daine held out his hand, but Lei remained sitting.

"Why not? I don't see any pirates on the horizon. What's wrong with you?"

Daine withdrew his hand and sat down on the deck, facing her. He ran his finger down the scar on his left cheek. "Perhaps I am taking this too seriously. It's just . . . we're going to Xen'drik."

"Really? That explains the boat." Daine glared at her, and she held up her hands. "Sorry."

"You're just proving my point. There's nothing funny about this. We don't know what to expect in the weeks ahead, but we need to be ready for anything."

"I'm not ready?" Lei said, a little heat rising in her voice.

"I guess . . . you were with me during the war. I know you can handle yourself in a fight if you have to, but you're not like Pierce and me. Pierce was built for war. I was raised in a house of mercenaries and learned the first forms as soon as I could lift a sword."

"Good for you," Lei said, "and who was it who fought a minotaur with her bare hands?"

"That's my point, Lei. You can fight if you want to, if you have time to prepare, but it's when—"

There was a flash of steel, and the point of his dagger was at her throat. She didn't even see him draw it.

"Life doesn't always give you warnings. I just want to make sure you're ready for anything."

Lei knocked the blade aside. "So what's your suggestion, *captain*? Don't trust anyone? Stay on edge every moment of your life?"

"Lei—"

"You don't know the first thing about my childhood, Daine. You were raised by soldiers? My parents worked in an isolated warforged enclave, and by the time I was eight I'd only met a dozen humans. My first friends were steel and stone, and the games we played were games of war. Perhaps I am too trusting. Perhaps my life has been too sheltered. Deception doesn't come naturally to the warforged—it has to be learned, so I'm not used to worrying about my friends pulling daggers on me. I assure you that when I'm facing an enemy I know how to deal with him." She narrowed her eyes, and Daine yelped and dropped his dagger. The metal glowed red with the heat of her anger, then slowly faded back to black. Lei stood and strode over to the rail, glaring out across the water.

Daine watched her, rubbing his hand. He could handle a sword with ease, but words—words were another matter. He'd known Lei for almost three years, but he'd never thought to ask her about her childhood. His history with his own family, the mercenaries of House Deneith, was a bitter one. After years of serving in the Blademark, he'd become disgusted with the moral ambivalence of the dragonmark houses, which typically put the pursuit of gold above all else. Daine often wondered what would have happened if the dragonmark houses had used their influence at the start of the Last War, if they'd taken sides—could they have ended it quickly, without the terrible loss of life of the past century? Had the thought even crossed the minds of any of the barons, or had they only seen the profit, as House Cannith built weapons for all nations, House Deneith fueled the fire with its mercenary armies, and every other house found its own way to profit from the conflict?

When it came down to it, he'd let his disgust with his house cloud his judgment of Lei. He remembered his own childhood, and he'd always assumed that Lei's naïveté was the result of pampering and luxury, far from the suffering of the war. Now he tried to imagine a child among an army of warforged, going through their drills and preparing to be sent to the field. He rubbed his scar again, stood up and walked toward her.

"Lei."

Silence.

"Lei, just listen." Daine clenched his burned fist, hoping the pain would focus his thoughts. "I didn't mean to upset you. I should know that you can handle yourself. After what we went through in the Mournlands, even the last few months . . . I know what you're capable of."

She continued to watch the water. She might have been a statue—or a warforged sentry, standing watch.

"It's just . . . I feel . . ." He slammed a fist onto the rail in frustration. "Fine. It's Jode."

Lei looked over, green eyes wide. She said nothing, but the question was obvious.

Daine took a deep breath. "I let him go, Lei. I could have stopped him. Perhaps if I'd gone with him, things would have turned out differently, but even before that . . . I never pressed him, never forced him to learn to fight." Each word was a weight on his tongue, each one heavier than the last.

Lei's anger melted in the face of his despair. "He was a healer," she murmured, "a dragonmark. He wasn't a target on the battlefield . . ."

"I was his friend. I could have taught him what I know. I could have made him learn."

"No one could make Jode do anything he didn't want to do."

"It's not just Jode," Daine said. "In my dreams—Jholeg, Krazhal, Jani, even thrice-damned Saerath. All dead."

"All soldiers," Lei reminded him. "Now you're going to take responsibility for everyone who died in the war?"

Daine looked away. "People die in war. That's unavoidable, but could I have done more? I can't even remember what happened at Keldan Ridge. Did I lead them into disaster? Am I doing it again? I could have made you and Pierce stay in Sharn."

"Oh, and Sharn is the safest place in Khorvaire? If it's Sharn without you or Xen'drik with you, I'll feel safer in Xen'drik." She put her hand on his shoulder, and ran her finger along the tense muscles of his neck. "You can't take responsibility for everything, Daine. We're in this together."

Now it was Daine who said nothing.

"Come," Lei said, taking his arm and pulling him away from the rail. "Let's go another round. Let me show you what I can really do. I think a few bruises are just what you need to clear your head."

Daine nodded, but the faces of the dead were still fresh in his mind.

❋ ❋ ❋ ❋ ❋ ❋ ❋ ❋

"Better," Daine said.

"Bold talk for someone lying on the ground," Lei said, the

point of her staff pressed against his chest.

"This is practice. If I don't let you get away with something occasionally, you'll never learn the technique."

"Oh, so you *let* me trip you?" Lei lowered the staff and offered her hand, pulling Daine to his feet. Despite her slender frame, she was surprisingly strong.

"Believe what you will," Daine said with a smile. "Now you're still leaving yourself open—"

He was interrupted by the ringing of the deck bell. *What now?* he thought. Moments later, crewmen were scrambling across the deck.

"Look at the main sail," Lei said. "The wind just turned, and only the captain could order that. I think we're coming to a halt."

"Why? I don't see any land." Daine studied the horizon. "Wait. What's that?"

There was a patch of purple weed floating off the starboard bow—a mass of seaweed some twenty feet across.

"It seems like it would be easy enough to steer around," Lei said, "unless . . . it's some sort of marker."

"We'll see," Daine said. "Perhaps you'll have a chance to put our practice to work."

Lei's assumption was correct. A moment later, the magical wind that filled the main sail died completely, and the vessel stood at rest on the water. Crewman lowered the anchor and threw something else over the side . . . a package of some sort? Daine wondered if this was some sort of sacrifice to the Devourer, the sinister god who embodied the destructive power of nature. Few people admitted to worshipping any of the Dark Six—the malevolent deities of the Sovereign Host—but he'd known many soldiers to say an occasional prayer to the Mockery when the odds were against them.

The captain came down from the wheelhouse, walking toward the knot of crewman. Daine caught up with him.

"What's going on?"

"Nothing for you to be concerned about," Helais d'Lyrandar said. "Routine procedure before entering Shargon's Teeth, though perhaps it would be a good time for you to visit the mess."

"Why's that?" Daine wasn't the most sensitive man, but even he could see that the captain was nervous. "I don't know anything about routine procedures, so perhaps you could enlighten me."

The captain scowled. "I don't have time to talk to passengers right now. Stay out of the way!" He made his way to the knot of sailors standing by the anchor.

"He's in a friendly mood," Lei said.

"Stay ready," Daine said. He walked slowly along the railing toward the knot of sailors, then a hand gripped the rail right in front of him.

It was covered in leathery green scales, still wet from the sea, each finger tipped with a sharp claw. A moment later a second hand appeared, and a horror pulled its way up to the edge. It was a hideous blend of man and armored fish, with two gleaming yellow eyes set above a wide mouth filled with needle-like teeth. A leather harness was wrapped around its torso, and a short barbed trident was slung over its back. Swearing, Daine drew back to strike—and suddenly found himself falling to the deck. Lei had tripped him with her staff. Before he could react, there was a hue and cry; the captain and the sailors had spotted the creature.

"Don't hurt him!" the captain cried, and for a moment Daine thought Helais was talking about him. Then the creature pulled itself over the rail and onto the deck, and Daine realized that its presence was expected.

"Well, you were right," Lei said, prodding him with her staff. "I did get to put our practice to work."

❂ ❂ ❂ ❂ ❂ ❂ ❂

The visitor's name was Thaask, and it seemed that the captain had met him before.

"He's a sahuagin," Lei said, as they watched the captain talk to the creature.

"I thought sahuagin lived on a diet of fresh sailors." Daine had heard tales of the fish-folk before, but he'd never seen one—and in all the stories he'd heard, these sea devils were a force to be feared.

"Sure, and ogres eat babies," Lei said, "but not the ogres in

Malleon's Gate. It's dangerous to make assumptions."

"What do you think this is about?" Daine said, watching the creature. The conversation with the captain seemed cordial enough, but something about the creature set him on edge.

"Helais said that we were about to enter Shargon's Teeth. From what I've heard, that's dangerous water—full of hidden reefs and . . . well, sahuagin. My guess is that the captain is paying for protection. Or a guide."

Lei's instincts were correct. A moment later, the captain handed a leather purse to the fish-man and gave a slight bow. Thaask echoed this with a slight nod of his angular head. The captain turned and spoke to the crew, and the sailors scattered across the decks, raising the sails and pulling up the anchor.

"If we're entering the Straits, we're almost to Stormreach," Lei said. "It won't be long now."

"It can't be soon enough for me . . . now what?"

Thaask was coming toward them. He had a strange, lopsided gait; it was clear that he preferred swimming to walking. He spoke, but the sound was a croaking gargle; Daine couldn't make out the words. Daine still had his sword in his hand, but Lei stepped in front of him.

"What did you say?" Lei said. "I couldn't understand."

Thaask spoke again, slower and more clearly. "I give you greetings, daughter of air. Many storms have passed since last we met."

Daine shot a sharp glance at Lei, but she seemed to be just as surprised as he was. "Since last we . . . I'm afraid I don't know what you mean."

The sahuagin made a rasping sound that could just as easily have been a laugh or a cry of outrage. Eventually it spoke again. "I forget the way that age takes you creatures of earth and air. You would not wear the face in my memory if you were the one I met before, so you must be the daughter."

"What are you talking about?" Lei said, her voice beginning to rise. Daine put a hand on her shoulder.

"Aleisa. This name is known to you?"

"That's my mother!" Surprise diffused the growing anger, and Lei loosened her grip on her staff.

"It is she whom I took you to be. As a guardian of these

waters, I never forget my charges, and you and she are one and the same."

"You met my mother? Sailing to Xen'drik?"

"Yes. Perhaps thirty of your years ago. An interesting one, she was, strong currents flowing, not like the man who was with her; he was ice in the deepest water, cold and still."

"My father . . ." Lei said. She glanced at Daine. "I told you that they'd been to Xen'drik." She turned her attention back to Thaask. "What can you tell me about them? Why were they traveling?"

"The cold one did not speak to me, but Aleisa and I talked often. She was curious about the secrets hidden in the deep waters, the ruins of those who went before. As we spoke, she told me of her own questing."

Daine found the whole conversation hard to swallow. Here they were in the middle of the Thunder Sea, speaking with a walking fish that just happened to have met Lei's parents. "Lei. This is some sort of trick . . ."

"No," Lei said, holding up her hand. "Thaask, please. What was she looking for? It would mean a great deal to me."

"Mean a great deal, hssh? When one has a thing of value, it is customary to offer a trade."

"I knew it," Daine growled. "He's just trying to catch you in his net and reel you in, Lei." He took Lei's arm, but she pulled away and stood her ground.

"This is my choice. What is it you want?"

"Your mother gave me a gift—a stone of music, which would play when held. It was taken from me long ago by a tooth of the Devourer. I would have such a thing again."

Lei nodded. "I could probably make you such a thing by the time we arrive at Stormreach."

"I trust you to hold to this bargain, for the honor of your mother," Thaask said, "and I will tell you what I know between my warning rounds. Two things were foremost on her mind, and I can speak of those now, before my work begins."

"Please!" Lei said.

Daine sighed and sat down on the deck.

"She traveled with the other in search of the ruins of those who went before. Her people had given life to the unliving, to create weapons of war—"

"The warforged, yes, I knew they worked on warforged."

"She said that the old land held many secrets of those gone before," Thaask said. He steepled his hands, tapping his yellowed claws together in a sharp click. "Her folk had plundered this knowledge to use in their creations, but she believed that there was far more to be found—that her kind had skimmed the surface without plumbing the depths. She wanted to find ways to improve these spawn of war, but she did not want to share her knowledge with her kin, whom she thought blinded by gold."

"You said she spoke of two things."

"Yes," Thaask hissed. "The spawn of war, but also a child of her own. A daughter, she wanted. I told her of the spawning pits of my people, and she spoke of her desire for a daughter. It was a subject of sorrow for her, one of great difficulty, but one much on her mind. I am pleased to see that she met with success: She must be quite pleased."

"She's dead," Lei said quietly.

"Yes, the great destruction on your land. We are glad this has come to an end; more ships sail this way, more needing protection of my kind, but my sorrows for her loss. I found her enjoyable company."

"A subject of sorrow . . . what do you mean by that?"

"Difficulty with the spawning. I do not understand your reproductive cycles, but I know that the spawning often brings no children, and so it was with her. She felt that soon would change."

Lei said nothing, but Daine saw her eyes grow wide, as if she'd just remembered something disturbing. "I'll have your stone for you by the end of the voyage, Thaask." Her voice was tighter than it had been a moment ago.

"You have my thanks. Speak again, when you wish it."

Lei said nothing; she simply turned and walked to the hatchway, her expression blank and distant. Daine glanced at the sahuagin, who bobbed his head in something that might have been a shrug.

"Did I offend?"

"I don't know," Daine said, "but I intend to find out."

# CHAPTER II

**A**re we going to talk about this?"

Daine caught up with Lei below decks as she entered their cabin. Pierce was standing in a corner of the room reading a book, and he looked up as the two entered. Lakashtai was nowhere to be seen; the kalashtar woman often disappeared during the day, and said that she preferred solitude for her meditations.

"No," Lei said. "There's nothing to talk about."

"Is there a problem?" Pierce said, setting down his book.

"No problem," Lei responded, glaring at Daine.

"You're in a good mood, for someone with no problems," Daine responded. "What's gotten into you?"

"I said I'd make a music stone for Thaask, and it's going to be hard to do in time, especially with most of my tools at home. I should have considered the situation more carefully."

"Creating a magic stone is your idea of a good time. I practically need to pry you out of the basement at swordpoint to get you to have a little fun. The conversation was going fine, and then he said something about your mother, and the next moment you're running for the hatch. There's something you're not telling me."

"Who said you had a right to know?"

"Damn it, I'm not trying to interrogate you!" Daine said. "If you don't want to talk, fine, but if you're in pain, of course we want to help."

"Fine." Lei sat down on the bunk, and all the energy seemed to flow out of her. "What do you know about the history of the warforged?"

"I didn't ask for a history lesson."

"You want to know about my family, that's what you get. Most people think Aaren d'Cannith created the first warforged, and in a sense, he did. He developed the multi-composite construction of the warforged, the blend of wood, stone, metal, and organic material that is still used today."

Lei was always fond of lecturing, and talking was clearly calming her nerves, so Daine decided not to press the matter. "Organic material? You mean flesh?"

"No, of course not, but wood is actually organic. Pierce, if you would, your arm—see those cords at the joints?"

"I always thought that was leather," Daine said.

"Leather would likely rot or tear. Aaren derived this material from studying the livewood tree, which remains alive even after it is cut from the ground. These cords are much like tree roots—flexible, tough, even able to respond to magical forms of healing, though not as effectively as flesh and blood. These roots form the bulk of a warforged soldier's muscles, if you will. The important thing is that the creation forges would actually cause these roots to grow at an accelerated rate, limiting the amount of steel and other materials needed to build a soldier."

"Great, and what does this have to do with anything?"

"Merrix took the first steps toward the warforged, but his creations lacked true sentience. It was Aaren, his son, who created the first warforged—who adapted the creation forges to breathe true life into metal and wood, but Aaren had no interest in creating soldiers. He wanted to understand the nature of life—to try to fashion a creature with a soul."

"House Cannith was only interested in war," Pierce rumbled.

"That's right. Aaren's forges were taken from him. The best artificers of the house were set to work, ordered to find a way to duplicate and adapt his creation to produce superior soldiers. My parents were part of this effort. I grew up in a small, hidden forgehold, and I never saw a human child. My parents were always busy, devising new tools for the warforged or new body designs. I spent my childhood with the warforged themselves, discovering the world as they did; but no warforged remained at the hold for long, and my friends would all go off to war. There was a time . . ."

Her voice shook; she paused, and closed her eyes. Before Daine could move, Pierce reached out and put his hand beneath hers. She smiled wanly and squeezed his hand, then continued.

"There was a time when I envied the warforged, when I wanted to be a warforged. At least they had a purpose. I felt like no one wanted me around."

"Thaask said your mother wanted a daughter . . ."

"I know! But that's not how it felt. She was warmer than my father, it's true, but she was always busy, and she and my father were always preoccupied with new designs, with the next idea. I guess I began to think of myself as a redundant model. They could always improve the next generation of warforged, but the daughter . . . they had to live with what they had."

She took a deep breath. "Things improved when my dragon-mark manifested. It appeared when I was nine—years before the normal age. At that point, my training began in earnest. I was sent to Sharn, to the towers of the Twelve, to Cannith enclaves across Khorvaire. I barely saw my parents again after that, and I didn't give it much thought. At last I had my purpose! I performed much of the usual work of the day, building wands for the battlefield, helping with the warforged. Eventually I caught the eye of Hadran d'Cannith."

Daine held up a hand. "If you don't want to talk about him . . ."

"Why stop now? I never loved Hadran. Never. He was wealthy and powerful, and it was a good match. It was my duty. Really, I never thought twice about it, but then my father interfered. He said that he wouldn't consent until I'd served four years serving on the battlefield as warforged support."

"What?" Daine vaguely recalled Lei saying that she never wanted to be a soldier, but he never guessed that her parents would have ordered her into such danger.

"He never asked me. He never explained his reasons. He simply gave his orders, and like a good soldier, I followed them, so I ended up with you."

"What does this have to do with Thaask?"

Lei looked away, and her voice tightened in her throat. "Just hearing him talk—knowing that there was a time when she wanted a daughter as much as she wanted that better warforged—it just hurts. Knowing that that love was there once—but somehow, I never received it, and now I'll never see her again."

Daine didn't know what to say, so he just put an arm around her shoulder and pulled her close. She clung to him, and soon tears began to flow. For a moment they just stood there, Pierce watching to the side. Then Lei broke away.

"I'll be all right," she said, sniffling and rubbing her nose. "It's over now, and I need to start work on that stone."

"All right. I'll leave you to it, but if you need anything . . ."

"I'm fine. I'll be fine."

Daine looked at Pierce. "Up for a little combat practice on the deck?"

"As you wish."

Pierce picked up his flail and followed Daine out of the cabin leaving Lei alone with her thoughts. She took her tools out of her backpack and found a focus stone that would serve for the job, but the image of her parents hung in her mind. Not the memories of a lonely child, trapped in a world of war and steel, instead she was haunted by the memory of a dream, lying on a slab next to Pierce while her parents discussed her progress. Perhaps it was just a manifestation of her insecurities—a fear that she was nothing more than another experiment, a failure to be cast aside? Somehow she felt that there was more to it, and it frightened her.

She rubbed the back of her neck, passing her fingers across her dragonmark, and set to work.

# CHAPTER 12

**D**aine's first vision of Xen'drik was Shargon's Teeth—a chain of islands rising out of the water, surrounded by sharp peaks of black basalt.

"Teeth of the Devourer," Thaask said, stepping up to the rail next to Daine. "When he hungers, the Teeth shatter the hulls and bring the ships down."

"I thought you were here to keep that from happening," Daine said.

"As he wills." Thaask ran a claw across his teeth; to Daine it looked like a ritual gesture. "Should he call storms, my path would not save you."

"Where would that leave you?"

"I and mine scavenge the ships that sink to the bottom. We are the children of the Devourer, and we claim what he leaves behind."

"So you want us to sink? And we're paying you to be our guide?"

Thaask gave a croaking rasp, which Daine had come to believe was a laugh. "What has this little ship to offer? If the elders wished it, sea and stone alike would rise to shatter this vessel. Nothing travels the waves save by our leave. There are those beneath the sea who take their pleasure in pulling down your vessels, but those of my school have no wish for war between the land above and the deep water, not now. We serve as guides across the water. If the Devourer wishes to claim your ship, we

75

will take what he leaves. If not, we take what you give and build the trust between our kind. We gain by either path."

"You said you didn't want war between the surface and the water *now*. . . ."

Daine let the sentence hang, and there was a moment of silence. Thaask turned to face him fully, and the sunlight gleamed across his scales. "As he wills," he said, drawing a claw across his teeth.

The sahuagin dove off the edge of the ship, returning to the sea to scout the waters ahead. There was a creature waiting for him there, a huge ray with fins that made Daine think of wings. This beast served as Thaask's mount, sliding through the water with speed that hinted at supernatural origins; Thaask clung to the ray's back and it darted forward, making it seem as if the *Kraken's Wake* was standing still. Daine watched the shadowy shape disappear into the depths, and wondered what lay hidden in the deep waters.

❂ ❂ ❂ ❂ ❂ ❂ ❂

The attack came without warning. One moment Daine was standing at the railing of the ship, an instant later, he was engulfed in cold shadows that drew the heat from the world. He was weightless, falling, and though he could see nothing, every instinct screamed that he could strike deadly ground at any moment.

*Let me take you from this place.* The voice was calm, soothing . . . Tashana. *Don't fight it. Take my hand and you can have refuge in your memories, safe from the death that awaits you here.*

Daine could feel her fingers just beyond his own, warm and welcoming. He clenched his fist. "None of this is real."

*Perhaps, but it is deadly all the same.*

The wind grew louder, and Daine felt that he was falling faster, though darkness was still the only thing he could see. *Surrender to me.* Tashana's thoughts were cold fingers drifting across his skin. *Let us return to your past. It's the only way you'll ever know the truth of that night—the only way you'll know if you were really to blame for the fate of your soldiers.*

Faces flashed across Daine's mind. Jode. Donal. For a moment he heard Krazhal cursing just behind him. Marshalling his thoughts, he forced the images away. "I know all I need. Now get out of my mind."

*Are you certain that's what you want? Do you know what you left behind?*

Impact. Not earth or stone, but water, even colder than the chilling wind. Daine's limbs were still frozen, and salt water flowed into his nose as the weight of his armor pulled him down.

*It seems I pushed too hard when I seized your mind,* Tashana said. *You've fallen from the railing. You don't have much time. Do you really want to spend it choking in the cold? Wouldn't you prefer to die in the company of friends?*

"I'm not dying!" Daine snarled. Then it struck him. He could feel the water flowing into his lungs, the paralysis gripping his body—yet he could still speak, still hear his own voice. "This isn't real!" he hissed.

Though Daine couldn't move his arms, he could *imagine* moving them. As his body slipped deeper and deeper beneath the sea, Daine pretended to reach down to his belt. One hand gripped the hilt of his sword. The other slipped into his belt pouch—and even as his belongings drifted out into the water, he wrapped his hand around the shard of green crystal.

Strength flowed into him, fire moving up through his hands and burning away the cold. A blazing green light consumed the darkness and Daine heard a keening howl as Tashana faded from his mind.

He opened his eyes.

His clothes were dry, and the air was as warm as it ever got on the *Kraken's Wake*. Light came from the everburning lantern on the wall. He was lying on his bunk, and Lei and Lakashtai were staring down at him.

"Daine?" Lei said quietly.

His left hand ached, and he realized he was clutching the crystal shard Lakashtai had given him so long ago—squeezing it so tightly he'd probably drawn blood. He opened his mouth to speak and choked on the empty air, words catching in his throat.

"Relax," Lakashtai said, placing her right hand over his. Warmth and relief spread through his blood. "You are safe now. Your will is strong, and we are with you."

"Safe?" hissed Lei, turning on Lakashtai. "You call this *safe*? You said that you could protect us—protect *him*. Is *this* your idea of protection?"

"Ur," Daine began, but words were still awkward.

Lakashtai released Daine's hand and turned to fully face Lei. Dazed as he was, Daine was struck by the contrast in their appearance: Lei was fire and gold, red hair and green leather, and he could feel her anger and passion. Lakashtai was cold, stark black and white, night and snow.

"I underestimated Tashana," Lakashtai said coolly. "She should not have recovered from our battle so swiftly."

"You *said* you could stop this," Lei replied.

"I can." Lakashtai passed her hand over Daine's left fist, still clenched tight around the crystal shard. He felt the stone grow warmer as her hand drew near. "The channeling stone is a shield. I just need to pour more of my strength into it—to spend more time in meditation. I can build a wall. I just didn't realize how high it needed to be."

Struggling, Daine managed to find the strength to raise his fist, touching Lakashtai's hand. "Thhh . . . Thank you," he finally muttered through numb lips.

Lakashtai looked down at him and shook her head. "No, Daine. I have failed: it was your strength that saved this day."

"Ours," he said, opening his hand to reveal the sparkling crystal shard.

Lei scowled and looked away. Lakashtai simply nodded.

"Keep the stone close," she said. "I must stay with you to protect your sleep, but I will do all that I can to ensure that they cannot strike again so long as you are awake."

Daine nodded, and rubbed his fingertips across the crystal. He turned toward Lei, trying to frame words in his mind. There *had* been a part of him that had wanted to let the world slip away . . . to stop fighting, to join Jode and the others. It may have been Lakashtai's stone that drove back the spirit, but it was thoughts of Pierce and Lei that gave him the strength to reach for the stone.

Lei had already left the room.

CHAPTER 13

THE
THUNDER SEA
*Lharvion 17, 997 YK*

Lightning shattered the night, and Lei winced as thunder rolled around her. The *Kraken's Wake* pressed forward through the storm, shuddering with the impact of each mighty wave. As Lei closed the hatch to the lower decks, a gust of wind broke through the invisible wards, almost knocking her down. Nature and magic were at war, and without the spells woven into ship and sail, the *Kraken's Wake* would be torn apart. The wind howled again, and Lei wondered how long the mystical defenses could hold against the anger of the storm.

The sooner I'm back below, the better, she thought, carefully making her way across the deck.

"I give you greetings, daughter of air." Thaask's harsh voice rang out over the wind. The sahuagin was standing by the rail, and he drew a claw across his teeth as he gazed up at the storm-clouds. "He hungers."

"He?" Lei cried over the wind. She gazed up at the clouds for a moment before she realized. "The Devourer."

Thaask said nothing. A massive wave rose out of the darkness, and Lei instinctively raised a hand to shield herself. Thaask just watched as the wave shattered against the Lyrandar stormbreaker wards, leaving only a dense mist.

Lei lowered her hand, slightly embarrassed. "I finished the sound-stone," she said, reaching into her pack and producing the carved sphere.

The sahuagin's eyes were pale and golden, set far apart on

79

his wedge-shaped head. He fixed her with one eye and held out a hand.

She pressed the stone into his palm. It was designed to draw music from the mind of the bearer, and as Thaask took the stone Lei heard faint strains over the wind and crashing waves—an eerie wail, the sound of glass and water. The sahuagin closed his eyes, listening in rapture. Then he hurled the sphere out over the water. For an instant she could still hear the music, then song and stone were swallowed by the darkness.

Surprise and anger were balanced against a lurching sense of loss. Lei had spent days working on the stone, shaping each groove with her mind and soul, and for an instant she felt as if *she* were the one flying into the maelstrom.

As the strange vertigo swept over her senses, another wave struck the ship and Lei slipped on the slick wood, sliding toward the railing. A strong hand caught her shoulder. Thaask was still facing the water, watching her from the corner of an eye as he held her steady.

Vertigo was replaced by comforting anger, and Lei knocked his arm away with a furious gesture. "Why did you do that?" she shouted. "I spent *days* on that stone—"

"When he hungers, loss is inevitable. The wise choose the loss." If Thaask noticed her anger, he chose not to acknowledge it. His eyes remained on the sky.

"You threw the stone in the water because you're afraid of the *storm*?"

Now Thaask looked at her, golden eyes glittering in the lightning-flash. "No fear. *Respect*. Sacrifice is loss. We make our sacrifice in faith, we choose what is lost. Challenge and he chooses." He looked back at the sky.

Lei opened her mouth then closed it again. The storm did seem to be abating, the wind dying down. Coincidence, no doubt, but she gave whispered thanks to Arawai all the same.

"The reefs ahead are dangerous enough when he is calm," Thaask said. "Your ship would not have survived his anger."

"So? I thought your people would loot the wreckage?"

Thaask turned back toward her. "You made the gift. You kept your word, and I serve the memory of those gone before."

For a moment they stood silently, watching the quieting

waves. Lightning still flickered on the horizon, but the seas were calm once more.

"I still don't understand," Lei said at last. "How can you worship the Devourer? In my land we respect Arawai, the goddess of the land. The Devourer—all he does is destroy."

"You create a goddess where none is needed. You have your gods of war and peace, but peace is what comes when war stays his hand. He is the fury of the storm, but he is with us in this calm. We were born from his belly, and when he hungers he will consume us again. It is the way of life: shape the current as you will; it will run its course in time."

"He'll kill you if you don't give up the things you love?"

The sahuagin turned to face her fully, and for a moment he opened his mouth, revealing a double row of razor teeth. "Do you share the faith of your forebears, child?"

His voice was louder, deeper, and Lei instinctively took a step back. At that moment she knew how smaller fish felt in the presence of the shark.

"Are you faithful to their ways?" Thaask hissed, taking a step forward.

"Yes," Lei said, holding her ground and staring at the sahuagin. "The Sovereign Host. I was taught to give thanks for their blessings."

"And to fear the dark, yes? The six? The Devourer. The Darkness. The One Unknown?"

"To *resist* those things," Lei replied, mustering her indignation. "Death, corruption, and chaos—yes, I was taught to stand against them."

Thaask brought his talons together in a sudden movement, creating a loud, sharp *click*. "You would not exist without them. Passion and madness, these bring change, and you are a child of chaos."

"What do you mean?"

Anger and curiosity warred within her. Part of her wanted to turn and go, to leave this savage who'd thrown her treasure into the sea, but she'd never actually spoken to anyone who worshipped one of the Dark Six before and interest lingered.

"You know of the force that brings change? The One who

Remains Unknown?"

Lei considered this. "The Traveler?" Of the Dark Six, this deity was the most enigmatic; the tales could not even agree on form or gender. The Traveler was said to walk the world, spreading chaos in his—or her—wake. Many old traditions of hospitality were designed to placate the unknown Traveler.

"Yes," Thaask hissed, letting his mouth hang open again just long enough to show his teeth. "Traveler. In the first days of my people, before we learned the rites of the Devourer, we were the slaves of a terrible force in the deep waters. A few implored the gods for mercy, for an end to this servitude. The One who Remains Unknown came to them in the depths and offered a sanctuary. With her guidance they wove a disk of roots and sat upon it, floating atop the waters."

"They made a boat?" Lei had never heard of sahuagin boats before.

Thaask nodded. "The waters are our home, and at that time there was no land. None had thought to rise into the air, and they never would have. The god's gift was the idea they could not see on their own."

"What happened?"

"The deep masters could not follow them. They were safe, but time above the waters sapped the strength of the people. Their scales fell and lungs grew weak." Thaask cocked his head, studying her. "The Devourer spoke to those who remained below, and with his strength they overcame the deep masters. Those who had fled could never return. They gathered floating roots and clots of mud, and slowly they built larger and larger shelters, until eventually those shelters took root and became lands. The world was divided into the nations of land and water, and so it has been to this day."

"So we're second cousins?" Lei considered the story for a moment. "But . . . because these people asked for help and trusted the Traveler, they ended up being banished from their homeland forever. Wouldn't they have been better off waiting with the others?"

"Yes, but there would have been no land above to bring profit to those below. The world you know would not exist. *You* would not exist. The powers of your six carry pain and danger, but these are the forces that shape the world, and many who breathe the air know this, those who spawned you among them."

*"What?"* Lei's hand dropped inside the one of the wide pockets of her pouch, and with a thought her staff was in her hand. Lei heard the faintest moan; it might have been the wind, or the soft cry of the darkwood dryad. "What do you mean by that?"

Thaask took a step back, keeping his teeth in view. "I promised you words in exchange for your stone, child, and the Devourer has claimed the stone. I have work to do, and you will have no more words from me. This vessel will leave the Teeth by tomorrow, and we will not meet again." He took a step sideways, standing to the rail. "Why don't you ask your gods?"

He slid over the railing in a blur of scales and leather. There was a splash as he struck the water, and an ululating cry from below—the call to summon his mount, perhaps.

When Lei reached the railing, the sahuagin was nowhere to be seen.

# CHAPTER 14

THE
THUNDER SEA
*Lharvion 18, 997 YK*

**T**haask was as good as his word, and the following evening the ship arrived at the port of Stormreach. Lei had finished her work, Lakashtai had emerged from her meditations, and all four of the travelers gathered on the deck to watch as the ship approached the colony.

The shore of Xen'drik was nearly as inhospitable as the Straits of Shargon. Stone columns and massive splinters of rock jutted from the water, and the coast was a sheer cliff. To the southwest, Daine could see a break in the cliffs, a jagged hole miles across. It looked anything but natural; it was as if a giant hammer had come down and blasted a gap in the rock, and knowing the legends of this shattered land, that may have been exactly what had happened.

It soon became clear that this unnatural gap was their destination. A handful of fishing boats were scattered across the rocky bay, and as they approached, a galley of an unfamiliar design came into view. The vessel was long and narrow, with a curving prow that rose high out of the water, and its sail was painted with a complex design of blue and silver lines—a dizzying labyrinth that drew the eye into its depths.

"An ill omen," Lakashtai said, watching the vessel head out to sea.

"How so?" Daine said.

"That is a Riedran ship, and the people of that land are the servants of the Inspired—and thus, the allies of our enemy.

Most likely it is mere coincidence we see it here, for Riedra has as much interest in the wealth of Xen'drik as any other land. The ship is heading away, but I fear to think what it may have left behind."

Lei shook her head. "Nightmares, brain eaters, sinister agents of doom—don't you ever have anything cheerful to say?"

"In times such as these, I prefer dark truths to pleasant deception," Lakashtai replied cooly.

A moment later, the colony itself came into view. Compared to the majestic towers of Sharn, this was an unruly sprawl. Buildings were scattered across the coastline as if dropped by a child. Every building was unique. Some reflected the traditions of different cultures; Daine spotted a building constructed in the Flamic style popular in Thrane and another that seemed to be the work of goblin hands. Stranger than the designs were the materials that were used. There were a few solid houses that might have been plucked from the streets of Fairhaven or Metrol, but many were odd patchwork buildings, using mismatched pieces of stone, chunks of driftwood, or what appeared to be rosy crystal. As they drew closer, Daine could see that a number of the structures incorporated pieces of ships' hulls, undoubtedly scavenged from vessels that foundered in the deadly harbor.

"The designs are most unusual," Pierce said, studying the coast. "Have there been many wars to cause such devastation?"

"This is not the result of battle," Lakashtai replied. "Stormreach is one of the few safe landings on this edge of Xen'drik—and safe is most definitely a relative term. As the people of Eberron took to exploring the seas, many ships were broken on this shore, and the survivors made their way to this place. In time people mastered the seas, and many found this place a welcome refuge. Smugglers and pirates sought a haven from the strength of Galifar, while explorers and scholars yearned for the treasures of legend. In recent years, prospectors have found the land to be rich in dragonshards and other valuable substances, such as the crystal material you see in some of the buildings. The dragonmarked houses came to Stormreach, and the princes of Khorvaire and Sarlona followed in their wake."

"Which nation claims the land?" Pierce said.

"Stormreach is its own sovereign state, and its lords are descended from the first settlers, but the laws are loose here, and you will find that justice is even harder to find than it is in Sharn. Each lord has his own guards, who do his bidding. The commoner and the traveler must make their own way in the world—force and guile are all that these people respect. We walk a dangerous path, and it will only get worse from here."

"I am pleased to hear it," said Pierce. Daine shot a quizzical glance in his direction, but the warforged had nothing more to say.

❦ ❦ ❦ ❦ ❦ ❦ ❦

Soon the *Kraken's Wake* pulled into the harbor, and sailors on the piers guided it to an empty slip. There were ships of many nations scattered across the bay. Daine saw a squat dwarven yacht, with a gilded sail and a jewel-encrusted dragon on the prow. There were a number of gnome merchant vessels, which seemed like delicate toys next to the larger Brelish freighters. Next was a black ship—an elven vessel from Aerenal, formed from darkwood and adorned with skulls. An actual tree sprouted in place of a mast, with a web of gossamer sails spread throughout its branches.

"Livewood," Lei said, pointing to it. "Remember? Sustained by magic. I wouldn't be surprised if there's a dryad in it."

"And the skulls?" Daine said.

"It's a common tradition among the sailors of the Aerenal islands," Lakashtai said. "Rather than rest on land, they prefer to have their bodies bound to the vessel they served on. If the proper rituals are used, the spirit can be bound to the skull, allowing the ship's priest to speak to the sailors and ask for advice."

"Charming," Daine said.

Moments later, the gangplank was lowered. The travelers already had their gear prepared; Lakashtai and the captain exchanged pleasantries and gold as Lei, Daine, and Pierce made their way across the plank.

"Solid land," Lei said, swaying slightly. "I never thought I could be so happy and so nauseous at the same time."

Lakashtai led them onto the street, which was loosely cobbled with an odd assortment of stones. The population was even more diverse than that of Sharn, and Daine could hear shouted conversations in three different languages. A pair of ragged goblins were arguing with a perfumed gnome woman dressed in bright silks; as the travelers passed by, the goblins drew knives and a gem-tipped wand appeared in the hand of the gnome. No one else spared a glance for the encounter, and Lakashtai caught Daine's arm even as he reached for his sword.

"This is not a place to go looking for trouble," she said.

He ground his teeth and pulled free from her grip but kept walking. A moment later, they heard the *fwoosh!* of magical fire and the distinctive smell of burning goblin.

"Do we have a plan, Lakashtai," Daine said, "or are we just walking the streets until we run afoul of the local gnomes?"

"First, we need shelter," Lakashtai said. "Then we need a guide. As you've seen, the streets of Stormreach are no place for strangers. As for your affliction, that will take time. I doubt the answer lies within the city itself, but someone here may hold the key. There are a few people I planned on speaking to when I thought I was coming alone. They know much of the mysteries of the land, and this would be the best place to start."

"Will we be staying with one of these friends of yours?" Daine said. He kept his eyes on the crowd; a tall man wrapped in a hooded black cloak caught his eye.

"None of these people are my friends," Lakashtai said, a smile drifting across her lips, "and I think it would be most unwise to put ourselves in their debt."

"Great," Lei put in, "so when it comes to shelter, do you even know where you're going?"

"I have a general idea," Lakashtai said. "While I have never been here, others of my kind have. Through our shared link to Kashtai, I can draw on traces of their memories. I think we'll find a reasonable inn down here."

"Great." Daine caught Pierce's eye and shifted his head; the warforged nodded slightly and drifted back to take up the rear. "Good food, you think?"

"I am afraid I am not qualified to judge such things," Lakashtai replied. "I am certain you would consider my diet to be quite bland."

As Lakashtai was talking, Daine bumped into Lei. When she glanced at him, Daine rubbed the palm of his left hand with his index and forefinger. *Web*, he mouthed silently.

Lei looked surprised but slid a hand into one of the pockets of her pack, coming up with a small clay disk.

"What's Kashtai have to say right now?" Daine said.

"It is not so simple, Daine. She does not speak in words. Her memories . . . they simply rise to the surface when needed. She is part of me."

"Well, not to question her guidance, but let's try a shortcut." Daine put an arm on Lakashtai's shoulder and steered her down an alleyway off the main street.

Lakashtai resisted at first, then shrugged and allowed Daine to lead the way. With a careful glance back Daine saw that the man in the dark cloak had followed as well—and he had a friend, likewise shrouded in black, with the distinctive shape of a shortsword visible in the folds of his cloak.

Not a problem, Daine thought. Two we can handle. Just a little further.

He was prepared for two, even three. He hadn't counted on five.

Just as Daine was preparing to turn on the two men shadowing them, three new figures stepped out of the shadows that lay ahead. They were dressed alike in loose black cloaks and robes hemmed in labyrinthine patterns of silver thread, faces hidden beneath hoods and silver veils. The man in the lead held a long, curved blade that appeared to be carved from a single piece of glass, and there was a glitter of chainmail beneath his cloak. The woman at his side held a blade of steel. These two were blocking the alleyway, but Daine caught a glimpse of the woman behind them and didn't like what he saw. She carried no weapons but held a crystal in one hand. Daine knew enough to recognize someone used to using magic in battle.

Daine cursed. These back alleys were a maze, and he'd chosen at random—how could these strangers have predicted his path?

"Lakashtai?" he said. "From now on, we're letting Kashtai choose the path."

# CHAPTER 15

**S**ervants of the darkness," Lakashtai hissed, her voice even colder than usual. "You know not what you do. Forsake your foolish path and turn away from your masters, while your souls are yet your own." A wave of coercive force accompanied her words—even Daine felt a momentary compulsion to do as she commanded, but if the strangers were affected by her words or her power, they gave no sign of it.

"It is you who have turned away from the light," called the man with the crystal sword. His voice was soft and clear, with an unfamiliar accent that gave a sibilance to his words. "We did not come to this place in search of you, lost one, but my lady came to me in dreams and warned me of your arrival."

"Feel like introducing us?" Daine said quietly. He hadn't drawn his sword yet; so much about Lakashtai was a mystery, and for all he knew these were second cousins.

"Warriors of Riedra," she said. "I give you this last chance. Leave. Now. For my wrath is as fearful as any nightmare."

"Mine too," Lei muttered, keeping her eyes on the soldiers behind them.

"You underestimate your power, katesh. Our lords are all-knowing, and they have not left us unprepared."

The sparkling crystal shard in his companion's hand flared with a burst of red light, and Lakashtai cried out in pain. She dropped to one knee, her face a mask of concentration and agony. Daine's hands flew to the hilts of his weapons, but the stranger spoke again before he could draw them—and even though he knew his thoughts were being manipulated, Daine felt compelled to hear him out.

"Surrender, fool," he said. "You cannot fight our power. It is you alone that we seek. Come with us now, and we leave your companions alive—even the foolish katesh. Do battle and we take you still, and their deaths are agonizing and slow."

"All right," Daine said quietly, turning to Lei and letting his eyes flicker back over her shoulder. "I'd hate for my friends to get tangled up in something that doesn't concern them." He looked at Pierce, tilting his head slightly. "Sorry, old friend, it's for the best. Just let me do what I have to do."

Pierce nodded solemnly.

Daine looked at Lakashtai. Her eyes were still closed, her teeth clenched, and her face was beaded with sweat. "Whatever you're doing to her, stop. Now."

"You are in no position to bargain. She will recover when we leave this place."

"Thanks, that's very reassuring, but those are my terms. If that's not good enough for you, I guess we'd better fight."

The man's eyes narrowed in the shadows of his hood. For a moment, Daine thought that he would refuse, but finally he nodded. "Very well."

The light from the crystal faded. Lakashtai slumped to the ground, catching herself with one hand. Daine glanced down at her; she simply nodded.

"Very well," said Daine.

He held out his hands and slowly walked toward the Riedrans. It had been an age since Daine had turned his thoughts to any higher power, but for a moment he considered a prayer to the Flame. In the end, he put his trust in himself.

The woman on his left sheathed her sword and produced a set of manacles. They were formed of crimson glass, and Daine could see no apparent locking mechanism—but it was the linking chain that caught his eye.

Perfect.

He held out his arms. As the woman leaned forward, he reached out—grabbing the chain and twisting to the side, tearing it from her hands. As he spun to the side he felt the tremble in the air as three arrows passed, catching the Riedran soldier in the chest and knocking her off her feet. There was no time for Daine to glance over at Pierce: continuing his motion, he lashed out with the manacles, wrapping the light chain around the crystal blade of the Riedran spokesman. The soldier tried to pull away, but Daine was too swift, too strong; one powerful blow sent the blade to the ground.

Daine spared a quick glance toward Lei. As instructed, she'd prepared one of the charms in her pouch; the two men who had been threatening her and Pierce were entangled in a mass of thick, sticky ooze. Pierce had an arrow nocked and was covering the astonished Riedrans.

Daine drew his sword. "Now, about surrender . . ."

The world dissolved into pain. The woman with the crystal had taken a step back, moving just out of his reach, and the crystal in her hand was pulsing with a baleful crimson light. Each pulse sent a wave of agony through Daine's nerves. He was dimly aware of his companions crying out—even Pierce.

"You were warned!" the spokesman said. Only his eyes were visible beneath his hood and veil, and they were blue splinters of pure fury. "Now they die!" He retrieved his weapon and pushed past Daine, making his way toward Lakashtai.

No, Daine thought.

The pain was overwhelming, a fire that paralyzed every muscle, but he found he could still feel his fingers clenched around the hilt of his grandfather's sword. He focused on that sensation, feeling the sword, and time seemed to slow to a crawl. He felt every aspect of the weapon: the balance of the blade, the steel wire binding the leather to the hilt, the silver eye glimmering on the pommel. Images of battle flashed in his mind, the hundreds of conflicts the blade must have seen. For a moment, he forgot the pain.

In that instant, he struck.

His thrust caught the swordsman just above the waist, tearing through his chainmail and punching a bloody hole in his flesh. Daine pulled the blade free, expecting the man to tumble to the ground.

He was disappointed.

The Riedran turned toward him; if the gaping wound caused

him pain, he showed no signs of it. The crystal blade flashed toward Daine, and he raised his sword just in time to block the strike.

Now Daine was on the defensive. In skill, they were almost perfectly matched; every thrust had a counter, every slash was blocked. Now the supernatural pain was pressing at Daine's mind, and with each passing moment it grew stronger. The mysterious strength Daine had drawn from his blade was fading, and it was becoming harder and harder to parry the strokes of the crystal sword. Daine took a step back, trying to reach the woman with the crystal. She was no fool, and even as he staggered toward her she darted away, staying out of his reach.

No, Daine thought, struggling against the pain. He fought to lift his sword, but every motion was torture. It can't end like this . . .

Then just as suddenly as it had begun, the pain came to an end. There was a flash of red energy, and the masked woman fell to her knees, clasping her hand. The crystal had shattered, and her skin was raw and studded with tiny shards. Even through the haze of agony, the cause was clear: her hand was transfixed by a short crossbow bolt, which must have hit the crystal dead center.

There was no time to lose. Forcing his heavy limbs to move, he lunged at the woman, landing a solid blow in her left shoulder. It was by no means a mortal injury, but at this point he just wanted to slow her down.

A new pain tore through his back: Daine had lowered his guard, and the man with the crystal sword had not let the opportunity go to waste. Caught between two foes, Daine drew his dagger and turned to face the veiled swordsman.

"Come on, then," he muttered, vowing to bury his blade in the man's heart with his last breath.

Fate had its own agenda. The lean man leapt forward, launching a lightning-fast thrust at Daine's throat. It never connected. There was a blur of motion, and another quarrel lodged itself in the man's leg, throwing him off of his path. Granted a moment's reprieve, Daine took a step backwards, setting his back against the wall of the alley. There was a silver streak, and Pierce's flail came flashing forward from the edge of his vision, knocking the Riedran to the ground.

*It's good to have friends,* Daine thought.

He took a deep breath and pushed himself away from the supporting wall. Pierce was fighting the swordsman, forcing the lithe assassin back down the alley. Lei and Lakashtai had also recovered and engaged the two soldiers Lei had trapped in the magic web. That left the woman with the shattered crystal. Though she was still clutching her injured hand, she was rising to her feet, and Daine had no idea what other powers she might have in reserve. He steadied his grip and prepared to strike.

*"Kolesq!"* a voice cried: the man with the crystal sword. As Daine lunged forward, the woman slapped her left wrist with her right hand. Her outline wavered, growing ghostly and translucent—in an instant, she was gone, and the point of Daine's sword struck the hard wall behind her. He swept the blade from side to side; he'd dealt with invisible foes before. This time, he felt nothing. It seemed she had fled.

She wasn't the only one. Glancing around, Daine saw that all of their assailants had vanished—even those trapped in Lei's mystical web.

"Status?" he called, sharply.

"Nothing serious, Daine," Pierce called.

*He never calls me "captain" anymore,* Daine thought.

"Minor injury," Lei said, and Daine spun to face her, his heart pounding harder. There was a shallow cut on her right arm, and she was clutching her lower left ribs. Daine knew that she could judge her own injuries, but he found himself by her side, studying the cut. "I can heal it . . ." she said, gritting her teeth. "Made wand . . ."

Lakashtai seemed to be in the worst condition, for all that Daine could see no physical injuries. She had fallen back against the alley wall, and was clutching her forehead. When she pulled her hand away, her face was paler than usual, her skin covered with sweat—the first time Daine had actually seen her sweat, he realized.

"Who . . . who shattered the crystal?" she said, her voice tight.

"That would be me," a voice said, just behind Daine. Even as he spun to face the new sound, a lithe figure slithered down the wall, landing smoothly on the alley path.

"My name's Gerrion," the stranger said, in a voice that sounded like laughter. "I understand you're in the market for a guide."

At a glance, the stranger was unremarkable; he wouldn't attract a moment's notice on the streets of Sharn. His clothes were threadbare and plain, patched brown breeches, tall leather boots in need of resoling, a light wool cloak that had once been a vivid burgundy but had faded under the relentless assault of sun and storm. On closer inspection, unusual details began to emerge. He was wearing a glove of fine leather on his left hand, oiled and polished with a loving care that his boots had never seen. The glove was deep black, with a wreath of vivid flames painted around the wrist and extending up the back of the hand toward the fingers; when he flexed his palm, the fire seemed to dance. But if Gerrion's gloves were distinctive, his face was even more remarkable. At first Daine had thought that the man was hidden by shadows, but he quickly realized that Gerrion's skin was gray—the cold color of faint smoke or the sky after a storm has just passed. His hair was a brilliant red with streaks of golden blonde; it fell to his shoulders and filled his hood, so that his head almost seemed aflame. His eyes were a gray so pale they were almost white, so that he seemed to have no irises at all. His eyes were slightly too large, slightly tilted, and his cheeks were high boned and perfectly smooth, with no trace of beard or stubble; after a moment Daine decided that the stranger had elven and human blood in his veins, though neither explained the strange tone of his skin.

"It seems we're in your debt," Daine said.

He had not sheathed his sword, and he was still ready to strike. Gerrion's right hand was concealed beneath his cloak. Daine had spent years as a bodyguard, and he could easily imagine the small crossbow it held.

"So pay me," Gerrion said carelessly.

He had the grace of a lazy cat; he leaned back against the alley wall, but Daine had watched him land, and he still remembered the crossbow bolt that shattered a tiny crystal. Gerrion might be in repose, but Daine had no doubt the man was ready to react to any perceived danger.

"Is that a threat?"

Gerrion rolled his eyes. He tossed back his cloak, revealing the expected crossbow—small, finely crafted, the wood of the stock polished to a fine sheen. With practiced grace, he pulled the quarrel and loosened the string, placing the weapon in a sheath on his right hip.

"If I wanted you dead, we wouldn't be having this conversation." He spoke with nonchalance, as if they were old friends discussing the weather.

"What is it that you want?" Lakashtai stepped up next to Daine. She was still drawn and pale, but her voice had regained its calm strength.

"That's a question with a long, boring answer, and it's not a tale I care to share with strangers in an alley, but gold will do for a start. I meant what I said before. You were right; you do need a guide in Stormwatch, and you'll find few better. If you need to go along the coast or into the jungle, I can arrange that too."

"Eavesdropping is always the best way to establish trust," Daine said.

"You only know I was eavesdropping because I told you; if I wanted to be deceptive, I could have come up with any number of better stories. As a matter of fact, I was looking for you, Daine."

"I'm supposed to be surprised that you know my name? That would play better if you hadn't admitted to the eavesdropping."

"Actually I was thinking another name might help matters. Perhaps Alina Lyrris means something to you?"

Daine had sheathed his sword, but in an instant it was out

again. "Something, yes, but not a name I expected to hear here."

"Well, your history is not my concern," Gerrion said, the hint of a shrug passing across his shoulders. If he was perturbed by the blade, he hid it well. "I received a message by the stones, warning me of your arrival and asking me to look out for you—Stormreach is not kind to strangers. The description was good, but it wasn't hard to spot you; a man traveling with a warforged and a kalashtar does stand out."

"What about—" Lei interjected, peering over Daine's shoulder.

"I'm afraid you weren't mentioned. I have no idea who you are—though it's a mystery I can't wait to solve."

Daine scowled. "Stand off a moment, would you?"

Gerrion made the slightest bow and walked farther down the alley.

Daine turned to the others. Pierce was standing a few steps away, an arrow already nocked in his great bow; Daine knew that the warforged was waiting for the word to strike. Lei was frowning, while Lakashtai remained as calm and enigmatic as always.

"What do you think?" asked Daine.

"I do not know this Alina Lyrris," Lakashtai said, "and I am troubled that this man knows of our presence. His thoughts are slippery, like polished glass, but he did us a great favor when he shattered the mindshard. I doubt that our enemy has another such object here in Stormreach, and it's not something they would sacrifice willingly."

"At this point, nothing Alina does can surprise me," Daine said, grinding his teeth. "She's a . . . I don't know what you'd call her. A spider, playing games with people's lives. This fellow has her stink on him, I'll give you that, but we did her a service recently, and I don't see any reason she'd sell us out. He's probably just what he seems—this would be her idea of a gift." A favor, he thought, taunting me with her help.

"Why doesn't he know who I am?" Lei said.

"Pierce, what do you think?" Daine said.

"If we need a guide, he is our best choice. We have no reason to trust anyone in this city. He has helped us once, and if this Alina did ask him to help us—it is my understanding that she is not a woman to be crossed lightly."

"Yes . . . that's certainly true."

"While he may have followed us without my knowledge, I assure you, Daine—I will be watching him now," Pierce said. Pierce was a scout and a hunter—if he had marked his prey, Gerrion wouldn't be sneaking up on them again.

"It sounds like we're decided, then," Daine said. "Lakashtai—do we have gold to spare for out guide?"

"I have some coin and letters of credit on the Kundarak Bank," Lakashtai said. "One does not come so far without gold in hand."

"Assuming you have gold to begin with," Daine said, running a finger along his all-too-empty purse. "Well, you're the mistress of coin. Perhaps you can see if our new friend can find us a trustworthy inn. I don't know about you, but I'd just as soon get out of this alley."

"Why doesn't he know who I am?" Lei said again.

❁ ❁ ❁ ❁ ❁ ❁ ❁

It took Lakashtai and Gerrion some time to work out the details of their arrangement; Alina might have told the gray man to look after Daine, but apparently she'd said nothing about the price of these services. Eventually they came to terms, and Gerrion took the lead.

"There are inns in Stormreach that make soup from the bones of unwary guests," he said, "but I know a place where you can sleep through the night."

Lakashtai walked alongside Gerrion, asking questions about the colony. Pierce stayed close behind their guide, listening to every word and taking his measure of the stranger. Daine held Lei back a step, just far enough so they could speak without being overheard.

"Are you all right?"

She nodded, tapping her healing wand. "I think we'll both pull through." She rubbed at a tear on her sleeve. "Though I'll need to do some mending, once we're settled in."

"That's not what I meant."

She frowned. "What do you mean?"

Daine gestured vaguely. "Everything! We're across the sea. There's no law here. We were almost killed a few minutes ago, and this gray man may be leading us into someone's soup pot."

"Where have you been for the last three years?" Lei said. "A week ago I was fighting bugs in the sewers. I'm starting to get used to it. Besides, this is *Xen'drik*. All my life I've heard stories. They say the old kingdoms of Xen'drik controlled powers we can't even imagine—mystical principles thousands of years beyond what my . . . House Cannith has developed." She stumbled for a moment; clearly the mention of House Cannith had brought back the memory of her own humiliation at the house, but she soon found her voice again. "Just look at this place. Where else could you find pre-Galifar Lhazaar architecture next to a Zil waterhouse? And . . . look at that."

At first, Daine thought the creature she was pointing at was a minotaur. It was a massive humanoid with hooves in place of feet; it wore a red tabard, and its exposed skin was covered with a coat of white fur. Its head was more like a ram than a bull; its horns curved back over its skull.

"I've never seen anything like it," She said. "Do you suppose there's an entire nation of them out in the jungle? Perhaps we could ask."

She stopped for a moment, but Daine took her arm and pulled her along. "Let's make sure we don't lose track of the others. I don't think we want to be left behind on the streets."

❧ ❧ ❧ ❧ ❧ ❧ ❧

"You're telling me this is the safest place in Stormreach?" Daine said. "I don't know about the innkeeper killing us in our sleep . . . I think the inn may do that on its own."

If not for the wooden door at the center, Daine wouldn't have recognized the structure as a building. At first glance, it seemed like a heap of twigs piled together by some massive bird—though on closer inspection, the boughs and branches were carefully interlaced.

Lei was already examining one of the thatched walls. "It's densewood," she said, running a finger along a twig. "The elves of Aerenal use it in place of stone—it's nearly as tough and durable as granite, but the elven buildings I've seen have all used blocks carved from densewood or long timbers. I've never seen a design like this. Try to break off a piece of one of those branches."

Daine grudgingly tried—and failed. It was just as Lei had said: the twigs were as strong as stone.

"Scratch at the walls all you want, I'm going inside," Gerrion said. "I don't know about you, but I intend to celebrate our new partnership."

The door was carved from a single piece of wood, and the hinges were densewood roots threaded into the labyrinthine walls. Some faint light filtered through them, but most of the illumination in the chamber came from a massive central hearth. As his eyes adjusted to the dim light, Daine saw that he was standing in the common room. Half a dozen patrons were scattered about the room spread around low wooden tables. The next thing Daine noticed were the cats. There were over a dozen felines of various shapes and sizes in the common room. Some were sprawled around the central fire, others peered out of nooks in the rough walls, and a few were demanding scraps from the more softhearted patrons. Daine was used to seeing a cat or two in an inn, or at least some creature that would keep the vermin down; halfling hostels were often protected by smalltooths, tiny carnivorous reptiles, but this was rather more than he was used to.

"Welcome to the Ship's Cat, travelers."

The voice was rough and deep but distinctly feminine. The speaker had the burly, muscular build that would have suited a blacksmith. Her brown hair fell in an unruly mane around her shoulders, and her large golden eyes glittered with reflected firelight. She was a shifter, and the blood of the wilds ran in her veins.

"Harysh!" Gerrion said. "I trust you have room for my four new friends?"

The innkeeper smiled, revealing pointed teeth. "Friends of yours are always welcome, Gerrion—though if you seek lodging, I'll need sovereigns on the table before I open my doors."

Gerrion gave a mocking pout. "I'd hoped that we'd finally put that behind us, hostess."

"Not likely. Now what can I get for you, travelers?"

Eventually Daine found himself tucked into a corner of the room, staring at a large gray cat that apparently had designs on his smoked tribex. The meat was slightly tough, but after days of hard tack and sea rations, it was delightful.

"Here we are," he said. "Stormreach. Xen'drik. We've found our little haven. We have a guide, and we've already encountered our first group of assassins. Now do you actually have a plan, Lakashtai, or did we just come here for the tribex?"

He immediately regretted lashing out at her, but he couldn't seem to help it. Ever since the mental siege had begun, his nerves had been wearing thin, and it seemed harder and harder to hold back his anger.

Lakashtai didn't rise to the barb. "I do not have answers for you, Daine, not yet, but I know where to begin. There is a sorcerer in Stormreach, and his vaults may hold the key to our problems. For now, I suggest that you enjoy your meal and get a good night's sleep. I suspect that we'll be traveling into the wilds before this is done—so enjoy these comforts while you have them. You'll all need your full strength in the days that lie ahead."

"If I may ask, my lady, what is the name of this mysterious stranger? I am well rested already, and I may be able to save you some time with your inquiries."

Gerrion had set his cloak on the floor, and Daine noticed a new detail in the flickering light from the hearth—a triangular tattoo at the top of the man's forehead, forming a sort of widow's peak. The tattoo was almost invisible against his pale gray skin and looked as though it continued back beneath his hair; while it was hard to see the details in the flickering light, the design appeared to be a complex pattern of interwoven flames.

"Hassalac Chaar," Lakashtai said.

Gerrion's eyes widened for an instant. "In that case, I hope you won't mind if I ask for some of my payment up front as well. There are debts I promised to pay before I passed away, and it seems that I should do this as quickly as possible. Shall we meet back here at the eighth bell?"

Lakashtai nodded, and after sorting through her belongings

she produced a few platinum coins for the guide. Gerrion gave a slight bow, flashed a smile at the innkeeper, and darted out the door.

"It's interesting," Lei said, watching him leave. "He looks like he has elven blood, but I've never seen any Khoravar with that skin tone before—or elf, for that matter."

"He's certainly in a hurry," Daine said. "Care to tell us more about this Hassalac, Lakashtai?"

The kalashtar woman glanced toward him, and Daine was surprised by the weariness in her eyes. The strength seemed to have flowed out of her, as if she had been holding herself together until the stranger had left.

"Not now," she said quietly. "There will be time to talk on the morrow. Let us find our shelter and rest: we have much to do tomorrow."

The innkeeper led them upstairs, and eventually Daine settled a small room that felt more like a rat's nest than a hostel. It was only as he was drifting into sleep that he realized—he hadn't seen Pierce since Gerrion's departure.

Long shadows filled the streets of Stormreach. Cold fire lanterns cast light into the darkness, but in the grimy avenues and alleys around the Ship's Cat these pools of radiance were few and far between.

The gloom suited Pierce's purposes, and he drifted from shadow to shadow as he followed Gerrion. He hadn't decided whether he trusted Gerrion or believed his claim to be an agent of Alina, but Pierce and his companions were in hostile territory. There were enemies about, and Gerrion was one of their only resources. If he were a traitor, Pierce needed to watch his movements. If he truly were an ally, he might need protection from their enemies. Either way, Pierce would be watching.

Pierce loved the hunt. Every thought, every sense, was focused on stalking his prey. This was what he was made for, and it came as naturally to him as breathing would to a human. Instinct guided him to every shadow, every patch of cover. Without even thinking, he analyzed every living creature in his field of vision, judging their apparent abilities of perception and the threat they might present in battle. It was calming, and for a time he let go of all of his concerns and questions, submerging himself in the pursuit of Gerrion.

Gerrion's behavior was anything but suspicious. He was in no hurry to go anywhere. For the next few hours Gerrion wandered the city. He brought a skin of wine to a group of beggars and passed half an hour with gossip and conversation.

He spoke with a few sailors and simple tradesmen, discussing the weather, the shipping news, word of various expeditions into the interior. Occasionally he brought up the name Hassalac, the man Lakashtai wanted to see—but it seemed like Gerrion was gathering information on his recent activities. If he was betraying Pierce and his companions, the signs were too subtle for Pierce to perceive.

While Gerrion seemed to have many friends in Stormreach, he had his share of enemies as well. More than a few people turned away with expressions of disgust when they caught sight of Gerrion, and a man with the look of a militiaman or mercenary soldier sneered and spat at the half-elf. It was hard for Pierce to tell if this anger was directed at Gerrion himself or if it was some sort of general prejudice toward his race. Over the course of two hours, Pierce only saw one other person with gray skin similar to Gerrion's; she was a beggar, and like Gerrion she also seemed to have some amount of elven blood in her veins; her rambling conversation suggested deep-rooted mental instability.

Eventually, Gerrion came to the harbor. He made his way onto a small sailboat, entering the cabin. The vessel was battered and worn, the hull covered with peeling black paint, and as far as Pierce could tell from the movement of shadows against the window-blind, Gerrion was its sole inhabitant.

Eventually the lamp within the cabin was extinguished. Pierce continued to watch the vessel for another hour, waiting to see if Gerrion would emerge or if a guest might arrive, but the harbor was silent and dead. A human might have found the wait to be excruciatingly dull, but such thoughts never crossed Pierce's mind. He was absorbed by the hunt, watching every sound, every motion, every ripple of water and shifting shadow. He was hidden against a mooring pylon, and between his superior view of the piers and his inhumanly sharp senses, no one should have been able to approach without his knowledge.

But she did.

"It is strange that we should meet in this place."

Her voice cut through the night, and if Pierce had been human he would have jumped in surprise. Instead he analyzed the situation. The speaker was close but out of sight; he considered the possibility that she was invisible but came to the conclusion that she was standing on the other side of the pylon he was using for cover. At such distances his bow would be useless, and he prepared to draw his flail should the need arise, but even as he made this calculation, he was also considering the voice itself. Though feminine in pitch and inflection, it had an echoing timbre that reminded Pierce of his own voice—words formed from the rippling of a flowing stream.

It was a voice he'd heard before.

She stepped out from behind the pillar and into the light of the two moons that were full in the sky. Pierce's instincts told him to draw his flail, but this time he restrained himself.

"Strange indeed," he said. "I had not thought to see you again or that you possessed the skills to approach me unseen—your talents have grown since our last meeting."

"Perhaps, or perhaps I wished to be seen."

She wore a cloak of stained gray oilskin, and her clothes were ragged burlap. With her scarf pulled up to cover her face, she would have passed unnoticed on the street. Just another beggar. Her scarf was pulled down, and the face beneath the hood was that of a warforged soldier, coated with dark blue enamel that blended into the shadows of the night.

"What brings you to this place, brother?" she said.

For a moment, Pierce was at a loss for words. He had never forgotten their meeting on the streets of Sharn, and he felt an unfamiliar thrill at seeing her here. The stranger fascinated him on many levels. While the warforged had no true gender, her feminine voice and posture were intriguing; it was not a physical attraction in any way a human would understand it, but she raised a deep curiosity, a question of how else she might differ from him. Her skills were impressive. Reflecting on the hunt, Pierce now recalled spotting her once or twice over the evening, but he had never realized her true nature or considered the fact that she might have been watching him. Just looking at her, he could tell that she would be a deadly foe. Her hands might be empty, but they were made of steel and mithral. Studying her stance Pierce could tell that she was ready to strike if he took hostile action.

"I am here to protect my companions," he said.

"Have you sold yourself to this gray-skinned breather, or do you still follow your old commander, bound by the chains of our ancient service?"

"I come in the company of friends, not as a slave following a master." Pierce said. "Perhaps friendship is a concept you cannot understand."

"I know it well," she said, taking a step closer to Pierce. His instinct was to step back, moving away from her reach, but he chose to hold his ground. She was a foot shorter than he was, and she gazed up into his crystal eyes. "Those creatures of flesh created us to die in their wars. Believe what you will, you are nothing but a tool to your so-called friends. You are the shield: the strong wall that protects them from harm and the first to be sacrificed when the onslaught comes."

"I think I know my companions better than you do," Pierce replied. The first stirrings of anger burned at the back of his mind. "I fought in many battles alongside the captain, and I am still here. I would not be, if not for the magical gifts of my lady Lei."

"Listen to your speech, brother. Your captain. Your lady. There is no war, not any more. You owe fealty to no one, but you have forged your own chains. Tell yourself they are your equals—your friends—if you wish, but in your deep thoughts, they remain your masters."

Pierce looked away, breaking the eye contact. She was twisting his words, but there was some grain of truth to it. Though he had consciously sought to set aside these terms of rank, at his core he still saw Daine as his commander. There was comfort in that hierarchy, in that sense of purpose, but even as his doubts grew, so did his anger.

"You know nothing of my life," he said.

"I *lived* your life, brother. I served in their war. I believed in the cause. I was almost destroyed more than once, only to be brought back from the darkness by their smiths and their spells, but that gift of life was not given freely. They made me to serve and brought me back so I could kill and die for them again."

Curiosity warred with anger. "How did you serve? You carry

no weapons. Have you set aside the path of war along with your former loyalties?"

"Things are not always as they seem." She crossed her arms before her chest and clenched her fists. Blades of black metal snapped out of her forearms. "I was born to kill generals and princes. I am the sword in the shadows, and many fell by my hand. I was built to bring death to creatures of flesh, and now that I am free, I choose my victims."

"You did not live my life," Pierce said. "I was not made to kill—I was made to protect. Now that I am free, I choose who I will defend."

There was a flash of motion. A tiny creature came darting out of the sky, a delicate silver construct no larger than a dragonfly. It settled on the assassin's chest. Pierce had heard of such devices but never seen one; they had been built to transmit memories and images from one warforged to another, facilitating communication between spies and scouts. The stranger's eyes dimmed for a moment as she listened to a voice Pierce could not hear.

"So you are not alone?" Pierce said. He did not know the range of the messenger, but he was certain it could not fly across the sea.

"I did not cross the Thunder Sea just to argue with you, no. I have my own purposes here, and it is time I returned to my work." She took a few steps back. "So return to your captain and your lady. Just remember—these creatures of flesh and blood are not as strong as we are. They are vulnerable to so many things: disease, hunger, the ravages of time. They will die eventually, and in a land as dangerous as this one, there are many ways it could happen. Defend them if you must, but we will be waiting for you when they are gone."

She turned and sprinted down the pier, moving with astonishing speed and silence. A moment later she had passed through the harbor gate, and Pierce was alone again.

Daine's sleep was troubled. He dreamt of a thousand floating eyes surrounding him, peering, probing, trying to press inside his mouth and ears. There were multifaceted insect eyes, yellow eyes of cats and wolves, human eyes the size of his fist. He could feel the alien gaze as if it were a physical force, icy fingers tracing strange patterns across his skin.

He woke with a cold shiver. The room was dark, and he could still feel the chill touch of the eyes against his skin.

"I am sorry."

Lakashtai was sitting on the floor next to his bed. She was still wearing her cloak, and even as Daine's eyes adjusted to the dim light her face was hidden in the shadows of her hood. A sleek black cat was draped across her lap, and it peered up at him with yellow eyes that seemed all too familiar.

"I was arrogant, and I did not anticipate the actions of our enemies," Lakashtai said.

Daine could not see her mouth, and her voice was a whisper in the darkness. For a moment he wondered if he was still asleep, and he stared at the cat with new suspicion. It ignored him, armored in feline pride.

"The crystal shard Gerrion shattered was a weapon designed to fight my people," Lakashtai continued. "The pain you felt was but a taste of its true power. Kashtai . . . the attack has weakened my bond to her spirit, and without her strength my powers are diminished. I thought that I would be protecting you, but now I fear that I shall be the one that requires protection."

"The eyes . . ." Daine said, struggling with his thoughts.

"They are the least servants of il-Lashtavar. The Dreaming Dark can capture the spirits of those who die while sleeping and bind them in mindless servitude. Tonight, they are the hounds of Tashana, and they seek your dreams on behalf of their mistress. I have wrapped you in mystery, and I believe that you escaped unseen."

"I'm safe?"

"For the rest of this night, I hope. I cannot shield you completely, but I can hold them at bay . . . for the moment, at least, but I cannot promise dreamless sleep in the nights to come."

She stood, and in her dark cloak she seemed little more than a shadow. The cat seemed to have vanished. "Return to your rest. Hard times lie before us, and you must marshal what strength you can. We will need you in the times to come."

Lakashtai walked over to the door, and her passage made no sound, but even as she left, Daine heard another whisper at the back of his mind.

*Beware the gifts of the Traveler, my friend. Remember the words of the wind.*

"Jode?" he muttered.

For a moment he struggled to rise, to look around the room, but sleep weighed on his thoughts like an anchor, and he found himself falling down against the blankets. His last memory was of a pair of yellow eyes shining in the darkness.

☙ ☙ ☙ ☙ ☙ ☙ ☙

If Daine had other dreams that night, he could not remember them in the light of the morning. He was the last of the companions to rise, and when he made his way downstairs the others were waiting for him. Gerrion and Lei were engaged in an animated conversation about the history of local ruins. Lakashtai sipped at a cup of tal, lost in her own thoughts. Pierce watched from a corner. Daine considered asking about his nocturnal patrol, but he knew Pierce would tell him if there was anything he needed to know. While he had come to think of Pierce as a friend and not simply a soldier, they rarely talked; they understood each other, and speech was unnecessary.

"These will strengthen you for the tasks ahead. Eat quickly," Lakashtai said, pushing a bowl toward him.

It was filled with berries drenched in a watery white liquid, and Daine studied the unfamiliar fruit dubiously. Each berry had a thin yellow shell with a vertical black slash, and at a glance it looked disturbingly like a mass of eyes glaring up at him.

Lei glanced over from her conversation and smiled. "If the local fare is too rich for your delicate palate, I can see about getting you a bowl of gruel, Master Daine."

Daine scowled and began to eat. He tried not to think about his dream and the eyes crawling into his mouth.

"Now that you have rested, there is no time to waste," Lakashtai said. "We must conclude our business in Stormreach as swiftly as possible. The Riedrans may have other concerns than hunting you, Daine, but I think it best that we leave quickly."

"This Hassalac can cure me?"

"It is not so simple. Hassalac has gathered many relics of the past. It is possible that he has already found the weapon we require to drive the darkness from your mind, but he is arrogant and proud, and he will not help us out of kindness. It is my hope that a suitable gift will serve as our gateway to his vault."

"So we're going on a bold expedition to the market?"

"Hassalac is a powerful and wealthy man, and the things that he desires are not sold in the market square. Fortunately our guide is familiar with Hassalac and the lay of this land, and Gerrion has suggested a suitable gift. This is not a time for discussion. Finish your meal swiftly, and let us set ourselves in motion; I shall explain everything in time."

Daine shrugged and turned his attention to his bowl of sour milk and bitter berries. Beneath the table a gray cat with glittering silver stripes rubbed against his leg, purring in strange fluting tones.

❀ ❀ ❀ ❀ ❀ ❀ ❀

Stormreach was a different place by the light of day. With the sun in the sky, Daine could see the buildings that dominated the center of the city . . . although building was a generous term. Stormreach was filled with ruins: remnants of stone and densewood, vast archways and broken walls.

"Tens of thousands of years," Lei murmured. "These were the homes of giants. Imagine what these walls have seen."

At the moment, Daine had little interest in history; he was more concerned with the Riedran warriors. While Lakashtai said they'd need time to recover, there was no way to know how many allies they had in the city. Daine studied each weed-choked wall, each stranger to cross his path. Many of the settlers had used the old walls as the foundations for their homes and businesses; these ranged from shabby tents to solid stone structures that looked like they could last another thirty thousand years. Pox-ridden beggars, vendors hawking strange and disturbing foods, and colorfully dressed missionaries all sought to bar their path, but Pierce pushed the strangers aside.

Gerrion led the way. He followed a strange path, and his choices seemed almost random. Wide roads alternated with narrow alleys where they needed to walk in single file, and Daine was certain they were moving in a wide circle instead of a straight line. The war had taught him that the shortest path was not always the safest one, and this time they did not encounter any ambushes.

"I think it's about time you told us who this Hassalac is," Daine told Lakashtai, as they made their way past a band of dwarves—miners, by the look of it. The sharp stench of roasting lizard-meat filled the air, fighting with the salty tang of the ocean. "Judging from our guide's reaction last night, I gather there's a story to tell, and I'm not going into this blind."

"Hassalac Chaar," Lakashtai said. "The Prince of Dragons. The most powerful sorcerer in Stormreach, or so it's said—possibly one of the mightiest in the world. He claims that the blood of dragons runs through his veins and that this is the source of his power."

" 'Prince of Dragons?' Don't tell me he actually has dragons as servants." Daine had never seen a dragon, but he had heard the legends. It was said that a single dragon could lay waste to an army.

"No," Lakashtai said. "It is just a title, derived from his beliefs about his bloodline."

"That's something, I guess, and he collects old things?"

"Yes. This was my original purpose in coming to this place—to gain access to his vaults and study the relics that he has acquired, to learn if he has found anything better left unknown."

"Like what?"

"In ancient times, Xen'drik was ruled by a race of giants. Their civilizations lasted tens of thousands of years, and in that time they learned much of magic. They developed mystical weapons and tools far beyond the capabilities of the wizards of Khorvaire."

"You're worried that he's found some sort of weapon built by these giants?"

"No," said Lakashtai.

There, was an angry roar coming from behind them. Glancing over his shoulder, Daine saw a massive, filthy woman—at least ten feet tall and heavily muscled—howling at the dwarves. The miners scattered, leaving the giantess alone with the nervous lizard-meat vendor.

"So that's a giant?" Daine said. "She doesn't look like much of an archmage to me."

Lakashtai shook her head. "The fall of giant civilization began with an attack from the outer planes—from Dal Quor, the region of dreams. Mystical portals brought a host of quori spirits to this world. It was an army of nightmares, fear given form."

"The work of your il-lushtavar?"

"Il-Lashtavar, and no, it was not. The plane of Dal Quor goes through cycles, ages in which the very nature of reality is reshaped and redefined. The Dreaming Dark is the spirit of this age, but we can only imagine what came before. This is why I have come—in the hopes that among his treasures, Hassalac has recovered tools of these ancient quori, something that will tell us more about their society."

"How does this help me?"

"The giants fought the forces of Dal Quor and in time defeated them. The giants developed some sort of terrible weapon that altered the orbits of the planes themselves. Once a skilled wizard could travel into Dal Quor or summon its spirits to do his bidding. The giants shattered the bonds that bind Dal Quor to Eberron, and today it can only be reached in dreams."

"Where's that leave Tashana?" Daine said. "She seemed like a little more than a dream in that fight on the docks."

"She is a vessel for a spirit of Dal Quor, and this fiend grants her terrible power. It would be far worse if it could manifest physically; as it is, the quori must act through mortal hosts."

"I hate to ask again, but how does any of this help me?"

"The giants fought a war against nightmares, and they won. Their ultimate victory was due to the weapon that shattered the bonds of worlds, but they undoubtedly used lesser tools in the battle—and if they could defend against quori attacks, they might be able to drive the spirit from your mind. It's possible Hassalac already has such a tool; if not, it is my hope that he has a map."

"Because . . .?"

"I do hate to interrupt," Gerrion said. "Actually, I kind of enjoy it, but that's beside the point. We have arrived at our destination, my lords and ladies."

The building before them was a dome-shaped structure built from large clay bricks. The walls were worn smooth by the passage of time, and Daine guessed that it was one of the oldest structures in Stormreach. In place of windows, large blocks of pinkish crystal were embedded in the walls. Each crystal slab was engraved with a unique symbol, and studying the symbols Daine realized the nature of the building. Glancing at the arched doorway, he saw what he had expected to find—a familiar eight-pointed cross.

"This is a temple to the Sovereign Host," he said. "What are we going to do—pray for our gift?"

"Not at all," Gerrion said. "You're going to steal it."

# CHAPTER 19

XEN'DRIK
STORMREACH
*Lharvion 19, 997 YK*

"**Y**ou want us to rob a *temple?*" Lei said. She looked at Daine. "Surely you're not going along with this."

Daine shrugged. "Where were the gods when Cyre was destroyed?"

"You can't expect the Sovereigns to take sides in mortal wars. Cyre, Breland—they watch over us all."

"Not very well."

"Stealing from priests—how much lower could we sink?"

Gerrion was watching the interchange with a smile. "Fair lady, I assure you that the master of this temple has sunk far lower than you ever could. If it is any consolation, he obtained the object we now seek through theft."

"Why should I believe you?" Lei said.

"Well, since I was the one who stole it for him, I would hope you'd take my word on the matter."

"Who did you steal it from?" Daine said.

"Hassalac Chaar. That's how I know it's something he wants."

"Of course." Daine ran a hand across his forehead. Lakashtai and Pierce both watched in silence. Daine guessed that Lakashtai had known about this all along; Pierce, on the other hand, saw no reason to speak. "So you know your way around Hassalac's estate?"

"Oh, no. I stole the scale before it ever reached the Dragon Prince. I have my talents, but I wouldn't be so foolish as to invade Hassalac's sanctum. Not to discourage you, of course."

Daine glanced at Lakashtai; she raised her eyebrows, and this minimal motion conveyed her indifference as clearly as any shrug. "Fine. This is your game, Lakashtai, and I'll follow your lead."

Lei was still studying the multicolored hierogram above the gate. "I . . . suppose. What are we looking for?"

"A single scale from a blue dragon, a foot across, one and a half feet tall. Straps have been placed on one side, allowing it to be used as a buckler; the other bears the symbol of the Sovereigns."

Lei considered this. "A foot across? But the dragon would have to be . . ." She trailed off, struggling to calculate sizes in her head.

"If you believe Master Sakhesh, it's a scale of the god Aureon himself."

"Oh!" Lei said. "They're draconists!" The prospect seemed to cheer her.

"Care to explain that to us lowly soldiers?" Daine said.

"There's a sect that claims that the Sovereigns walked the earth before they rose to the heavens," Lei said. "The draconists say that these dragons were the mightiest children of Eberron and Siberys, and that after defeating the demons of Khyber they ascended to a higher state of being. I've never actually met a draconist, but I've seen a few of their icons."

"It's a belief that's alive and well in Xen'drik," Gerrion said. "They say Master Sakhesh hopes to become a dragon himself some day, and his faith is founded on greed. The dragon church is one of the oldest buildings of Stormreach; this is a hard land, and the first settlers relied on the magic of the priests for survival. The church has a proud history of extortion, and Maru Sakhesh is a great believer in tradition."

Daine didn't care if people cast the gods as dragons, humans, or fruit, but it seemed to make all the difference to Lei; this revelation had removed her doubts. "What's our plan?"

"Gather around," Gerrion said, "and I'll tell you what to do."

❀ ❀ ❀ ❀ ❀ ❀

Gerrion did not accompany them into the church. The situation was plain enough to Daine; this wasn't the first time that Gerrion had robbed this temple, and Sakhesh would not welcome him. Daine glanced over at Lakashtai. Much of this plan depended on her mental power, and in her weakened state she might not be up to the challenge. Her expression was serene, and if she had any doubts she hid them well.

A small antechamber led into the circular nave of the church. Benches filled the center of the chamber. Nine altars were spread along the walls, each altar placed beneath one of the crystal blocks in the walls; pink light filtered down through these crystal cubes. Traditionally, each altar would bear the symbol of one of the nine Sovereigns; here the altars were engraved with images of dragons, elaborately carved and inlaid with enamel and jewels. Daine was no expert on religion, but he knew that the central altar was typically dedicated to Aureon, and here it bore the image of a rearing blue dragon wreathed in lightning.

*Do not speak.* It was Lakashtai's voice, quiet and clear. Too clear—there was no trace of an echo in the great hall. *Think of me, and I shall hear your thoughts.*

*Great,* Daine thought. *I needed more voices in my head.*

*Who invited you?* It was Lei's voice. *Wait—? Daine?*

*I have linked us all,* came Lakashtai's thought, and there was a strange burst of emotion like the mental equivalent of a frustrated sigh. *Someone approaches, so do turn your attention to the task at hand.*

The priest was tall and heavyset, a man used to good food and easy living. He wore a robe of black silk with a golden cowl, and colorful dragons danced along the hem.

"Travelers have come to the house of the Nine," the priest said, his voice low and resonant. His golden hair was scented and oiled, but lines of age could be seen beneath the powder on his face. "Olladra smiles on us all to lead you to this place. I am Maru Sakhesh, and in this place I speak with the voice of the Sovereigns. I fear the midday service is hours away, and many of my acolytes have yet to arrive, but perhaps you have come in search of more—*personal* services."

Daine had no idea what the old man was talking about, but

something about this speech sent a shiver down his spine. The old man's voice had power, but there was something fundamentally repellent about him. There was no emotion in his gaze, just cold calculation. This man might worship dragons, but looking into his eyes, Daine knew that to the priest he was no more significant than a worm.

"We have, good priest," Lakashtai said. She met Sakhesh's gaze, and Daine caught the faintest gleam of green light burning in her eyes. "We set sail tomorrow for the city of Trolanport. We have done well in our travels, and we wish to make offerings to Kol Korran and Olladra to thank them for their bounty and to ensure our safe return."

She gestured at the empty air beside her, and for an instant Daine saw a host of servants, laden with coffers brimming with coins, gems and platters of rich foods. He blinked, and the image vanished.

"As you can see, we have brought a variety of goods," Lakashtai continued. "Some we wish to sacrifice directly to the Sovereigns themselves, but it was our hope that you would guide us through the ritual of Olladra's Feast—joining in the celebration, of course. Naturally, we would make a donation to the temple to compensate you for your time."

Maru Sakhesh stared at the space she had indicated, and his eyes widened. "As Olladra wills!" he said cheerfully. "It is not my place to refuse her bounty." He indicated a heavy wooden table at the very center of the chamber. "Let me sort through your goods, and then we can begin."

*It is done,* came Lakashtai's thoughts. *He has a strong mind—I do not know how long I can maintain this vision. Move swiftly and as silently as possible. Sound may break the trance.*

Sakhesh was inspecting the row of servants that existed only in his mind, sniffing at imaginary delicacies.

*Pierce, Lei—you can both hear me?* Daine thought. Affirmations quickly followed. *Flail out, Pierce—if we encounter enemies, it will be close quarters. You take the rear. Lei, you're with me. Watch floor and door for any sort of defenses. Any opposition, I want you back behind Pierce. Understood? Go!*

There was a large wooden door at the far end of the room. Lei examined it and nodded. Daine grasped the door and pulled gently—there was the faintest creak of old hinges, but nothing the priest would hear over his loud conversation with Lakashtai and her imaginary companions. Daine ducked through, leading with the point of his sword, but there was no one on the other side—just a spiral staircase dropping down beneath the temple.

Daine gestured with his dagger, and Lei cautiously stepped past him, moving slowly down the stairs.

Normally, it would have been Pierce leading the way; the warforged was built for stealth and speed and could withstand the most punishment if it came to a battle, but Gerrion had warned them to expect magical countermeasures. As she made her way down the stairs, Lei cleared her mind of all stray thought. Her task was much like listening for a sound on the edge of hearing, a slight tone that an untrained listener would never notice. What she sought could not be caught with eye or ear. It was something that could only be felt in the mind: a shiver in the soul, the faintest trace of the unnatural in the air. It was beyond most people, but Lei had shaped flows of magical energy as a child, and she could she sense the world hidden in the shadows of reality.

She paused at the bottom of the stairs, stopping the others with a sharp gesture. Had she truly felt it, or was it just an echo in her imagination? She reached out with her thoughts, sending the faintest pulse of mystical energy through the air. Suddenly a web of pale blue light burst into view—a dizzying pattern of glowing lines and words in the script of dragons, forming a wide circle that completely blocked the narrow hallway.

*Glyph,* she warned the others. It was a spell frozen in time, waiting to unleash its power on any creature that passed over it. The seal could hold any number of unpleasant effects. It might paralyze its victim, explode in a burst of deadly fire, or summon a fiend to dispatch the intruder. Studying the walls and floor, Lei couldn't see any scorch marks or signs of physical damage, so odds were good that the glyph wouldn't explode—but there were many lethal effects that would leave no marks on the surroundings.

*Move swiftly. I cannot hold him long.*

Lakashtai's thought pulled Lei from her reverie. *I know, I know! Give me a moment.* Daine put a hand on her shoulder, squeezing slightly, and she gave him a brief smile. "I'm all right," she whispered, feeling an irrational desire to keep her words from the kalashtar upstairs.

She drew a deep breath and turned her attention back to the glowing glyph. She closed her eyes and extended her perceptions, calling on the same techniques she used to craft her own magic. She touched the seal with her mind and slowly traced its path with her thoughts, running along each strand of energy until she reached the end. Every gleaming thread was bound together to form a greater whole, and she contemplated the beauty of the magical web. Finally, she directed a burst of energy at the heart of the seal—a blade that would either cut the thread or cause it to explode.

Slowly, she opened her eyes. The glyph had faded away. To the others, the experience had only taken seconds, but she was exhausted; it seemed as if days had passed since she first looked at the glyph.

*Broken,* she thought to the others and continued down the hallway.

❋ ❋ ❋ ❋ ❋ ❋ ❋

*If Gerrion's directions are correct, this is the chamber we're looking for,* Lei thought. *I can't sense any traps, but it is mystically sealed—the work of House Kundarak, if I know my auras. I imagine Sarkhesh has a token to deactivate the seal.*

"Remind me why we didn't just kill him and take the key?" Daine muttered.

*My, thief to assassin in less than an hour. You really are making quick progress,* Lei thought. *Now let me work on this door—I'm going to need to prepare an unbinding charm, and it's a difficult task.* She pulled a small brass wand from her belt pouch and began whispering to it, weaving the energies she would need to break the arcane lock.

*Three acolytes have arrived.* It was Lakashtai. *I have managed to draw them into my illusion, but there is a limit to the number of minds I can affect—should anyone else arrive, there will be trouble.*

*Lei's working on it,* Daine shot back. A moment later Lei completed her task and touched the wand to the door, producing a brief flicker of light. The door slowly creaked inwards.

Daine pulled Lei away from the door. *Pierce, point.*

Pierce had his long flail in one hand, the chain wrapped around the haft. He pressed the flail against the door, slowly pushing it open. Then he darted inside, swift and silent.

*Safe*, came his thought.

Daine was the next to enter, blades drawn in spite of Pierce's assurances. He glanced around, and his heart sunk.

The room was full of dragons.

There were wooden dragons, wyrms carved from gold and ivory, statues in a host of shapes and sizes. The doorway was flanked by two copper statues, and each of these rearing dragons was taller than Pierce. Dozens of chests and caskets were scattered around the chamber, seemingly without rhyme or reason. A mail shirt hung from the wall, white scales bound to leather. If there was a blue dragon scale in the room, it was hidden from view.

*Lakashtai?* Daine thought. *You may have to maintain the ritual for longer than we'd planned.*

# CHAPTER 20

For a moment they were stunned by the spectacle. Daine had seen greater wealth in his life; he still remembered Alina Lorridan Lyrris' garden of jewels in Metrol, but with Alina, one never knew what was real and what was illusion. Here treasures were scattered about with no concern for art or appearance. A gilded statuette with ruby eyes the size of Daine's thumb was propped against a rolled tapestry.

"Blue scales," Daine said, pulling his thoughts together. "Pierce, watch the door. Lei, I need to know if these chests are safe—it must be in one of them."

"We could fit a lot of this in my pack," Lei said, studying one of the chests. Her pack was a treasure of her childhood, though Daine didn't know if she'd made it or inherited it; in the past, they'd hidden Pierce inside of it.

"I always knew you had the makings of a thief," Daine said. "Greed suits you."

He opened the chest as soon as she moved on. At first it appeared to be filled with shards of broken pottery, covered in gleaming enamel; as Daine sifted through the fragments to make sure no scale lay beneath, he realized that they were the remnants of enormous eggs.

Lei blushed. "I—this isn't about gold. I've just never seen a collection like this." She tapped the lid of a steel coffer. "Leave this one alone. I'll come back to it."

Daine nodded, sifting through a hamper of cloth bundles—

old flags or battle pennants, he thought.

"That's a Seren sculpture over there," she continued. "I've only heard of them, and if what Gerrion said is right, this man doesn't deserve these things."

"Let it go," Daine said. "If we only take the scale, he might not even notice it's missing until we're gone. I don't care about his faith; I'd just as soon we didn't have to deal with the wrath of the gods right now."

"Very well," Lei sighed. "Oh, this is interesting—"

"*Daine!*" Pierce's thought was a hammer in his skull.

Copper flashed in the light of the cold flame lanterns, smashing the table beside Daine into splinters. A copper dragon crouched before him. It was the size of a tiger, and its head bobbed with the fluid grace of a snake, but its eyes were cold metal. A second ago, it had been a statue frozen at the door. Now it was all too alive—and if Pierce hadn't slammed into it the instant it began to move, it would have been Daine lying beneath the creature instead of the shards of a shattered table.

The attack happened too quickly for Daine to recognize the nature of his foe. Without thinking, he drew his sword and launched forward in a lunge, striking the beast directly between the eyes. His wrist ached with the impact, and the point barely nicked the surface of the living statue. Then the creature was upon him. The blow slammed him to the floor. The dragon's claws were pressing down through the rings of his chainmail, just piercing the skin of his chest. Metal jaws stretched wide and descended toward his face—but as glittering teeth filled his vision, there was a resounding *clang!* and the head was knocked aside. Pierce stood over him, and the spinning chain of his flail was a wall of steel in the dim light.

*We don't have time for this!* Daine thought. While Pierce's blow didn't seem to have caused any serious damage, it had struck the creature off balance. Daine threw his weight into it, twisting to the side and knocking the dragon to the floor. *Lei, keep searching!*

Now the dragon was crouched in a corner of the room, and Daine could see his image reflected in its dead metal eyes. Any doubts about its nature were laid to rest: this was a creature of magic and metal, not flesh and blood. Somehow, it disturbed

Daine in a way the warforged never had. At least the warforged were human in form and voice, and in some ways they weren't so different from men in armor. Occasionally, especially when drunk, Daine had forgotten Pierce's true nature, calling him to join the revels, but there was nothing natural about this creature. It shouldn't even have been able to move. There were no joints, no hinges—it was solid metal, yet it had the flexibility of flesh.

There was a moment of stillness as the enemies watched each other. The only sound was Lei's quiet curse as she fumbled with the lock on a stubborn coffer. Then the creature leapt forward, crashing into Pierce. The warforged raised his flail just in time to catch the dragon's foreclaws, holding its upper body at bay, but it lashed out with its hind claws, and there was a terrible screech of metal on metal. Copper claws gouged Pierce's armored plates and tore into the leathery cords that lay beneath.

The warforged did not cry out in pain, but the extent of the injury was plain to see. Cold fury welled up in Daine's heart. Pierce might have saved his life only moments ago, and that was just one time of many. This thing would not be the end of his friend. His anger pulled him forward, and as Pierce struggled to hold the dragon at bay Daine reversed his grip on his dagger and slammed it into one of the creature's eyes. This dagger was no ordinary blade; forged by a mad smith of House Cannith, it could carve through steel as easily as cloth, and no mundane metal could match its edge. The blade sunk deep into the dragon's head, with no more resistance than he would have felt from a block of soft cheese, but the dragon had no brain within its skull. It twisted its head, and pure anger gave Daine the strength to hold onto the dagger and pull the blade from the creature's head. Its left eye was a ruin, but it didn't seem to be affected in any way; Daine leapt back just in time to avoid the snapping jaws.

*Status, Pierce,* he thought.

The warforged was on his feet, but he gave no response. The beast was continuing to tear at Pierce with its hind claws, and Daine could see the shredded cords at his waist. Were Pierce a creature of flesh and blood, his entrails would be dripping from the dragon's talons, but the warforged wasn't down yet. He lacked the strength to push the beast away, but he twisted to the side, using its weight against it. As the dragon fell to the floor Pierce brought his flail down, wrapping the long chain around one of its hind legs. The copper beast tumbled to the floor, scattering coffers with its wild thrashing. Pierce dropped to one knee—clearly his injuries were taking a toll on him, and he still hadn't responded to Daine's telepathic query.

Anger gave way to concern, but there was no time for either. Daine darted forward, slashing with his dagger. Slivers of copper fell to the floor. It was clear that the creature did not possess any sort of vital organs: if Daine was going to do anything, he'd have to take it apart piece by piece. It might not use its eyes, but perhaps the loss of its head would prove more of a handicap.

It was easier to devise such plans than to put them into practice. In an instant the dragon was fully facing him. It lashed out with its tail, catching Pierce directly in his injured midsection; the warforged soldier crashed into the wall and lay still. Now the dragon glared at Daine with its ruined gaze. Daine crossed his blades before his chest. Perhaps if he caught it in mid-leap, he could use its force against it, drag the dagger across its neck . . .

In the end, it wasn't the dragon that leapt. There was a flash of motion and then Lei was on the creature's back, clinging to its neck. Her mouth was twisted in a terrible grimace, and Daine could see the air rippling around her hands; for a moment he remembered the battle at Keldan Ridge and a warforged soldier exploding at her touch. The dragon thrashed around, trying to reach her, but she held on with grim determination; Daine was afraid to strike at the beast for fear of hitting Lei in the melee.

He needn't have worried. The creature gave no howl, no cry of pain. It simply froze in place, becoming dead metal once again. Lei slumped against its neck, breathing hard.

"Lei!" Without even thinking about it, Daine reached out for her. She fell into his arms, still gasping for breath.

"I've got . . . scale," she said, her head pressed against his shoulder. It took a moment for Daine to remember the purpose of the battle. "Let me . . . Pierce."

Daine steadied her on her feet, and for a moment he just held her as she caught her breath. All thought was lost in a maelstrom of emotion, anger and concern wrapped together with something deeper. Then he let her go and they ran to Pierce. The warforged lay against the wall, seemingly as inert as the dragon statue. His waist was a gaping ruin of shredded cords coated with a translucent, sticky fluid, but Lei just knelt beside him and ran her hands over the torn ligaments. Daine had seen her work with warforged before, and he knew there was still hope.

*Lakashtai, what's going on?* He thought.

Nothing. Suddenly he remembered Pierce's failure to respond.

*Lei? Can you hear me?*

"Lei?" he said.

"Yes?" She didn't look up from her work.

"We've got trouble."

"I should say that you do," came a voice from the hall.

Maru Sakhesh was wreathed in flame. The fire did not touch his dark robes or the arch of the doorway, but Daine could feel the heat against his skin, and he wondered for a moment if it would only burn the flesh of a foe. The priest held no weapons, but as he clenched his fists, his burning aura grew brighter.

"The season of flame is upon us," Sakhesh hissed, his voice low and deadly. "You have chosen an excellent time to die."

"We've got other plans," Daine said.

He'd felt a momentary shred of doubt when Sakhesh had appeared; no matter how he tried to justify it, the fact was that they were thieves and the priest was defending his property. Daine had no intention of being burned to death, and he needed to find Lakashtai. He wasn't sure he'd call the kalashtar woman a friend, truly, but she was a companion, and she'd saved his life. He couldn't fail again.

Daine leapt forward and lunged at Sakhesh, the point of his blade directly in line with the priest's heart. Sakhesh was an old man, and he didn't have any room to evade the blow. He didn't try. He didn't even flinch when Daine struck. His black silk robes had the strength of steel, and Daine's blade slid to the side without penetrating. The priest's fiery halo flared with light and heat, and a column of fire lanced along Daine's sword to surround his arm. Daine leapt back, but his shirt was smoldering, and his arm was sore and burnt.

"Be at peace," Sakhesh said. He clenched his fist, and Daine was caught in a vise-like, invisible force. He struggled with all his might, but he could not move. Sakhesh stepped toward him, throwing his arms wide. "Surrender. Give yourself to the fire, the breath of the true Sovereigns."

CHAPTER 21

Lei was still examining Pierce's injuries when Sakhesh entered.

*First sahuagin, now draconists,* she thought. As a child she had been taught to believe in the Sovereign Host, and like every heir of House Cannith she had receive the ritual blessing of Onatar, the Lord of Fire and Forge. She wasn't an especially devout worshipper, but the Sovereigns didn't ask much of their followers. Nonetheless, she felt a certain disdain for this priest and his radical beliefs. Dragons were amazing creatures—but they weren't gods. The fiery aura gave her pause, but his magical powers didn't vindicate his beliefs; a wizard could summon fire without following any god. Magic was a power many could draw on, and the faith of the priest was but one path to power.

Even before Sakhesh spoke, his intentions were clear to her—they weren't getting out of the room without a fight. She might be able to get Pierce back on his feet before Sakhesh could strike, but with only seconds to work, she could only perform minimal repairs, and if Pierce suffered more damage in such a state, he might be destroyed for good.

Pierce had to sit out of this battle, but she didn't.

As Daine leapt forward, Lei closed her eyes and concentrated on her armor, merging her thoughts with this magical aura that encased and surrounded her. Green leather studded with golden rivets, this armor was her most treasured possession. It had been a gift from her mother, given to Lei when she left her parents' enclave for her first assignment. Aleisa said that it was an heirloom of the house, crafted by the legendary artificer Alder d'Cannith. There was power in the vest, a reservoir of energy she called upon when weaving her enchantments, and the vest itself was mystically malleable. Lei could weave temporary effects into any object, but this usually took a considerable amount of time: with her vest, it was a matter of seconds. Now Lei drew on the concept of fire, the basic principles of heat and flame. Touching the vest with her mind, she took its aura and twisted it, shaping it, creating a shield that would protect her from all forms of heat.

She opened her eyes. Mere seconds had passed. Daine was frozen in place, paralyzed by another spell. Sakhesh was walking forward, preparing to wrap Daine in his burning embrace. He hadn't even spared a glance for Lei.

That was a mistake.

Lei spun in place as she rose from the ground, and her darkwood staff was a black blur as it smashed into the priest's head. There was a burst of flame, but it dissipated harmlessly around her; even her staff was protected by the magical aura of her armor. Sakhesh cried out in pain and stumbled away from her, one hand rising up to shield his head.

Lei threw herself forward, striking again and again. The priest had his own magical shield that helped turn the brunt of physical blows, but he simply wasn't prepared for the sheer ferocity of Lei's attack. Neither was she. She felt as if she was being swept away by her own anger; she was guided more by instinct than conscious thought. Jode's death, Daine's affliction, Lakashtai's cool condescension, and now Pierce's injuries and these battles in a strange land—it had been building up inside her ever since they'd arrived in Sharn almost a year ago. Now she had an outlet for all that rage and frustration, some arrogant man who wanted to kill Daine and didn't even understand how to show proper respect for the Sovereigns.

Sakhesh was no fool. He was no match for her physically, and he knew it. He fell back, circled the room, and tried to put obstacles between them. He clenched his fist, and Lei felt his hand trying to grasp her mind and freeze her in place, but his magic paled before her fury, and the spell shattered against the wall of her will. Gouts of flame were dispersed by the magic of her armor, and every moment that passed she landed another blow.

Finally, Sakhesh fell to the ground. His flaming aura had guttered and died. His face was a mass of bruises, and Lei was certain she had felt a rib crack on her last blow. Now a new feeling rose within her . . . a strange sense of shame. Was this really who she was, a thief, who would break into a man's home and beat him? The point of her staff was lowered, ready to strike—but she paused, her anger finally fading.

Sakhesh glared at her, forcing himself up with one hand. Blood dripped from his mouth, and she could feel the raw hate in his gaze.

"*Fool!*" he spat. "You cannot fight me."

"I think I just did." She wondered if she should strike him again, silence him, but now that her fury had faded the idea of beating a fallen foe seemed repellent.

"You have won *nothing!*" A shattered tooth fell from his mouth as he gasped out the words. "You . . . you will lay down your weapon and return what is mine. Now!"

"And if I don't?"

"With one word . . . *one!* I can turn my fires on your warforged, burning him from within. You cannot stop me in time."

He was right. He'd fallen back when he'd dropped to the ground, and now she was too far away. He could cast one last spell before she could close, and Pierce was horribly damaged. Surely this . . . it couldn't be worth it.

"Very well," she said.

"Now *drop your—*"

He never finished the sentence. Even as he shouted his final demand, the point of a black dagger spouted from his throat.

"Trouble speaking?" Daine said.

He planted his boot on the priest's back, grasping the hilt of his dagger as he pushed down with his foot. The blade was slick with blood as it emerged, and Sakhesh sank to the floor without another word.

Lei stared at Daine. In the battle with Sakhesh, both she

and the priest had forgotten about him, and he'd finally broken free of the magical paralysis. Daine looked down at the corpse beneath his boot and the spreading pool of blood, and she wasn't sure if his expression was one of sorrow or cold resolution.

"I guess I'm an assassin after all," he said. He knelt next to Sakhesh and wiped his bloody blade on the priest's robes. "Get Pierce on his feet and that scale in your pack. We need to go. Now."

❀ ❀ ❀ ❀ ❀ ❀ ❀

Daine took the lead as they charged up the stairs. Pierce was still wounded, and they couldn't afford to take the time to fully repair his injuries. Lakashtai might be dying. Sakhesh could have called for help. There was no time to lose.

Daine leapt over the top of the stairs, sprinting into the nave. His sword was out, adrenaline surging as he looked for the next foe.

Lakashtai was in the center of the chamber. She was kneeling over three bodies in the robes of temple acolytes, and as Daine drew closer he saw that she was binding their wrists and feet with silk cord. She looked up as he approached.

"I expected you sooner," she said. Her clothing was singed, and there were burns across her left arm, but her voice was low and calm. "I apologize about the loss of thought-speech, but he took me by surprise. I imagine that your actions triggered some sort of warning. I chose to feign defeat; I couldn't match them alone in my current condition, but these three posed little challenge."

Daine looked at Lei. Neither had anything to say. Pierce stood silently behind them.

"Come now, move quickly!" Lakashtai said, standing up and striding toward the door. "This was only the beginning. The true danger is still to come."

# CHAPTER 22

That went about as well as could be expected," Gerrion said cheerfully. "I am sorry about your warforged."

"He's not *my* warforged," Daine said, stepping out of the way of a cart pulled by a lizard the size of a horse.

"No? My apologies. I've never been to your land, and we've seen only a few of these creatures here in Stormreach; most of them are servants at the Cannith enclave. If it doesn't belong to you, why is it here?"

*Good question,* Daine thought. "It was his choice. He's a person, Gerrion, not some lump of metal."

The gray man gave an easy shrug. "I suppose, but he was built from a lump of metal, wasn't he?"

"What were you built from?" Lakashtai said coolly. "What brought sun and shadow together in you?"

For a moment Gerrion's smile faltered—he recovered quickly, but not quickly enough. "I couldn't say. With all the sailors and merchants passing through this town, a foundling in Stormreach is like a pebble on the beach."

"Pierce was built by design, while you were built by accident," Lakashtai said. "The soul is what matters, not the origin of the vessel."

"What makes you think he's got a soul?"

"What makes you think you do?"

That thought kept Gerrion silent for a full two hundred feet.

Gerrion had been waiting for them when they emerged from the temple. Lakashtai wanted to meet Hassalac immediately. With Sakhesh dead, she felt it was more important than ever that they conclude their business and leave Stormreach as quickly as possible. Gerrion assured them that there would be no battles in Hassalac's domain or that if there were, that two more people wouldn't make a difference. They paused long enough for Lei to produce the dragon scale shield, and for Lakashtai to study it and confirm that it was indeed the object that they sought. Then Lei and Pierce had returned to the Ship's Cat, where Lei could take the time she needed to repair Pierce, and so it was Daine, Lakashtai, and Gerrion who finally arrived at Hassalac's door.

❦ ❦ ❦ ❦ ❦ ❦ ❦

"That's quite a . . . door." Daine said. Black marble pillars stood to either side of the portal, and ruby-eyed dragons forged from gold peered down from the tops of the pillars. With the number of tomb raiders and treasure-seekers that came to this place, the fact that these statues were still intact hinted at some sort of magical defense. A massive door of dark densewood hung between the two pillars. Mystical symbols were engraved along the edge of the frame and inlaid with silver. There was no sign of handle or hinges, just a dragon's head of silver bearing a heavy knocking ring in its jaws. "But somehow I expected a mansion to go with it."

"That sort of thing just attracts thieves," Gerrion said.

The door stood on a square marble platform, perhaps ten feet across, but there were no walls. It simply filled the space between the pillars. Daine peered behind it and found that the back was identical to the front, including the silver knocker.

"You're sure about this?" Gerrion said to Lakashtai.

"Yes, though you need not accompany us if the prospect fills you with fear."

"Oh, fear and I are old friends," Gerrion said, "and despite our past grievances, I doubt Hassalac would harm me . . . well, harm me too seriously. He knows the value of my services, but I do prefer to keep our dealings at a distance, just in case. Besides, if you don't return, someone needs to tell the lovely young lady you left back at the Ship's Cat."

"We will return," Lakashtai said. "I have confidence in the skills of my companion."

"Of course you do!" Gerrion flashed an innocent smile at Daine. "Then let's be on our way."

He approached the door and lifted the knocker, striking three times. "I'm sure you recognize me," he said to the air, "I bring two who wish to speak with Master Hassalac Chaar. They know the risks of entry and are prepared to face them for the honor of this audience."

"What risks?" Daine muttered to Lakashtai. She made a dismissing gesture.

A moment passed in silence. And another. Gerrion stood at the door, smiling slightly.

Daine's suspicions began to mount. "Oh, I see how this game is played. We paid you last evening, and I'm sure those coins have already gone to pay your debts. You even get us to kill one of your enemies. Now you bring us to your magic door, and what do you know, the doorman doesn't want to speak to us. Not your concern, is that it? You've done the best you could?"

Gerrion shrugged. "Well, if Hassalac doesn't want to speak to you, there's really nothing I can do about it. You don't force his hand."

The battle with Sakhesh had left Daine in a poor mood for petty cons. "If this Hassalac really exists, you'd better take us to his house right now, or I'll be using force on *your* hand."

"Daine—" Lakashtai began, but Daine cut her off.

"I'll bet you don't even know Alina, do you? You just somehow linked me to her and figured it was a good angle to play, or perhaps this is her idea of a game."

Daine's sword was a flash of steel in the sun, but Gerrion's crossbow was already drawn and leveled. The half-elf could only loose one bolt before Daine could close the distance, but the vision of the shattered crystal remained fixed in his mind.

"You have a keen mind, old soldier," Gerrion said, "and I admit, I've played this game before, but not today. I can smell the path to profit, and there's far more to be made working with you than against you. While I understand that you once escaped from Lyrris' wrath, I don't care to test my luck against the gnome."

"Then what are we doing here?"

"Waiting," Gerrion said. "I'd have thought you'd have learned to do that in your war."

Then, without a sound, the door simply vanished. The space between the pillars was filled with dark mist.

"There," Gerrion said. "Was that so terrible?"

Daine studied the portal for a moment. Nothing could be seen through the black smoke, which chose to ignore the rising winds. "Lakashtai . . ."

"This is what I expected, Daine. This is the gateway to our true destination. When we pass through, we shall emerge elsewhere, and I would suggest that we move quickly." She glanced at the sky for a moment. "I believe a storm is coming."

"I'm going first." Daine's sword was still in his hand, and he drew his dagger. With one final glare at Gerrion, he stepped into the shadow.

❧ ❧ ❧ ❧ ❧ ❧ ❧

The darkness flowed around him, and Daine felt a shiver of fear as he remembered Tashana's psychic attack, but it lasted only a moment. The pressure grew, and for an instant he thought his bones would snap—then it was gone, and the world returned.

He was in the wrong place.

This was no merchant's manor. It was a subterranean passage, with walls of dark stone and packed earth illuminated by the light of guttering torches. Daine took in the surroundings in an instant, but his attention was focused on the creature that stood before him—a massive reptilian humanoid with the build and bulk of an ogre. Its skin was covered with thick black scales. Its fanged jaws could make a single mouthful of Daine's head, but its halberd was more of a concern. The long blade at the end of the haft was strangely curved and bore some sort of engraved pattern, but what Daine saw was the point leveled at his chest.

*Gerrion!* Daine cursed all lying half-elves. He wasn't sure what game Gerrion was playing, but this was no time for questions.

Lakashtai could arrive in seconds, and she was still wounded from the battle at the temple. *If she arrives at all.* Perhaps Gerrion had been counting on Daine to go first, leaving him alone with Lakashtai for whatever schemes he had in mind.

Distance was the first concern. The reptilian warrior was almost twice Daine's height, with the reach to match. Daine charged forward, knocking the halberd's point aside with a blow of his sword. The creature roared in fury, and Daine winced from the sound; the deadly blade swept forward in a stroke that could cut him in two.

Anger was what Daine was counting on. The wild swing was just what he'd expected, and he dropped down below it. Now the beast's strength worked against it, and the force of the blow carried the halberd crashing past Daine and into the wall. Painfully aware of each passing second, Daine threw his energy into a lunge, praying that the creature kept its vitals in the same place as a man. He landed a solid blow in the creature's gut, but now he realized that it was wearing a shirt of fine black chainmail, almost invisible against its scales.

*Flame!* When Daine's sword emerged, the tip was covered with dark blood—but the strike was not as deep as Daine had hoped, and the fight was far from over. He raised both blades just in time to block the beast's countering stroke, and the force of the blow almost knocked his sword from his hand.

In that instant, Daine let go of conscious thought, drawing on instinct and rage. Somehow he found the power to match the lizard warrior, pressing his sword against the halberd and holding it in place. Summoning every ounce of strength, he lashed out with his dagger, striking the halberd where the steel blade met the wooden haft. Wood was no match for Cannith-forged adamantine. The head of the halberd clattered to the floor of the passage, leaving the lizard holding a simple wooden pole.

*Don't expect one blow to win every fight.*

Daine didn't need his grandfather's words to know this battle was far from over. The beast had lost its blade, but with its strength the haft alone was a weapon. It threw its full weight against Daine, and he fell back against the wall of the cavern, but now time was on his side. He could move more freely in the narrow cavern, and he ducked away from the creature's brutish blows, darting in with thrust after thrust. The beast began to slow, blood flowing from a dozen wounds. Finally Daine saw an opening and slammed into the creature with all the force he could muster. It staggered and fell to the ground. Daine put a foot on its chest and raised his dagger for the finishing blow.

"STOP!"

*What now?* Daine felt the pressure of the mental command even as he recognized Lakashtai's voice. Her power was certainly diminished; he could easily have resisted the order if he'd chosen to, but he froze, the point of his blade against the fallen warrior's throat. It watched him silently.

"What have you done?" Lakashtai said, running down the passage from the portal.

She knelt beside the creature, laying a hand over one of its wounds. Her eyes glowed with emerald light and the beast relaxed, sinking back against the ground.

Daine's heart sank. "Don't tell me this is a friend of yours."

She turned to glare at him, her eyes still burning. "I do not know him, but you of all people should know that people of power employ guardians."

"And live in mansions!" Daine gestured at the rough walls of the passage. "I'm supposed to believe this is Master Hassalac's manor?"

The light faded from Lakashtai's eyes. She was silent for a moment, then looked away. "Yes . . . it seems that I am at fault in this. I should have told you what to expect; I sometimes forget the limitations of your lonely memory."

"Fine. I think. Now what?"

Lakashtai turned back to the fallen beast. "I apologize for our actions," she said softly, and even though Daine was beginning to recognize her powers he still felt a swell of sympathy. "My companion knows nothing of the one that you serve. I ask that you forgive us and escort us to your master."

The creature nodded and slowly rose to its feet. It indicated that they should follow it with a motion of one curved claw, then lumbered down the passage.

"I did not realize I had such a champion to protect me," Lakashtai said, her ghostly smile flickering into view, "but please, keep your sword in its sheath for the rest of this visit."

# CHAPTER 23

K uryeva!" the goblin merchant called, leering with rotting teeth as he offered his wares. "A fine skin of kuryeva to warm the darkest night!"

The street was a riot of color and noise, swirling around Pierce and Lei. In plotting their route back to the Ship's Cat, Gerrion had taken pains to send them along crowded streets, believing that the Riedrans would avoid a fight in a public place. As damaged as he was, Pierce found himself wishing that they'd taking a quieter path—a pack of assassins seemed preferable to the milling crowd.

"Gurk'ash! Gurk'ash meat and milk, a luxury no traveler should do without!"

"A comb for the lady? Such lovely hair should be treated with care."

Pierce stepped in front of the last speaker, a dwarf with greasy gray hair and a patchy beard. He reeked of sweat and ale. Comb-seller or no, given the man's knowledge of hygiene Pierce suspected that larceny was his true goal.

Even as he pushed the dwarf aside, Pierce recognized the foolishness of his actions. Lei had shown herself to be quite capable of dealing with the cutpurses of Sharn. Given his current condition, if it came to a fight he would be wiser to let Lei take point. While Lei's magical talents had restored him to consciousness, Pierce was still grievously damaged: combat would be most unwise.

Pain was a familiar feeling for Pierce. Shame was not.

The sensation of physical injury was quite different for warforged and humans. Pierce was aware of the damage that he suffered. Just as he could feel the stone when he touched a wall, he could feel the claws that tore through his innards. After the shock of the initial blow, the pain lingered, a continuing reminder of his condition. It was simply a part of how he perceived the world. He could sense each root-like tendril that ran throughout his body. He knew that six of the cords in his waist were severed, while four more were severely damaged. There was a long gash on the mithral plate of his upper left torso, and the alchemical reservoir below had suffered minor damage. There was no escape from this knowledge: even when he was fully repaired, he would feel the minor shifting in his ligaments with every motion, the constant balance of the self-replenishing fluids that kept his organic components flexible. For a human, it would be like sensing every second of the aging process, being constantly aware of the growing voice of hunger and thirst, feeling even the faintest touch of rot and cancer as they laid claim to his body, yet these things didn't bother Pierce. This was a part of his existence and always had been.

While Lei could restore Pierce's body, his pride was another matter. Pierce's life to this point had been defined by his ability to perform his task and protect his allies. This was not the first time he had been seriously damaged, but it seemed that he had failed on multiple levels. First there was the frustration of the malady that had befallen Daine. Pierce could face any foe on the battlefield, but this concept of an enemy within dreams— Pierce could not even sleep, let alone dream. His inability to help Daine had been gnawing at his mind for the last week, far worse than any physical pain, and now he had failed again. He was a scout, and he'd fought Valenar commandoes in the woods of Cyre, yet he'd been surprised by Riedran assassins last night, and he'd fallen prey to the psychic attack that Daine had found the strength to resist. Now he'd been nearly torn apart—by another creature of magic and metal.

Was he flawed, or was lack of action to blame—had the relatively peaceful life of the last six months dulled his skills?

"Are you all right?"

Lei's voice pulled Pierce from his reverie. "Yes, Lei," he said. "My apologies. My injuries remain a distraction."

"I'm sorry to leave you like this," she said, refusing to meet his gaze; Pierce could sense her indignation. "With the day still ahead of us… you know." She looked away.

"I do," he replied. "Do not be ashamed. You must conserve your magical energies, and your skill with hand and tool shall suffice for this task. I have faith in your talents: a few moments more and we shall arrive at our inn, and you can begin the work."

She smiled, and for a moment Pierce didn't feel his pain.

Distracted as he was, Pierce could still recognize a threat. A large man—not quite large enough to have orcish blood in his veins, but carrying both muscle and fat on his frame—was purposely approaching them. He wore a shirt of rusting chain-mail beneath a soiled gray tabard. There was a halberd in his hand and leather-bound club at his belt. A guard or watchman, Pierce concluded. With some bemusement, he noticed a smaller figure trotting next to the heavyset man—a bedraggled halfling wearing a miniature version of the same uniform, carrying a tiny halberd that Pierce could have used as a walking stick.

"Just what have you been up to, orasca?"

It was the halfling who spoke, his voice a nasal whine. His skin was remarkably dark, while his eyes were a pale shade of blue. He wore the hood of his tabard up, but as he spoke Pierce got a good look at his face and saw that the halfling's left ear was missing; scar tissue covered the back of his head, seemingly the result of a grievous injury. Pierce wondered if the man had fought during the Last War, and if so what had caused him to abandon the Five Nations for this place.

Lei took the lead. "I'm sorry, is there a problem?"

"There are always problems in Stormreach," the little man replied, studying her with an appraising gaze. "Your warforged looks like he might have been involved with one of them."

"Oh, I doubt it," Lei replied. "I purchased him from the smith down the way with the black barrel over his door. I don't even think he's been on his feet for a month, so I don't see how he could have caused any trouble."

"Is that so, tincoat?" the halfling probed at Pierce's injured cords with the point of his halberd, sending new signals of pain across Pierce's consciousness.

Pierce simply nodded.

"Well then," the watchman examined Pierce again. "Selling such trash to visitors to our fair city—a crime, is what it is. I can't allow it, lady."

"I'm quite satisfied—"

"I didn't ask," the halfling said sharply, turning the point of his halberd toward Lei.

The larger man sniggered loudly.

The instant the halberd turned on Lei, Pierce was considering courses of action, weighing the odds and merits of a direct strike versus an attempt to trip or disarm the little man, yet these were guardsmen. He and Lei had been involved in a robbery. To fight the watch as well...

"I think the safest course of action would be for you to give us your gold and goods, lady," the halfling continued. "That should keep you from making any unwise purchases in the future."

Lei and Pierce exchanged glances. Lei didn't have much money on her, but her enchanted pack was extremely valuable, and her staff was irreplaceable.

"Stormreach guard, yes?" the halfling snapped, seeing their hesitation. "When the guard asks, you give."

Pierce could see that Lei wasn't going to surrender to these two. He had grown accustomed to her temper, and if she was going to fight, he would stand by her side. He loosened the chain of his flail, ready to strike—

And the guards fell down.

It took a moment for the event to fully register in Pierce's mind. A lithe figure stood over the fallen guards, wrapped in tattered burlap and a stained gray cloak. Her face was hidden beneath a deep hood and motheaten scarf. He hadn't seen her approach; she must have stepped up behind the big man. A single kick for the halfling, a swift jab in a tender spot for the bulky man... both were stretched out across the muddy cobblestones, dead to the world.

Lei simply stared at the newcomer. The point of her staff was lowered, and she studied the stranger with a watchful eye.

"They will live."

Pierce only recognized the voice, because it had been on his mind so much of late. It was softer, more... human. If he hadn't been contemplating their earlier conversations in his mind, he would never have thought this woman was warforged.

"What do you want with us?" Lei said.

"I suppose gratitude would be too much to ask. I simply wanted to keep your companion from fighting in his current condition."

"So you attacked the guards," Lei said.

"As you were about to," the stranger stated calmly. "Do not worry about retaliation. The guards of this town are little better than bandits, and they'll find easier prey."

Studying the people around them, Pierce thought it was more likely that the guards would be robbed. The faces of the onlookers were cold and hard, and a scruffy boy with wild black hair spit on the halfling and laughed.

"Nonetheless," the stranger continued, "I imagine we should go our separate ways." She inclined her head to Pierce. "A shame to see you like this, brother, but I suppose it is the price of your service. A strong wall indeed—and yet the first to be sacrificed, it would seem."

"Brother?" Lei said. But the woman had already gone, swallowed up by the crowd. Lei glanced at Pierce. "Can you explain that to me?"

"No," Pierce replied, but the words remained in his mind, echoing the conversation on the docks the night before. Was she right? Was he just a tool, a shield? Was she following them? Why did he find himself wanting to see her in battle again—to test her limits against his own?

"Then let's get out of here," Lei said, with an uncomfortable glance at the growing mob. "I want to get you properly repaired before the next disaster strikes."

Pierce nodded, and they made their way through the crowd. Pierce could hear the people close ranks around the fallen guardsmen.

He didn't look back.

The reptilian guard led them through a labyrinth of twisting passages. Though the caverns appeared to be natural, Daine noticed a few places where the stone had been smoothed down or where a tunnel appeared to have been widened. Torches were embedded directly into holes in the stone; Daine could feel the heat of the flames, but as the tunnels stretched deeper and deeper, he could only imagine that they were sustained by magic. The only sounds were the scrape of the beast's talons against the stone, and the labored hiss of its breathing.

"What is it with this town and dragons?" Daine muttered to Lakashtai. "I thought Sakhesh was obsessed with his little eggshell collection, but at least he didn't live in a cave."

"Have you ever seen a dragon?"

"Has anyone?"

"I have not seen one with my own eyes, but I carry the memories of those who have. It is easy to understand why people like Sakhesh would consider them to be divine. A dragon—it carries a sense of majesty that I have seen in no other mortal creature."

"Except me?"

Lei would have rolled her eyes at the comment, but Lakashtai didn't even acknowledge it. "Long before human civilization arose in Sarlona, Xen'drik was the realm of giants. In the dawn of their civilization, these giants learned the art of magic from the dragons of Argonnessen, and with this knowledge they created wonders you cannot begin to imagine."

"If these dragons are so great, why haven't they taught us these magical secrets?"

Lakashtai shook her head. As always, the movement was minimal, yet somehow Daine *felt* her deep disappointment, as clearly as if she'd heaved an enormous sigh. "Where are the giants today? Power without wisdom can be a terrible thing. The giants unleashed terrible forces to bring an end to their war against the spirits of Dal Quor. They disrupted the very alignment of the outer planes—the fundamental order of reality itself. It brought an end to the war, certainly, but it devastated the land, and we may still be suffering the consequences of their rash action."

"But they beat these nightmare creatures."

"Perhaps, but that is the danger of fighting immortals. The quori still exist, even if they have been banished to the outer darkness of reality. The empires of the giants are only memories."

Daine considered this. "I thought we were talking about dragons."

"The giants did not fall to the horrors of Dal Quor, but it was the beginning of the end. The elves had long been slaves of the giants, and in the wake of the quori incursion, many of the slaves rose in revolt."

"The dragons?"

Lakashtai spared a glance. "You have no patience. All things come in time, and all things fall in time. The elves slowly turned the tide against their former masters, and it became clear that the civilization of the giants would not survive. In their pride, the greatest wizards among the giants decided to unleash the same powers that had been used on Dal Quor against Eberron itself. The consequences of such actions—it is impossible to say. The world could have been torn apart, and it would have been, if not for the dragons of Argonnessen."

"Finally. So dragons beat giants?"

"To say the least. The details are largely unknown, even to the elders of the kalashtar. The ancestors of the elves of Aerenal had fled before the disaster came. The dragons swept across the land, and all that can be said for certain is that when they left, the civilization of the giants was ash and ruin. In the present day, the giants are largely savages—or at the least, no more sophisticated than your people."

"Thanks," Daine said.

"Many look to that power—the strength that leveled one of the greatest civilizations in the history of Eberron—and seek to claim it for their own. Many believe that these secrets are hidden here in Xen'drik."

"Including . . . " Daine paused in midspeech, distracted by another group coming down the tunnel toward them. The strangers had a reptilian guard of their own, and Daine only caught a glimpse of the silver hem of a cloak, fluttering as its wearer moved.

It was enough. Daine grabbed Lakashtai's shoulder, pulling her back. His sword was in his hand.

"What an unexpected surprise." The soft voice was all too familiar. The lizardfolk had shifted to the sides of the tunnel so the two groups could pass one another. There, ten feet away, stood the Riedran man who only last night had threatened Daine with a crystal sword.

"Put the sword away, Daine." Lakashtai's voice was firm. "This is no place for a battle, and he knows it."

Indeed, the Riedran had not drawn his weapon. His hood and veil were drawn down, revealing finely chiseled, slightly effeminate features. His dark hair was drawn back into a single braid, and in the flickering light there seemed to be deep blue highlights mixed among the black strands.

"Of course. Master Hassalac disapproves of those who spill blood in his manor." He smiled at Daine, who had the uneasy feeling that the Riedran—and Hassalac—knew about his ill-advised battle with the guard. Daine slowly returned his blade to its leather sheath, keeping his eyes on the stranger.

"What brings you here?" Lakashtai's voice was as close to cordial as Daine had ever heard it. They might have been at a dinner party.

"Oh, the same thing as you, I imagine," the man said. "I have heard so much of Master Hassalac's collection—I had hoped for the chance to see it with my own eyes." He studied Lakashtai, his gaze lingering over the sack that held the dragonscale shield. "Perhaps you'll have better luck."

"Perhaps we will. Providing we do not keep our host waiting."

The Riedran nodded slightly. "Please, do not let me detain you. I'm sure we'll meet again soon."

He tapped his guard on the shoulder, and they squeezed past Daine and Lakashtai. Daine's hand was resting on the hilt of his dagger, and he yearned to draw and strike as his enemy squeezed past him; in the confined space, it would be impossible to miss. One mistake was enough. He kept his back to the wall and watched the Riedran walk down the passage; the man never looked back.

One he was out of sight, Lakashtai nodded to their escort, and they began walking again.

"I don't like it," Daine said. "If we have to go out the way we came in—we're sure to be ambushed."

"Perhaps."

"Perhaps? There's no 'perhaps' about it! Remember last night? That little exchange about taking me alive and killing the rest of you?"

"That was when he still had his weapon, and he doesn't know my condition." She turned to face him, and to Daine's surprise, actually smiled. "Besides, you were born as a bodyguard, weren't you? I'm sure you'll think of something."

"Staying out of buildings with one exit would be a good start," Daine growled.

"*Hassalac Chaar.*" The voice of the reptilian guard was harsh and loud, echoing across the passage. It took a moment for Daine to recognize the words hidden within the rasp.

The tunnel opened into a large cavern, and Daine stared in disbelief. Here at last was the luxury he'd expected to see at the entrance. Zil glamerweave carpets were spread across the floors, each displaying colorful shifting patterns of light and shadow. To Daine's left, dark wine was flowing down the tiers of a silver fountain; soft cushions were spread across the floor, along with low couches whose craftsmanship spoke of elven artistry. To Daine's right, there was a statue of a coiled golden dragon, easily twelve feet in height. If this one comes to life, I'm running, Daine thought.

But for all these fine touches, it was still a cave. Stalagmites protruded from the ground, polished to a mirror sheen or gilded in gold or silver, and he could still feel the hard stone beneath the floor.

A half-dozen of the blackscaled lizardfolk stood along the edges of the chamber, halberds held to attention. A young man stood in the center of the room, almost glowing with health and perfect beauty. His silk doublet and breeches were the color of rust, and his gloves and boots were well-oiled leather. At least a dozen garnets glittered in the torchlight, winking from necklace, belt, and cuff. Despite himself, Daine was impressed; this man couldn't have been more than eighteen years old, and to command such respect and resources at such a young age was no small feat, even if he chose to live in a cave.

"Greetings, Lord Hassalac," he said, inclining his head politely. "We thank you for seeing us."

A chorus of rumbling growls ran through the lizard guards. The man smiled, revealing perfect teeth. "I am afraid you are mistaken. My name is Kess. I have the honor of managing Master Hassalac's household."

Daine shot a glance at Lakashtai, and the glitter in her eyes told him that she'd known the situation from the start. He cursed all absent-minded kalashtar.

"Of course," he said, without really knowing why. "That was the message I wanted you to give to your master on our behalf."

"You may tell him yourself, if you wish. I am simply here to provide you with warnings. Do not interrupt my master when he is speaking. Do not approach within five feet of his throne. Do not attempt to use magic, or—" he glanced at Lakashtai. "other abilities in his presence. Do not draw any weapons. In fact, you may want to leave those with me."

"That's all right," Daine said.

"Very well, but let me be clear: these warnings are for your own good and are critical for your survival. Master Hassalac can kill you with a word, should he desire, but these precautions—they have already been woven into the stone itself, and if you violate any of my instructions, the consequences will be instant and severe."

"Can we get on with it, then? No offense, but I'll be just as happy when we're through with this conversation."

The guide glanced at Lakashtai, who nodded. He turned around, and as he did so, the patterns of the glamerweave carpets shifted—a river of fire burst into life, running down the center of the room. Kess walked onto this glowing bridge and led the way down the cavern. They passed other strange luxuries. A preserved gorgon stood on display, firelight glinting on its iron scales and bull-like horns. A trio of white granite statues was clustered together; each was about the size of a goblin, but their features had been worn down by time and weather, and it was impossible to guess the artist's intent.

Finally they reached an obelisk of polished red marble, fifteen feet in height. An image of the sun was engraved on the back, with a dragon coiled on the disk. Kess dropped to one knee before the monument.

"Master Hassalac! I bring two more before you."

"*WHO SEEKS HASSALAC?*" Daine could feel the voice in his bones. Deep and powerful, the bass rumble seemed to shake the floor itself. Daine realized that the voice was coming from the other side of the obelisk, that the stone was most likely the back of an enormous throne. Lakashtai's stories of giants flashed through his mind.

"I am Lakashtai of the kalashtar." In the wake of the thundering proclamation, Lakashtai's voice was little more than a whisper, but as always, though she spoke quietly, her words were clear and sharp as crystal. "I come with my companion, Daine of Cyre, in the hope that you will honor us with your words."

"*YOU WASTE MY TIME. I COULD BE CONTEMPLATING MYSTERIES BEYOND YOUR COMPREHENSION.*"

"I am aware of this, Master Hassalac. We have brought a gift to show our appreciation for your time and our hope that you will heed and honor our request."

"*PRODUCE YOUR OFFERING.*"

Lakashtai produced the steel coffer from the sack she was carrying it in. She lifted the lid, revealing the dragon scale that lay within. Daine hadn't seen the shield himself; looking at it, he could see how Sakhesh might think it a piece of a god. This was no dull leather—it glistened, as if the scale were a shard of blue crystal with a flame burning on the other side. Daine had no training in the arts of magic, but when Lakashtai opened the coffer, even he could feel the energy that flowed from the scale.

Apparently Hassalac could feel it as well. *"YOU MAY APPROACH."*

The path of fire extended, circling around to the right of the obelisk. Daine noticed that it stayed five feet away from the stone, and he resolved not to test Kess's warnings. He let Lakashtai take the lead this time; he'd had enough of making embarrassing mistakes. Following Lakashtai, he walked around the edge of the great throne, coming face to face with Hassalac Chaar, the Dragon Prince, the mightiest sorcerer in Stormreach.

He had to choke to hold the laughter in.

**A** moment earlier Daine had wondered if Hassalac was a giant. Little could be further from the truth. The mighty sorcerer was a tiny, gaunt figure; by Daine's estimation, Hassalac wouldn't be much over two feet tall when standing. Hassalac's skin was covered with rust colored scales, and his long snout was reminiscent of both lizard and dog. His head was crowned with two short black horns.

He was a kobold.

Eberron was home to a surprising number of humanoid species. Khorvaire alone possessed over a dozen distinct humanoid cultures, from the dwarves of the Mror Holds to the orcs of the Shadow Marches. Ogres, halflings, gnomes, trolls—out of this multitude of creatures, kobolds were possibly the most pathetic. They were the smallest and weakest of the humanoids; even a goblin could bully a kobold, and where the goblins and their kin had carved out empires, the kobolds had never risen above simple tribes. Kobolds were cowardly and reclusive by nature, and for centuries they were seen only when they built up the courage to ambush miners or merchant caravans. During the Last War, House Cannith had recruited a number of kobold tribes as laborers, and Daine had dealt with the creatures on a handful of occasions. His strongest memory was of their incessant chattering, and their voices: high-pitched yapping, like the bark of some tiny dog.

"SO *YOU* ARE THE ONE WHO STRUCK KRYSSH!"

Hassalac's voice was no yammering yap. His words were like thunder. Even as Daine was wincing from the terrible sound, a wave of force slammed into him, throwing him back against the cavern wall. Hassalac was standing on his throne, his little hand stretched out before him; and Daine could feel that grip, magnified a thousandfold, crushing him into the stone.

"Master Hassalac, I ask that you forgive my companion," Lakashtai said. "He meant no harm and believed that he was defending me from danger."

"HE HAS THREATENED MY LOYAL SERVANT, AND HIS LIFE IS MINE! IT HAS BEEN TOO LONG SINCE THE SCENT OF BLOOD HAS FILLED THE AIR!"

Daine's struggles were useless. He couldn't move a muscle, and every second the pressure increased. Hassalac's voice faded to a dull, incoherent roar. *Thunder.* His vision blurred, and the world began to fade.

Then it was over. He fell to the ground, gasping for breath. His body was worn and sore, and the world's angriest blacksmith was using his head as an anvil. Lakashtai was speaking to Hassalac, but Daine couldn't make out the words through his fog of pain. Whatever she'd said, it had kept him alive . . . though at the moment death seemed preferable to the terrible pounding in his head. He saw that Lakashtai had produced the dragon scale, which floated through the air to the kobold's throne.

" . . . the company of that half-breed rat."

Slowly words began to take shape. Mercifully, Hassalac had lowered his voice. He still spoke in resonant bass tones instead of the squeaking yap of the kobold, but as Daine watched he realized that Hassalac's mouth wasn't actually moving when he spoke. The sorcerer wore robes of crimson velvet, and a braided ring of gold was wrapped around his throat. Rosy dragonshards were embedded in the terminals of this torc, and they pulsed with a faint light in time with Hassalac's words. Apparently the sorcerer didn't care for the sound of his own voice.

"We only met Gerrion last night, Master Hassalac," Lakashtai said, "but he helped us find you, and his advice played a vital role in the selection of this gift."

"HE IS A THIEF AND A GRAY WORM!" Hassalac roared,

and Daine winced at the sound. "Surely this is another of his tricks!"

"Calm yourself, Master Hassalac." Lakashtai's words were like cool water, and even Daine's headache seemed to subside at the sound of her voice. "Gerrion told us he was a thief. In fact, he said that he had stolen goods on your behalf on more than one occasion."

"Perhaps . . ."

"Besides, if Gerrion was plotting against you, why would he have revealed his presence? We bring no hidden purposes to your door."

The kobold scratched his chin with a polished claw, running his other hand across the dragonscale that lay across his lap. Rings glittered on his fingers. "Very well. I accept your tale, for now, so what is it you seek?"

"Your name is known even in Khorvaire and Adar, Master Hassalac. Your collection of treasures is a thing of legend."

"This I know. Make your point, for my patience wears thin."

"All we ask is the opportunity to study your treasures, Master Hassalac, to examine your collection, that we may know once and for all what wonders you possess."

Hassalac's mouth finally opened, producing a series of barking yaps that Daine recognized as kobold laughter. Lakashtai remained unruffled, and eventually the sorcerer's mirth subsided.

"You have manners, warm one," he said at last, "to bring a gift with your request. The one who came before did not, and he is lucky that I let him leave; I considered turning him into crystal and adding him to my treasures."

"We have no desire to take anything from you—"

"Except knowledge," Hassalac snapped, "and you know well that knowledge is the greatest treasure of all. My secrets are worth far more than mere silver or gold. In return for this fine gift, I shall allow you to inspect those relics placed on display in this chamber and to leave with your lives when you are done, but no one enters my vaults."

Hassalac's voice might have been magically generated, but it conveyed emotion well, and the threat hung in the air. Daine's hand was on his sword, but Lakashtai caught his eye and shook her head.

"We shall avail ourselves of your kind offer, Lord Hassalac. We shall not take long; I am certain that you yearn for your privacy."

"Than you are wiser than I thought." The kobold dismissed them with a gesture. "Go. And you—" he fixed Daine with his gaze, and for a moment Daine felt an icy hand around his heart. "Spill another drop of blood in my domain, and your death will be a slow one."

*Get in line,* Daine thought. "I understand."

Hassalac wasted no more words on them, turning his attention to the dragon scale. Daine followed Lakashtai into the main chamber, where Kess was waiting.

"Whenever you are ready, I will arrange for your escort to the surface. Take as much time as you wish. Although," he lowered his voice and glanced at the back of his master's throne. "I think you would be wise to act swiftly."

❦ ❦ ❦ ❦ ❦ ❦ ❦

Lakashtai spent little time examining the various treasures on display in the cavern. There were a number of worn statues, and a pockmarked spearhead that must have belonged to a giant; it was nearly two feet long, and the tip was stained and black. She devoted a few minutes to studying a chunk of crystal the size of Daine's head. She refused to speak or to acknowledge Daine's questions, but it had been less than a quarter of an hour when she summoned Kess and asked to leave.

As before, one of the lizard guardians led the way through the maze of tunnels. Daine tried to see if he could remember the way out, but passages kept branching, and he quickly lost track.

"Well, that was worthwhile," he said to Lakashtai. "After all, we only killed a priest and robbed a temple, and what did we get? To leave with our lives. Sovereigns be praised."

Lakashtai said nothing, but Daine had spent enough time with her to spot the faint smile.

"What? You're not disappointed?"

"Be silent," she said, though her tone was gentle. "You

should be grateful to Master Hassalac for sparing you after you harmed his guard. Merely meeting him was honor enough for the price that we paid."

" . . . Sure."

Eventually, they came to the gate of shadows. "You go," rasped the guardian.

Daine turned to Lakashtai. "So. There's a good chance your friends are waiting for us out there."

"Agreed."

"You're always appearing out of nowhere—is that some sort of a kalashtar trick?"

"It is a discipline I have learned, yes. I can cloud the perceptions of others, so they overlook my presence, but I cannot extend this shield to protect you."

"Don't worry about me," Daine said. "Supposedly I'm the one they're looking for, so hopefully they won't even care if they do see you. Now, I want you to go through first. Do . . . whatever it is you do. Get away from the doorway. Count to ten, slowly, and then start screaming at the top of your lungs."

"Screaming?"

It was hard to imagine the serene kalashtar in a panic, but Daine didn't want to argue. "Yes. Scream. Murder, fight, thief, whatever. Draw a crowd. They'll focus their attention on me, trust me on this. As soon as there are enough people around, we break off and head for the Ship's Cat together. This isn't an assassination; they want me alive. As long as there are people around, they can't grab me."

"As you wish." Lakashtai gave a slight bow to their reptilian escort. She walked into the shadow and disappeared from view.

Daine smiled at the guard. "Well, thanks. You've been a great help. Let me see if I have something for you . . ." He fumbled with his leather pouch, and produced a pair of copper coins. "Here," he said, tossing them to the guard.

The creature let go of its halberd with one hand to catch the coins, but Daine had deliberately thrown too low, and the coins clattered to the floor. The guard bent over to pick them up.

And Daine charged.

He slammed into the creature with all the strength he could muster. The lizardman was far stronger than Daine, but he was caught completely off balance. It fell, tumbling backwards—and the two of them went through the gate together.

The moment of transition was unpleasant, but Daine held his focus with grim determination. The next thing he knew, he was in Stormreach, the sun bright overhead. The guardian was sprawled on the ground, and nearby a woman was screaming.

Luckily for Daine, the guard had dropped its halberd in the melee, but the creature had long talons and jaws that looked strong enough to bite through bone. It rose to its feet with a roar. Daine ducked under the first swipe, but the second caught him along the ribs; his chainmail took the worst of it, but his side burned where the claws had left bloody furrows. He continued to dodge and weave, leaping out of the path of the creature's blows and slowly circling around it. Finally, he was back in position. He leaned against the marble pillar, doing his best to appear exhausted and out of energy—not something that required much effort. Sensing victory, the beast charged forward, roaring in triumph.

Daine threw himself out of the way, revealing the gate of shadows.

The creature was moving too quickly to stop, and it disappeared into the darkness. The instant it was gone, Daine dove off the stone platform and into the crowd that had gathered to watch the fight, heading toward the place he'd heard Lakashtai. If there were Riedrans about, the crowd held them at bay. Daine found Lakashtai with Gerrion and grabbed her arm.

"Let's go. Gerrion, back to the Ship's Cat—and main roads only."

Behind them, there was a roar as the angry creature burst back out of the gateway. Daine didn't look back as they hurried down the street.

"Hassalac said no blood," he muttered to Lakashtai. "He didn't say anything about bruises."

❦ ❦ ❦ ❦ ❦ ❦ ❦

Lei and Pierce were playing sundown in the common room when they arrived. Pierce was fully restored, and Lei had even cleaned his mithral plates. He rose as Daine entered.

"Is there trouble?"

Daine shrugged. "As far as I can tell, all we've done today is make enemies."

"Not at all," Lakashtai said. "We have accomplished exactly what I expected."

Daine frowned. "What? Hassalac threw us out."

"Of course."

"So what was the point?"

"Because now," Lakashtai said with a smile, "we can break into the vault."

# CHAPTER 26

XEN'DRIK
STORMREACH
*Lharvion 19, 997 YK*

It had all begun so well.

"Get up, damn you!" Daine grabbed Lei's shoulders and shook her, but she did not respond; her neck lolled against the floor. A bolt of energy punched a skull-sized crater in the wall behind him, the ray missed him by less than an inch, and his skin tingled from the passage of the beam.

*It's my fault. She came because of me. . .*

Two hours ago they'd been in the Ship's Cat. He could still taste the meat and ale, and hear Lei's laughter in the back of his mind.

Now she was dead.

❁ ❁ ❁ ❁ ❁ ❁ ❁

"I can't take this sober." Daine gestured to the innkeeper, and three cats followed the motion in silent unison.

"You must," Lakashtai said. "We leave as soon as you have collected your belongings."

"No. We don't." Daine turned to the shifter matron. "Good food. Strong drink. I don't care what it is. She's paying."

"Daine. This is not a matter for discussion."

"You're right, Lakashtai, it's not." Daine took a seat at the table. Lei glanced at Pierce, but neither said a word. "We go when we're all ready to go, and this time, you tell us the plan from beginning to end."

"You're a soldier, Daine. You know there are times when a

general has to keep secrets."

"How many times have I heard that before? When did we join your army?"

"When my enemy chose to attack you. You aren't in the army, Daine—you are the battlefield."

Lei snorted. "You keep saying that, but why? What could your doom and darkness possibly want from Daine?"

"We cannot afford to find out."

"That's convenient for you, isn't it?" Lei remained in her seat, but Daine could feel her mounting frustration from across the table. "We're fighting a war against *your* enemy for reasons only *you* understand. You've got us robbing temples, killing priests, and now fighting sorcerers. Lucky for us the law seems even more lax here than in Sharn. What's next? Overthrowing a king?"

Lakashtai was as imperturbable as ever. "If you had to kill a king to save your friend, would you?"

"How do I know *any* of this is to help Daine?"

"Enough!" Daine slammed a fist into the table. "If you want us to keep going with this, Lakashtai, we need answers. We're going to rob Hassalac? Fine, but I want to know why. You say this is for my benefit—how, exactly? Use small words." He glanced at Gerrion. "Isn't this a job for an actual thief?"

"I don't know who you've been listening to. I'm just a guide," the gray man said with a smile.

Lakashtai ignored the comment. "Gerrion has other duties to attend to. It is Lei's skills that will be required for this task."

The conversation was brought to a halt by the arrival of Harysh with Daine's lunch. The ale was served hot, mixed with honey and cloves. A large plate held boiled roots, dark brown bread, and a large empty space. With some surprise, Daine noticed a few strips of red meat floating off the right side of the platter.

"Displacer beast," the shifter explained. "The marinade preserves the effect for a few days. Just feel around the center of the plate, you'll find it. Trust me, it's worth the trouble." She inclined her head and returned to the bar.

"Apparently, nothing here is what it seems," Daine remarked, stabbing at empty air until he found the invisible meat. "So tell us, Lakashtai. What's the plan?"

Lakashtai studied the group spread around the table. Then, to Daine's surprise, she sighed; for an instant her cold mask dropped away, and she looked weary and afraid. She looked away, and the moment passed.

"I do not wish to speak in this place. Finish your meal, and let us begone. I shall explain everything as we travel, and if my plan does not meet with your approval, we can return to the harbor and seek passage back to Khorvaire."

Daine glanced at Lei and Pierce. The warforged soldier nodded gravely. Anger glittered in Lei's eyes, but she eventually nodded. "Fine, but after this . . . no more surprises."

"Of course."

❖ ❖ ❖ ❖ ❖ ❖ ❖

The second bell was ringing as they left the Ship's Cat. Lakashati led the way, and when they arrived at the main road she turned south, heading away from the harbor. Gerrion had left earlier, and he was nowhere to be seen.

"Lakashtai—"

"Wait until we reach the gates of the city. There are far too many ears in this place. We shall not enter Hassalac's domain without your approval; we could not, regardless of my desires."

"Very well."

Daine let Lakashtai lead the way, falling back to walk next to Lei. He offered her his hand, and she took it with a slight smile. Pierce was at the rear, studying the crowds. It seemed to Daine that Pierce was looking for something in particular—presumably, the Riedran soldiers they had fought before.

"Are you all right?" Daine murmured to Lei.

She smiled faintly and squeezed his hand. "I'm not the one with the beast in her head."

"I know, which makes this my problem, not yours."

Lei shrugged.

"I don't know. You just seem tense. Angry. And you don't have the excuse of bad dreams." She stiffened slightly at the comment. *Or does she?* She spoke before he could raise the question.

"I'm not allowed to feel angry about this? About what's

happening to you?" Lei shot a glance at Lakashtai. "I don't like this. *Any* of this. I don't like *her*. It's just . . . How do we know she isn't using you?"

"Let's see what she has to say. She did save my life."

"So you say. Why didn't you talk to us first?"

*Why hadn't he?* Looking back, it was hard to remember. He'd been afraid, even embarrassed, and what could Lei have done? The kalashtar—all the stories said that they were creatures of mind and dream, and it has just seemed like the right decision at the time.

"You tried to fight this. It didn't work, remember? She's held it at bay, and that counts for something."

"Still. She just happened to be going to Xen'drik? I just feel like we're doing her dirty work."

"A fortunate coincidence, I assure you." They'd been speaking quietly, but not quietly enough; Lakashtai had keen ears. "It was fate that brought us together, and sometimes we must trust in the whims of fate."

Lei scowled but said no more. She was holding her staff in her right hand, and the face carved on the shaft suddenly caught Daine's eye; its expression was an exact mirror of Lei's, as if the staff itself was angry. He gave Lei's hand a gentle squeeze, and the frown faded from her face—but the staff was still scowling. Had it always been like that? For a time, they walked in silence, taking comfort in the physical connection.

They arrived at a wide plaza, the very edge of the city. Stormreach was surrounded by a wall of dark stone, and a pair of tall gates stood across the length of the square. Merchants of many races displayed their wares from simple hide tents and worn blankets. These were the people who dared to live beyond the city walls, and their goods were simple things: strange fruits, dried meat, furs. A pair of gnome scholars dressed in the blue and red robes of a Korranberg college were studying the fragments of stone and pottery offered by a scarred half-orc wrapped in a lizardskin cloak. Despite the many traders, there were fewer people in the square than they'd seen in the northern city; Stormreach was a port town, and the harbor was where its people made their living.

Lakashtai didn't spare a glance for the traders. As soon as

they passed beneath the worn arch and past the walls of the city, she turned to the southwest, leading them off of the wide, unpaved road that led toward the farms. The ground was scrubland, hard earth choked with stone and weeds, and Daine could see nothing of any possible interest.

For a few minutes they continued to walk into the wilds, then Lakashtai began to speak.

"Before I knew of your troubles, Daine, my mission was to come to Stormreach to catalog the artifacts collected by Hassalac Chaar—to ensure that he had not found anything best left undiscovered. While it would be convenient if he has discovered a weapon we could use against the forces laying siege to your dreams, I truly hope that he has not. I can think of only one place where he could find such a thing, and there are powers there no mortal should have."

"So why—" Daine began, but Lakashtai silenced him with a raised hand.

"What we seek could only be found in one of the armories of the ancient giants—a place where they forged their weapons of war. My people have learned of one such place: the Monolith of Karul'tash. We do not know the location of Karul'tash, but I have spoken with explorers who have sold relics to Hassalac in the past, and I believe that he has a map that can show us the way."

"That's ridiculous," Lei snapped. "We came all this way because we hope he *might* have a map to a place that may or may not still exist? If he had a map, why wouldn't *he* have used it?"

"Because he will not have recognized its true nature. You will understand when you see it."

Daine shook his head. "None of this explains why we're in the middle of a barren field or why you had me kill a priest this morning."

"Gerrion spoke truly earlier this morning: a manor attracts thieves. Hassalac's abode is hidden, accessible only by teleportation, and only when he decides to open the gate."

"Why didn't we do something when we were *in* his home?"

"You saw his power, Daine. We cannot challenge him directly, but we did do something: we gave him a gift."

Daine frowned. "That helped us how?"

A new voice spoke. "You have tricked him into revealing his location?" It was Pierce. The warforged had been silent for so long, the sound took Daine by surprise.

"Precisely," Lakashtai said. "I possess the ability to see the auras that surround both objects and people—and if I charge an object with my energies, I can sense it from far away. We needed to present Hassalac with a treasure of such value that he would place it in his vault."

"You could have told us this earlier," Daine said.

Lakashtai stopped walking, and turned to face the trio. "I have no doubt that at least one of our Riedran foes can read minds, and Hassalac himself may have this power. I can shield my thoughts—you cannot. It was necessary to keep these details hidden until now."

Daine considered this. He didn't like it, but it made sense; after all, they did end up meeting a Riedran soldier in the tunnels, and it hadn't occurred to him that the man might be a threat even without taking physical action.

"Very well. So where is the vault?"

"Four hundred feet below us."

Lei blinked. "In this field?"

"Beneath this field, yes."

"Is there some sort of secret passage?"

"No." Lakashtai looked at Lei. "You will take us there. I can show you the path; can you not craft a device that can transport us across this space?"

"I . . ." Lei looked away, and Daine could almost hear the thoughts racing in her head. "I understand the basic principles that govern the movement of motion, but to transport all of us at once—I've never tried to channel that level of power before. If my calculations are wrong, or if I lose control of the threads . . . it could be dangerous."

Daine sighed. "*How* dangerous?"

"If we're lucky, the energy I'm binding would be released in a burst of light and heat—like a charge from a fire wand."

"And if you're unlucky?"

"We're transported somewhere else. Into solid rock, or perhaps four hundred feet up instead of four hundred feet down."

Daine glanced at the sky. "Well, at least the weather's good for it. Lakashtai, you're certain this is the only way to do this?"

"Yes, I believe that it is. Your only hope lies in Karul'tash, and if Hassalac does not have this map, we have no idea as to its whereabouts. In my weakened condition, it may only be a matter of days before Tashana overcomes the defenses I have woven and shatters your mind."

Daine turned to face Lei, placing his hands on her shoulders. She met his gaze, and he could see the fear in her eyes. "You've risked your life for me just by coming here. I can't ask you to do it again."

"You didn't ask me the first time," she said softly. "It's my choice. I'm not going to let you die." She looked away. "Now let me get to work."

She sat down on the rough earth and produced an assortment of crystals and wooden rods, which she spread out across the ground in from of her. Slowly she began to whisper, channeling the essence of magic with thought, gesture, and sound.

Daine watched her work. There was a chill in his heart he'd never felt in battle. *She can do this. She's never failed before.* "Any other surprises, Lakashtai?"

"None. We go to the vault and find the map. No doubt Hassalac will have defenses in the vault, but hidden as it is, I doubt that he expects too many people to enter the vault directly. Gerrion will be waiting at the harbor with a boat prepared to sail as soon as we are on board. He takes us along the coast, and we land as near to Karul'tash as possible. Now you know the extent of my plans."

Daine nodded, his eyes on Lei.

"I'm done," she said, and Daine felt a weight lifted from his chest. "I think . . . if something was going to go wrong, it would have. Gather around. You'll need to be touching me for this to work. And Lakashtai, I need the precise distance."

Daine drew his sword. "Pierce, flail ready. No telling what's waiting there for us."

Each of the travelers placed a hand on Lei's shoulders. Green light flashed from Lakashtai's eyes; Lei's brow furrowed for an instant, and she nodded.

They vanished.

CHAPTER 27

XEN'DRIK
STORMREACH
*Lharvion 19, 997 YK*

It was pitch black.

Should have seen that coming, Daine thought. Why leave lamps on for the thieves? "Light," he murmured, loud enough for Lei to hear. He heard the whisper as she wove temporary cold fire into her staff, but before this enchantment took hold, the area was filled with a pale green radiance. Glancing over, Daine saw that Lakashtai's eyes were shining like beacons, casting a cone of emerald light before her. "That's . . . disturbing," he said, keeping his voice low.

To his surprise, she winked at him, causing a temporary flicker of light.

They were standing in a vast cavern, far larger than the audience chamber they had seen earlier. To their right, tall shelves were lined with small chests and loose dragon scales; Daine recognized the casket that held the blue scale shield. The shelves to the left held books—but books unlike any Daine had ever seen. Most were three feet in height, with a width to match. These tomes were bound in lizardskin or thick leather, but most were crumbling with age.

"Giants," Lei whispered. "These must have been written by giants before the fall of Xen'drik."

"Which one has our map?" Daine said. "Tell me we don't have to read until we find it."

"The map we seek is not bound by leather and ink." Lakashtai glanced along the shelves, sweeping the cone of light across rows of books and long leather tubes that probably held enormous scrolls. "It is a large translucent crystal, about three feet in diameter. It must be elsewhere in this chamber."

Daine nodded. "Lei, Pierce—on point. Slow."

They crept down the aisle. Lei stayed just ahead of Pierce, and Daine wondered what she saw as she studied the currents of arcane energy. Moments passed before an end to the aisle came into view. They had come to the edge of the room, and a narrow corridor ran alongside the stone wall of the cavern. Lei paused at the edge in the intersection, kneeling down and passing her hand over the floor.

"What have you discovered?" Pierce asked.

Lei frowned. "There's a symbol here, a glyph of tremendous power. Set this off and you'd be dead in an instant—it would be like a hurricane blowing out a candle."

"Can you break it?" Daine said.

"Never, but . . . it's already been triggered. It's strange—it looks like it was set off, but there aren't any corpses."

Daine's grip tightened on the hilt of his sword. "So we're not alone?"

"It really depends how long it takes for the energy in the seal to rebuild itself. Perhaps intruders were in here earlier, and the guards already removed the bodies."

"Perhaps. We need to be prepared. Lakashtai . . . can you link our minds again?"

*Certainly.* The thought blossomed in Daine's mind.

*Good. Lei—left. Careful and quiet.*

They crept along the edge of the wall, slipping past rows of giant shelves. Up ahead, the labyrinth of shelves came to an end, opening into a wide chamber; Daine caught a glimpse of shattered statues and other large relics, but a sudden *stop* from Pierce brought them to a halt.

*There. At the corner of the last shelf. Blood.*

It could barely be seen in the magical light, but Pierce's eyes were keen. There was a dark stain at the base of the last shelf, just intruding into the corridor, a pool of dried blood.

Daine stepped forward, drawing his dagger. *Lei, is the hallway clear to that point?*

*I . . . I think so.*

Daine took his place next to Pierce. *Stand ready,* he thought.

He tumbled forward, executing a low roll that would hopefully drop him below the line of anyone who might be waiting with weapon in hand. He darted out beyond the shelves, coming to a halt behind a massive foot formed of blue marble—apparently, the last remnant of a colossal monument. Spinning around, he searched the hall for any sign of enemies, but there were none to be seen.

No living enemies, at least.

*It's safe,* he thought, stepping out from his cover. *Come take a look at this.*

Two corpses were spread across the floor of the chamber. They were two of Hassalac's reptilian guards—possibly the same two that had escorted Daine and Lakashtai earlier in the day, but the damage made it impossible to tell.

"Merciful Arawai," Lei whispered, dropping to one knee to study the closer of the two corpses. "What could do something like this?"

Barely half of the creature's body was left. It was as if it had stumbled into a wall of whirling razors—a force that had shredded flesh, bone, and chainmail with equal ease, scattering the remains in a bloody circle almost ten feet in diameter. The stench was awful.

"I don't know," Daine said, "but for the moment it looks like someone has cleared our path. This blood is dry, and we haven't seen any motion. Let's do this as quickly as we can and begone before anyone else comes to investigate. Lakashtai?"

The emerald gaze swept across the scattered relics. *There,* she thought, and the cone of light narrowed to focus on one object—a massive chunk of polished crystal, covered with strange sigils etched into its surface.

*All right. Pierce, ready your bow. I'll take point.*

Daine darted across the room. There were still no enemies to be seen, and the others swiftly followed. Pierce kept his distance, watching the shadows of the room; Lei and Lakashtai took up positions around the stone.

"I don't understand," Lei whispered. "I don't sense any sort of magical aura at all, and these symbols—that's no language I've ever seen or any school of arcane design."

"It's not magical," Lakashtai replied. "Memories have been embedded in the crystal. Unlocking them, opening them—it's a matter of thought. You must view the crystal as an extension of yourself, and reach into it as you would your own mind." She placed a hand on the massive shard, and it began to glow—a faint blue shimmer that soon grew to a strong, powerful radiance, flooding the chamber with light.

*Daine.* It was Pierce's thought, as slow and steady as his voice. *Look to the ground. Look for the traces.*

Daine studied the stone floor. He never would have noticed on his own, but after a moment he saw what Pierce was talking about. Blood. A faint trail of blood lead from the scaled corpses to the crystal he was standing next to. Whatever had killed the guards—it had come in search of the crystal map.

He turned to speak to Lakashtai, but Lei stopped him with a gesture. "Don't interrupt her," Lei whispered. "She's—finding her way through it, I think. It must be like reading a book."

Lakashtai's eyes were closed, and a swirling web of light danced within the heart of the stone.

"Fine. Get started on whatever you need to do to get us back out of here—I want to leave the instant she's done."

Lei waved her hands, encompassing the treasures around them. "*Look* at this place. Don't you want to explore it further? Think of what treasures might be down here?"

"What I want is to leave in one piece, instead of being split in half or having my candle blown out by a hurricane. Get to work. *Now.*"

Lei sighed, but found an empty spot against the wall of the chamber. She sat down, and produced the components she needed to generate another burst of teleportation.

Daine glanced around the chamber, studying the shadows cast by the statues and fragments of broken masonry. Was that a sound—the pad of soft leather against stone? With eviscerated corpses only a few lengths away, it was easy to imagine ghosts in the shadows. Still—

*Danger!* Pierce's thought rang through Daine's mind in the same instant that his arrow split the air. A dark-cloaked figure had stepped out from the cover of the tall shelves, one arm raised and pointing in Daine's direction. Pierce's arrow struck just below its upraised arm, driving into its chest and likely piercing a lung. It was a blow that would have dropped a normal man, but the intruder somehow stayed on its feet. Before Daine could fully comprehend the situation, a beam of light lanced toward him; missing him by inches.

Details slowly came together. A dark robe hemmed in silver, a glittering veil beneath a deep hood. It was one of the Riedrans—the woman who had wielded the crystal of pain. Daine could see others in the darkness behind her.

*Pierce. Hold your position. See if you can keep them pinned down.*

*Acknowledged.* Pierce loosed two more arrows, but the woman had darted back behind the cover of the shelves. Even as Daine tried to determine the best course of action, there was a distortion in the air next to him. What began as a ripple in the air became deadly reality; an instant later a man was standing next to Daine, and a crystal blade was flashing toward him. Daine turned just in time to block the blow with the edge of his grandfather's blade.

*I guess they don't want me alive after all.*

The Riedran swordsman moved with unnatural grace and speed, and like Lakashtai he seemed to be able to predict Daine's intentions. It felt like Daine was fighting a ghost; the enemy danced out of the way of every thrust and cut, leaving Daine slashing at empty air. For all these tricks, he lacked Daine's skill with the blade itself. Even though Daine couldn't touch his attacker, by dropping into a defensive stance he found that he could parry each blow. This dance continued for a time, and for a moment it was actually relaxing; there was no room to think of anything but the battle itself. Then his enemy's eyes flashed with blue light, and Daine's thoughts exploded in agony. It was as if a hammer had struck him between the eyes, and in that moment of distraction the Riedran broke past Daine's guard, striking directly at his heart.

Pain lanced through Daine's chest, but his chainmail saved him; Cyran steel held against Riedran crystal, and only the very tip of the blade pierced his flesh. The pain fueled his anger, and even as he dropped back into guard position, he thought *good trick—let's see how you like it. Pierce!*

Perhaps the Riedran was reading Daine's thoughts; it seemed

like he began to leap to the side, but he wasn't fast enough. He shuddered under the impact of Pierce's arrows, and in that moment Daine lashed out, a swift arc of steel that cut across his enemy's throat. Black cloth was wet with blood as the man fell to the ground, three long arrows projecting in a perfect line running down his spine.

This victory had its price. The instant Pierce turned from his post, the woman in the shadows struck again, and this time the dark bolt struck Daine directly. For an instant he felt the same sensation he had when Lei had brought them down into the vault, or when he'd stepped through Hassalac's gate—the cold disorientation that accompanies teleportation. This was immediately replaced by blinding pain. It was as if half his body had teleported a fraction of an inch, leaving the rest of him behind. Every muscle felt torn, his bones ached, and his mouth was filled with blood. It took every ounce of willpower to stay on his feet, and he knew that he wouldn't survive another blow like that one.

Even as his vision cleared, he saw a green glow at his side. Lakashtai!

*We have what we need. I shall do what I can against this one; see to our passage.*

*Right. Lei, what's the status?*

Daine turned toward Lei, and a new pain gripped his chest, worse than the magical bolt. Apparently the first beam hadn't been meant for him. Lei was sprawled across the ground, mystical components scattered around her and the glowing staff across her chest. Her mouth and nose were smeared with blood. Daine dove toward her, but even at a distance he could tell she wasn't breathing.

# INTERLUDE

*Darkness.*
*Cold.*

For all that the world seemed to be defined by this frigid silence, she somehow felt abstracted from this chill. It was the foundation of reality.

An eon passed before she realized that there was more. That she could feel a hard surface beneath her. She remembered Lei. Her friends. Her life.

She opened her eyes.

After an eternity of shadow, the light was blinding. Slowly her eyes adjusted. A magic lantern hung directly above her, mirrors within the casing shaping the light of the cold fire into a focused beam, shining directly down onto her. She tried to sit up, but her muscles wouldn't respond.

"You knew this time would come." A man's voice. Familiar. This was all familiar. Calling on every ounce of strength that she possessed, she managed to turn her eyes toward the source of the sound.

It was her father. Talin d'Cannith. Suddenly it all came back to her. The vision, almost a year ago now, when she had collapsed in the tunnels beneath Sharn. She was back in that same chamber, stretched out on a stone slab. There were other slabs around her, the shapes upon them hidden in the shadows.

"After all this, all we've put her through, you're just going to give up on her?" It was her mother. Aleisa. Lei couldn't see her, but she could never forget the voice.

"It's nature, nothing more." Her father's voice was calm. "We did all that we could for her, but in the end, it's a weakness of the medium." He bent over another slab, and when he stood he had something in his hand. A head? A warforged head? "This. This is how you defeat death."

Her mother stepped into view and struck the head from her father's hand. It fell to the floor with a clang, "Damn you! This is our *daughter,* not just another experiment."

Talin retrieved the fallen head and returned it to the slab. "Everything is an experiment, my love. You know that as well as I do. Some are just more . . . complicated than others."

"This isn't over."

Aleisa turned and walked over to Lei, gazing down on her. She was young, a woman Lei barely remembered from her childhood. It was a face Lei had almost forgotten, one that had been hidden by age and stress, but now, it was like looking into a mirror.

"It seems to be. You have to be prepared for the loss. I told you that at the beginning."

"No. She has the tools. She just doesn't know how to use them."

Now her father was looking down on her as well. She tried to speak, to question, but her jaws were fixed as stone.

"It is a shame," he said. "Such promise, such potential. So much time spent teaching, but all that is flesh must perish. We knew that from the start."

"Not yet." Aleisa laid a hand on the center of Lei's chest. Her touch was warm, and it seemed to drive away the pain and cold. "This is your battle, Lei. You have all the weapons you need, but you need the will to fight, and I can't give you that."

Talin watched, and she could read nothing in his eyes. "There's no more time."

"I know." Aleisa's voice was gentle, but resigned. "It's all up to you now, my daughter." Fingertips drifted across Lei's cheek. The light was fading, and her mother's voice was little more than a whisper. "Just remember that whatever happens— whatever happened—I always loved you."

The room faded away, leaving her in shadow, but Lei could *feel* something nearby: a bar of white light, even though that light was hidden by the darkness that surrounded her.

The cold began to seep back through her limbs, but now there was hope. Clinging to the sound of her mother's voice, Lei found the strength to raise her arm, to force her hand through the shadow.

She reached out for the light.

**G**et up, damn you!"

The voice was distant but growing loud. There was a sound of shattering stone. Suddenly the world exploded into pain. She remembered. She'd been weaving a charge of teleportation into the darkwood staff when there was a flash, a bolt of energy. She felt her body tearing itself apart as the power teleported pieces of her at a time. She was no healer, but she could feel the ruptures within—torn lungs that wouldn't fill with air, shattered bones, severed tendons—but even as she became aware of it, the pain was fading. Warmth spread from her left hip, rippling out across her body, bone and tissue mending in its wake.

She took a breath, and the air was ambrosia, filling her newly-formed lungs. Taking another deep breath, she opened her eyes.

❋ ❋ ❋ ❋ ❋ ❋ ❋

Tears did not come easily to Daine. The loss was like a fire; it burned all feelings away, leaving charred earth in its wake. All he had left was fury—cold hatred of those who had done this.

*From the sound, there could be more than six of them.* It was Pierce's thought, traveling through Lakashtai's mindlink. *They are spreading out—soon they may flank us.*

*Most will not have such power,* Lakashtai thought, *but they are armed, and they have strength of numbers. How much longer until we can depart?*

*Lei . . .* Daine couldn't bring himself to shape the thoughts,

172

but there was no time for pity. This was war.

Lei sat up.

Her skin was even paler than usual, and it shone with cold sweat. A thin stream of blood trickled from her mouth, and for a moment her eyes were dazed and unfocused. Then she caught sight of Daine, and for an instant her smile was all he saw, but there was no time for joy, even as there had been no time for pain. He barely realized what he was doing as he dove forward and pulled her to the floor an instant before a black bolt of energy filled the air where she had been.

"We've got to get out of here," he hissed, and now it was even harder to hold back the tears. "Can you do it?"

"Yes." Her breathing was ragged, her voice weak. "But the others . . . we need to be touching."

*Fall back! Now! We're leaving!*

Lakashtai was on the other side of a chunk of masonry, and she vaulted across it, a smooth, graceful motion that brought her down directly next to Lei. Pierce backed away from his post by the shelves. As Pierce retreated, a Riedran leapt out from the near corridor, a curved steel blade in each hand. Pierce paused just long enough to loose a single arrow, striking his foe directly in the right eye. The soldier moaned, falling to his knees and clawing at the shaft. Others were emerging from the shadows, but Pierce was already sprinting toward his companions.

"Staff . . ." Lei whispered.

Daine saw the darkwood staff lying amid the objects she'd scattered across the floor and snatched it up. It seemed unnaturally cold, but there was no time to worry about this, and he pressed it into Lei's hand. She clung to his arm with her free hand, her lips twisted in a pained smile. Lakashtai and Pierce were there in a second, each reaching out to lay a hand on her shoulders.

Riedran soldiers were pouring out from behind the shelves in a flood of black silk and steel. Daine met the gaze of a black-robed woman, her arm outstretched and energy flaring around her fingertips, but even as he saw the blast flying toward him, the surroundings melted away.

● ● ● ● ● ● ●

After the dim light of cold fire and Lakashtai's glowing eyes, the brilliant sunlight was as stunning as the pain from Daine's injury. They had emerged on a side street, black mud paved with chunks of stone pried from an old, rust-colored ruin. A vendor dropped the purple fruits he was holding, staggering back against the thorny weeds covering the nearby wall, and a trio of colorful birds was startled into flight. The other people on the street didn't even spare a glance; apparently Stormreach truly was a place where the fantastic happened every day.

*We must move quickly,* Lakashtai thought. *Clearly we have concerns beyond Hassalac, and they may have others who can teleport. To the harbor.*

"Are you injured?" Pierce said, looking to Lei. "I can carry you if you require assistance."

"No, I'm . . . I'm fine."

Miraculously, it seemed to be true. She began to lope after Lakashtai, and despite her initial unsteadiness, now she appeared to be in better condition than Daine himself. He staggered along, doing his best to ignore the pain that came with every step. *Maybe Pierce could carry me.*

Pierce took the lead as they made their way through the city, and most people were quick to move out of the path of the charging warforged. They drew a few stares from council watchmen and mercenary soldiers, but there was no hue and cry in their wake, and they made it to the harbor unmolested.

*It's the third pier,* Lakashtai thought, but Pierce already knew where they were going. He'd seen Gerrion's boat the night before, and even if he hadn't been able to recognize the battered black hull in the daylight, the gray man was standing on the deck waiting for them.

"We're sailing in *that?*" Daine said. "Maybe I'll stay and take my chances with the Riedrans."

"That is your choice," Lakashtai said, as she made her way across the wobbly gangplank and onto the deck. "I wish you pleasant dreams."

"Great," Daine sighed. He followed Lei across the plank, looking for holes in the sails.

"Welcome aboard the *Gray Cat,*" Gerrion said with a grin,

once all four of the companions were aboard. "Everything is cleared with the harbor lord, and I've stocked the hold. Oars couldn't hurt until we catch the wind; Master Daine, Pierce, if you'd care to lend your strength to the cause we can be on our way."

Perhaps the Riedrans weren't pursuing them. Perhaps the Riedrans were stranded in Hassalac's caves. Whatever the truth, there was no sign of their enemies as the *Gray Cat* moved away from the docks and out into the water. Daine gritted his teeth against the pain that flared in his shoulders with every stroke of the oars. Gerrion was manning the lines, and soon he found the wind. As Stormreach fell away behind them, Daine pulled in his oars and finally fell asleep.

❂ ❂ ❂ ❂ ❂ ❂ ❂

When he awoke, Lei was leaning over him. She was sitting on the deck behind him holding a short wand in her hand. He felt a soothing warmth as she passed the wand over his skin and realized that his pain was all but gone.

"Lucky for both of us that I finished the wand before our trip," she said, smiling faintly.

There was no time for thought as he sat up, wrapping his arms around her. For a moment, he thought it was all another of his mad dreams, but she was there. "You're alive. You're still with me."

She gently pushed him away. "Careful. I'm not quite done with you yet—your injuries were quite severe. I'm amazed you made it to the docks."

"What happened?"

"From talking to Lakashtai, it appears that some of the Riedrans we were fighting have the power to shift the location of matter with their thoughts alone. This was—a sort of partial teleportation. It's an interesting—"

He put a hand over her mouth, stopping her in mid speech. It was all he could do to keep from laughing. "What happened to *you*?"

"Oh!" She glanced away. "Well. It seems that I was struck with the same form of attack that you were."

"You were dead, Lei. One moment you weren't breathing,

the next you're running ahead of me."

"I don't know, exactly." Her eyes were distant, and her voice had dropped to a whisper. "I . . ." she held up the wand in her hand. "This is livewood. It's a perfect vessel for healing energies. By binding power into the wand, it becomes a reservoir of healing, magical power that can be released later—"

"Lei. I know what a wand is."

Lei nodded, the corner of her mouth twisting down. "Yes. Well. I was carrying the wand. I thought we might need it. As best as I can tell, when I was struck by the attack, the wand healed me."

"You were unconscious. It wasn't even in your hand."

"I . . ." She shook her head. "I know. Someone needs to activate a wand to release its power, but somehow — I can't explain it. It's as if the wand acted on its own, as if it sensed my need."

"Is this a breakthrough, my lady?"

Dusk was beginning to fall, and Daine hadn't noticed Pierce in the shadows. He might have just arrived, or he could have been there for the entire conversation. *My lady,* Daine thought to himself—it's been a while since I've heard that.

"No. I don't think so. I don't know. Everything I did . . ." She studied the wand in her hand, holding it gingerly. "There's nothing unusual about the design. A wand can't act on its own."

"And you felt nothing else? I too once stood on the edge of life and death. Did you . . . dream?"

Lei glanced at Pierce for a moment, and Daine could see the tension building in her. She shook her head. "I can't talk about this right now." She looked back at Daine. "I . . . I need to be alone right now."

He just nodded. Confusion, pain, joy—his emotions were a storm within him, and at the moment he just wanted to close his eyes and let it all go. He gave her arm one more squeeze, then she stood up and walked away. Daine let his head drop back against the deck, glancing up into the sky. The boat rocked beneath him, and the sound of the surf seemed to wash away his thoughts. Pierce was standing over him, as silent as any statue, and the face of the warforged was the last thing he saw before he drifted off to sleep.

CHAPTER 29

THE
XEN'DRIK
COAST

*Lharvion 20, 997 YK*

When Daine opened his eyes again, the sky was dark; the faint glow on the horizon hinted at the approaching dawn. Someone had draped a blanket across him, but he still felt a shiver run across his skin. Though the images were quickly fading, the night had been filled with disturbing dreams. Probing eyes, beating wings, masses of tentacles barely held at bay by a fading shield—he had been standing in the center of a hurricane, and with every passing second it threatened to come crashing in upon him. Even now, with the sun rising in the distance and the fresh tang of warm, salty air, he still felt a cold and inevitable dread. The darkness was there, waiting, whenever he closed his eyes. How could anyone fight something like that?

"More bad dreams?"

Lei was next to him, wrapped in a ragged blanket of her own. Lakashtai had yet to emerge from the cabin, and Pierce was nowhere to be seen. Gerrion was back at the wheel, but his eyes were fixed firmly on the coastline.

Daine just nodded, sitting up and leaning against the side of the boat.

She glanced away, looking out into ocean and night. "I . . . I know how unsettling that can be."

"Really? What's trying to destroy your mind?"

She looked at him, and for a moment he wondered if he'd crossed a line—if there was something she wasn't telling him.

She'd been on edge for weeks, and her expression seemed . . . haunted. He reached out, laying a hand on her shoulder.

"Lei—what's wrong?" He kept his voice low, trying to avoid drawing Gerrion's attention.

She shook her head and looked away again, but she raised her left hand and clung to his arm. "I don't know," she said, a quaver in her voice. "It's all so—chaotic. What's happening to you. Lakashtai. She—I just don't like her, but I wonder if I'm just jealous because she can help you and I can't, and by the Nine, I *died* yesterday! I should be in the claws of the Keeper right now." The dawn light caught the first glitter of a tear in the corner of an eye. "How am I supposed to feel?"

Daine put his hand on her cheek, turning her face toward him. Her fingers tightened around his wrist. "Lei . . ." his words felt like iron in his throat, but he forced himself to stumble on. "You've helped me in ways Lakashtai never could. I'd never have made it this far without you."

She closed her eyes, and a tear ran down her cheek. He could feel her shivering.

"I don't know what's happening to me," he said. "I don't know what will happen, but we'll survive it. We always do. A month from now, Lakashtai will be ominously helping some other poor soul, but still we'll be together."

"I know." The sun broke the horizon, and the light turned her hair into a halo of copper flame. She opened her eyes again.

A moment passed before he even realized he was kissing her. The crashing water, the warmth of the rising sun, the feel of her skin against his—it merged together in a rush of emotion, a flood of sensation that swept all thought away.

Then she pulled back.

"This . . . we can't," she said, and now the tears were flowing. She put her hands against his chest and pushed him away, and she couldn't meet his gaze. "You *know* that. We can't."

Daine was still dazed by the moment, by the release of the emotions he'd kept buried for so long. "What?" He kept his hands on her shoulders, and struggled against the urge to pull her back to him. "Why?"

She sighed, and despite the warmth of the sun she was shivering even harder than before. "I—I care about you, Daine. You know that. You've got to know that. You . . . Pierce . . . you're the only family I have left."

"Lei—"

"I always thought that there was something, that—behind your mockery of my life, my betrothal—that you felt something for me, even if you couldn't say it. Even if I wouldn't. What would have been the point? My path was already set in stone."

"Lei. We were at war. You had a husband waiting for you. I . . . don't think I even knew what I was feeling."

"What does it matter?" she cried. She pushed him with unexpected strength, breaking his grip and knocking him back. "You *told* me! You're *Deneith!* You *know* what that means!"

Caught by surprise, Daine had struck his head against the edge of the boat. Between the motion of the water and the ringing in his head, it was difficult to focus his thoughts. "I renounced the house before I even met you. It's not part of who I am."

"*Of course it's a part of who you are!*" Lei rose to her feet, flinging the blanket aside. "It's not something you can just abandon. It's in your *blood*, and our blood can't mix."

Understanding washed over Daine. The politics of the dragonmarked houses were a complex dance of power, and Daine had assumed that this was what Lei was referring to. Now he remembered the stories he'd heard as a youth.

"You're not serious. You're worried about *mixed marks?* I don't even *have* a dragonmark!"

"The potential is still in you. My blood would fight yours, and our child would suffer. Remember the Tarkanans?"

"Who's talking about *children?*" Daine's head was pounding, and not just from the blow. "I just thought we could comfort one another."

"I'm from the House of Making," Lei said. "We always look to the future."

"You *were*."

Lei's eyes narrowed, and Daine knew he'd gone too far. He opened his mouth without knowing what he was going to say, just hoping to find some way to pull back that terrible mistake.

And the boat shook.

"Get *down*, both of you!"

In the heat of the moment, Daine had forgotten the others on the boat. Belatedly, he wondered how much Gerrion had heard, but he soon had other concerns. The sky was clear and the wind was steady, but the water was rising hard. Daine had little choice in the matter; a wave slammed into the side of the *Cat*, and the force sent him tumbling to the deck.

*It's on the wrong side of the ship*, he realized. *The waves are moving against the tide.*

Pierce made his way up from the stern. His bow was drawn, and he maintained his footing with surprising grace. "There is motion in the water," he said, as he reached Lei and Daine, "but I see nothing solid. It is as if the water itself has chosen to attack."

"I'd say that's exactly what's happened," Gerrion said.

Another wave slammed into the boat, and the deck tilted precipitously. Pierce stumbled, but kept his footing while Gerrion clung to the wheel. Daine managed to seize one of the loose lines with one hand, grabbing hold of Lei with the other. She glared at him but clasped his wrist with both hands.

"Care to explain that?" Daine shouted over the crashing surf.

"There's always been angry water across the coast, ever since the disaster that shattered Xen'drik," Gerrion said, struggling with the wheel. "I've never heard of troubles this close to the coastline. It'll make a great story, if any of us live to tell it."

"So what do we do?" The boat shook again.

"Sink, apparently, unless you think you can kill the sea with your sword."

"Elementals," whispered Lei, barely audible over the crashing waves. "Daine, I need stability. Tie . . . tie the rope around my waist. Quickly!"

*At least someone has an idea*, he thought. She let go of his wrist and wrapped her arms around him, and for a moment he forgot the crashing sea and the angry words that had passed just a moment earlier. Then the ship shuddered from another blow, and he quickly turned his attention back to the task at hand.

As soon as Lei was lashed to the line, she reached back and

opened one of the side pockets of her backpack. A sheaf of long arrows leapt out of the pocket in response to her mental command. She knelt down on the shaking deck and laid the arrows across her legs, her features contorted in deep concentration. Daine could see her lips moving, but he couldn't hear the whispered words over the thundering waters.

The water surged, and the deck tilted sharply. Daine clung to the rope, almost hanging in the air, and even the surefooted Pierce stumbled and needed to steady himself with one hand.

"If you're going to do something, do it quickly!" Gerrion called.

Blue fire played around the arrows in Lei's hands, and her eyes snapped open. She thrust the bundle toward Pierce.

"Strike the waves!" she shouted. "Whatever moves against the current! There can't be many of them—look for the motion and shoot into it!"

Pierce snatched the glowing arrows without comment. He held his footing atop the shifting deck; fitting an arrow to the string, he made his way to the side, sighting into the raging surf. As the next wave rose up against the tide, Pierce released the shaft, loosing a second arrow before the first had even struck. There was a burst of blue light as the arrows struck the water and a deep, low moan like the creaking of old wood—and as the light faded, so did the wave, dissolving into the sea. Pierce launched a second volley into the water, tracking a blur of motion, but if there was anything in the depths it escaped his aim. His third strike bore fruit, and another inhuman groan rose up from the water. He drew back the last of the enchanted arrows, searching the water for any sign of motion, but the moment of violence had passed. The water was calm again, with only the slow motion of the tides and the sound of the wind on the water.

Daine let his breath out slowly. "So . . . just another day in Xen'drik?"

"A parting gift from our friend Hassalac, I imagine," Gerrion said. "He never was one to leave a debt unpaid. I suppose it took him some time to find the boat."

"I studied elementals in my first visit to Sharn," Lei said, as she worked at the rope knotted around her waist. "The key is breaking the binding energy. We're lucky they were so small; a larger spirit would have capsized the boat in an—"

The water erupted around them.

The ship fell to the side, and no amount of agility could help Pierce; Daine saw his warforged companion disappear into the boiling water. Daine was still clinging to the rope, and now he found himself dangling in the air, clutching the slick line as he hung over the violent surf. A massive wall of water had risen to the north, completely obscuring their view of the horizon. The crest of the wave was over twenty feet in height, and there was no doubt in Daine's mind that it held the end of the *Gray Cat*.

It refused to break.

It simply hung in the air, a cobra waiting to strike. Doom poised above them, as Daine managed to wrap the line around his forearm, and Gerrion clung to the wheel. It was merely a question of whether the wave would finally fall before the vessel completed capsizing.

Then, as quickly as the disaster struck, it came to an end. The towering wave didn't break; it fell back, gently subsiding into the sea. Daine caught a glimpse of a vast, dark shape moving through the depths, and then, inexplicably, the *Gray Cat* was rising up. Water fell from deck and sail as the ship righted itself, finally standing straight and true. Now the ocean was truly calm, and the wind had died completely. The *Gray Cat* had survived, but it was dead in the water.

*Pierce!* Daine scrambled along the edge of the deck, still clinging to the rope. Daine had fallen asleep in his chainmail shirt, and he'd never been a strong swimmer; leaping into the water with armor on was a sure path to a watery death, but Pierce didn't need to breathe. He had to be alive. Of course, Pierce had never learned to swim. For a moment Daine had an image of the warforged sinking to the ocean floor, slowly walking back to Stormreach.

He had to be alive.

"Can you see him?" Lei was still holding the rope around her waist. If she'd managed to get the knots undone a moment ago, she would have been swept into the ocean by the second wave. Now she held the rope belt, uncertain whether she trusted the new calm enough to undo her lifeline.

"I do so hate to lose crew," Gerrion remarked, "but we might want to set to the oars and get out of these troubled waters before something worse comes along. Better to lose one than five."

Daine ignored him, studying the still waters for any sign of motion. Was that a glint of metal, deep in the darkness? Rising to the surface?

It was—but he was not alone. A vast spout of water rose up from the sea, but this was no wave, and it didn't even shake the ship. A shower of spray washed across the deck, obscuring their view, then they saw her through the mist.

A woman was gazing down at the *Gray Cat*. She was at least thirty feet tall, dressed in a long flowing robe—a robe formed of water. As the mist cleared and the sunlight struck her, Daine realized that the gown was a part of her. Her clear blue skin was still water, and her long white hair was bubbling surf; the surface of the gown was flowing water, the current giving the appearance of textured cloth. The hem of the gown disappeared into the sea.

And Pierce was in one liquid hand.

For a moment, Daine was stunned by the sight. She was beautiful and strange, as close to a god as he'd ever thought to see. This only lasted a second: his friend's life was at stake, and there was no time for awe. Even as he wracked his brain for a plan—wondering if there was time to act before she could strike the ship, whether Lei's magic arrows could affect such a magnificent creature—she reached down, placing Pierce on the deck of the ship.

*Be not afraid.* The voice swept across them like the tide itself. It was the sound of a gentle brook, of a tumbling waterfall, and Daine couldn't say whether the sound was shaped into actual words or if they simply somehow *knew* what it wished to tell them.

"Pierce, are you hurt?"

"No, Daine. It was an interesting experience, but I am none the worse for it."

Bursting free of the rope at last, Lei ran over and wrapped her arms around the dripping warforged, even as she stared up at the watery figure.

*Distant forces turned the waters against you, but I have calmed the restless spirits.* The voice was soothing, as calm and hypnotic as slow waves at sunset. *My mark is upon you, and you will reach your destination without further trouble.*

"You know this because you know our destination?"

*There is little I do not know, Daine with no family name. Your journey is just beginning. Darkness is at your heels, and your journey will take you through death and dream. Water will not harm you, but this is the season of fire.*

"I'd heard that," Daine said, glancing over at Lei. He questioned her with his expression, but she just shook her head. "How do you know who we are?"

*We have met before, Daine, aand we will meet again before this is done. I watch and I wait, and I act when I can—but there is little I can say and less I can do.*

"Well, I thank you for saving my vessel, good spirit of the seas," Gerrion put in.

The waters composing the spirit grew darker, and her voice was thundering surf instead of gentle tide. *I do nothing for you, child of the Sulatar. You have your own destiny, and it is not my place to change it. Count yourself lucky that you do not travel the seas alone this day.*

Gerrion bowed his head, stepping back to the wheel. "My humblest apologies, great lady." Daine and Lei exchanged looks.

*The time for talk is done, and the currents draw you to your destiny. Remember: sometimes the oathbreaker is more trustworthy than the ally, and a brother can be both enemy and friend. I will see you again beyond the gates of night.*

With that, she was gone. Whatever force was binding her body relaxed, and a fountain of water crashed down into the surface of the sea, spraying salt water across the deck of the *Gray Cat*.

No one spoke. Even the usually garrulous Gerrion was at a loss for words; he kept his eyes away from the others, and Daine wondered what a "Sulatar" was. The wind slowly picked up, billowing out the sail, and the ship began to move.

Daine slowly walked toward Lei and Pierce. Lei was fussing over the warforged, studying every joint; she did not look at Daine as he approached.

Motion in the corner of his vision brought Daine to a halt, and he turned toward the small cabin at the back of the boat. Lakashtai stepped out of the hatch.

"I was engaged in deep meditation," she said, taking in the soaked sail and the bedraggled travelers. "Did something happen in my absence?"

Daine glanced at the others then shrugged. "Stormy weather," he said.

CHAPTER 30

THE
XEN'DRIK
COAST

*Lharvion 21, 997 YK*

**W**hether it was the result of mystical protection or simple good fortune, the day passed without further incident. Once Daine thought he saw a vast dark shape moving beneath the water, but predator or spirit, it did not rise to threaten the *Gray Cat.* The storms that lingered over the Thunder Sea held their distance, forming a dark wall to the north.

Though the waters were calm, the moods of the passengers were anything but. Lei had been avoiding Daine ever since the attack, devoting her attention to Pierce and pointedly looking away and falling silent the few times he approached. He could have forced the issue, but the *Gray Cat* was too small for privacy, and Daine didn't want to continue the conversation around Gerrion or Lakashtai. In the end, he didn't know what to say.

It had been many years since Daine had been a member of House Deneith, and it simply wasn't a part of his identity. He had chosen to leave. In part this was a protest against the actions of the house itself. Cannith, Orien, Deneith: if the houses had joined together in support of the rightful queen of Galifar, the civil war might have ended before it had ever begun, but the war was an opportunity for the houses. The conflict brought many opportunities for profit: Deneith mercenaries, Jorasco healers, Cannith smiths—every house had an angle to work in the war. Greed and lust for power came before any sense of decency or compassion or loyalty to any land.

The policies of the house were only one factor in his

decision. Long before his dreams had come under siege, he'd been haunted by nightmares of the things he'd done in the service of the house. Spilling blood for gold was bad enough, but when he thought back to his younger years in Metrol, to Alina's hall of mirrors—the memories still burned. It had been Jode who'd pulled him up from that moral abyss, and now all that remained of Jode was a glass vial in his pocket.

When he left the house, Daine had scored the Deneith emblem off the pommel of his sword. It had since been repaired, and he'd chosen to leave it intact—out of respect to his grandfather if not to the house itself, but he no longer considered himself to be a member of House Deneith, and it had never occurred to him that it might have meaning to Lei. She was right; regardless of his feelings, the blood of the house ran through his veins. Daine might not have the dragonmark of the house, but the potential was still there in his blood. Daine had never concerned himself with history, but every child of the houses knew the stories: mixing the blood of two dragonmarked houses could result in aberrant marks, children with strange powers who could grow up twisted by madness or disease. Daine had been a cynical child and had never put much stock in the stories, but a year ago, they'd encountered three people with aberrant dragonmarks, and it had been a troubling experience. Daine thought about the man covered with sores and boils, the little halfling giggling and talking to her rats. If Lei and he were joined—was that the gift they would give a child?

Did he even want a child?

"You have troubles enough to deal with. Do not invite more."

Lakashtai's soft voice startled him out of his reverie. Gerrion was sleeping, but apparently the kalashtar knew something about sailing. She stood behind the wheel, her cloak billowing in the wind. The burns along her pale skin had vanished; Daine wondered if she had come to terms with Lei at some point, or if healing was just another of her powers that he didn't know about. Lei herself was nowhere to be seen and was most likely asleep in the cabin. Pierce was standing at the bow, but glanced back when he heard the conversation.

"I don't need you prying in my mind while I'm awake," Daine said with a glare.

"Neither of us has any choice in the matter," she replied. "It is the price of your protection. I have touched your dreams, and it is difficult for me to ignore your most powerful emotions. You might try being grateful for a change. I do not enjoy the feeling of your thoughts and emotions intruding on my own, but my only alternative is to kill you."

"If there is a battle, it will not be Daine who falls." Pierce was cleaning the chain of his flail. His voice was as calm as Lakashtai; it was hard to believe that they were discussing murder.

"In my current condition, you are more than a match for me, Pierce. The pain from the shattered crystal still burns within me, weakening my bond to Kashtai, but I speak without malice. Without my help, your friend will die, and all your strength and skill cannot save him. His death would be a thing of agony and madness, serving the cause of a greater darkness. It would be a mercy if I killed him."

"You're just full of compassion, aren't you?" Daine said.

Lakashtai glanced at him. Her eyes weren't glowing, but even at this distance the vivid green was remarkable. "If I did not care about your fate, I would not be here now, and the only part of you that matters would have died a year ago."

Though her voice was calm and level, Daine thought that he could hear traces of pain behind it, and he felt a touch of shame. Lakashtai's imperious manner made it easy to forget that she might have feelings beneath her serene mask, and even her beauty was as disturbing as it was alluring, but she was right—and she deserved better from him.

"I didn't mean to stab at you. It's just that I'm used to fighting my own battles, and somehow, this talk of killing me just doesn't fill me with goodwill."

"I understand, but it is not the way of my people to shy away from a difficult truth."

"Then why do you do this?" Pierce said. "If killing Daine would have been a merciful act, why did you agree to help? How was it that you were even in a position to assist him in the previous incident?" His expression was fixed in metal, and his voice was steady, but the signs of suspicion were there—his grip on the haft of his flail, the tension in his knees.

"Coincidence, if you believe in such things." Lakashtai turned to Daine. "I am sensitive to the winds of fate, and when I first saw you in the King of Fire, I knew that our destinies would come together, though I did not know how. When you sought me out, plagued by the mind wraith, I did what I would do for anyone; that technique is an abomination, one used far too often by il-Lashtavar. Once again, I felt the premonition—the sense that there was a bond between us, so I left the crystal beacon in the hope that I would feel you when there was a need. I did."

"Arriving just in time to kill me," Daine said.

"If that is how you wish—"

"No. No, I'm sorry," Daine said, with a dismissive wave. "You're right. I might already be dead if it weren't for you. Let's just forget about it."

Pierce turned his attention back to his flail, but Daine could see that the warforged was still watching Lakashtai as he oiled the chain and spiked head.

❋ ❋ ❋ ❋ ❋ ❋ ❋

Gerrion eventually returned to the helm, and they turned toward the land, following the coastline and eventually heading up a wide river toward the interior. The oars came out, and all energy was devoted to driving the boat up the channel. At first, Daine thought the reputation of the region was overrated. The shores were covered with thick vegetation, but it seemed no worse than the rainforests of Breland; there were no beasts bursting out of the underbrush, no ancient ruins with walls of gold.

Then they reached the ice.

It began as a chill in the air. Tendrils of mist and steam drifted across the water. A light dusting of frost could be seen on the trees, and this quickly gave way to deep snow. Looking down the river, Daine saw a wall of fog and falling snow, shrouding water and shore alike in white shadows.

"I don't understand," Daine called to Gerrion, his breath steaming in the frigid air. "How can the weather be so severe?

An hour ago we were in a jungle—would this weather kill the plants?"

"Xen'drik doesn't play by your rules, my friend," Gerrion said. "We're lucky the river hasn't turned to lava."

"Are you serious?"

"Certainly. It's rare, but I've heard of stranger things happening. For the most part, it's stable, but when you pass into one of the soft zones—well, you never know what you might find."

"Xen'drik's ancient kings possessed terrible powers," Lakashtai said. "They fought a war with dream and nightmare; that conflict left its scars on reality. Tomorrow, this region could be green and tropical again, or perhaps the soil will turn to stone and the trees to glass."

"And the people?" Daine said.

"Best not to find out."

Snow began to cover the deck, and Daine found he was striking chunks of ice with his oars.

"I don't much care for the looks of this," Gerrion remarked. "Ten crowns says the river's frozen solid up ahead, and I don't feel like being caught in that."

"I could try to create some sort of heat shield," Lei said, laying off her oars for a moment. "I couldn't cover the entire boat, but perhaps I could fix a small ball of fire just in front of the ship. I don't know how long I could keep it up, but it would make an interesting experiment."

"No . . . There's no telling how far this goes or how long it will last." He turned to Lakashtai. "My lady, if you don't mind a slight risk, there is another way for us to reach your destination."

"Speak."

"I know the region you described from your map. There is—a magical path, more or less, that could get us closer to this monolith. There's a small cove nearby, where I could set anchor. While I do hate to leave the *Cat*, it's a harbor I've used before, and it's as safe a landing as one can find in this place. It won't be pleasant, given the weather—but this path should allow us to leap inwards. Even if the river isn't frozen, this would save us a few days travel."

Lakashtai glanced at Daine. "Well, captain? Any tactical advice?"

The deck was covered with snow, and Daine's face was numb. An icy wind was beginning to rise. "This doesn't look good, and I don't much want to drag this boat across a frozen field. I say listen to the guide."

Gerrion gave a quick bow. "Always the best advice. Lay on your oars, then—hopefully we can reach the cove before the river is completely frozen."

❋ ❋ ❋ ❋ ❋ ❋ ❋

The temperature fell with the approach of night, and twice they came to a halt, until Lei carved a path with magical flame. Frost formed on Pierce's outer shell, and the creatures of flesh and blood drew their cloaks tight against the cold, but even as the sun slipped away, Gerrion pulled the vessel off of the river. Strangely, the waters of the inlet were less choked with ice; it was as if some hidden force was warming the water, and Lei's mystical flames were not needed. The shore was hidden behind shadow and snow, but Gerrion proved his worth as a guide, steering through the darkness. At last the ship struck soil, and Gerrion and Pierce heaved the anchor off the side.

"If you have any warmer clothing, now's the time to find it," Gerrion said. "The path's only a few hours walk from here, and I'd sooner press on than camp in this mess. Olladra willing, we'll be back in the warmth by midnight."

"We are not alone." Pierce's quiet voice drifted from the cold. Daine could barely see Pierce through the snow, but the warforged had his bow in hand, an arrow to the string. There was a blur of motion in the night, a splash as Pierce leapt down from the deck. "There is another boat at rest here, struck aground harder than ours."

Daine squinted into the darkness. He could barely see the outline of the vessel. He sighed: if anyone was out there, they'd surely have noticed the arrival of the new boat. "Lei, light—disposable."

Pale light pushed back the night, emanating from a copper coin in Lei's palm. She pressed the glowing disk into Daine's hand, and he flung the coin off the deck, creating a pool of light in the darkness. Daine searched for any signs of movement, any reaction in the night, but he saw nothing.

Pierce was right: another boat was at rest some 20 feet away. Slightly larger than the *Grey Cat*, it was a two-masted vessel with a squat, rounded hull covered with black tar. *At least it's not Riedrans*, Daine thought—at least the ship was simpler and far uglier than the elegant vessel Lakashtai had identified as Riedran when they'd first arrived in Stormreach.

There were no signs of movement beyond the lapping water and no lights on the ship.

Drawing his sword, Daine leapt off the prow of the *Gray Cat*. Icy water splashed around his boots, and Daine ground his teeth against the cold as he made his way to the shore.

Pierce materialized next to him, a mithral ghost in the snowy night. He raised a hand, gesturing toward the boat. *Follow, silently,* his gestures said.

Daine shadowed Pierce, moving as quietly as he could. The warforged kept his bow ready, but a moment later he paused, nodding his head toward the icy ground.

A human body lay on the ground. It was half-buried in snow, and fresh blood was spread across the white blanket.

CHAPTER 31

XEN'DRIK
THE
FRIGID SHORE
*Lharvion 21, 997 YK*

**D**aine swore silently. He'd seen worse in the war, but those were times he'd done his best to forget. At first it seemed that the corpse had been cleaved in two, but the truth was far more disturbing. Only half of the body was intact. As for the rest—what Daine had taken for bloodstains were actually the pulped remnants of flesh and bone. It seemed that the man's body had been caught beneath a wheel of razor-sharp spikes, and from the pattern of the spray the wheel was spinning at a tremendous speed. Daine knelt next to the corpse. The snow hid any distinguishing features that were left to him and obscured his clothing. Daine was reaching out to brush away the concealing snow when Pierce gave a sharp gesture.

*Enemy. Holding position—possible ambush.* He pointed toward the beached boat.

Lei had come up from the shore, and she was stopped short by the sight of the devastated body. "Claws of the Keeper," she whispered. "What could do something like this?"

"Whatever it is, it's long gone," Daine said. "This boat's probably been here for days. Weeks, even." As he spoke, he signaled with his fingers, drawing Lei's attention to their hidden foe. *Moving in. Give ranged support—nonlethal if possible.*

"Good," Lei said. "We've got enough to worry about with the cold, but I would like to take a moment to study . . . this, if you don't mind. I'd like to know what's out there."

She knelt beside the corpse and drew a crystal and a short

wooden wand from her pouch. Doing her best to ignore the grisly spectacle and focus on her work, she ran the carved stick around the edge of the crystal and concentrated on infusing the shard with the energies she needed.

Daine could hear Lakashtai and Gerrion emerging from the river, but there was no time to explain, and in any case neither of them was familiar with Cyran military signals. Best to move quickly and hope they were smart enough to recognize the situation on their own. Under optimal circumstances Daine could have crossed the distance in the blink of an eye, but the deep snow slowed his movement. Moving calmly and carefully, he made his way to the hull of the opposing vessel. He took a deep breath, the chill air sharp in his lungs, and dove around the bow.

Nothing. Just shadows and blowing snow.

Pierce himself had disappeared. Daine hoped that he had drawn any enemy's attention away from the warforged, allowing him to do what he did best. Daine put his back to the boat, studying the ground for any signs of tracks or recent motion, then he saw it—a small figure almost hidden in the falling snow and the shadows of night, a gnome or perhaps a human child. Daine couldn't see a weapon in the silhouette, though in this age of magic the enemy without a weapon could be the most dangerous foe of all. This might be the child of the dead sailor, but Daine couldn't take any chances.

"*You!* Step forward, hands where they can be seen." Daine had his blade leveled at the shadow in the snow, and he was tensed to leap into the darkness. "Come forward slowly. If you engage in any sort of hostile action, you'll have three arrows in your chest before you have time to blink."

"I never blink." The sound was like hissing steam in a kettle of tal—a warforged voice. The stranger slowly moved into the pool of light that emanated from the glowing coin.

Behind Daine, Lei drew in a sharp breath. It was all Daine could do to restrain himself from lashing out, striking the construct before it could come closer.

Beneath the layer of shimmering frost, the plates of the 'forged were blackened metal, engraved with strange patterns and words in a language Daine didn't know. While its hands were empty, dozens of two-inch blades were folded back against its arms and torso, and Daine knew from experience that these could rise up and lock into place to serve as deadly weapons. Its arms were long and spindly, out of proportion with its childlike torso, and its head was the narrow wedge of a rat or weasel, complete with a mouth full of steel teeth. It was not the strange appearance of the construct that caused Daine's fingers to whiten against the hilt of his sword. He'd seen a warforged like this before. He'd destroyed one, maybe more than one.

At Keldan Ridge.

"Where did you come from?" Daine snarled. Every instinct urged him to strike before the creature could act. Memories rose in his mind, fresh from recent nightmares—this rat-like construct leaping the barricade, only to be shot down by Lei. It couldn't be the same one. They'd left it in pieces, but he'd never seen any warforged like this anywhere else—and it sure didn't look like the work of House Cannith. "What are you doing here?"

The warforged had a slightly hunched posture, and its neck was just a little too long and too flexible. It turned its head to the right, scanning the landscape.

Daine lashed out with his sword. The scout had kept its distance, but Daine wasn't trying for a solid blow; he just tapped the point of his blade against the edge of the creature's head. It jerked back, its blades snapping into attack position.

"Answer my questions. *Now*."

"You are no threat."

"That's why I have friends. Pierce? Two."

Nothing happened.

Then there was a blur of motion, as two long arrows came out of the snow to strike the strange warforged, catching it in the lightly armored cavity just below its right arm. The warforged hissed so loudly that Daine thought Pierce had struck some sort of reservoir of steam trapped within its body.

It was a perfect shot—but Pierce had hesitated. *Why?* "I'm waiting for an answer, as is my threatening friend."

"You cannot destroy me." Even with the arrows half-buried in its torso, the warforged spoke with eerie confidence. Daine was used to dealing with warforged. Pierce was his friend—and he was far from the only warforged Daine had served with during the war, but most warforged were designed to resemble humans. This thing—it violated those principles. Its posture, its proportions, its teeth—it was all wrong, and Daine found it unsettling on a level he couldn't really explain.

"Maybe not, but I'm really looking forward to trying," he said. "I'll ask you one more time. Why are you here? What did you do to him?" Daine gestured at the frozen corpse with the point of his sword.

"I serve my purpose, breather." It brought its arm down sharply, snapping off the shafts of the arrows embedded it its right armpit. "Nothing you do matters."

"I . . . I don't like the thought of it, but if we subdue it, I might be able to torture it," Lei whispered, just behind him. Daine kept his eyes on the stranger, but from Lei's tone, he could tell that she was disturbed by its presence. "Warforged don't feel pain in exactly the same way that we do, but if I slowly damage its lifeweb—it certainly won't enjoy it."

"That won't be necessary." Lakashtai had arrived as soundlessly as always. "It may be a creature of metal, but it is still driven by thought and emotion. Let me see what I can draw from this shell."

Daine kept his sword as Lakashtai stepped forward, the point in line with one of the creature's crystalline eyes. She moved with catlike grace through the deep snow, and the thick flakes slid off of her cloak; swathed in pure black, she seemed to be a sliver carved from the night itself.

The warforged shifted its weight slightly. The pale light glittered on its bladed arms. "Pierce, Lei—if it moves, kill it," Daine said.

"Be still, little one," Lakashtai said softly, her eyes gleaming in the depths of her hood. "Stone and steel were not meant to move."

The blades snapped down against the scout's arms, and it did not move as she stepped closer.

"Your thoughts—they extend far beyond this one form," Lakashtai murmured. "It seems we have something in common, you and I. Let us follow that path and see where it leads."

The blades of the warforged fluttered in place, rising slightly only to snap back down again.

*Snap.*

*Snap.*

*Snap.*

Lakashtai's eyes were closed. She seemed peaceful, at rest, but after spending a week in her company, Daine could see the strain—the faint furrow of her brow, the occasional twitching of her lips. *She doesn't want us to know her limits,* Daine realized. It might be pride; it might be a cultural tradition, but he knew so little about what she could do or how the psychic attack had affected her. Was there danger here? What was this battle he couldn't even see?

*Snap.*

A chill gust of wind blew snow in his face, and Daine blinked.

*Snap.*

Wood sang through the air as Pierce and Gerrion loosed arrow and bolt. Any one of these shafts would have dropped a normal man but not the warforged. Its arms spread wide as it charged toward the kalashtar, and the impact of Pierce's bolts barely broke its stride.

Lakashtai must have sensed its hostile intent in her last moments in its mind, and she tried to throw herself to the side, but she wasn't fast enough. Too late, Daine realized the purpose of the creature's disproportionately long limbs. It wrapped its arms around Lakashtai and twisted to face them, using the kalashtar as a shield

"I do not die after all," the warforged hissed, "and you see no more. Drop weapons. I leave."

The blades on the creature's arms were digging into Lakashtai's flesh, and blood dripped on the snow. Her mouth was twisted in pain, but she made no sound.

"Do it." It was Lei. She stepped forward from behind Daine, her hands held out in front of her. "All of you. Throw away your weapons."

*Keldan Ridge.* Daine nodded and tossed his blades aside.

"You're hurting her," Lei said, slowly walking toward the warforged. "Let me take her and ease her pain."

Crystal eyes watched her, peering out from around Lakashtai's waist. "No. We leave. Perhaps she survives, returns. Perhaps not."

"You can't take her with you."

"You are mistaken."

"No," Lei said.

She reached out, and her fingers barely brushed the back of a mithral forearm. There was no burst of flame, no flash of light. The warforged simply fell apart. Connective cords snapped. Razor-sharp blades scattered across the snow like fallen leaves, leaving spatters of blood in their wake. In an instant, all that was left were chunks of wood and stone scattered around a bloody kalashtar. Lei didn't even look at Lakashtai; she was watching the light fade from the crystal eyes of the warforged.

"I'm afraid I'm not," she whispered.

Lakashtai stood stiffly, refusing to surrender to pain. The blades of the warforged had torn into her skin where it had grabbed her, and a few of these razors remained in the wounds. Lakashtai carefully drew each blade out, letting them fall to the snow. She closed her eyes, breathing calmly and deeply, and the blood stopped flowing from the gashes. A moment later the clotted blood flaked and fell away, leaving smooth, unblemished skin. The only hints that she'd ever been hurt were the slashes in her cloak and the tunic beneath. Despite her stoicism, she shivered slightly as the wind lashed her pale skin.

Daine found the sight slightly disturbing for reasons he couldn't explain. He was used to supernatural healing; the touch of Jode's dragonmark had saved his life on many occasions, and Lei had crafted a number of healing charms over the years, but Lakashtai—what limits did she have? What else could she do? He dug his swords out of the snow and strode over to her.

"Pierce is looking for tracks, Lei's studying the warforged, and Gerrion is searching the boat," he said. "Did you learn anything from our little friend?"

"We must leave quickly," she said. "Lei did not kill it—him. This body is just a fragment of what we face. There are others, and they know we are here."

*Wonderful. Now* warforged *are after us?* "Do you know what they want? Are they looking for me?"

"No. He did not know who you were, but there was recognition." She glanced off into the snow, looking for the shape moving through the shadows. "Pierce. Only Pierce was of interest."

*He knew Pierce? Is that even possible?* He remembered that moment of hesitation when he ordered the attack and felt a chill that had nothing to do with the cold.

Gerrion jumped down from the deck of the ship. "Three dead on board. Stormreachers, all of them—guides and servants." He smiled. "Less competition for me, at least."

"Glad something good could come of it." Daine said. "Lei! We need to get moving!"

She nodded and stood up, a scrap of metal in her hand. Before she turned around, Pierce appeared next to Daine, seeming to materialize out of the snow.

"It is difficult to follow any tracks in these conditions," Pierce said. "The wind is quickly covering any traces of movement, but a group of people—five, possibly six—headed southwest sometime within the last few hours." He gestured off into the blowing snow.

Daine found his hand was on his sword, and he forced it away. *This is my friend. He's saved my life a dozen times.* As he looked at the metal mask that was his companion's face, Daine felt traces of doubt. *He's not human. He's not even flesh and blood. What is going through his mind? Is this even Pierce, or could he have been replaced by some other warforged?* It was a ridiculous thought, and Daine felt vaguely ashamed for even allowing it to cross his mind; he could just as easily worry that Lei had been replaced by a changeling, but still. *Only Pierce was of interest.*

Pierce was still waiting for a response. "Good work," Daine finally said. "Gerrion! If you know where we're going, lead the way. If not . . ." He glanced down at the ruined corpse spread across the snow. "Well, it doesn't seem to be a good day for guides."

"Not to worry, captain," Gerrion said with a chuckle. "I'll see what I can do about getting you out of the snow. This way."

The others followed Gerrion into the wind. They were heading south, and Daine was relieved to see that the path veered away from the trail Pierce had uncovered.

⊛ ⊛ ⊛ ⊛ ⊛ ⊛ ⊛

They were walking through a frozen jungle.

Vast trees towered above them, draped in thick vines and moss. Huge, tropical flowers were crusted with frost, strange blooms weighed down with snow. The cold was worse than anything Daine had ever encountered in Cyre, and the icy wind felt like shards of glass digging into his skin. His fingers were stiff and numb, and he prayed that he wouldn't have to try to wield a blade before they found warmth.

"What did you find?" he called out to Lei.

He would have preferred to keep the conversation quiet, but there was no hope of whispering over the howling wind. Besides, who was he trying to hide from? Gerrion might have saved their lives in Stormreach in the first fight with the Riedrans, and Pierce—even if he did listen to any of these lurking fears, Pierce's hearing was keen enough to pick up a whisper on a battlefield.

"I've only seen a warforged like that once before," she called.

". . .at Keldan Ridge." He completed the sentence for her.

"Yes. It had none of the standard markers indicating the forge of origin, purpose, nationality, or anything like that. I've seen a lot of 'forged who've had those marks removed since the war, but that usually leaves traces. This one—whoever made it wanted to keep its origin secret."

"Why would anyone do that?" he shouted, as the wind picked up.

"I don't know! The whole design—it doesn't feel right. It's as if someone was playing a game, designing a warforged like you might craft a doll for a child, just to see how it might look with teeth and longer arms, but creating new designs is a difficult and expensive process. Once Cannith came up with a reliable design, that's what they used. A few variant models were produced—the adamantine soldier, the smaller scout—but you don't make a new warforged just to see what happens."

"I saw you take something from the body—what was it?"

Lei rummaged in the side pocket of her pack and produced the scrap of metal. It was curved, and flat on one side. After a moment, Daine realized that it was part of the scout's head—a wedge of steel engraved with an abstract glyph, perhaps a letter in an alien alphabet. Every warforged had a similar mark on its forehead; Daine had always assumed it was a unit insignia or maker's mark.

"It's called—"

"It is a ghulra." Pierce said, interrupting Lei. The warforged had been taking up the rear, and he had silently drifted up behind Daine. "The mark of life."

Lei glanced over at him. "That's right. Each mark is unique. No one knows why. It's something inherent to the design, something shaped when the body and spirit are fused."

"What do you mean, 'no one knows why'?" Daine said. "Didn't your people—House Cannith—design the warforged in the first place?"

"Well, yes . . ." Lei said, letting the sentence trail off.

"The true origin of the warforged is a mystery," Pierce's deep voice was clear even through the wind. "Many say that House Cannith scavenged the most important elements of their work . . . from Xen'drik, actually, that even Merrix and Aaren d'Cannith did not truly understand the source of the warforged spirit or how they had bound life to metal and stone."

"You've picked up more history than I realized," Lei said.

"I have been reading. The history of the warforged was a logical place to begin."

Daine was still thinking about what Pierce had said. "If Cannith scavenged the knowledge from the past . . ."

"It could mean that there were once warforged in Xen'drik, or at least, something quite similar to the warforged. There may be much about my people that House Cannith does not understand."

*My people.* "Pierce, did you know that warforged, the one we killed on the beach?"

"I had never seen it before, Daine."

There was no hesitation, and of course, Pierce had no expression to read. In a warm, well-lit room Daine might have been able to draw some conclusion from Pierce's stance; even the warforged had body language, though it took time to understand it. If there was anything suspicious about Pierce's behavior, Daine couldn't see it.

"Lakashtai said that it recognized you."

"That seems unlikely. It may have mistaken me for another warforged of my line."

*Perhaps*, Daine thought. He'd never seen another warforged soldier of precisely the same model as Pierce. He'd always assumed this was simply a factor of age; Pierce had been on the battlefield before Daine had learned to talk, but a few other thoughts nagged at the back of his mind. He remembered an encounter with Director Halea d'Cannith at the forgehold of Whitehearth; she had been prepared to offer five elite 'forged units in exchange for Pierce. *What did they want with one old 'forged?*

Even as he tried to shape a question, they stepped out of the snow and into sunlight.

● ● ● ◉ ● ● ●

It was like stepping through a curtain. One moment Daine was surrounded by swirling snow and bitter cold. An instant later he was in a forest, lush and green and with the steamy humidity of any Brelish jungle. His skin tingled, protesting the sudden change in temperature. Looking back, he could see a white wall of the frenzied storm, but not only could he no longer feel it, he couldn't even hear it. The roaring wind had been replaced by the buzz of a thousand insects and the calls of strange birds.

Daine scanned the trees for signs of motion. He glanced at Pierce, and the warforged gave a slight shake of his head. Daine relaxed slightly—if Pierce couldn't spot a threat, they were either safe or there was no hope for them. Gerrion was pressing through the brush, cutting a path with a long knife. He held a glowing crystal sphere in his left hand, charged with cold fire.

"What's next?" Daine called. "A desert?"

"If you're willing to go a few days out of your way," Gerrion said, "but this region is relatively stable. We just need to find—ah, here we are."

He slashed through a final patch of dense vines, and they stepped out into a long, natural corridor running east to west. The path was almost twenty feet across; the ground was covered in brambles and vines, but clear of trees.

Daine stepped out of the forest and felt stone underfoot. "A path?"

"A road. Older than your species, most likely. Though if you want a history lesson, I'm sure one of your friends can do a better job than I."

Daine glanced back at the others. Lei was talking to Pierce, and she was smiling for the first time since their fight aboard the *Gray Cat*. The unexpected conflict had momentarily pushed the tension aside—but for the moment it was probably best to let it lie. Lakashtai was walking just behind Daine, her hood pulled low to hide her eyes. Judging from past experience, Daine was sure she'd heard them—if she wanted to talk, she would.

"I always preferred swords to books," he said to Gerrion. "You want to tell me where we're going, exactly?"

"No, not really." Gerrion spun his dagger in the air, as they walked along the ancient road, deftly catching it and setting it in motion again.

"You're going to, anyway."

"I wouldn't want to spoil the surprise."

"I hate surprises," Daine said.

"Give it a chance," Gerrion replied cheerfully. His dagger was a web of steel flowing from one hand to the next, remaining in constant motion.

"Then let's talk about something else."

"Oh, let's."

"You want to tell me what a Sulatar is?"

Gerrion froze, and in that moment of shock, he failed to catch the spinning dagger. Daine caught a glimpse of steel flashing toward his eyes, then the blade stopped, suspended in midair. Lakashtai reached up from behind them, plucking the dagger from the air.

"An Elvish word," she said, handing the weapon back to Gerrion. "It means 'bound flame.' In the older dialect, you could interpret it as 'one who binds fire,' I suppose. Why is this significant?"

Daine glanced at Gerrion, but the half-elf had returned the dagger to its sheath and picked up his pace, pulling ahead of them. "The spirit on the water called our friend Gerrion a 'child of the Sulatar.' Seems to be a touchy subject."

"Child of the bound flame," Lakashtai mused. "Child of the firebinders. It is a shame I did not see this spirit myself."

"How did you manage to meditate through the boat being tipped over, anyhow?"

"It's . . . not that simple. My soul was submerged within, leaving the body temporarily unattended."

"It also mentioned a 'season of flame.' Does that mean anything to you?"

Lakashtai ran a finger across her perfect lips. "Interesting. I don't see why it would be relevant, but it is—"

"We're here!" Gerrion called. "I told you it wouldn't be far from our path, and trust me, it will be worth the time."

There was a clearing up ahead almost two hundred feet across. A long, flat mound stretched across the space, rising up six or seven feet from the road.

"Who built this?" whispered Lei, coming up behind him.

"Built what?" Daine said.

"Look around you."

He did. A long mound, surrounded by trees. Trees with no branches. Trees with strange inscriptions winding around their trunks.

"Look up."

There was a roof over the clearing. Nearly forty feet from the jungle floor, it was now falling to pieces—but its original purpose was perfectly clear. The trees weren't trees at all; they were pillars carved from the trunks of massive densewood trees, set around the mound. The mound itself—dirt and weeds had risen up around it, but it was a platform of light stone.

"Daine, Lakashtai!" Gerrion called down to them. "Come up here—I'll show you why we made the trip. As for you, Lei, you should study the notched pillar in the corner. For a scholar like yourself—well, I think you'll be fascinated."

Daine shrugged and climbed up the steep edge of the platform, then reached down and helped Lakashtai make her way to the top. "What's so interesting . . ." He stopped as he saw what he was standing on.

It was a map.

Two hundred feet long, one hundred feet wide, it seemed

to have been carved from a single vast slab of stone—though Daine couldn't imagine how such a thing could be quarried or transported. There were craters across its surface where chunks of densewood had fallen from the canopy, but much of it was still intact. The serpentine shapes of rivers wound down from the edges toward the center, and mountain ridges rose up a few inches from the base. He could see the spires of towers surrounding tiny cities.

It was as if he were a god, straddling the entire continent.

"Why are we here again?" he called, making his way over to Gerrion. The half-elf was examining a small castle that seemed to have been painted in black enamel. "It's something to see, I'll give you that, but I thought we already knew where we were going. It's too big to be useful anyway—the only way I could make any sense of it would be from thirty feet in the air."

"I suspect that wasn't a problem for its creators," Gerrion replied. "Besides, just think: years from now, you'll be telling your grandchildren about the time you saw the biggest map in Xen'drik."

"I trust you have a better reason than that," Daine replied.

Lakashtai had been studied their surroundings intently, illuminating the map with the eerie light radiating from her eyes. "There," she said, pointing to a massive densewood boulder a few feet away. "Our destination is in that crater."

Gerrion smiled. "I hope that's not a bad omen, but, even if we can't get there directly, we'll still be able to save a few days' travel."

"What are you talking about?" Daine snapped. "You drag us through the snow to see a map just to show us a place we already know how to get to? How does this save us time?"

"Patience, captain," Gerrion replied. "Allow me to demonstrate." He dropped to one knee and reached for the tiny castle.

Before Gerrion's fingers reached the carved tower, there was a burst of motion on the treeline. There was no sound, no burst of fire or smoke, but a patch of vines vaporized as if caught in an intense explosion. Five people strode into the clearing. Four were identical: warforged scouts, duplicates of the hunched creature they met on the frozen beach. These scouts were spread in a semicircle around a huge cloaked figure at least nine feet tall and with the build of an ogre.

"*Be still.*" The voice was like a rush of sand or metal particles thrown against the wind. It seemed to flow all around them, carrying across the clearing with no need for volume. "*Throw down your weapons, and you may yet live.*"

Daine's blades were in his hands in an instant, and he was charging, ready to leap from the platform and join up with Pierce and Lei on the ground. Then Gerrion placed his hand on the dark tower, and everything changed.

# CHAPTER 33

The forest was on fire.

The temperature had jumped, and the emerald green that cloaked the trees was a blaze of orange. This sheet of fire had swept forward, and Pierce, Lei, and the strangers vanished beneath the fiery curtain. Daine cried out in wordless anguish, barely halting his progress before he tumbled into the flame.

No. Not flames—tall grass, weeds painted in red and orange. As his eyes adjusted to the light, he realized that their surroundings had completely changed. The trees were draped in the colors of autumn, and the trees and shrubs themselves were clearly different. The clearing was far smaller than the last one had been.

Daine could see Gerrion out of the corner of his eye, and he turned toward the half-elf, his sword still in his hand. Lakashtai was even swifter. She lashed out with her foot. The kick caught Gerrion in the side of the head and slammed him to the broken earth. Lakashtai brought her knee down in the small of Gerrion's back, pressing him into the ground. Her right fist was poised above his head, wrapped in a halo of baleful green energy.

"Explain swiftly or I will tear the answers from your mind," she said, her voice cold and hard.

"Helped you . . ." Gerrion gasped.

"*Lei and Pierce!*" Daine said. "What did you do to them?"

Lakashtai traced one finger across the back of Gerrion's neck, and he convulsed in pain.

"You're closer . . . closer to your goal," Gerrion said. "The map. Magical . . . teleportation. We escaped your enemy, moved closer."

Lakashtai hissed and shoved Gerrion's head into the ground with a swift blow of her hand. "How *dare* you? Abandoning the others to save your own miserable skin."

As angry as Daine was, he was still surprised by Lakashtai's viciousness. The kalashtar was usually so calm, and she'd hardly seemed to care about Pierce or Lei. Now Gerrion was writhing on the ground as the light flared around her fingers.

"Don't kill him! We still don't know what he's done."

"Nor do we need to, because he's about to undo it. Aren't you, *guide?*" Lakashtai released Gerrion and stood up, her face twisted in anger. The halo around her hands slowly faded.

"I can't," Gerrion moaned. "Look . . . down. Ground."

The stone beneath their feet was just a cracked shard of an ancient plaza. Once it might have been a mirror of the map they had seen before, but if so war and weather had destroyed it long ago.

"There's no going back," Gerrion said. He'd rolled onto his back and was slowly catching his breath, and his gray skin glistened with cold sweat. "I thought the others were on the map. I swear. It's too late. Now it would take us more than a day to get back to the boat, and even if the others survive, there's no telling where they'll have gone by then. Just find the Monolith. Do what you came here to do."

"Unacceptable!" Daine said. "I don't care what happens to me. We are NOT leaving them behind." He pondered. "The boat. They'd return to the boat. It's the only place we all know. They'll return there and wait for us."

"If they survived."

"Pray that they did." Lakashtai said. She had regained her composure, but Daine could still *feel* her anger, like a burning itch at the back of his mind. "Now get on your feet and show us the way back, and the next time you feel like doing something clever—don't."

Gerrion slowly rose to his feet. "I didn't mean to abandon

them. Truly. I thought they were on the map." Whether it was pain or sorrow, his voice was still shaking, and he kept his gaze trained on the ground. Daine was still filled with anger, but the half-elf seemed so dejected, so pathetic, that it was difficult to hate him.

But he could certainly try.

"Just show us the path. Now," Daine said.

"We can't travel through the night."

"Can't we?" Daine said. He glanced at Lakashtai, and a flicker of emerald fire played across her fingertips. "Somehow, I just don't feel like sleeping."

"You don't understand. This is the forest of fire. There are things that come in the night—forces even you can't fight. We need to take shelter."

"Even if that's true, I don't see many safe havens out here. Don't tell me there's a comfortable inn nearby? The Fool's Rest?"

Gerrion closed his eyes and took a deep breath. Finally he opened his eyes and stared at Daine, trying to keep his voice level. "There is a settlement nearby. Hunter-gatherers. I've dealt with them before and I'm sure I can convince them to give us shelter." His voice finally broke. "I didn't mean for this to happen, I swear! I just wanted to help. If you want to return to the boat, we'll go back, but you'll never make it without me—and I promise you, travel into the night and you won't live to see the morning."

Daine struggled with his emotions and fears. In his mind, he saw Jode in the sewers of Sharn, and he couldn't bear the thought of leaving Lei to the same fate, but the voice in the clearing had offered a chance to surrender. Even if they were outmatched, it was possible Lei and Pierce were unharmed—and they knew how to take care of themselves. He had to believe they were still alive, and for all his bravado, he was tired, and a march through the night would leave him with no energy to battle whatever they might find on the other side. He glanced at Lakashtai.

"What do you think?"

She shook her head ever so slightly. The anger had evaporated, and once again she was calm and collected. "This is

Xen'drik. No doubt there are dangers in these jungles we know nothing about. It seems we must trust him. This may have been a mistake after all." She glanced at Gerrion, and her eyes flashed. "Be warned, another such mistake could be fatal."

"Of course," Gerrion said. He wiped his brow and ran a hand through his hair, smoothing out his pale locks. His manner was still subdued, but he had recovered a hint of his former jaunty demeanor. "Follow me then. We'll reach the city within an hour, and be on the path again by dawn."

The gray man waded into the field of orange grass, retrieving his light-sphere. The vegetation was densely packed, and progress was slow. "There should be a path once we reach the treeline," Gerrion said. "These weeds—they're seasonal. Rapid growth."

Daine's thoughts were still on Lei and Pierce and the strange metal giant they might be fighting even now. *They were warforged. Lei can fight warforged.* Even through the fog of concern, he could still see what an excellent opportunity this was for an ambush. Tall grass, poor lighting—Daine could barely see the trees themselves, let alone anything that might be hidden around the treeline. Swordsmen crouching in the weeds, a few archers scattered among the trees. Wait until the enemy reached the center of the meadow—*there*—then strike.

He was off by five feet.

He dropped down the instant he heard the *whiirr*. Something flashed over his head, a spinning object thrown with considerable force—an axe? Knife? He ducked down into the grass. "I'm going to *kill* you, Gerrion!"

*Daine.* Lakashtai's thoughts filled his mind. *I have been struck with a wooden weapon with sharpened points. The wound . . . it is not deep . . . but . . . I fear poison. Were you . . . injured?*

*No,* he thought. He kept still, his blades before him, listening for any sound of motion. Their enemies would be spread across the field. In the darkness, perhaps they thought that he'd been hit and had fallen to the ground. If they were using poison, they would wait for the venom to take full effect before closing in. *Did you see Gerrion? Was he part of this?*

No response. He heard the sound of shifting grass, but he thought it was a body falling to the ground, and the light suddenly faded.

*Lakashtai?*

Nothing.

*So. Attacked by unknown enemies. Either Gerrion has betrayed us, or he's just led us into a trap. Perhaps Pierce and Lei were the lucky ones.*

He waited, listening.

*Do they think we're all dead? Could they have left?*

No. It didn't make sense. Surely anyone who would go to this effort would want to confirm the kill—or to strip the bodies. If Gerrion was involved, he knew Lakashtai had gold.

Then he heard it. The faintest whisper of wind in the grass—but there was no wind. Someone was moving toward him. Possibilities flashed through his mind. Riedran soldiers? More warforged? Psychotic kobolds? The stranger wasn't carrying any sort of light, and the footsteps were almost silent. Daine carefully set his sword on the ground, shifting his dagger to his right hand. This needed to be close and quick. Once he would have drawn comfort from the Silver Flame. Now he cursed any god that might be listening.

The wind blew through the grass again. A dark figure emerged, a slender silhouette set against the night sky. There was the faint gleam of moonlight on long silver hair, on skin dappled in patterns of black and white. That was all he saw before he struck.

He swept her legs out from under her, and she tumbled to the ground. Daine felt a thrill of relief as he leaned down on her neck and placed the point of his dagger against her throat.

"Drop your weapons and don't make a sound," he whispered.

He was talking to empty air. It was like trying to hold water; one instant his arm was against her neck, the next he was staring down at the earth and she was standing beside him. Her features were still hidden in shadow, but she held a long knife in each hand.

Daine threw himself backwards, and the twin blades struck earth. He snatched his sword from the ground and rose to his feet, throwing himself into first guard position.

Three other people were spread around the clearing—and as dark as it was, Daine could see that Gerrion and Lakashtai were not among them.

*Oh, this isn't good.*

He knocked the woman's daggers out of line with a sweeping blow from his sword and slammed into her, throwing her back into the grass. Something *whirred* past his head and he ducked down into the weeds. *So much for subtlety.* As his opponent rose to her feet he slammed the pommels of both blades against the side of her head. She staggered for a moment, and he struck again, the metal balls making a sickening crunch against her unarmored flesh. She fell, dropping her blades, but he couldn't stop now; he followed her down and struck again, smashing her head against the ground. Daine felt the faintest twinge of guilt, but he'd seen and done far worse in the past—if she was lucky, she'd live through the night.

He might not be so fortunate.

Sheathing his sword, Daine wrapped an arm around the woman's chest and stood up. For all her speed, she had the build of a scrawny teenager, and in the heat of battle she seemed almost weightless. He backed toward the remains of the shattered plaza, bringing his dagger up to her neck.

The other three strangers had disappeared. Dropped down into the weeds, no doubt.

"I don't want to hurt her," Daine called out. "Show yourselves and we can talk this out. We didn't mean to come here, and all I want to do is to leave with my companions."

Nothing. The treeline was a wall of shadows, and there could easily be a hundred enemies hidden in that darkness.

"I don't know who you are, and I don't care," Daine continued, watching the grass and waiting for movement. "We're going north. Back to our ship. Leaving."

"You lie."

One man stood up, facing Daine across the clearing. He spoke with an odd, lyrical cadence, blending the syllables of the common tongue together as if they were part of the same word. Like Daine's captive, the man was little more than a silhouette in the darkness, although he wore some sort of opalescent breastplate that shimmered in the light of the moons.

"Where are your friends?" Daine said, keeping his eyes on the grass. "Surprises make my hands twitch. I think this lady will be much safer if they show themselves."

"You show your heart," the shadowy figure said, "speaking of peace, but threatening death."

"I do that when people try to kill me and my friends. If the others don't show themselves now, you'll see what that's like."

There was a pause. Daine had the sense that the man was staring at him—but it was too dark for him to see the stranger's face. Putting on his best scowl, he traced a line across his captive's neck with his black dagger.

"If that's what you want . . ."

"Halt!" The man did sing, then, or spoke in a language Daine didn't know—though something about it seemed hauntingly familiar. The other two figures appeared, both closer than Daine had expected; they must have been creeping up in the darkness. One held a pair of daggers; the other carried a long chain, similar to the weapon of a Darguul chainmaster, but lighter. "You will die with her."

"Not a lot of alternatives, and I never planned on dying alone." Daine took a few more steps back, trying to keep the woman between him and his enemies. "I'd be happier if no one died tonight."

"You say again, but you travel with others."

"So do you." There was an object in the stranger's right hand, held at his hip—a weapon, probably, but just out of sight.

"North, you travel. To the glass city."

"If that's what it's called, sure, that's the plan. The jungle's a dangerous place at night. Perhaps you've heard about that."

The two warriors flanking Daine had not moved; they might just as well have been shadows. The speaker slowly raised his hand, revealing a curved, dark object with three prongs. "Perhaps you speak truth. I cast away the weapon."

"Good. Get your friends to drop theirs, and we might be able to have a real conversation."

The slender man didn't drop the weapon—he *threw* it, sending it whirling through the air, but while Daine was surprised, the throw was well to Daine's left—a warning shot, at best.

"What was—"

Before Daine could complete the sentence, the world went white as something heavy smashed into the back of his head.

There was a sharp pain in his neck, replaced almost instantly by a cold, spreading numbness. Daine tried to tighten his grip on the woman, but his hands seemed to have plans of their own; even as he tried to get his arms to move, the silver chain flashed in the moonlight, snatching the dagger out of his grasp. Then he was on the ground, the numbness spreading across his body. There was a wooden object lying in the dirt next to his face—a wheel formed from three curved spikes. *Did it . . . curve back?* He thought.

That was his last thought for some time.

CHAPTER 34

XEN'DRIK
THE STONE
MAP: PIERCE
*Lharvion 21, 997 YK*

Pierce and Lei were on the ground when the strangers appeared.

Following Gerrion's suggestion, they had gone to study one of the massive stone pillars supporting the pavilion while Gerrion, Lakashtai, and Daine climbed onto the plaza. The column was more than ten feet across, and covered with worn inscriptions. Lei was examining the faded words and muttering to herself. Pierce was watching the treeline, bow in hand, and so it was that he saw a wall of weeds and vines silently explode, as if caught in a whirlwind.

Pierce caught the briefest glimpse of the four figures in the shadows of the trees, but he didn't wait for them to emerge. He stepped back into the narrow space between the pillar and the elevated plaza. Instinct said to ready an arrow, but he held back long enough to grab Lei's shoulder and pull her along. She glanced up in surprise, and he gestured, using the military symbols she'd learned in their time together: Enemies. Four. North. Silence. She nodded, and her right hand slipped down to the longer of the two wands that she carried at her belt—a slender piece of oak tipped with a glowing pink crystal. An instant later they heard the hissing, metallic voice, flowing around them like a gust of wind.

*Be still. Throw down your weapons, and you may yet live.*

Now Pierce had an arrow nocked. He slid around the wide pillar, until he caught a glimpse of movement—a warforged scout like the one they'd seen on the beach, its arms studded with blades. In an instant, Pierce considered distance, wind, and the trajectory of his opponent. Even in the dark of night, Pierce was confident that he could strike his foe; he was already considering his second attack, how the enemy might respond in the time it took Pierce to draw and loose a second arrow. He felt a faint twinge of doubt—why were these warforged here? Were they connected to the stranger he'd met at the docks of Stormreach? But he forced it aside. This was war. This was his purpose. All he needed was Daine's order, and the battle would begin.

The order didn't come. Seconds passed as Pierce and Lei stood ready, waiting for some sign or signal. Finally the voice came again.

*Now your companions abandon you. How . . . human.* The voice was like a sandstorm, particles thrown against the wind to form coherent words. *But you remain, brother. Reveal yourself. Your destiny awaits.*

Abandon? Brother?

Were they looking for him?

Lei was staring at him, puzzled and concerned, and Pierce found himself gripped by unfamiliar emotion. Usually, his path was crystal clear. Follow orders. Protect his companions. He knew the principles of war, of stealth, the quickest ways to kill, but *destiny*—it wasn't a word he had ever given much thought to. He had a purpose, and it was a purpose he had served for almost thirty years. What else could there be?

Over the last year, Pierce had spent much of his time reading, learning about the history of the warforged and the nature of magic, but only now did he truly understand the power of curiosity.

The scout was slowly moving forward, and Pierce could hear the others making their way across the clearing. The larger figure was apparently wearing chain mail or something similar; the air was filled with the sound of metal clinking against metal.

"Your bow!" Lei hissed. She held out one hand. "Quickly!"

Pierce knew what she was planning. Lei could weave magic into a weapon to enhance its power against a specific type of creature, causing even a glancing blow to inflict a terrible injury. If all of their enemies were warforged, such an enchantment could turn the tide of battle, but now strange words loomed in his thoughts. Brother. Destiny.

"Pierce!" Lei snapped. She reached out for the bow, and to his surprise, he found himself stepping back, moving out of her reach. Her eyes grew wide.

He said nothing, relying on military signals to frame his request: silence. Hold position. His mind was aflame with doubt, with fear—was he placing Lei in danger?—but he found himself turning around and slowly stepping out from behind the pillar.

The four scouts were spread across the clearing. They were identical, and as Pierce moved into view they turned to face him in perfect unison, blades rising up and locking along their arms.

It was the man in the center of the clearing who drew the eye. He towered over the scouts; he must have been nine and a half feet in height with a solid, powerful build. His intimidating bulk was enhanced by his cloak, which flowed around him—though it was a still night, with no breeze to justify this motion. Pierce's instinct said the man was warforged, and certainly there was no sign of flesh on the stranger's body, but neither could Pierce see any wood, metal plates, or the root-like tendrils that served as the muscles of a warforged. At this distance, he seemed to be covered in chainmail—but Pierce could see nothing beneath the glittering links except darkness.

*At last.* The stranger's voice seemed to radiate out in all directions, a dry whisper raised to the sound of a mighty wind. His face was hidden from view. At first Pierce thought the stranger was wearing a hood, but instead there seemed to be a cloud of smoke or mist centered over his head, or perhaps a dense cloud of fluttering insects. *I let you slip through my fingers once before, little brother. That will not happen again.*

Once before? Pierce had never seen this creature, though there was something strangely . . . familiar about his voice. "Who are you?"

The stranger's entire body seemed to *ripple*, and his armor clinked and chimed. *I am death to that which bleeds. I am the wind that scours flesh from bone. I am Harmattan, and I am your brother.*

"Harmattan? I see no family resemblance," Pierce said, "and the wind is not part of my family tree."

*Are you so certain? Do you know what forces went into your making? Do you know why you were brought into this world?*

"To protect the nation of Cyre."

*No. That is what you were told, by fleshlings who knew nothing of your true purpose or potential. That is their use for you—it is not your destiny.*

*Daine!* He glanced back, but the plaza was completely empty. There was little cover, and it was too large for Daine to have left it without Pierce hearing the sound of boots on stone. "Where are my friends?"

*Your ... companions ...* His voice was dry, but he indicated his disdain with a slow drawling of the word. *...left you, it seems. Teleportation, I suspect. Apparently they didn't care enough to bring you along. What else would you expect, from a former soldier? In his mind, you were built to die for him.*

The dull heat of anger was as unfamiliar as curiosity. "So far I have heard nothing but arrogant mockery. If you know anything about me, speak quickly."

*What I know is far less important than what you may learn in my company.*

"I do not understand."

*How could you? You have spent your life among creatures of flesh. In their eyes, you are nothing but a tool, a sword to be used in battle until you are broken or cast aside.*

"Perhaps it is you who doesn't understand them."

*And you do?* Harmattan's cloak rippled like smoke, setting off another series of chimes. Pierce realized that the cloak itself was made from metal fragments—making it all the more impossible for it to flow so freely. *Your essence is magic, not flesh and bone. Your life is the product of artifice, not blood and lust. You are warforged—but do you even know what this means? You will never find out among humans.*

As strange and foreboding as this Harmattan was, he had an undeniable charisma. His windy voice was almost hypnotic, like listening to the surf at night. And his conviction rang through each sentence; there was no question that he believed these words. Curiosity rose again. Pierce knew that Daine and Lei relied on him, but he rarely seemed to be a part of their conversations. He could feel emotions passing between them, but often the triggers made little sense to him, and there were so many little things—the endless quest for food, for shelter. The hours he spent alone as they slept. What would it be like to be among others who had no needs of these things?

Then he looked at the scouts, with their metal teeth and spiked arms. There might be something to Harmattan's words—but were these the creatures he wished to learn from?

"I will consider your words," he said at last, "but for now, I think I will remain with my friends, so unless you intend to help me find them, you may as well be on your way."

*We have given much to find you, little brother. You are more important than you know. I told you, you will not slip away again.*

"Oh, I think he might." Lei stepped out from behind the pillar. Light burst from her staff, illuminating the clearing and the long wand in Lei's hand. Pierce flexed his fingers around the arrow he held at the ready.

Harmattan *rustled* again. *You*, he said, and there was a note of amused recognition in his voice. *Of course, I should have known you would stay close to your . . . protector. What sort of friend have you been? I see your scars on his soul. I assure you, you will find me a more dangerous foe.*

"Let's find out."

Lei raised the wand and there was a brilliant flash of electricity. The bolt smashed into Harmattan. Chips of blackened metal went flying, and when the smoke cleared Pierce saw that the blast had punched a hole straight through the stranger's chest almost a foot across.

He was still standing. He hadn't even shifted position, and as Pierce and Lei watched in surprise, the gaping hole slowly filled itself in. It was then that Pierce realized: Harmattan wasn't covered in a coat of metal shards. His entire body was composed of tiny pieces of metal. He was like a statue made of sand. Some force was holding these particles together—and within seconds, he had simply readjusted his mass to erase the gaping wound.

*Satisfied?*

"No."

Lei released a second bolt. This one struck the stranger in the head. No creature of flesh and blood could survive such a blow, but when the flash had faded, Harmattan was still standing. The mystical energy had evaporated the cloud of mist hiding his features, and now Pierce could see the stranger's head—the head of a warforged soldier. It was blackened, but intact, and Pierce guessed that it was forged from nearly indestructible adamantine, but it was far too small for Harmattan's massive body; it was about the same size as Pierce's own head. It was floating above his torso, hovering at least three inches in the air.

Lei's wand only held enough energy for two blasts, and now that charge was drained. She slipped it back into her belt and gripped her staff in both hands. Pierce had an arrow drawn, and he kept his eyes on Harmattan, wondering if a simple arrow would have any effect on the strange creature.

Neither of them saw the slender figure slip out of the shadows behind Lei until it was too late. A metal elbow slammed into the base of Lei's skull, followed by a powerful fist. Lei staggered forward, nearly dropping her staff, and turned to face the new foe.

"So you are his lady."

The warforged had abandoned the robe and cloak she'd used as a disguise in Sharn and Stormreach, and Pierce had to admire her design. The blue enamel on her plating seemed to shift with the shadows, blending into the darkness. Her frame was light and willowy, built for deadly speed instead of brute force. As she spoke, adamantine blades slid into place.

"You should have killed me when you had the chance," Lei said.

The air rippled around her fingers, and Pierce remembered the scout she had destroyed earlier that day, aand he remembered another battle—a struggle beneath Sharn, when she had turned that same power against him.

"STOP!" He cried, his voice rising to its maximum volume. He unleashed his arrow, striking the ground between the warforged and the artificer. "Lei. Do not fight, and you—if you harm her, I swear that I will destroy you."

There was a moment of silence. Then the dry voice washed across the clearing. *Indigo.*

The assassin took a step back, her blades disappearing into her arms. "As you wish."

Pierce felt a strange fascination as he watched her. The

bladed scouts, this Harmattan—they seemed so alien that it was hard to think of them as being members of his own race, but the blue woman—there was something about her, a feeling he couldn't explain.

"Lei," he said. "Daine has abandoned us. It seems we will be traveling with these people."

Harmattan *rustled* again, and Pierce realized that it was what he did instead of laughing.

# CHAPTER 35

**D**aine was surrounded by darkness.

He couldn't feel anything. He couldn't see or hear. He was stranded in endless gloom.

Just a month ago, his first thought would have been *am I dead?* Dolurrh was said to be an empty void, a net that pulled in the souls of the fallen and held them until all memory and thought had faded away. A few weeks ago, Daine might have felt traces of panic, fear that this was the end.

Instead, his first thought was *darkness again?*

His second thought was to evaluate the qualities of the void, with the attention a connoisseur might give to a fine Aundairian vintage. When he was attacked by Tashana, the shadows were cold and viscous. That darkness was like tar—he could struggle against it, but there was so much pressure he could barely move.

Here, there was no pressure at all. He seemed to have no body. Trying to move an arm—there was no struggle. It wasn't cold, because he couldn't feel any sort of temperature. There was nothing at all. All he had were his thoughts.

His next thought was *am I dead?*

Before confusion could turn fully to fear, he heard a sound. A distant voice, raised in song. At first, it was pure music. Slowly Daine began to make out individual words, though he could not understand the language. As he concentrated on the song, he began to feel sensation returning, as if his spirit was flowing back into his body. There was no strength in his limbs, but at least he could feel his arms and legs again, his heart beating in his chest. The song continued, but now he realized that it wasn't a song at all—it was a conversation. There were two voices, alternating and pausing. The language was fluid and lyrical, but the patterns weren't those of music, and though the accent was strange, the cadence too quick, he recognized the language.

Elvish.

Daine had never learned the Elvish tongue, but he'd fought Valenar soldiers on the southern front, and he'd learned to fear the sound of an Elvish battlecry. The shadows that attacked them—slender, swift, and now he thought about it, shorter than most humans—elves. He was certain of it.

Feeling had returned to his arms and legs—enough that he could sense what an uncomfortable position he was in. He was lying flat on his stomach, with his face pressed against moist earth. His arms were stretched behind his back, his legs pulled up, and his wrists and ankles bound together. He tried pulling at the bonds, to no avail; the cord was strong, the knots tight. As slight as this motion was, he apparently attracted some attention; the singing voices broke off, and he heard someone kneel down next to him. Taking a deep breath, Daine lifted his head and opened his eyes to look at his captor.

He'd expected to see an elf: pale skin, pointed ears, fine features, large eyes with green or violet irises.

He was half right.

It was still deep night, but there was a clear path to the sky above, and the moons cast their light on the man kneeling over him. The figure staring down at him looked like an elf—at least, in silhouette, but his eyes were blank white, with no trace of veins, pupil, or iris. Half his face was missing. No, his skin was jet black, darker than any man Daine had seen, and almost invisible in the shadows, but it was covered with corpse-white patches, patterns that were too regular to be natural. The left half of the man's face was a white mask, a stylized skull that covered much of his skin. As Daine's eyes adjusted to the dim light, he saw that the stranger had markings on the right side as well—fine white traceries running under his right eye and out to his long, black ear, than dropping down the side of his neck.

Words, perhaps, or some sort of mystical inscription.

From his vantage point with his chin in the dirt, Daine could see little beyond the stranger's head. The man had pale, silver-blond hair drawn into thick braids, and he wore an odd cap over his forehead, apparently made from the iridescent shell of a white lobster.

"You'd better let me go. Now."

"Why do I do this?" It was the voice from the previous battle; this was the man who had thrown the curving stick at him. As before, his words seemed to flow together, and Daine had to struggle to make sense of it: *whydu'Iduthis*.

Daine tested his bonds again. "When I get mad, I . . . bite people."

A smile flickered across the lips of the strange elf. He sang a phrase in his liquid tongue, and Daine heard hisses around him—apparently the laughter of the other elves.

"Tell me of yourself," the man said. "What you come to steal, your oath to the firebinders. Tell me and your death will be swift."

"Tempting offer."

"No offer," said the elf, pale eyes gleaming. "Promise."

He stepped back, allowing Daine to get a better look at his enemy. The elf was dressed for the jungle heat. Much of his skin was exposed, inky black marred by intricate white designs. He wore a few pieces of armor, pale white shell attached to straps of leather. In addition to his cap, he wore long vambraces over each forearm, shinguards, a plate covering his upper torso, and an armored loincloth. He wore a belt of dark leather, with a wooden throwing wheel hanging down along each hip. Daine could see the hilts of some sort of swords or knives, but the weapons were slung behind the elf's back, and Daine couldn't get a good look at them.

A moment later, the elf knelt down again, but now he was holding something in his hand. At first Daine thought it was just another piece of white chitin—until it *moved*. It was a scorpion—a pale scorpion, which must have been hiding in the man's armor.

"Xan'tora aids and inspires," the elf said. "She shows the hunter's path, silent motion and deadly strike."

"Charming," Daine said. "When I was growing up, I had a lallis hound, myself."

The elf set his hand down, and the scorpion scurried off onto the ground. A moment later Daine felt the tiny creature climb up his shoulder and onto his back, its footsteps faint drops of rain through his clothing. He shivered, remembering the swarms of insects beneath Sharn.

"Xan'tora listens as I ask my question. You do not answer, you feel her blade. One touch brings pain. Twice is far worse. You should not survive a third—though some time passes before the pain ends." The elf paused to let this sink in. "Why are you here?"

"I told you, we're just trying to find our friends and *leave*." Daine waited for the scorpion's sting, but apparently the answer was sufficient.

"Then what have you done already? You do not belong in our land. You come only to steal, to desecrate. If you are to leave, you must have already taken."

"I'm sick. We thought we could find a cure . . . somewhere around here. Then our thrice-damned guide touched the wrong stone and we found ourselves here."

"Sickness?" The elf took a step back, speaking in Elvish, and a dagger appeared in his hand—Daine's dagger. "What is this sickness? You seem to be in health."

"It's a disease of the mind. It doesn't spread." He sighed. "Look. We haven't taken anything of yours. All we want to do is leave. Just undo these ropes and you'll never see us again."

"Because you go to the city of glass?"

"Yes! Do you want to search our belongings?" He glanced at the point of his own dagger, in the hand of the elf. "Assuming you haven't already? From where I'm lying, we don't seem to be the thieves here."

The elf's eyes narrowed, and Daine felt a needle in the small of his back—the jab of the tiny stinger, pressing through the links of his chainmail and piercing his shirt. Where the last dose of poison had a chilling, numbing effect, this venom felt like acid; Daine could swear that his flesh was melting around the wound, and fire spread through his blood.

"We aren't here to STEAL!" he growled.

The elf watched him closely, as if he could read his pain. "It may be as you say, but you are friend to the firebinders. Tell me what they plan."

"I don't know any firebinders!" Daine cried. His back was in agony, and he could feel his heart pounding.

"You *travel* with their child!" The elf hissed, and for the first time he truly seemed angry. "They are fools and foul, blind to the wisdom of the wilds, but to sell their blood to the outlands—I had thought it untrue, until it was seen."

"I don't know what you're talking about." His inquisitor raised a hand, and Daine braced himself for another jolt of poison, but the elf paused.

"No? You are not the servant of the firebinders? Speak truly, or Xan'tora strikes again."

"I don't . . . know . . . what you are talking about!"

The tattooed elf tapped the fingers of his left hand against the blade of the dagger. "You have spirit. More than the last of your kind I killed. Perhaps you are not a thief, but only a fool."

"Those are my only choices?"

"Prove to me that you are no servant of the firebinders, and I may release you and your mate. Are you willing of this?"

*Mate?* "Of course I am, and what's that going to involve? Eating hot coals?"

The elf held out his hand, and the scorpion crawled off of Daine's back, returning to its master's wrist. "I am Shen'kar, Vulk N'tash of the Qaltiar." He rose to his feet. "If you have been misled, I offer you this chance to return to the righteous path and leave our land. Lie to me, and I will hunt you in this life and the next."

He called out in Elvish, and Daine heard his comrades answering the call. A moment later someone cut the cord binding Daine's wrists and ankles together, but even as he stretched, he felt a new rope being tied around his left foot.

"What's this?"

"You promise the proof," Shen'kar said. "He wakes and is ready. Now is the time to show." He exchanged a few more words with his companions, and the hilt of some sort of weapon was pressed into Daine's hand. "Your mate still sleeps; we stand with her and watch. Prove your words. Flee and she dies."

Now the cords binding his ankles together were cut, but there was a separate tether around his left shin. He tested it—the knots were tight, but there was no pressure on the rope. Two of the dark elves pulled him to his feet; glancing sideways, he saw that one was the woman he had fought earlier. Her black skin was tattooed with a series of white streaks that reminded him of tears, and he could see the cuts and contusions on the side of her head where he'd bludgeoned her. She stared at him, her large eyes blank and impossible to read.

"Little time," Shen'kar said. "Prove swiftly. Then we decide your fate."

His two guards stepped away. Shen'kar darted forward, Daine's dagger in his hand, and Daine felt the cords binding his wrists fall apart. He flexed his arms, wincing at the stiffness, feeling the weight of the weapon he'd been given—a heavy wooden baton with a carved hilt.

"Act," Shen'kar sang. "Kill the firebinder."

Daine turned around. He saw that he'd been bound with vines, not ropes. The vine still wrapped around his left ankle ran a short distance across the clearing, to the leg of another man. The captive's arms were bound behind his back, and he was gagged with a thick vine, like a horse with a bridle. Daine took a step back and the cord between them snapped taut, pulling the victim into the moonlight.

It was Gerrion.

CHAPTER 36

XEN'DRIK
THE
NORTHERN
JUNGLE
Lharvion 21, 997 YK

Lei was exhausted.

The tireless warforged were marching through the night, heading deeper south through the jungle. Lei's hands weren't bound, but there was no question that she was a prisoner. Hydra was shadowing her, following to either side, arm blades set and ready to strike. The little warforged was hungry for vengeance, but so far Pierce and Harmattan were holding him in check. Harmattan had agreed to spare Lei's life—but only so long as she could keep up with the others. To her surprise, Pierce had agreed to this.

There were six warforged in the band that had captured them, but as it turned out, there were really only three. The four scouts weren't just identical in appearance—they were controlled by one mind, a force that called itself Hydra. Lei had never heard of such a thing, but the evidence was incontrovertible. The scouts often moved in perfect unison, and when they didn't speak at the same time, they would finish one another's sentences. They even had the same ghulra—the mark of life on the forehead, a symbol that was supposed to be unique to each warforged. The consciousness of Hydra stretched across all of his bodies, and he had fought them on the icy beach. He'd felt the pain when Lei had destroyed that body—and given the opportunity, Lei was sure he'd take vengeance. Hydra rarely spoke, but he was always watching Lei with at least one set of eyes.

Harmattan was a greater mystery, a ghost of metal and wind. His body was formed from bits of broken armor, shattered blades, arrowheads, and splinters of steel too small to be identified. He had no skeleton, no frame—he was just a mass of metal pulled together by magic. What had first appeared to be a cloak was simply an extension of his body, a curtain of metal shards held aloft by invisible force. His head was surrounded by a cloud of powdered steel, his eyes glowing within this darkness. This halo had reformed soon after the attack, but the brief glimpse of his floating head was still fixed in Lei's mind. It was blackened and worn, but it touched a chord within her. She couldn't place it yet, but she was certain she'd seen that face before.

The third warforged was called Indigo, due to the dark blue enamel covering her body. Lei had grown up among warforged, and she'd seen a few "female" constructs, but it was still slightly unnerving; the male voice was far more common. Like all warforged, her body had no indications of gender, but she was lean, wiry, and remarkably graceful. Compared to the armored bulk of the typical warforged soldier, she did have a feminine appearance, and Lei could see why her creator might have given her a woman's voice. She was swift and silent, and she and Pierce had quickly taken point and disappeared in the jungle. It was clear that she'd spoken with Pierce before. Lei had always thought of Pierce as a brother, and she'd never considered that he might have secrets; deception and treachery were human traits. Now she wondered what else he had been hiding and whether she'd been a fool to trust anyone.

*You are weary.* Harmattan's words emerged from his body, ground metal carried on the wind. *Why fight with your flesh? Your death is inevitable. Ask, and I will end your suffering.*

"I'm fine."

Harmattan rustled. *You struggle with every step. How long until blood and bone collapse beneath you?*

"I can stay on my feet as long as I have to."

*You know that's not true. You walk toward your grave. Every step is more difficult than the last, and even if you survive this day, how many more do you have? In a century, your Pierce will still walk the earth, while you will be the dust beneath his feet.*

Lei gritted her teeth and said nothing. Her stomach was knotted with hunger, and her knees and ankles ached—but she'd be damned before she admitted her weakness to this *thing*.

*There is no shame in it,* he said, as if reading her thoughts. Perhaps he was. *It is not your fault you were forged of flesh instead of steel. You did not choose your design, and you are not to blame for your flaws. Why struggle against them? Death lurks within you, waiting to overtake your beating heart. Submit. Surrender. I can end it swiftly.*

"Why do you care so much?" she snapped. "Or do you have this conversation with every human?"

*Is that what you are?* He rustled again. *I suppose that it's Pierce I am thinking of. He cares about you, that much is clear, and it holds him back. If I kill you—he's not ready for that, but if you ask for death, if you choose to end your pointless struggle . . . it will be best for both of you.*

"Well, thanks so much for looking out for us. I'll make sure to let you know if I want to take you up on your generous offer."

*Do you remember Blacklion, Lei? The broken forge?*

Lei stopped in her tracks. Blacklion was the forgehold where she'd spent most of her childhood—the Cannith workshop where she'd first manifested the Mark of Making. "How do you know about that?"

*I was born in Blacklion, Lei, just as you were. I'm sure you saw thousands of warforged while you were there—It's hardly surprising that you don't remember.*

She stared at him, trying to see the face hidden in the shadow. There was something gnawing at the back of her mind, but she couldn't quite grasp it. "Somehow I think I'd remember you."

*It took time for me to reach my full potential . . . though Pierce is taking even longer.*

"You—you're saying that Pierce is like *you*?"

*Keep moving, child of flesh. We still have far to go and no time for your weakness.* He pressed a massive hand against her back and pushed her forward. *Pierce has his own destiny, but we have been shaped by the same hands, and there is much he has yet to discover.* He raised his voice, continuing over her question. *The broken forge of Blacklion. Surely you remember the abominations it produced?*

She nodded, slowly. The creation forges were built during the Last War, and few members of the house understood the enchantments involved. One of the forges at Blacklion was unreliable, but with the demands of the war, it was often used anyway. Most of the time the warforged it produced were satisfactory, but she still remembered the failures—cripples and creatures with deformities that could never be shaped from flesh. She remembered a torso with a half dozen arms flailing about, crushing the skull of an attending magewright, and her father, stepping in and shattering the horror with a touch.

*You destroy failures, Lei. It is the way of your house—and the way of the world. It is a mercy to end the suffering of such a thing. I merely offer you that same mercy.*

Lei searched the trees ahead, looking for some sign of Pierce. She kept walking, and for the moment her anger burned away her exhaustion. "Is that what your Lord of Blades says? It's a mercy to destroy humanity?"

The eerie *rustling* came again, a flutter across his form. *We are guided by a force far greater than any one warforged, and I was not talking about humanity. I was talking about you.*

"Then who—"

Her complaint was cut off by a song. A woman's voice, faint and full of sorrow. Lei's staff. She couldn't quite hear the words, but somehow she knew their meaning. *Death surrounds you, beyond your metal guardians. Strike the shadows, for the truth is not what it seems.* Lei could feel anguish sweeping over her, and she knew this pain was trapped within the staff. She could almost touch the spirit within, but somehow it was just beyond her reach.

Lei had stopped the instant the song began, frozen by the despair that flowed from the staff. Hydra raised its arms, and she could see Harmattan's gleaming eyes watching her from within the shroud of steel.

*What is it?*

"Danger." Was he asking for her opinion, or did he know more about the power of the staff?

Harmattan hissed a command in a language Lei didn't recognize. The four scouts spun in place, forming a perimeter with a pair of eyes at each cardinal point.

*Stay between Hydra, little one. We may as well protect you until you choose to die.* Harmattan strode out of the circle.

Lei scowled but held her ground. The staff was murmuring quietly, singing of circling death.

An instant later a long, low shape melted out of the undergrowth and raced toward the warforged. Lei caught a glimpse of a lean, black panther-like creature racing forward on six legs. A pair of long, whip-like tentacles flowed out from its shoulder-blades, each tipped with vicious bone hooks. Its gleaming red eyes met hers, its lips drew back in a snarl—and then she saw one of Hydra's spiked arms pass right through its skull.

There was no blood, no sound of impact, and no reaction from the creature. Instead, it lashed out with its tentacles. It seemed to be flailing at empty air, until the attacking Hydra staggered back. A gouge appeared across his chest, accompanied by the sound of bone scraping against steel.

Lei remembered Daine's last lunch at the Ship's Cat—the meat that had appeared to be floating off the plate. *Displacer beast!* The creature she could see was just an illusion, a reflected image of the invisible predator that lurked nearby. Hitting such a creature would be a matter of luck as much as skill, trying to guess where it was by the blows it landed on its victims.

The hunter wasn't alone. Even as Lei and the warforged turned to face the attacker, three more of the beasts leapt from the shadows. Two of Hydra's sentinels reeled from invisible blows, and a powerful stroke dug a furrow into Harmattan's chest—a wound that vanished an instant later. Lei paused, gripped by indecision. Should she join in the battle, or leave the warforged to fight on their own?

The conflict was over before she had time to decide. Harmattan seemed to *explode* outwards. A whirlwind of razor-sharp metal swept across the path, and Lei heard the sound of tearing flesh and agonized howls that fell silent within seconds. The steel hurricane swept around Lei and Hydra, leaving the mangled corpses of the four beasts in its wake. For an instant, Lei saw the head of the warforged soldier floating in a maelstrom of metal. Then the whirlwind collapsed in on itself, coalescing into the solid humanoid form of Harmattan. A rattling, intense shiver ran through his form, scattering blood and bits of flesh onto the ground.

*Just like a dog*, Lei thought. Her mind was almost blank with shock from what she had just seen. The displacer beasts had died in an instant, and their corpses could barely be recognized. She'd thought of Harmattan as a ghost earlier, but now she wondered—*How can you fight something like that?*

Indigo leapt out of the jungle, her adamantine blades extended. Pierce appeared behind her, an arrow to his bow. He glanced around the battlefield, studying the carnage.

"Excellent work," Hydra hissed, four voices speaking at once. "Without your skills, we should certainly have been destroyed."

"I am certain your role in this battle was *exactly* as significant as mine," Indigo replied. Harmattan rustled, and she inclined her head toward him as her blades slid back into their sheaths. "My apologies to you. Pierce and I should not have let this go undetected."

Pierce was keeping his eyes down on the ground, examining one of the devastated corpses. His bow was lowered. *He's . . . embarrassed,* Lei realized, and it certainly wasn't like him to let a threat slip by.

*It is done,* Harmattan said, *but it seems we need more eyes in the darkness. We are close, and we cannot afford to miss the door. Hydra. Spread out. Three point search, serpent spread.* His glowing eyes turned toward Lei. *I think that I can watch our little cousin.*

Indigo and three of the Hydras scattered into the jungle. Pierce paused for a moment and glanced at Lei, but he followed Indigo without speaking.

Lei shivered. Harmattan was deadlier than she'd thought possible, but right now . . . right now, it was Pierce that frightened her.

# CHAPTER 37

I *knew* we couldn't trust you!"

Gerrion was lying on the ground, and blood from his earlier wound was running into his eyes, but even with his hands bound behind his back, Gerrion was not to be underestimated. He twisted to the side just in time to avoid the blow, and Daine's club dug a furrow in the earth. Daine had put too much strength behind the attack, and as he recovered, Gerrion launched a sweeping kick at Daine's knees. As quick as he was, the half-elf wasn't fast enough, and Daine darted back out of the way.

"Get up," Daine growled. "I want to knock you down again."

Gerrion slowly rose to his feet. His jaws worked around his gag, but all he could manage were unintelligible grunts. Daine had already broken a few of Gerrion's ribs, and there was a faint froth of blood around the gag. Gerrion had a pleading look in his pale eyes, and he shook his head frantically, but Daine couldn't decide if this was a protestation of innocence or a simple plea to end the pain.

On consideration, he decided that he didn't care.

"What's that? Something's wrong?" He took a step closer to the wounded half-elf.

Desperate nodding.

"It's not what it seems?"

Gerrion shook his head, blood slowly trickling down his cheek.

"Tell that to Lei, you gray bastard!" Daine smashed the club into the side of Gerrion's face, and he felt a cheekbone give way.

Gerrion staggered, but he was tougher than Daine had anticipated. He took a step back, but instead of falling he lashed out with a foot, moving with surprising speed given his condition. This time, Daine wasn't his target; he struck with his left foot, and even as Daine stepped back, Gerrion looped the trailing vine around the club, pulling it from Daine's grip and sending it flying.

It was a valiant effort, but Gerrion could barely stand—while Daine was driven by pure fury. An instant later, Daine slammed into Gerrion with his shoulder, sending the half-elf tumbling back to the earth.

"I *said* I'd kill you!" he shouted.

He aimed a savage kick at Gerrion's broken ribs, and the half-elf jerked in pain. Reaching down, he grabbed the nearest heavy object—a chunk of rock that might have been the toe of a giant statue—and brought it down with terrible force, again and again. Finally he stopped. Panting, he straightened up and looked at the elves who were standing around Lakashtai. He let the stone fall to the ground, and he tried to ignore the ruin at his feet.

The dark elves watched in silence. Lakashtai was still unconscious; she lay on the ground before the elves, her wrists and ankles bound together.

"Satisfied?" Daine said, wiping his bloody hands on his sleeves.

Shen'kar slowly walked forward, his scorpion-shell armor gleaming in the moonlight. He still held Daine's dagger in his hand. "A fierce battle. For one of tainted blood, the firebinder fought well."

Daine spit on the gory corpse. "Not well enough."

"Truth. You say he betrayed you?"

"All I know is that he lured us away from our friends—and I'm sure he didn't have our best interests at heart." He kicked Gerrion's corpse. "I don't know what you've got against these firebinders, and I don't care. Just cut me free of this traitor and we'll be on our way."

Shen'kar studied him, or so Daine thought; the apparent lack of pupils was deeply disconcerting. "That is not to be." He drew one of the weapons from behind his back—a rod of dark wood, set with fangs along the edge—or were they scorpion stingers? Behind him, the other elves had produced blades and chains.

"We had a deal!"

"We agreed to decide your fate after this battle, so we have. Even if you had not brought pain to Xu'sasar, even if you were not despoilers of the land, you sought the city of glass in the season of fire. We can give you no mercy."

"But I killed this . . . firebinder!"

"Yes. Perhaps that will earn you rebirth as one of the Qaltiar. Let us send you to the testing grounds." The dark elf raised dagger and rod and took a step forward.

"Wait. Wait!" Daine cried, holding up his empty hands. "Very well. I accept my fate, but before you kill me, there is something I took from your people—something you should have back."

"What is?" Shen'kar said, curious.

"This," Daine said, smashing him in the face with the wooden club.

❀ ❀ ❀ ❀ ❀ ❀ ❀

*A few minutes earlier . . .*

"Act," Shen'kar sang. "Kill the firebinder."

Daine studied Gerrion. The tattooed flames around his face, his short but clearly pointed ears, his eyes—slightly too large, strangely pale. The gray skin. He'd seen half-elves before, and for all he knew, Xen'drik was filled with gray-skinned elves. Now he guessed that Gerrion's coloring was a faded mirror of his elven parent.

He tested the weight of the baton in his hand. Gerrion was unarmed, his wrists bound behind his back. It would be a simple matter to kill him. Perhaps these elves *would* let him go. Perhaps he and Lakashtai could find their way through the jungle on his own.

In his mind's eye, he saw a man with a crossbow standing in an alley in Stormreach. Gerrion had aided them against the Riedrans, without any promise of aid. As angry as he was about being separated from Lei and Pierce, Daine couldn't help but believe that it had been an accident. If Gerrion had meant to harm them, he could have simply left them to die in that alley.

"Act with speed," Shen'kar called again. "Lest Xan'tora be sent to touch your mate."

"She's . . ." Daine stopped himself. *This isn't the time to argue.* Mate or not, the last thing he wanted was for the elves to poison Lakashtai—at the very least, he needed to buy time. He dropped into a battle stance, bringing the club up into a low guard position and slowly circled to the left, away from the elves.

Gerrion watched him warily.

Daine studied the elves. They had little in the way of armor, mostly pieces of shell or chitin attached to strips of leather, but they were armed, there were four of them, and they had poison on their side—and possibly magic or trickery they simply hadn't revealed. He was bound to Gerrion, and Gerrion wasn't even armed. He sighed. Perhaps it was a no-win situation. Could he kill Gerrion, if it would save Lei?

*We need Gerrion. We cannot find our way through the jungle alone.*

*That's right! You can't kill me!*

The thoughts were those of Lakashtai and Gerrion, pressing into Daine's mind. He kept circling, trying to keep his face blank. *Lakashtai? You're awake?*

*Yes. I believe that I can escape these bonds, but it will take time.*

*Gerrion—Don't just stand there! Back away. Keep your distance, and Aureon's shattered teeth! Tell me what is going on here!*

The half elf met his gaze and gave the slightest nod. As Daine moved forward, Gerrion darted back, pulling at the tough vine that bound them together. Hopefully Daine's slow movement seemed like sensible caution.

*These . . . they aren't the elves you know from Khorvaire. Thousands of years ago, the elves fought the giants that ruled this land. Giant wizards captured elves and experimented on them, created their own soldiers to go places the giants could not. It's said that they wove dark magic into the elven form, and that these are the result. The first elves call them the drow.*

*I'm going to attack,* Daine thought. *Careful.* He lunged forward, launching a few cautious blows—the goal was to appear to be testing Gerrion's reflex, not yet attacking in earnest. The half-elf leapt back, and Daine just brushed his cloak.

*These . . . The leader called himself 'vulk n'tash of the qaltiar'. That means 'scorpion wraith of the broken oath.' Whatever you do—I wouldn't place much trust in his word.*

"Just die, you bastard!" Daine cried, darting forward again, pulling his blow at the last moment so Gerrion could slip away. *So why's he got it in for you? What's a 'firebinder'? And fight back next time I come close—kick me or something.*

*My mother was human. They don't like halfbreeds. There's a longer story, but somehow I don't think this is the time.*

Daine charged forward but allowed himself to be caught off-guard by Gerrion's well-placed kick. *Agreed. Lakashtai—can you just put them to sleep or tell them to let us go?*

*I could not exert direct control over so many—and the elvish mind can be difficult to command. I could perhaps slow them for a time, but they would not be completely helpless.*

*Hold that thought. What else can you do that could affect them all? If I don't start hurting Gerrion—I don't want to have you get hurt as well.*

*I can shift their perceptions . . .*

*And make us invisible?* Daine thought hopefully.

*No, nothing so great. I might be able to hide an object in your hand, make your armor seem to be clothing, turn a whisper into a shout, shift the color of skin or hair, but I could not hide you.*

*Could you . . . make a scrape appear to be a bloody wound?*

Daine could feel Lakashtai contemplating the idea. *Yes. I think I could.*

*Then this is what we're going to do . . .*

●　●　●　◉　●　●

The battle was carefully choreographed. Daine barely touched Gerrion, but Lakashtai assured him that the drow were seeing a brutal fight. She made the club seem to disappear when Gerrion "disarmed" him—but it never left his hand, and as soon as she had slipped free from her bonds, Daine and Gerrion brought the battle to a close.

*I told you not to trust him,* Gerrion thought as Shen'kar drew his weapon and pronounced Daine's fate.

*Whatever.* Daine smashed the drow across the face with the club, and before the surprised elf could react, he brought the club down on his enemy's wrist, forcing him to drop Daine's dagger. With one fluid movement, Daine dropped to one knee, snatched the dagger, and cut the vine binding him to Gerrion.

Shen'kar was not surprised for long, and Daine barely raised the club in time to parry the spiked rod. The drow warrior cried out in Elvish, his fury marring the beautiful speech.

*You don't want to know what that was,* Gerrion added helpfully.

Though smaller than Daine, Shen'kar was swift and skilled. Daine slashed at the drow's weapon with his dagger, hoping to split the rod, but the elf dodged the blow as if it were an approaching ox, and before Daine could raise his guard he felt the scrape of chitin spikes against his cheek. Fire burned in the wound, and Daine mustered his strength to ignore the pain of the poison.

The other elves were spreading out. The chain-wielder set his weapon in motion, creating a whirling disk of steel.

*Lakashtai, if you've got something prepared, now would be the time.*

*Very well.*

For an instant, the night was lit up with an emerald glow, and Daine felt a wave of power pass over him, pressing against his thoughts, then releasing them. The elves froze in place. Daine aimed a quick blow at Shen'kar, but to his surprise, the drow warrior ducked down beneath it.

*Don't fight!* Lakashtai thought. *They can't act directly, but they can still defend themselves. Flee as fast as you can—if we're lucky, we'll have a minute or two before they recover!*

*Gerrion?* Daine thought. *I believe you're the guide.*

*So why aren't you following?*

Gerrion was already halfway across the clearing. They raced into the jungle, leaving the dark elves behind.

❦ ❦ ❦ ❦ ❦ ❦ ❦

They ran hard and fast, redoubling their efforts when Lakashtai reported that the elves had broken free of the trance. Branches tore at Daine's skin, and more than once he stumbled on the uneven terrain, but Lakashtai was always just behind him, pulling him up and pushing him on. His injury ached, but it seemed that he'd only received a tiny dose of venom—the pain wasn't nearly as bad as when he'd been stabbed by the scorpion itself.

Daine couldn't say how long they ran, but eventually Gerrion slowed to a walk. "I think . . . we should be safe now. We're almost to the city."

Daine could smell smoke in the air, and now that he was moving more slowly, he could see an orange glow in the sky ahead. "There?"

"Yes. We've probably been spotted by the patrols already—let me see if I can summon guards." With that, he called out, a long, loud verse in Elvish—and Daine couldn't help but notice that he spoke with the accent of the elves they'd just left behind, not the slower speech of the Valenar.

A moment later, another call came in response, echoing through the jungle. "We're safe," Gerrion said. "Even if we've been followed, they won't attack us once my friends arrive. Come daylight, they can help us find the others."

Daine nodded and took a deep breath, struggling with his beating heart. "I won't say no to a bed and a meal. Here." Gerrion's arms were still bound behind his back, and Daine cut the vines.

"My thanks, and for your efforts earlier."

Daine shrugged. "You saved me before. I guess this makes us even."

People were approaching, and from the noise it was clear they weren't the silent stalkers they had fought in the clearing. There was flickering light, most likely from a torch.

It wasn't a torch—and when the soldiers finally reached them, Daine was in for another surprise.

They were drow.

The soldiers wore leather jerkins studded with bronze scales and conical bronze helmets with chunks of black glass embedded around the rim. Beneath the helmets, their eyes were large and white, with no iris or pupil. Their skin was jet black, as black as the obsidian chunks decorating their armor, and tattooed with brilliant patterns of flame—designs much like those Gerrion wore. The "torch" turned out to be the weapon of the leader—a short spear with a long, blackened head that was wreathed in crackling flames.

Daine put himself on guard, and only then did he realize— *My sword!* He'd reclaimed his dagger from Shen'kar, but he'd left his grandfather's sword behind. *Elves!* He cursed.

"Daine! Stop! They aren't going to hurt us!" Gerrion jumped between Daine and the soldier, speaking rapidly in Elvish. The soldiers lowered their weapons, and the captain with the flaming spear spoke with Gerrion.

*They recognize Gerrion.* Lakashtai's thoughts drifted into Daine's mind. *He says that he has brought us to see the high priest, a man named Holuar. The warrior seems suspicious—something to do with thin blood—but he is going to show us the way.*

*So . . . not all of these dark elves are vicious scorpion killers?*

*It would appear that way.*

"My apologies," Gerrion said, turning back to them. "I should have made that more clear. These are my father's people—the Sulatar. Comparing them to the savages we met earlier . . . oh, it's like comparing Cyrans to barbarians from the Demon Wastes. Trust me, you'll get that bed and meal."

One of the elves wasn't wearing armor—a scout, Daine supposed. The captain spoke to her and she raced off into the darkness, most likely to deliver word of their arrival. The other soldiers spread out around them, spears and bronze swords at the ready. Their faces were grim, and Daine found his hand back on the hilt of his dagger.

"They don't seem that happy to see us."

"It's not you. I told you—the jungle isn't safe at night. We're just lucky we didn't stumble into any cesspits or briarghosts on our way here."

Indeed, the elves turned their attention outward, and the captain led the way with his flaming spear. They continued on in silence. The smell of wood-smoke grew stronger with each passing minute, then they came to the edge of the jungle and saw the city.

It was a castle sculpted from glowing volcanic glass. The orange glow Daine had seen in the sky was coming from the walls themselves, and Daine could feel heat radiating out from the city, but the glowing walls were only one of the strange features of the castle. It was enormous; the gates were at least thirty feet high, and the walls might have been fifty feet in height.

And it was a ruin.

The towers that rose above the walls were shattered and broken, and the walls themselves were cracked and uneven. Set against the vast walls, the dark shapes of the elves seemed like insects crawling around a broken toy.

A troop of elves was waiting for them as they approached the gates. A dozen soldiers in bronze armor stood in a semi-circle, arranged around a man and a woman. The man wore a black robe and what appeared to be a prayer shawl inscribed with letters of flame. There was an obsidian crown with three tall spikes on his head, and Daine guessed that this was the priest Holuar. The woman next to him was a warrior. She was holding a double-bladed sword—a shaft of wood with a long blade on either end, much like the double scimitars of the Valenar elves. However, these blades were straight—and wreathed in flame. Her armor was quite different from her comrades. She wore chainmail made with lines finer than Daine had ever seen, but the metal was glowing cherry-red with heat. It should have seared her alive, burning flesh and bone—but it didn't seem to harm her in any way. Her helmet was sculpted to resemble a bonfire, and her pale eyes were surrounded by tattooed flames. She met Daine's gaze and showed her teeth in what might have been a smile—but probably wasn't.

The priest and the warrior exchanged a few words with Gerrion; Lakashtai immediately began to translate.

*The man with the crown is Holuar. The woman is their war leader, Zulaje.*

*War leader. Well, good to know they're peaceful hunter-gatherers.*

The woman pointed the blade of her sword at Gerrion, but the priest spoke sharply and she stepped back, scowling. Gerrion raised his hands in a placating manner.

*Holuar welcomes Gerrion, but Zulaje is suspicious of him. She believes he is wasting time again.*

*Again?*

Daine could feel Lakashtai's frustration. *Let me try to forge a stronger link between us—to allow you to draw on my knowledge of the language.*

There was a sharp, twisting pain in Daine's head, and he almost cried out. For a moment all sensation was blocked out by the pain. Then the sing-song voices of the elves returned—but he realized that he understood the words of the song, the meaning of pitch and inflection.

" . . . Foolish prophecy?" said the woman, Zulaje. "We should be eradicating the oathbreakers, not wasting our time on legends."

"You know nothing but the sword." Holuar was old; his face was not wrinkled, but it was gaunt and drawn, and his voice was rough. "This is where our destiny lies. This is the vow that gives our lives meaning. You are certain?"

"I swear it on my father's blood." Gerrion was more serious than Daine had ever seen him. All traces of the laughing rogue had vanished. "The child of war, the voice from the past. There can be no doubt." ·

"Then let us put them to the test." The old priest glanced at Daine, and waved his hand to the guards. "Take them."

# CHAPTER 38

XEN'DRIK
THE SU'LASA
*Lharvion 22, 997 YK*

**D**o you remember your first kill?" Her voice was a whisper, drifting over the calls of waking birds.

Dawn was rising over the jungle. The vegetation around them was painted in orange and red, the fiery colors of autumn. Pierce and Indigo slipped through the underbrush, and Pierce was impressed by his companion's grace and skill.

"No." Pierce said. "I served Cyre for over two decades. Perhaps it is age, or the damage I suffered, for I was damaged often."

"Soldiers," Indigo said dismissively. "I remember each of my victims. When my human companions slept, I would recall those past struggles and consider what might come. I assume you have fought your companions in your mind? Your Lei, your captain?"

"He is not my captain anymore."

"True . . . but you did not answer my question." A blade flickered out of her forearm, and she cut through a wall of vines with a quick slash. When Pierce said nothing, she continued. "There is no shame in it. It is what you are: a weapon, made to kill. An ally today may prove a threat tomorrow." She did not turn her head, but he could feel her gaze. "Surely we have battled in your thoughts?"

"Many times."

"What was the outcome?"

"Satisfactory. You are a dangerous opponent, but I can match you."

She did glance at him then. He studied her ghulra, the twisting sigil carved into her forehead, fixing it in his memory. "You know less of me than you think. Perhaps we shall put your projections to the test, once this business is concluded."

"What is this business? A door embedded into the earth. What could bring you all the way to Xen'drik?"

"Harmattan will tell you, when he feels you can be trusted."

There was a rustle in a nearby tree, and both warforged turned. Pierce had an arrow drawn and ready, but Indigo had already loosed a bolt from her shortbow. A shape fell to the ground—a small monkey with orange and gray fur, which had been hidden amid the bright foliage.

"Was that necessary?" Even as he turned, Pierce had a sense of the size of the creature from the sound and motion in the brush. The monkey hardly seemed a threat.

"You have been long away from battle, or you never fought the war as I did." Walking over to the corpse, she put her foot on its chest and pulled the bloody arrow out of its skull. "Wizard's familiar, shapechanged foe—we cannot take any chances."

It was true—Pierce had fought the Valenar at Felmar Valley, and the elves had often used ravens and other birds as spies. Perhaps his instincts had grown dull, living in High Walls. Still, there was something about the twisted body, broken on the ground—something felt wrong. He pushed the thought away. "And you? Do you know all the answers, or do you just do what Harmattan tells you?"

Indigo returned the arrow to the string, and continued to move forward. "Harmattan serves all warforged. I trust his judgment."

"You criticized me for following my friends. You seem to have traded one leader for another."

There was a cold edge to Indigo's voice. "What reason did you have for your service? None. You fought because you were ordered to, because you knew nothing else. You never had the courage to find your own path. I follow Harmattan, yes, but Harmattan is one of us, and the warforged are his only concern."

"He does not look like 'one of us.' "

Indigo cut away another patch of vines, studying the

ground. "He was born a soldier, and he fell in battle—destroyed by humans, as you or I might have been, but he refused to die. He rebuilt himself. He is proof of our power, of our own divinity. Humans made us to die. Harmattan can lead us to true immortality."

"Or perhaps Harmattan was made to be immortal. We are all different. Soldiers, scouts, war-wizards—we were made to serve different purposes. Perhaps this was his."

"You have no faith," Indigo replied. "You have spent too much time surrounded by flesh and blood. We are beings of magic, brother. We were not shaped by the hand of man. Humanity was the vessel that brought us to this world, but our true destiny is only beginning to unfold—and it is a mystery the human mind could never hope to comprehend."

Pierce let the matter drop, and for a time they walked in silence. In some ways, he found her company to be more comforting when they weren't talking. It was simple to match his movements to hers, to give himself to the hunt—to allow his instincts to take over, search for the silent step, the trace of their quarry, any sound or threatening motion. Even as he watched the surroundings, he found his thoughts drawn to battle—imagining what a fight with Indigo might be like. He remembered the brief struggle in Sharn, when he'd locked his flail around her neck—but she claimed that she had let him seize her. He'd seen her speed when the displacer beasts attacked, when she shot the monkey. Perhaps he could trip her, pull her down to the ground . . .

There was a glitter against the soil: glass or metal, and again, just ahead, a broad panel, hidden under a blanket of vines and roots.

He tapped Indigo's shoulder and gestured. She followed the motion, signing back. Stand. Cover. I close.

Slinging her bow, Indigo allowed her adamantine blades to slide from their sheaths. She approached the reflective patch, silent and swift. There was no other sign of movement, no roar of magical energy. Slowly, she cut away the vines and weeds, revealing a wide circle of black volcanic glass almost twelve feet across. It seemed out of place in the otherwise lush jungle, but there was little to be done with it—it was just a patch of dark glass. Though now as he looked again, he saw a small symbol carved in the very center of the circle.

He took a step forward, and Indigo raised her hand. "Do not touch it. This is what we have sought."

"I thought that we were searching for a door," Pierce said. He saw no outlines of an opening, no indication of moving parts.

"We have found one." Indigo studied the glass for a moment, then there was a blur of motion as a tiny object flew from her chest. It was the messenger drone Pierce had seen in Sharn—a tiny metal dragonfly. "It will find Hydra," she explained, "and he can lead Harmattan to our location. Now we wait."

"Certainly. We cannot risk making a decision without Harmattan to guide us."

Indigo glanced at him. "The mystical charge stored in the glass would destroy either one of us. Only Harmattan understands the true nature of the portal."

"So. He cannot trust you with his secrets either?"

Her eyes flashed. "I do not need to know the answer to every question."

Strange words for the champion of freedom, Pierce thought, but he did not speak. He didn't want to fight with Indigo—not this way. Was he so different, in his loyalty to his friends? Would he have expected an explanation from Lei, if she had asked him to perform such a task?

Lei.

There had been blood on her cheek when he'd last seen her, sprayed from the corpse of a displacer beast. Perhaps she hadn't felt it; perhaps the blood was on her cloak and only seemed to be marring her skin. Her expression was full of confusion—and anger.

Was that such a surprise?

Why did it matter? He had protected Lei for years. He was protecting her now: It was Daine who had abandoned them both, and only Pierce's actions saved Lei from Harmattan. He would see that she was set free when they reached a point of safety. He had served her well, and now . . . now he wasn't a servant.

Why did it feel so wrong?

Indigo was watching the treeline. Her bow was back in her

hand, an arrow nocked. She was like a crossbow—a deadly mechanism, primed and ready to kill. Her task was all that occupied her thoughts, and he envied that inner peace.

"Do you remember your first kill?" he said.

"Of course," she replied, tracking the motion of a bird at the far range of sight. "I remember all of my victims, but the first—that was sweet."

It was not a word Pierce would have used to describe his victories. "How?"

"Tannic d'Cannith, the artificer who first woke me from my sleep. He worked with me in the early days, as I was imprinted with the skills of my trade. Of course, all of my opponents were warforged—soldiers learning the ways of battle."

Pierce remembered nothing of his birth, but he had heard of this practice from other warforged. Cannith artificers and craftsmen would stage wargames, setting warforged against warforged in full battle. It prepared the 'forged for the true experience of battle, for the painful sensations of injury and deactivation. Most of the fallen could be repaired—though occasionally a soldier would suffer an injury too severe to be restored.

"From the beginning, they used us to die in their stead. I was trained to kill princes and lords, but it was warforged who suffered the first blows from my blades."

He couldn't remember these wargames, but Pierce had certainly fought other warforged on the battlefield. All five nations of Galifar made use of warforged soldiers. Keldan Ridge was the only time he'd faced an army of warforged, but he'd destroyed many enemy warforged in the heat of battle. The momentary thought of Keldan Ridge reminded him of the strange scout, Hydra. What was his tie to that accursed place?

"Tannic was pleased with his work," Indigo continued, "always close at hand, always suggesting ways our performance could be improved, but he grew careless with his choice of words. Looking back now, I think that he considered us his children. One day he was explaining human anatomy, pointing out the swiftest ways to kill a human, and he encouraged me to strike at those killing points, and so I did."

"You struck your creator?"

"I killed him. They had grown careless: there were mage-wrights ready to repair the warforged, but no healers for the humans. When I watched his blood spread across the tile floor, I understood death for the first time. I knew what I was, and I knew the weakness of the flesh, the vulnerability of those who had created me."

"I'm surprised they let you live."

She didn't shrug, but Pierce could hear the ambivalence in her tone. "We were too valuable for such things. My adamantine blades were probably worth more to the forgehold than he was, and it was his poor choice of words. Even then, I believed that my purpose was to serve the house and the nation it would sell me to. I began to imagine the others who would fall at my blades, and I took greater pleasure in the rest of my training, but it was years before I realized that *I* could choose who would live and who would die."

"As long as Harmattan agrees with you."

"Do not worry about Harmattan showing mercy to flesh and blood, brother. If he spares a breather, rest assured he has a reason."

They fell into silence again. For a moment Pierce saw Lei's face in his mind, but his thoughts were interrupted by noise—a massive figure crashing through the jungle.

Harmattan was coming.

CHAPTER 39

**W**ake up.

It was Jode's voice. Faint, distant, but as familiar to Daine as the voice of his father.

*Wake up!*

The scent of smoke was strong in the air. He could hear a rhythmic pounding, the sound of metal on metal—a column of armored soldiers, marching nearby. There was a terrible pain in his left thigh, as if he'd been stabbed. His other injuries seemed to have vanished.

He opened his eyes.

The night sky was hidden by dark clouds, lit from below by distant fires, but Daine knew that light wasn't coming from an elven city. He could hear torn tents flapping in the slight wind, and he could feel a rough pallet beneath him.

This was Keldan Ridge. The camp on the hill.

He sat up, sending a pulse of pain through his injured thigh. "Jode?"

The campsite was deserted, and Jode was nowhere to be seen. He rose slowly to his feet. The sound of armored footsteps grew louder, and he saw that a column of warforged was marching in a circle around the camp. These were the warforged he'd fought in the battle, and they formed a moving wall of metal bristling with blades and spikes.

"This didn't happen," he said, only half expecting an answer.

251

"Are you certain? Perhaps you just don't remember it."
The voice was an all-too-familiar purr. The woman standing
next to Daine pulled her hood back. Her silvery-white hair
reminded him of the wretched elves, but her skin was as pale
as snow.

"Tashana," he said.

Wrapped in her cloak, she seemed more shadow than substance; either she was surrounded by a thin layer of dark mist,
or she was only a shade herself. She met Daine's gaze, and her
eyes gleamed. "Your protector grows weaker by the hour, and
now that you're imprisoned it's only a matter of time before I
shatter her defenses and break you."

She reached out to touch his face, and he found that he
couldn't move. Suddenly it was Lei beside him, and he felt a
disturbing thrill as she stroked his cheek. He tried to speak,
but he was frozen in place. "But what about our houses?"
she said, glancing coyly to the side. She laughed, becoming
Tashana again as she pulled her hand away.

"Ah, Lei," Tashana said as she pulled up her hood. "We'll
have some fun with her, you and I. It was I who killed her
betrothed, you know, and I'll do worse before I'm through with
the two of you."

Daine was burning with fury, but for all his anger, he still
couldn't move.

"Who are you playing with now?"

The voice came from behind him, from further away, and
it drew an angry hiss from the woman at his side, but it was a
familiar voice—Tashana's voice. He flung his fury at the force
that held him paralyzed, and he felt something give.

*Wake up.*

And he did.

❋ ❋ ❋ ❋ ❋ ❋ ❋

Daine awoke in darkness.

Again.

"Why couldn't I get captured by *light* elves," he muttered.

At least this time, the darkness felt natural—a simple absence
of light, as opposed to some supernatural force or the fading
effects of poison. He was lying on a smooth glass floor, and

after twitching his fingers and toes he decided that everything was where it should be. He sat up.

"*Gaah!*"

The ceiling of the cell was less than three feet high, and his forehead slammed against the glass ceiling. He stretched out his hands, tracing the walls of his prison. It was a small hollow, a little over six feet long and about three feet high and three feet wide. Every wall was made of smooth glass, with no trace of a door. There were two small glass bowls lying next to him—one filled with water, and the other with what seemed to be thick gruel.

" 'Oh, trust me, you'll get your meal and your bed.' " Daine slammed a fist against the wall. "The gray rat just never bothered to mention they'd be in a thrice damned *prison cell.*"

Silence was the only response.

He patted his clothes. The shirt beneath his chainmail was stiff with sweat and blood, and he could only imagine how bad he must smell. His dagger and the club were gone, but they'd left his belt pouch alone.

*Wake up,* he thought. Perhaps it was all still a dream.

He reached into his pouch and searched through its contents: a few copper crowns, the keys to the inn and to his trunk back in High Walls, a shard of green crystal, and a small glass vial filled with blue liquid—glowing blue liquid.

He took out the vial and set it on the floor next to him. The light was faint, but in the absolute darkness of the cell, it was a startling change. His earlier suspicions were confirmed: there were no signs of door or window, just smooth black glass all around. With the aid of the glowing vial, he found a few tiny holes in the ceiling, smaller than his smallest finger—air holes, presumably, to prevent him from suffocating.

He examined the two bowls under the blue light. The water seemed clear enough, and the gruel looked lumpy and unappetizing.

"Care for some gruel?" he asked the bottle.

*The best thing about dying? Never eating gruel again.*

"Sure, but you're missing out on this great water. I'm sure it's a fine gnomish vintage."

*Ooh, you're right. Maybe you could just pour some in the bottle.*

It wasn't Jode, but staring at the vial, with Jode's dragonmark stamped on the seal, it was comforting to imagine what his old friend would say if he were still around.

*I think the elves are just trying to wear you down. After all, you put up such a fierce fight—they're probably afraid of you.*

Daine swallowed a mouthful of porridge. "I didn't see you lending a hand."

In truth, the struggle could hardly be called a fight. Once Gerrion joined the elves, Daine and Lakashtai were outnumbered by more than ten to one. Daine was weak from poison, and Lakashtai had expended a great deal of mental power in the earlier battle. The priest had bound Daine in chains of cold fire, and someone had clubbed him from behind; the last thing he'd seen was Lakashtai facing the woman with the flaming blades.

*Hard to lend a hand when you don't have any, but I healed you, didn't I?*

Daine paused to consider this. It was true. The gouge on his cheek was gone. The sickly weakness from the poison had faded away. Aside from the terrible hunger in his belly—which the gruel was addressing, however unpleasantly—he felt fine. "Really?"

*Of course not. I'm dead, remember? The elves must have done it.*

"Why would they do that?"

*How should I know? They were talking about prophecies, legends and testing you. Maybe they want you healthy for it.*

"I thought the test was fighting those guards."

*Well, that would have been a big failure.*

"I failed you."

*I didn't give you much of a choice, did I?*

Daine looked at the little bottle. "You were there for me when I was at my worst. I should have—I should have known. I should have taken better care of you."

*Enough self pity. I'm the dead one. You've got other things to think about.*

"Like what? Digging my way through a wall of glass?" He sorted through his belongings and produced the crystal shard. "I'm sure this will do the job."

The words had scarcely left his lips when he felt a wave of intense heat. An orange glow suffused the wall to his right, and as he watched the wall melted away. Instead of simply flowing down toward the ground, the molten glass spread out in a circle—flowing up and sideways in defiance of gravity.

An instant later the glass was cold again, leaving a round exit from the cell. The chamber beyond was lit by flickering firelight, and Daine could see dark figures standing around the door.

"Out," a voice called—a woman's voice, deep but sweet.

Daine quickly thrust his belongings back into the belt pouch. Grabbing the gruel bowl, he slid out of the alcove.

The chamber beyond was formed of pure black glass. *Haven't these people heard of wood or stone?* The floor was slightly rough, providing traction. The walls were smooth and reflective, but Daine could see a double row of rough circles along the wall. *More cells, I suppose.* The upper row of circles was six feet off the ground, and Daine idly wondered how you'd get someone into a cell that far up. There were no exits that he could see—just a huge hearth filled with a roaring fire on the far wall.

There were four guards standing around the cell when Daine emerged, but his eyes were drawn to their leader. It was the woman he'd seen beyond the walls, the warrior with burning blades. *Zulaje.* She was almost a foot shorter than Daine and couldn't be more than half his weight. Her hair was hidden beneath her bonfire helm, which appeared to be made from soot-coated gold. At the moment, she was holding her sword in a neutral posture, but Daine could see the graceful tension of her grip, the way her feet were spread, knees slightly bent—she was ready for battle, and she knew how to wield that weapon. Her chain armor was still orange with heat, and the fiery tattoos spread across her face seemed to burn as she stared up at him.

"Your presence is sought," she sang softly, flowing her words together as Shen'kar had. "Waste time and you die, and you waste time already."

"Oh, I hate to waste time," Daine said. "Lead on. You don't mind if I finish this on the way, do you?" He indicated the bowl of porridge. "I love gruel, and let me tell you, it doesn't get much better than this."

Zulaje glared at him disdainfully then turned her back without saying a word. Two of the guards took up positions on either side of Daine, spears lowered; the other two remained by the row of cells. Zulaje led the way across the room, and as they approached the hearth, Daine saw that it held no logs nor any fuel at all that he could see; it was a wall of searing flame, deadly and pure. The drow woman whispered to the fire, and it slowly died down, revealing a long, dark hallway. After the party had crossed the threshold, the flames sprung up again, as fierce as before.

*Firebinders,* Daine thought. He took another swallow of gruel. He turned to the elf to his right as they walked down the hall. The man's face was devoid of expression; he might have been carved from volcanic glass.

"Really great," he said. "Do you eat this yourself?"

The guard said nothing.

"Really. Have you tried the prison food?"

Daine guessed that the man didn't speak the Common tongue of Khorvaire, but he wasn't waiting for an answer. Instead, he was waiting for the soldier to glance toward his commanding officer, hoping for a cue on how to deal with the noisy human—and a moment later, he did just that.

"See what you think."

Daine brought the bowl up in a sweeping motion, flinging cold porridge into the guard's face. Reversing the motion, he then brought it down in a vicious arc, slamming the obsidian bowl into the man's fingers. The guard didn't cry out, but he pulled back his hand—leaving only one hand on his spear. Dropping the bowl, Daine grabbed the spear in both hands and jerked backwards, yanking the weapon free from the dazed man's grip. The elf opened his mouth to cry out, to warn his fellows—but he wasn't fast enough. Daine jabbed the point of the spear into the man's throat, silencing his cry before it could begin. The elf fell to his knees, gurgling and clutching his neck.

The other elves didn't need any warning; the motion alone had been sufficient to attract their attention. Zulaje and her companion turned to face Daine, and he barely had time to step back against the wall.

"Tend the fallen, Xuxajor." Zulaje was speaking Elvish, but Daine found he could still understand the words—whatever

Lakashtai had done before, the power was still in effect. "I will take this one."

Daine slowly backed away, keeping the bloody point of his spear leveled at the drow woman. "I don't know what this is about or what Gerrion has told you," he said, "but it's a mistake."

"This I know," Zulaje said softly. She held her weapon in a vertical guard, concealing her true reach. She slowly moved toward him, keeping her blades in slight but constant motion; the pattern of the burning steel was hypnotic and distracting. "Too long have we looked to the world beyond—it is time for our flames to sweep across this land."

Daine tried to keep his eyes on Zulaje, to ignore the flickering flames. Her smoldering red armor was almost as distracting, pulsing with inner heat. "I don't want to hurt you."

"No fear." She ran her unarmored right hand up along the shaft of her sword, and wrapped her fingers around the burning blade. The flame tattoos around her eyes glowed with an inner light, but she showed no signs of pain. "I am the child of fire. My blood burns, and you will not spill it this day." She released the blade, restoring her two-handed grip. "Come. Holuar's worm calls you the child of war. Let us see if you are worthy of the name."

"I'd say cousin, at best." She's overconfident at least, he thought. That's something.

He let her move forward another foot. Then he launched into a full lunge, a deep thrust with the short spear.

Zulaje reacted instantly, spinning her blades to form a shield of fire, but Daine was prepared, and he swiftly spun the tip of the spear, matching her speed and spiraling toward her.

Close—but not enough. She leapt back just before the tip of the blade could strike her chest. She bared her teeth and slashed crosswise at his spear, but Daine pulled back before she could shatter it.

*Overconfident . . . with good reason.* "Well, I've shown you my trick as the cousin of war. What've you got, fire child?"

He was hoping to goad her, to provoke her into rash action. Her response surprised him. She hissed a word in a crackling tongue, and a moment later a wreath of crimson flames spread across her body.

She darted forward, a burning shadow wielding a shaft of light. As surprised as he was, Daine still had the presence of mind to make a swift thrust against her charge, and this time the spear struck true, but even as he felt the point pierce armor and strike flesh, a gout of flame flashed out along the shaft of the spear and across his skin.

*He was on fire!* He could feel the searing heat as his clothing caught flame and smell the stench of burning hair. At the same moment, Zulaje landed a solid blow on his spear, and the pole shattered in burning shards.

Rolling back, Daine slapped himself with his hands. His scalp was burned, his clothes were charred and burnt through in places, but after a few moments, he'd managed to put out the fire.

Zulaje was standing above him, one point of her weapon leveled at his head. He could only see her silhouette as she gazed at him through her burning shield.

"The tradition of flame brings you to Holuar, outlander, but you need no legs to fulfill the prophecy. Will you walk?"

Daine sighed and slowly rose to his feet. "Fine." Zulaje stepped away as he stood, and he could see that she'd perfectly matched his reach.

"Then you will walk ahead, with my blade at your back." She gestured for him to move forward.

The other guard had disappeared, along with his injured comrade; Daine imagined he had gone in search of a healer. A trail of blood drops could be seen running down the hallway.

"I would tell you that his death will mean your own." Zulaje's voice was barely audible over the crackling flames that surrounded her, "but I suspect he'll outlive you either way."

# CHAPTER 40

XEN'DRIK
THE SUL'ASA
*Lharvion 22, 997 YK*

**H**armattan studied the patch of glass on the ground.
*Can you feel it, little brother?*

"Feel what?" The supposed door seemed completely unremarkable, and Pierce was more concerned with Lei. She was surrounded by Hydra on the far side of the clearing, and Pierce could see her glaring in his peripheral vision.

*The spirit bound within the door. Watching. Waiting.*

Pierce looked down at the glass. "It's alive?"

*Alive as an airship is alive. A half-life at best, but it is a beginning. Study the glass. Look for the fire within, the reflection of a flame you cannot see. That is the spirit within. It was bound over forty thousand years ago. For tens of thousands of years it has waited for the key, destroying any who sought to force passage.*

"Destroying?"

"I did tell you not to touch it," Indigo said.

*It holds the power of an inferno. Look closely. There. Burnt bone. A tooth.*

Harmattan was right—looking across the clearing, Pierce could see a layer of ash and fragments of charred bone spread beneath the undergrowth.

"How do we open it?"

*We do not, little brother. You do, and in the simplest way possible.* Harmattan held out his hand, and there was a rustling and rattling as the shards of metal that comprised his body shifted. A moment later, a small amulet rose out of his palm. *With the key.*

Pierce looked down at the medallion. He'd seen similar objects before: it was an essence disk, a magical tool designed to enhance the abilities of a warforged soldier.

"Why me? Any warforged could use this."

*Not this one. This is a relic of this ancient land, a key of a most unusual nature. Only a warforged designed to interface with it can make use of it. Hydra, Indigo—it will not interface properly with their auras.*

Pierce wanted to look at Lei, but he couldn't bring himself to do so. "What makes you think I can use it?"

*Because I could, if I still had a body, and you are my brother.*

"Indigo also calls me her brother."

*She speaks of our larger family, of the bond between the warforged, but you and I—we were built by the same hands, for a purpose beyond mere battle. Do you remember your creation, your first awakening?*

"No," Pierce said. "I . . . I have always assumed that age or damage has clouded my memory."

Even as he spoke, he remembered his vision beneath Sharn, when Lei had almost destroyed him. The room with six tables. Lei, lying on the slab next to him. The woman's voice, whispering.

"Protect my daughter."

*Perhaps.* Harmattan's voice broke the reverie, *or perhaps the knowledge was buried in your mind. Your mind is a magical engine, little brother—how do you know which memories are real?*

"This makes no sense. If I am the only one who can use the key . . . you came to Xen'drik without me. If we had not met, your mission would have failed."

*Faith. The warforged were not born by accident, little brother. We are part of a grand design, older than human civilization and far more ancient than House Cannith. When this key was placed in my keeping, I was assured that one would arrive who could use it—and so we found you.*

"What grand design? Who gave you the key?"

*These are not my secrets to tell, and you are not ready to hear them. You must learn faith, brother. Only then will your destiny be revealed.*

*Was he mad?* Pierce had never heard of warforged going insane, but if Indigo's story was true—if Harmattan had truly pulled himself back from the brink of death—such an experience would be bound to challenge the strongest mind. Pierce remembered the ravings of the changeling Hugal, who claimed that the people of Cyre could harness the power of the Mournland and turn it against their foes. Was Harmattan insane? On the other hand, his power was undeniable. Was a higher power acting through him? Did it have plans for Pierce—and for all the warforged? He glanced at Indigo, but she said nothing.

He took the essence disk from Harmattan's massive hand. "What do you want me to do?"

*Bond with the disk, than walk to the sigil. Stare into the glass until you see the flames, then command the door to open.*

"You said the door would destroy any creature that tried to force it."

*The key will protect you.*

"You may trust your nameless benefactor. I see no reason to do so."

*It doesn't matter. You have no choice. You will do as I say. It is why you are here.*

"I am not your slave, and if you destroy me, you still cannot open your door. I want information. If you expect me to use this key for you, you will start by telling me who gave it to you."

"Why are you doing this?" Indigo said, watching from the side.

"When I was a soldier, I served without question. You promised freedom. Do you even know what that is?"

Harmattan rustled. *You are a fool, little brother. You cannot fight fate, and you cannot bargain with me. I have been given all the tools I need, even if I did not see their value right away. I have you . . . and I have her.* Harmattan's glowing eyes turned toward Lei. *Disobey me, and she dies.*

Even as the words hung in the air, Pierce's mind was racing, evaluating the positions of the combatants and the actions he could take. The results were disillusioning. Despite his bold words earlier he wasn't sure he could defeat Indigo, though he would have the momentary advantage of surprise. Lei was surrounded. Even if Pierce could reach her in time and somehow scatter Hydra, he had no idea how to defeat Harmattan.

"Why should I care?" he said. The calculations had taken less than a second; hopefully Harmattan hadn't noticed the hesitation.

*So you don't care after all? Good.* He gestured, and two of Hydra's bodies grabbed Lei's arms. *Hydra!* he called. *I'd like to make a point to our brother Pierce. Please remove one of his fleshling's fingers.*

An instant later Lei cried out in pain. "Damn you!" she screamed, moaning.

Pierce moved toward her, but Harmattan slammed him to the ground with a single blow. He had no skeleton, but whatever force bound his body together gave him tremendous strength. *Do I tell Hydra to bind the wound, little brother, or should I move down to the wrist?*

*Protect my daughter.* It was a voice from a dream, but now Pierce realized that it had been with him all along, that on some level he'd known it was his purpose when he'd first laid eyes on Lei. *Protect my daughter.*

"I told you that I would destroy you if you harmed her."

*Fate seems to have other ideas.*

"Very well. I will do as you ask, but you will pay for this."

*I think not. I am doing this for you, little brother, and for all of us. In time, you will realize this. One day, you will kill her at my command.* He turned back toward Hydra. *Search that pack of hers. I suspect she has rope and bandages. Restrain her as you bind her wound—she won't be coming with us.*

The scouts pulled the wounded Lei to the ground, but even as they worked a rope gag into her mouth, she straightened up, staring straight at Harmattan. "I remember you," she said. "*I know who you are!*" The rope was pulled tight between her teeth, and any further words were lost.

*We have work to do, little brother. Hydra will stay with your fleshling to keep her safe. Of course, he will also be with us—and he will be watching you. Challenge me again, and she will pay the price. Now let us begin. Open the door.*

For now, there was no choice. Pierce set the amulet against his essence node, a small hollow in his sternum. He focused his thoughts and reached out to encompass the disk. There was a shifting of metal as the medallion was drawn fused to the node, and he felt its energy flowing into him—very old, very alien, nothing like the scouting disks he'd used in the war. An instant later, the bond was complete. He looked over at Lei then stepped onto the circle. Gazing down into the obsidian surface, he could see a faint flickering—patterns of flame in black and white fluttering in the shadows. As he watched, these grew more focused and pronounced.

*Open,* he thought. He could feel the disk grow warm, feel his thoughts being translated into some ancient tongue and spread across the ether.

The glass began to glow.

The shimmer of heat rose up through the air. As Pierce watched, the glass around his feet began to melt and flow, but it was contained, channeled—and a moment later it was cold again, and a spiral staircase led down into the darkness.

*You see, little one? No danger at all. Now let us go. Indigo, join Pierce in the lead—I don't want him setting off any defenses.*

Indigo walked up to Pierce. She'd slung her bow, and her blades were extended. She moved with a precision the human eye would never appreciate, and even now Pierce found her fascinating.

"Let go of this doubt," she said. "We are your family. We belong together, and we shall change this world."

"All we need to do is follow our orders," Pierce said, drawing his flail.

"It is our fight," she replied, studying the stairs and trying her foot on the first step. "Our leaders should not have to compel our loyalty. It is our duty to our race."

"How many times has a human made that same speech?"

Indigo had no reply. She made her way down the spiral staircase, and Pierce followed in silence.

Gerrion had dressed for the occasion.

The threadbare rogue Daine had met in Stormreach had been replaced by a dashing dandy. His clothes were black glimmersilk embroidered with red and orange flames, and he wore tall boots of red leather. His hair had been oiled and washed, and it was like a wreath of fire around his face. Only two traces of his old identity remained: the crossbow in his right hand and the glove on his left, black leather painted with interwoven flames.

"Daine!" He said, "I hope you enjoyed your rest and your meal. I do try to keep my promises." He studied Daine with a critical eye. "Are those burns I see? Have you been getting in fights again?"

"*Bastard!*" Daine yelled. He leapt forward, heedless of Gerrion's crossbow, ready to strangle the half-elf with his last breath, if that's what it took

He never reached the traitor. He'd forgotten about Zulaje, and even as he charged forward she swept him off his feet with a blow to the back of his legs. She could have easily severed his tendons, but she used the flat of the blade, so instead he found himself tumbling to the floor. He managed to catch himself before his face struck the floor, resting on his forearms.

"Bastard, but ours," Zulaje sang from behind him.

Gerrion smiled down at Daine and shrugged. "I'd stay there, if I were you. From what I hear, she's been in a bad mood."

From his vantage point on the floor, Daine saw that his adamantine dagger was tucked into the wide belt Gerrion wore around his waist.

"Why, Gerrion? Why would you do this to us?"

"You know nothing of my life," Gerrion said, and his voice was suddenly cold and deadly. He clenched his left fist, and the painted flames danced across his knuckles. "I lived in Stormreach for twenty years, waiting for your arrival. You and your lady are the key—the key that will lead me to immortality."

"And Lei?"

"Irrelevant. For decades I have waited for the child of war and the woman of two worlds, the man guided by voices from the past, who will open the way to our future. broken from his family, yet—"

"Oh, enough already!" Daine said. "I get it, so I'm—broken from my family? What do you know about that?"

"I did not lie to you earlier, Daine . . . well, not very much. I made many contacts in my decades in Stormreach, and Alina Lyrris *did* ask me to look out for you. She told me a great deal about you. Then you slew Sakhesh, and my hopes were confirmed."

"So you really do work for Alina, and you're going to cross her? You're even stupider than you look, and that's saying a lot."

Gerrion rolled his eyes, rising to his feet. "You have no idea what is at stake here. The wrath of a gnome half a world away? By the time we're finished, a whole nation of gnomes could not harm us."

"Sounds to me like you don't know many gnomes, but—"

A flaming blade smashed into the ground in front of Daine's face. "Silence, worm!" Zulaje called. "The Keeper of the Burning Gate approaches. On your knees for the speaker of law!"

"Do you want me to get *up* on my knees?" Daine asked. "Far be it for me to be rude to the speaker of law."

His only answer was the point of a red-hot blade, pressing into his back. He winced but didn't cry out. "Right. Stay down. Understood."

He could hear footsteps approaching—a troop of soldiers,

by the sound. Raising his head, he looked past Gerrion. He'd been so consumed by anger, he hadn't even noticed the chamber he was in.

It was enormous.

All surfaces were polished obsidian. The ceiling was a curved dome that rose nearly forty feet off the ground. He could see fire mirrored in the glass . . . but he was looking straight up, and there was no conflagration below to be reflected. It was as if the memory of fire had been trapped in the ceiling, a dim image of what had gone before. There were a few huge braziers scattered around the floor, providing more than enough light for Daine to see. A vast altar—twice the size of any he'd seen in a human church—was flanked by two basalt statues. Each of these figures was twenty feet high. They appeared to be squat, heavy-set men, each holding a greatsword, but the statues had been defaced, features chiseled away. At this point they were little more than massive silhouettes, black and featureless, towering over the chamber with swords at the ready.

A column of dark elves filed into the chamber, entering from a wide hallway to the north. The old priest Holuar walked at the head of the troop, carrying a long stone staff. Two acolytes followed him; their heads were shaved, revealing rings of flame tattooed around their scalps, and each carried an incense burner on a long chain. A squad of soldiers walked behind them. In the midst of these troops, Daine saw another familiar face: Lakashtai. The kalashtar had been stripped of her cloak, and there were burns and bruises across her pale skin, but her expression was as serene as ever, and she walked with no signs of a limp or pain. She inclined her head slightly when she caught sight of Daine. It was then that he noticed the unusual collar around her neck, an assembly of bronze, leather, and obsidian.

*Are you all right?* Daine thought, trying to push his thoughts in her direction. He'd grown so used to telepathic conversation that he expected an immediate response, but this time, there was none. Lakashtai smiled slightly as their eyes met, but if she could hear his thoughts, she gave no sign of it.

Holuar walked to the center of the chamber. Moving slowly and solemnly, he struck the floor of the chamber with his staff, calling out in a tongue Daine did not recognize. On the third blow, fire burst up around him. A pattern of golden flames spread out across the floor, a complex seal some thirty feet across and inscribed with words in a forgotten language. The fire flowed around Daine's feet, but the flames were cold.

"Firebinders!" Holuar called out, speaking with surprising volume for such an old man. He was talking in Elvish now, but somehow, inexplicably, Daine understood his meaning.

*Lakashtai?* he thought, but there was still no response.

"In ancient times, our masters gave us the power of the night and mastery of fire."

*"Fire and sword,"* the drow murmured.

"In ancient times we brought fear to the foe, spilling blood with fire and sword. The rebel, the monster, the breaker of oaths—all fell before us, and our masters were pleased."

*"Fire and sword."*

"Promises they made, of the reward that was to come. When the war was over, the Burning Gate would be opened, and we would be shown the path to paradise, to the realm of our power and eternal life."

*"Fire and sword."*

"The foul dragons snatched our destiny away from us. Even as our masters prepared the path to paradise, the jealous wyrm-kings descended on this land, devastating all in their path. Our masters were laid low, all knowledge and wisdom torn from their minds, but the dragons underestimated us. They saw us only as servants, as insects, beneath their notice. They did not see the gifts we had learned from our masters."

*"Fire and sword."* Daine almost joined in on the chant himself.

"We have drawn truth from the darkness. We have learned what must be done. When the season of flame is upon us, the opener of the way will come."

"Fire . . ." Daine caught himself. No one else was speaking, but they were all looking at him.

Holuar continued. "The cycle of flame has come and gone, more than six thousand times, and still we wait. No more. The blood of fire and blood of water brought our emissary into the world."

Gerrion stepped forward.

"You were sent to the place of storms, to watch for the child of war, led by the voice of the past. Have you fulfilled your duty?"

"Yes, speaker."

A murmur ran through the soldiers. Holuar struck his staff on the ground.

"Silence!" He pointed the staff at Gerrion. "You have failed us before, child. Do you have assurances?"

"I do, lord speaker." Gerrion turned to face Daine. "This one was born into a house of warriors, but he split from his house and lost his nation. The child of war, broken from his family, a man without a home. He is led by a voice from the past—a voice that speaks directly in his mind. He is accompanied by a woman of two worlds, who holds the key to that voice. She has been holding it at bay, and surely she can unleash it."

The murmuring rose again, and Holuar silenced it once more. "Continue."

"He brought down the priest of dragons, a mighty wielder of flame, and the water rose up to greet him." He paused here, as if trying to find the words. "A woman of water, speaking in the common tongue!"

Holuar glanced over toward Daine. "You have something to say, Zulaje?"

"Nothing I have not said before, Lord Holuar. I fear that this gray worm wastes our time, as he has done so often before. I fear that this legend holds us from our true destiny. How many generations have we stood at the threshold of the Burning Gate, when we could be spreading our fire across the jungles?"

"Beware, Zulaje," Holuar hissed. "Do you speak of abandoning our vows? Perhaps you wish to join the savages of the Broken Oath, since you have no respect for our way."

Zulaje walked forward. "I have more respect than you know, old one. I respect the power we have gained from our devotion." She spun her double sword, creating a dazzling wheel of fire. "I respect the fury of the flame—it is you who seeks to cage that fury, and even some among your own order grow weary of it. Let us return to the ways of *fire and sword*. Let those we fought so long ago fear us once again."

"ENOUGH!" Holuar roared. He slammed his staff into the

ground, and the cold fire flared up. "Six thousand cycles we have waited. Six thousand! And I tell you, Zulaje, the season has finally come. I have heard it in the crackling voice of the flame, as I have lain in trance. The time has come, war leader. The opener of the way walks this land. Even I have doubted in the past, but not today. This is the season that the Burning Gate will open."

Zulaje stilled her blade and inclined her head. "Then let us test our child of war, Lord Holuar."

He nodded. "Let the two be joined, and lead them to the labyrinth."

Zulaje spun, and the tip of her flaming sword stopped an inch from Daine's face. "Stand," she said in the Common tongue. "Unnecessary movement brings pain."

As he stood, the guards escorted Lakashtai over to him. Her hands were not bound, and she reached out and let two fingers trail across the back of his hand—a slight gesture, but he could feel the warmth in it; for her, he knew, it was the equivalent of an embrace. He took the hand and squeezed it, and she smiled slightly. The guards surrounding them lowered their spears, and marched them out of the room.

"Are you well?" Lakashtai said quietly. "You seem to have lost your eyebrows."

Daine tried to look up, but he couldn't see. "I had an accident with fire, but I'm all right. Should we be talking out loud?"

"We have no choice, I'm afraid. This collar—should I use my mental abilities, it will unleash a burst of flame that will burn through my neck, or so the man who put it on me said, and I know that he believed it."

"*I* didn't get one of those. I feel so unimportant."

"More likely, they need you alive," Lakashtai said. "They may have concluded that you'd do something rash and kill yourself quickly, if you were equipped with such a device."

"That does sound like me," Daine admitted, considering his aborted escape attempt. "What do we do now?"

"We wait, and we see what this test is. Perhaps you are this chosen one they seek. I have heard far stranger tales."

"Really? I've got two crowns in my purse that say otherwise."

She smiled again. "Then I hope we'll have time to put my

claim to the test, but now, it seems we have arrived at our destination."

The hall was a vast obsidian corridor, with no decorations or furnishings; it stretched forward into darkness, stretching on for hundreds of feet. A series of catwalks crisscrossed overhead, and Daine could see drow soldiers watching from above, crossbows at the ready. The ceiling stretched a short distance above the catwalks. Huge chunks of it were missing, revealing a view of a cloudy sky.

"Maybe it'll rain," Daine said to Lakashtai.

There was a line carved into the floor, and the guards prodded and pushed until Daine and Lakashtai crossed over it.

"Child of war!" Holuar called. "It is your destiny to open the Burning Gate, to unlock the path to the world beyond, but the way is blocked by hidden peril." He produced a small bronze orb from the sleeve of his robe and flung it forward. The sphere fell to the floor, rolled fifteen feet, and suddenly dissolved into a pool of molten, bubbling metal. "The deadly walls cannot be seen and shift with every passing moment. Only the voice that speaks within you can guide you safely through, so listen, and walk, and find the way to victory."

Daine turned around. "Invisible walls of death?"

Holuar spoke in the unknown tongue, and a wall of fire sprang up along the line carved in the ground, separating Daine and Lakashtai from the drow. The flames rose up to meet the catwalks and completely split the hallway. As Daine watched, it began to expand, creeping toward them inch by inch.

"Ah." Daine said. He glanced at Lakashtai. "Any ideas?"

# CHAPTER 42

XEN'DRIK
THE SUL'ASA
*Lharvion 22, 997 YK*

**W**hat is this place?" Pierce said.

The warforged had descended deep below the surface before coming to a large obsidian chamber with rough floors and a smooth, curved ceiling. The walls were filled with the reflections of ghostly flames—and it was these false fires that spread light across the room.

*A vault,* Harmattan replied. Though Pierce and Indigo had taken the lead, Harmattan and three of Hydra's bodies were close behind. *This land has seen many wars and rebellions. This is a storage facility, holding supplies . . . though we have come here to rescue a prisoner.*

"A prisoner?" Pierce considered the level of brush they'd cut away to reveal the entrance, the thick layer of bone and ash. "How long has he been trapped down here?"

*Over thirty thousand years. Our quarry is no creature of flesh and blood. I told you, little brother. Our roots are far older than House Cannith.*

Harmattan gestured to Indigo. There was only one tunnel leading away from the entry hall, and she began to creep down it, Pierce at close behind. After a few steps Indigo paused, holding up a hand.

"Look at the ceiling," she said. There was a fine smattering of fracture lines across the glass. "There is power in the hall—a sentry spirit, as there was above. I believe this hallway is set to collapse."

*Better the treasures be lost to all than stolen, it seems. Little brother, let Indigo show you to the perimeter of the sentry's watch. Contact it. Tell it to . . . maintain, and lest you think of giving other instructions—failure in this matter will prove most painful for your dear lady.*

Indigo traced a line across the floor with a finger, and Pierce stepped up to it. He looked out into the hall, studying the illusory flames on the walls. As before, the flames grew brighter. There was something, a presence, like a wisp of smoke at the back of his mind. Maintain, he thought, conjuring images of stability. A wall. A block of ice.

"I believe that it is safe," he said at last.

*Hydra, take point once. Indigo to follow.*

As one, the three Hydras took a single step forward and turned to face each other. A second passed. "Very well," they said together, and the one to the left walked toward Pierce. He limped slightly; of the three, he had suffered the most damage when the displacer beasts attacked.

As Hydra crossed the sentry line, Pierce felt the faintest tension, as if a thought was trying to worm its way out of his mind. Maintain, he thought, pushing back against the pressure. Indigo followed the first Hydra, but the ceiling held above her.

*Well done. Follow Indigo. I'll be right behind you.*

The passage curved to the east, slowly dropping further below the earth. Finally it came to an end, opening into a large, dark room. There were no flames bound into the walls of this chamber, but Indigo was prepared. She tapped her left shoulder, and a ball of cold fire rose up into the air. This drifted just behind her head, casting a cone of light out in front of her.

They were in a vast, empty hall. The walls and floor were made of a tough ceramic material that absorbed light and sound. It was impossible to judge the length of the chamber; it seemed to be a void stretching off into infinity. There were no objects in the hall, nothing that could be used to judge size or distance . . . until Pierce saw the guardian.

The sentinel was an enormous man, twenty feet tall. He had a heavyset bulk reminiscent of a dwarf; he was massively muscled, and his shoulders were more than seven feet across. His skin and robe were jet black, as was his spiky hair and bristling beard, and his mouth was set in a permanent sneer, but even as Pierce raised his flail, he realized that the fierce expression was still as stone, and the giant's eyes were fixed straight ahead. This sentry was an obsidian statue.

Statue or not, it was superlative work. It appeared to have been carved from a single block of glass . . . or given what he'd seen at the stairs, perhaps it had been *shaped* instead of carved. It held an immense greatsword above its head, almost seventeen feet in length. Staring into its blank eyes, Pierce thought of the spirits trapped in this vault, and he wondered—could this thing be alive? He reached out with his thoughts, trying to sense the emanations he'd caught before, but he felt nothing.

Just as well, he thought.

*Indigo?* Harmattan had entered the chamber.

"The chamber appears safe. However, the compartments are warded. Breaking these wards—it will not be a simple task, but it is possible."

Even as she spoke, Pierce saw the compartments she was speaking of. The walls of the hall were covered with them: square, flat panels recessed into the surface of the walls, each marked with characters in an alphabet he didn't know. After a moment, he realized that these were the same language as the markings he and Lei had found on the pillars back by the stone map.

"We cannot open these doors with the key?"

*No,* Harmattan hissed. *The key . . . it is not so much a key as a lock-pick. It was not created by those who made this vault but rather by their enemies. Unfortunately for us, those who built the vault thought to add a second system of defense.* He began walking along the edge of the northern wall, studying the panels. Indigo stayed with him; Pierce started to explore the other wall, but once he drifted too far from Indigo the darkness became too deep.

*This is the one,* Harmattan said. He stood aside, and Indigo produced a series of small tools; Pierce had seen Lei use similar items when breaking down protective wards.

"Our prisoner is in there?" Pierce said, still puzzled.

*Yes,* Harmattan replied. *With his help, we shall unlock the gates of Karul'tash, and then—we shall see what fate has in store for us.*

*Karul'tash*—the name was familiar, but Pierce couldn't place it. He watched Indigo. She worked in silence, her attention completely focused on the task. A moment later, the sigil in the center of the panel began to glow, and this light spread out in a vertical line. Once the door was bisected, the panel swung inwards with a faint *hiss*. The chamber within was rectangular, padded with dark fabric. It held one object: a metal sphere two inches in diameter. It was forged from silver or mithral and polished to a mirror finish, its surface studded with red and gold dragonshards.

*Yes,* Harmattan said. *We have found it.* He reached forward and drew the sphere out of the vault; it was almost lost in his massive hand.

"This is a prisoner?" Pierce said.

*It is a vessel—a housing for sentience, not unlike our own. It—*He paused abruptly and raised the sphere closer to his glowing eyes. *Something is wrong. I can barely sense the energies within.*

Indigo glanced at the sphere. "Perhaps we chose the wrong vault. It would be dangerous, but I could try to open another."

*No. This is the key, and we would not have been sent all this way or found our brother Pierce, if this was not the path of destiny. There must be an answer.*

Harmattan looked at Pierce and extended his hand. *Perhaps—*

And the sword came down.

The glass giant in the center of the room had sprung to life. It had no joints, but it moved anyway, as if obsidian were as flexible as flesh. The massive great sword slammed through Harmattan's right arm and completely severed it. Whatever force was binding the arm together dissolved, and it disintegrated into a mass of metal shards, falling to the floor. The sphere was thrown from his hand and rolled into the darkness.

Harmattan *hissed* in rage. Even as the glass giant raised its sword for another blow, Harmattan flew forward, exploding into a whirlwind of steel. The shattered remnants of his arm were swept up off of the floor to join the storm of razors. The maelstrom struck the statue with the sound of a hundred knives on glass, and slivers of stone scattered through the air.

*"INDIGO, STAND READY!"* Harmattan's voice thundered through the chamber, louder than Pierce would have thought possible. *"PIERCE, HYDRA, FIND THAT ORB!!!"*

Pierce had seen the sphere fall, and he traced the path

through the darkness. Behind him, he could hear the blade of the glass warrior smashing into the floor. Harmattan might be indestructible, but he was at his deadliest when fighting creatures of flesh; he was slowly chipping away the surface of the statue, but it would take time to bring it down.

"*NOW!*"

Turning, Pierce saw that Harmattan had drawn back from the giant and was reforming his humanoid shape. Indigo spun forward, her adamantine blades glittering in the darkness. Pierce had seen Daine cut through stone and steel with his adamantine dagger, and Indigo's swords were just as strong. She moved with inhuman speed and precision, dodging a blow that would have split her in two and rolling between the statue's legs. Coming up behind it, she slashed at its ankles, and her blades carved deep gouges in the stone.

The animated statue was faster than Pierce would have thought possible. Even as Indigo regained her balance from the blow, the giant caught her with a swift kick. The blow swept her off her feet and threw her back into the darkness.

For a moment, Pierce was torn. It was Harmattan who had threatened Lei. Pierce no longer knew what he believed about his destiny, his family, or his people, but he couldn't stand by and watch Indigo die. He charged, drawing his flail and setting the chain in motion. Daine would have called out, issuing a triumphant battlecry. For Pierce, purpose was enough. The sentry had turned away from him to finish Indigo, and Pierce swung the flail as hard as he could, striking the damaged ankle with a resounding crash. Glass shards flew through the air. Despite his strength, Pierce's weapon was mere steel, and it didn't have the bite of Indigo's strange blades, but he had drawn its attention. It turned toward him, the obsidian blade spinning down . . .

And Harmattan dove between them.

His razor cloak was spread wide, and it absorbed the full force of the blow without breaking. It was a wall of steel, and it came between Pierce and death.

*Careful, little brother,* Harmattan said. *Your role in this game is far from over.*

Pierce simply stepped to the side. Indigo had returned, and

her blades were almost invisible as she slashed at the giant again and again.

"Brother!" she called. "Strike from the opposite side!"

He did, timing his blow to match hers. His flail could not match her blades, but his strength made the difference, and the obsidian leg shattered beneath the combined assault. For a moment the giant turned, trying to maintain its balance and spot the tiny creatures below, then it toppled. The terrible injury must have broken the animating magic, for it stiffened as it fell, and when it struck the ground it shattered into hundreds of pieces.

"Satisfactory," Indigo said, looking at Pierce. "You are a dangerous opponent, brother, but do you truly think you can match me?"

"Perhaps we shall put my projections to the test," Pierce said. He felt a strange . . . *pleasure* as he spoke the words. He had fought in more battles than he could remember. He had even served with warforged before, but with Indigo—somehow, their movements complimented each other perfectly. It wasn't battle—it was music.

*Enough,* said Harmattan. *The sphere! Where is it?*

"I have not yet found it," Hydra said, speaking from three corners of the hall. "If you could produce more light . . ."

Illumination filled the chamber—a cold glow emanating from Harmattan himself. *Be quick.*

Pierce returned to the region he had been searching before, over by the entrance to the hall. He contemplated the broken hallway beyond, touching the spirit that held the ceiling in place.

"You fought well." Indigo had followed him. "But it was foolish of you to join the fray with such an ineffective weapon."

"I couldn't let you fight alone."

"Why is that?"

Before Pierce could speak, Hydra called out, his three voices hissing across the darkness. "No! What is she *doing?*"

For a moment, Pierce stared at Indigo. She was beautiful, in a way no human could ever be. A weapon, swift and deadly. Just as he was.

"Stay down," he said, and knocked her off of her feet with a savage blow from the butt of his flail. He was already turning as she fell, racing down the tunnel as fast as he could. *Maintain*, he thought.

*PIERCE!* It took only seconds for Harmattan to respond. Pierce could hear metal tearing against glass as his brother followed him, but he didn't stop to look until he reached the chamber on the other side, with the spiral staircase rising upwards.

In his whirlwind form Harmattan was far faster than any man. He was already halfway across the hall when Pierce turned. Pierce could see the gleaming eyes within the storm of razors, beacons of fury. *PIERCE!* He howled again, a loud and deadly wind.

*Release.*

And the shattered ceiling came tumbling down.

It was over in an instant. Where there had once been a passage, there was simply a wall of rubble. Pierce thought of Indigo and wondered if she'd been caught in the tunnel or if she'd remained in the far chamber—and which would have been the greater mercy. He remembered the beauty of the motion as she struck the giant's ankle with both blades.

*Protect my daughter.*

He took only a moment to make certain that silver orb was safe in his belt pouch, where he'd put it before turning to fight the giant. Then he slowly made his way up the long spiral staircase leading to the surface.

Pieces of Hydra were scattered across the clearing. It was a familiar sight, and Pierce knew what had happened even before he saw Lei. She was unbound and ungagged. She held the dark-wood staff in her bandaged right hand. The left was pointed at him, and the air around it rippled with magical energy. Her face was a mask of fury.

"*You*," she said. "We fought before, Pierce. This time you won't be coming back."

CHAPTER 43  XEN'DRIK
THE SUL'ASA
*Lharvion 22, 997 YK*

**A** drow warrior was watching Daine from the catwalk, crossbow at the ready. More than anything else, she seemed bored—supremely uninterested in the spectacle below.

*I guess they don't think much of my chances.*

"Can Tashana guide us through this?" Daine said.

"What?"

Daine had never seen Lakashtai look confused until now. Perhaps it was the loss of her hood and cloak, which had always seemed to serve her as spiritual armor. Without it, she was a woman in a torn tunic, her pale skin glistening with sweat from the fire. Fear and uncertainty just seemed to add to her beauty; in that moment, she seemed more human than ever before. Looking at her, Daine felt that he was seeing her for the first time, and for a moment he was at a loss for words, but the searing heat from the wall of flame was a painful reminder that time was running out. He tore his gaze away and forced himself to pull his thoughts together.

"You heard Gerrion. This whole prophecy hinges on this voice in my head—the one you've been 'holding at bay'. That's what's supposed to get us through this thing alive." He glanced out across the apparently empty hall. "Or maybe it's some sort of twisted game, and there's no maze out there at all."

Lakashtai shook her head. "That's ridiculous. Tashana can only touch you when you're dreaming, and even if you gave her possession of your body, she doesn't have the power to guide you through this labyrinth."

The wall of flame was drawing close, and Daine's skin was slick with sweat. Reaching into his pouch, he drew out a copper coin. "I don't know," he said. "I can't say as I'm keen to give that witch more of a hold in my mind, but the elves seem pretty sure about it—and I don't see how things can get any worse."

"She can't help us, Daine."

"What makes you so sure? Is there a thousand-year-old prophecy backing *you* up?" Daine threw the coin in front of him; it flew three feet and disintegrated, dissolving before his eyes. Daine sighed and took a step forward, staying just ahead of the encroaching flame.

"They're *wrong*, Daine. I know Tashana. You don't. She can't help us. She wouldn't if she could, and I'll kill us both before I give you to her."

"A few more minutes and you won't have to." Daine took out another coin and tossed it to the left; it went five feet before vaporizing. "Come on. I've got five more crowns to my name . . . That'll buy us some time."

It took two more coins to find a path that led ahead, getting them five feet further from the creeping wall of flame. Daine shivered—it was a strange feeling standing in an empty room, but knowing that death could be just an inch away.

"I wonder if these 'shifting walls' can move on top of us while we're standing still," he mused.

"Most likely." Lakashtai idly traced a finger along the edge of the leather collar wrapped around her neck.

Daine looked up at the catwalk stretching above them. On a whim, he flung one of his remaining coins at the drow guard; it struck her squarely in the forehead. She glared down at him and spat, and her aim was just as good as his.

"Interesting," he said, wiping his face. "No barriers above us. If we could just get up there . . ."

"A simple task," Lakashtai said.

"*How?*" He could feel the temperature rising as the burning wall drew close once more.

"I could levitate myself. I believe I could support both our weight."

"So *do* it!"

Lakashtai shook her head. "A simple task under normal circumstances, but should I engage my mental abilities, I will trigger this collar, and it will burn through my neck."

The flames crept closer.

Daine gritted his teeth. "Any ideas that would actually *work*?"

Lakashtai gazed into the distance, and the creeping fire was reflected in her emerald eyes. "It is possible . . . I could try to divert the energy generated by the collar, converting it into a less dangerous form of energy—light, perhaps. However, the act of raising this shield would itself trigger the collar—I might not survive long enough to complete the manifestation."

The flames were a foot away. "Lakashtai, I've only got two crowns left . . ."

"I believe I could survive. If . . ." She met his gaze, and he could see the uncertainty in her eyes. " . . . If you would share the pain with me."

"What?"

"I could . . . empathically transfer the experience, spreading the agony between us, but I do not know the power of the collar. It could kill us both."

The flames were licking at Daine's back, and it was becoming hard to breathe. "Just *do* it!" he shouted.

Lakashtai seized his hands. Time slowed to a crawl. The roaring flames faded to a dull whisper, and all he felt was the touch of his skin against hers. Staring into Lakashtai's eyes, Daine felt a deep sense of peace, of serenity. As her eyes began to glow, he felt . . .

Agony.

In an instant, reality came tumbling back. The hot air seared his lungs, but it was nothing compared to the blinding pain that was tearing into his neck. He could feel the skin charring, the terrible heat eating away at the flesh beneath. He drew in breath to scream . . .

And it was over.

The torment had forced all thoughts from his mind. A dark shape pressed against him, a woman, covered with sweat. She wrapped her arms around him.

"Hold me," she said.

"Lei," he whispered, pulling her close.

Then he was in the air. He clutched at the woman, and as sense and memory came flooding back, he recognized Lakashtai. He almost let go of her, but they were ten feet off the ground and rising quickly, and reflex made him tighten his grip.

Within seconds they had risen to the level of the glass catwalk. Though the pain was no worse, Daine's neck was still in agony; the cracked skin ached with every motion, but he couldn't afford to give into the pain. The guard had seen them, and she was already raising her crossbow.

Summoning all his strength, Daine let go of Lakashtai and *shoved* her, using the force to fling himself backward onto the catwalk. Even as the dark elf leveled her weapon, Daine was tumbling toward her. He felt a flash of pain as the quarrel grazed his back, tearing a furrow across a shoulder-blade, but then he was upon her. The elf was small and quick, her black skin crisscrossed with spiraling flame tattoos, and she dropped her crossbow and grabbed at her sword as Daine rose up before her, but she wasn't fast enough. Daine slammed into her, throwing all his rage and pain into one mighty blow. She fell back, struggled to find her balance—and failed. She spun off the edge of the catwalk, and disappeared into the massive wall of flame that stretched out below.

"That's what you get when you play with fire," Daine muttered, as the scream faded.

*Daine, quickly! Toward me!* Lakashtai's thought forced its way through his mind. *We don't have long!*

She was right. The wall of flame had been a deadly threat—but it had also served to shield their actions from view. The battle had drawn the attention of Gerrion and the others, and if Gerrion's archery wasn't threat enough, Daine was certain the old priest could bring magic to bear.

The thought proved all too prophetic. Even as Daine turned toward Lakashtai, he heard the old elf calling out to the powers of flame. Daine threw himself forward as a pillar of fire struck the platform behind him, melting the space he had been standing on.

*Quickly!* Lakashtai was standing thirty feet further down the bridge, her neck swathed in a halo of golden light. A drow soldier was charging at her with his spear lowered, but the kalashtar raised her hand and stood her ground. A cone of sparkling green light blazed forth from her palm, and the elf staggered back and fell; as Daine drew closer, he saw that each sparkling light had been a shard of crystal, and this storm of glass had shredded the flesh of the unfortunate elf.

"Hold tight," she whispered, wrapping her arms around him once more.

This time Daine could see clearly, and for a moment he found it strangely difficult to obey the command, but she was holding on to him, and as she began to rise into the air reflex took over and locked her in his arms.

Lakashtai had brought them beneath one of the gaping holes in the ceiling, and now they rose up and out of the chamber. The roof was surprisingly thick, but a moment later they were out in open air, gazing out across the orange and red canopy of the jungle. From this perspective, the castle was a ruin. The battlements were uneven, the towers were shattered, and there were a dozen holes in the roof, but as old and damaged as it was, there was one thing that truly stood out: it was on fire.

The entire fortress was built from obsidian, and the outermost walls were brilliant orange. The heat was even worse that the wall of flame. The roof around them looked like it might actually be molten; Daine couldn't see what was keeping it from flowing down into the chambers below.

For a moment they hung there, just above the burning castle.

"What are you waiting for?" Daine whispered. His neck ached, and he was all too aware of the pit below them. "Let's go!"

"It is not that simple," Lakashtai replied, studying the molten glass. "It is a trivial matter to move across the vertical axis, but horizontal motion is—"

"Just do *something!*"

"Lift up your feet."

"*What?*"

*Do it!* The thought was a command, and the next thing he knew, Daine's feet were wrapped tightly around Lakashtai's waist. To his utter surprise, she actually closed her eyes . . . and charged forward into the glass.

The roof was just as hot as it appeared, and her feet sunk deep into the molten surface. She should have been burnt to ash, but instead, there was a flash of light.

*The shield!*

It seemed that the mental field she had created to protect against the collar extended across her entire body. As Daine watched, she pulled her foot free and took another step forward. Her feet were surrounded by a blinding radiance, as the heat of the molten glass was transformed into pure light. Step by step, Lakashtai pulled them across the boiling roof, until they finally reached the edge of the wall.

"One moment more," Lakashtai said, her voice barely a whisper.

She had opened her eyes, and for the moment the serene mask of the kalashtar had fallen; her face was filled with pain and pure determination. She stepped off the edge of the shattered battlement, and they fell toward the earth.

Seconds later they hit the ground. Lakashtai's powers held to the last second, but as soon as they touched soil she released Daine and fell forward. She would have collapsed if he hadn't caught her by the shoulders to steady her.

"It's all right," he said. "Let me carry you."

He swept her off her feet and ran for the cover of the foliage. Behind him, he could hear sentries calling out in the musical tongue of the elves, but he didn't stop to try to decipher the meaning, and a moment later he was hidden in the cool darkness of the jungle.

❧ ❧ ❧ ❧ ❧ ❧ ❧

The next hour was a blur as they forced their way deeper into the jungle. Daine didn't even try to find a path; he just tumbled recklessly forward, trying to put as much distance as he could between them and the burning castle. He plunged on, struggling to ignore his aching muscles and the collar of seared flesh around his neck, but he could only stay ahead of the pain for so long. Eventually he stumbled and collapsed to the ground, his breath coming in ragged gasps.

*Relax.* Lakashtai was fighting to catch her breath, but she had at least regained her mental composure. *We can afford a moment's rest.* She reached up and touched the leather collar. Daine saw a flash of emerald light around her fingers, and a new bolt of agony shot through his nerves. When his vision cleared again, Lakashtai was holding the collar in one hand. The leather had been cleanly severed.

*I'm sorry,* she thought. *I needed to cut it loose before my shield failed.*

Beneath the collar, Lakashtai's neck was a mass of charred skin and burnt muscle; it looked every bit as bad as Daine felt. He touched his own skin and winced in pain—but as bad as it felt, he didn't seem to have the physical injuries he saw on Lakashtai . . . just the pain. As he watched, Lakashtai raised her hands and wrapped them around her neck; she closed her eyes for a moment, and when she removed her hands, the wounds were gone, her skin fresh and unblemished, but he felt exactly the same, his skin throbbing with the imagined burns.

"I wish I could take the pain back from you," she said, opening her eyes, "but I can only perform such adjustments on my own flesh. We would not have escaped without your courage and strength, and I hope you can bear this torture a little longer."

"I'm fine," Daine said, trying to keep his voice steady.

She took his hand, and for that moment, at least, the pain seemed to fade. "You saved my life, Daine. I will not forget that."

Her gaze was intense, and Daine forced himself to look away. "I'd say that we both did our share of saving."

She placed her hand on his cheek, slowly turning his face back toward hers. Her hair was disheveled, and there was blood and ash on her face, but her eyes were brilliant jewels. "Daine—"

Then the world exploded.

"I have *had* it with fire!" Daine shouted. The bolt of flame had just missed them, but Daine had been caught in the splash and he slapped at a few smoldering patches on his clothing.

*"Do not move!"*

The words were Elvish and coming from the air. A second later, the source of sound and flame came into view. At first Daine thought he was looking at an airship, a Lyrandar airship being ridden by giants, but it was a sled, not a ship—a narrow sled of dark wood, about nine feet in length. A ring of fire was wrapped around the waist of the sled, just like that of a Lyrandar airship—a burning ring of elemental flame, the power that held the vehicle aloft. One elf was lying down on his stomach, stretched out along the front of the sleigh. He wore a strange helmet formed of brass and obsidian, studded with what Daine guessed were dragonshards. This helmet concealed his eyes, but his dark skin and the fire tattoos left no doubt as to his nature.

A second elf stood just in front of the burning ring. He held a dark staff inscribed with symbols of brass. It was attached to a rotating stock set into the center of the sled. Daine knew a weapon when he saw one, and considering this was pointed at them, it wasn't hard to guess where the bolt of flame had come from.

"On your knees!" The firesled hovered in midair, and the staffsman adjusted his aim.

*Any more tricks up your sleeve?* Daine thought.

*I am afraid not,* Lakashtai thought, *and the shield I had manifested has faded. I can offer no protection.*

*Then I guess it's up to me,* Daine said, dropping to his knees.

He glanced around the trees, looking for *something* he could use as a weapon, praying for inspiration to strike. At first, he saw nothing. Then there was a flash of motion, a glitter of metal in the darkness.

A long silver chain lashed out from the trees and wrapped around the throat of the staffsman. Even as his hands flew to his neck, he was pulled from the sled; he fell screaming to the ground, the chain dangling behind him. Realizing he was in danger, the pilot set the vessel in motion, but it was too late; there was a *whirring* sound, and Daine saw two dark disks strike the drow. The ring of fire burst into life, and the sled leapt forward. A moment later, Daine heard the roar of a distant explosion; whether he'd been killed or simply wounded, it seemed that the pilot had lost control of his vehicle.

Daine stood and turned to Lakashtai. "Let's go," he said. "Quickly—"

It was too late.

Three dark shapes detached themselves from the shadows. Pale chitin armor gleamed in the light of day. The leader held a three-pronged throwing wheel in his right hand, and a scorpion sat on his left.

"Our paths cross again, outlander," Shen'kar said. "Now we speak of fire."

# CHAPTER 44

Lei let go of her staff, and it fell to the ground. She didn't need it to deal with Pierce. Her hands were far more dangerous than any weapon—if she could touch him, she could tear him apart from within.

While she'd fought Pierce once before, she didn't expect this battle to follow the same path. The first time Pierce had been driven into a rage, unhinged by the powers of the mind flayer Chyrassk. Now he was in full control of himself, and he knew her capabilities as well as she did. As soon as her words had registered, Pierce dropped his flail and backed away from her. His bow was in his hands, though he was pointing it at the ground. He was fast, and under normal circumstances she'd never be able to close the distance to touch him, but she'd had a few moments to prepare. She'd magically enhanced her own speed and even woven an enchantment that would protect her from Pierce's arrows. She was ready for the traitor, but she needed to act quickly. Surely the others would be here at any moment.

"I do not wish to hurt you, Lei," Pierce's voice was calm and somber. "This has been a confusing time, but I have always sought to protect you."

"What do you call this?" She held up her maimed hand, with only a stump in place of her smallest finger. Hydra had bandaged the wound, but the injury still throbbed, and she was terrified to think how it might affect her work.

287

"That . . . is my fault. Harmattan used you to manipulate me. He threatened to kill you unless I agreed to help him."

"So you did all of this for *me*," Lei said.

"No. No, I did not. I was uncertain, curious to know what my life could be—what it would be, without you or Daine." He paused. "There are things you and I will never share, Lei. I understand that, but I am a warforged, and I was made for a purpose. That purpose was to protect you."

"*Liar!*" The loss of Daine, her wounded hand—Lei's thoughts were a maze of pain and anguish, and she barely followed Pierce's words. It was a trick. He was delaying, covering for the others who would soon emerge. She charged at Pierce, hands out, already envisioning the powers she would draw on to destroy him. She knew what he would do: dart to the side, loose a volley of arrows, try to maintain the space between them.

He didn't.

He didn't try to run from her, and he didn't raise his bow. He simply stood there, even as she laid a hand on his chest. He just watched her. His face was as expressionless as always, but she had learned to read his moods in his stance and the tension in his limbs. He wasn't going to fight.

For a moment she stood with her hand pressed against his torso. She could feel the cold metal, and in her mind she could sense the energies within—the pattern that gave life to stone and steel. A voice screamed inside of her: *Destroy him! Destroy all of them!* She'd thought it would be easier, but she'd thought he would fight back. Looking at his face, it was hard to hold onto the anger. Instead, she found herself thinking of the night they'd arrived in Sharn, when he'd carried her sobbing from the doorstep of Hadran's manor, of the battle at Keldan Ridge, and of the vision she'd had the first time they fought.

She slammed her left fist against his torso. "*Fight*, damn you!"

"I cannot." Pierce placed a hand over hers, pressing it against his chest. "Destroy me if you must, but I will not fight you again, nor will I allow you to come to any harm that I can prevent."

Blinking back tears, she held up her left hand, the maimed finger plain to see.

Pierce looked away. "Do what you must, my lady. If my failure cannot be forgiven, let my punishment be swift."

Lei clenched her wounded hand, feeling the burning pain. She gathered the energies once more. She reached out with her mind, feeling the familiar patterns of his lifeforce, the tapestry she'd mended so many times before.

For a moment they stood in silence. Then, slowly, she took her hand off his chest. "Where are the others?" she said at last.

"Destroyed or trapped below. It makes no difference. They will not trouble us again."

Lei looked at him. "How? What defeated them? How did you escape?"

"I defeated them," Pierce said, "though I had to wait for you to free yourself."

Lei thought about the way Pierce had been speaking with the blue warforged, and an ember of suspicion flared up again. "I thought they were your new family."

"I have a family," Pierce said, "and you are a part of it." He walked past her, and picked up his flail, replacing it in its harnesses. "Earlier, you said that you knew Harmattan. What did you mean?"

"I . . ." Lei paused.

She wanted to explain, but somehow it was difficult to force the words out. It had been a year since her strange dream, and she'd never mentioned it to Pierce. Somehow, when she tried to speak, her brain and her tongue just refused to act.

Pierce noticed her discomfort. "What is it? Are you in pain?"

"I . . ." Lei closed her eyes and collected her thoughts. "I had a vision last year, beneath Sharn. I've had others, since then. I . . . I think my parents may have created Harmattan."

Pierce nodded slowly. "Why is that?"

"In one of my dreams . . . My father, he held up a piece of a warforged, a head. I remember him saying 'This is how you defeat death.' Harmattan keeps his face hidden, and when I saw it that once, it was battered and scorched, but it was him. I'm sure of it now. I don't know how they did it, but my parents made him."

"And they made me."

She nodded, slowly.

"I have had one of these visions as well, but I do not think it was a dream. I think it was a memory."

Lei shook her head. "No . . . my visions have drawn on current events, on my surroundings. They're just dreams. They must be." She remembered a jeweled blade poised above her eye, and she shuddered.

Pierce considered this carefully. "If not memories . . . what if these are visions of the present?"

"What?"

"Perhaps someone is watching us. Monitoring you from within."

*This is our daughter, not just another experiment!*

The words echoed through Lei's mind, but her mother wasn't the only voice she heard.

*All that is flesh must perish,* her father said, *we knew that from the start.*

Harmattan hissed: *You destroy failures. It is the way of your house, and I was not talking about humanity. I was talking about you.*

"You said you saw Harmattan—as a severed head," Pierce continued, "but he was built with the body of a warforged soldier. You were an adult when I saw you. Did you see Hydra in your visions?"

"No."

"Yet in many ways, Hydra was just as strange as Harmattan. Would you have any idea how to create such a warforged?"

"No," Lei said. "A personality spread between multiple bodies? I can't begin to imagine it. The sensory input alone would overwhelm a normal spirit."

"But you said you'd seen similar designs . . ."

Lei completed the sentence. "At Keldan Ridge."

"You're certain it wasn't a Cannith forgehold?"

"At this point, I'm not certain of anything," Lei replied, "but there were so many strange varieties of warforged there— economically, it didn't make any sense. You don't hand-craft warforged, and they didn't have the house markings."

"Can anyone else create warforged?"

"Not without the Mark of Making, no. Except . . ." Lei paused. "I'm sure you've heard the stories—that the secrets of the warforged are hidden in Xen'drik, that Cannith expeditions built the first creation forges using knowledge stolen from Xen'drik. My parents came to Xen'drik, too. The sahuagin guide on the *Kraken's Wake,* he said something about it . . . 'She wanted to find ways to improve the warforged, but she did not want to share this knowledge with her kin.' " *And she spoke of her desire for a daughter,* Lei thought, but she kept the thought within. "What if . . . what if there was a conspiracy in House Cannith, a group that was creating new warforged for some purpose aside from selling them?"

"Did you not say that Aaren d'Cannith despised what the house was doing with his creations?"

"Yes . . . yes, I did," Lei said, "but Aaren hated the idea of war. I can't imagine him building the army we saw at the ridge. Besides, he was excoriated."

"So were you . . . and your parents."

Lei's eyes grew wide. "You're right. My parents. I never understood why Merrix would move against them, but what does Merrix know about them? Do you think . . . do you think they might still be alive?"

"I do not know, Lei. All I know is that Harmattan was doing the bidding of another. Perhaps if we follow his path, we can learn the identity of this hidden master."

Lei nodded, and she crossed the clearing and retrieved her staff. "What do we know about Harmattan's plans?"

"He was searching for this." Pierce produced the silver sphere, and it glittered in the sunlight. "He called it a prisoner. He said it would 'unlock the gates of Karul'tash.' "

"Karul'tash?" Lei frowned. "Karul'tash. The Monolith of Karul'tash. That's where we were going. That's where Lakashtai said we could find what we needed to help Daine."

"Then if we only had Daine, I would call this a sign of destiny."

"Let me see that," Lei said. "It seems familiar, but I just can't place it. A sphere . . . Xen'drik . . ." She took the orb from Pierce's hands and almost dropped it in surprise.

It recognized her.

The instant she touched the orb, she felt a wave of thought pass over her—a sense of identity, almost like looking at a human face. It was distant, faint, but she knew that there was a consciousness within the sphere . . . and that it was aware of her. The sense of recognition was not strong. It wasn't the feeling she'd get from seeing a friend, but rather one of seeing a man in a familiar uniform, of knowing *that's a member of the Sharn Watch.*

"Hello?" she said cautiously.

"Greetings?" Pierce replied.

Lei shook her head and pointed at the orb. "I was . . . did you feel anything when you were holding it?"

Pierce shook his head.

Lei turned her attention back to the orb. She could sense that it was aware of her, but there was something . . . in the way. It was like looking at a lantern covered by a blanket. Reaching into her backpack, she produced a pearl; she'd found these stones to be an effective focus for divinatory energies. Touching the pearl to the silver sphere, she reached out with her mind, studying the orb.

It was beautiful.

Seen through the lens of magic, it was an intricate web of golden threads, burning with pulses of light. "It's an . . . information matrix," she said, wonderingly. "I think it's alive—not quite alive as you, but self-aware. Conscious. Just imagine—this must have seen the civilization of the giants!"

"How can we communicate with it?" Pierce said.

"That's the strangest part. I think . . . it looks like it's designed to interface with a warforged, to attach to your essence node, but it must be tens of thousands of years old."

"So it seems that Cannith didn't create the warforged after all."

"I'm not sure I'd go that far," Lei said. "It may be that Cannith explorers adapted a few design elements from Xen'drik golems, and the essence node was one of them."

"There is only one way to be certain. Attach it to me."

"We have no idea what it might do to you!"

"Harmattan said it was the key."

"He also said it was a prisoner!" Lei exclaimed. "It could be a demon, a monster—who knows what?"

"Study it further. Do you think there's a danger of it seizing control of my body?"

Lei closed her eyes, reaching out through the pearl. "I . . . I don't think so, but it's difficult to say. The design is like nothing I've seen before."

"Attach it to me. If it can lead us to this Karul'tash, perhaps we can find Daine and the others. Lakashtai said nothing about a key, so she may not know it is necessary. It could be our only chance to find them."

Lei grimaced, but eventually nodded. She examined his torso, and Pierce released the metal disk he had attached earlier.

"What's this?" she said, pulling it loose.

"Harmattan gave it to me—it is the key that opened the gates of this vault."

"Interesting," she said, tucking it in a pouch. "Now . . . here it goes."

She pressed the orb against his socket in his chest. As she watched, the node shifted shape; metal softened and flowed in to surround the sphere. After a few moments had passed, the orb had been almost fully absorbed into Pierce's body—only a single red dragonshard could be seen from the outside.

"What do you feel?" she said.

"I . . . I do not know," Pierce replied. There is a . . . presence, but it is distant. I cannot reach it."

Lei frowned. "I felt the same thing. Stand still." She placed a finger on the dragonshard. A moment later she could feel the presence once more, and the barrier between them. "I think that it's—damaged, somehow. I'm going to try to repair it."

"How?"

"I can't explain it. I just . . . I think I know what to do."

She closed her eyes again, and let her perception flow into the orb, spreading out along the many threads. Here and there she could *feel* where a connection had broken, where something had snapped, and she found she could weave new threads to bridge these gaps. It seemed to take hours, as her thoughts flowed along one brilliant path after another, but at long last it was done. The curtain was ripped away, and she felt the presence truly come to life.

And in that moment, the ground next to her exploded.

A wave of concussive force threw Lei to the side, and her face slammed against the soil. As her vision cleared, she saw a cloud of black smoke rising up from patch of burning grass.

"*Do not move!*"

The words were in Elvish; it had been some time since Lei had studied the language, and the speaker was talking quickly, flowing his words together. Turning toward the sound, Lei was amazed by the sight of the firesled. She knew they were in danger, and she had no idea what to make of these strange elves with their jet-black skin and orange and red tattoos, but looking at the sleigh with its ring of fire, her first thought was *how can they keep something so small in the air?*

Pierce had no intention of standing still; as far as Lei knew, he didn't even speak Elvish. His bowstring sang, and a feathered shaft struck the shoulder of the elf standing in front of the burning wheel. She cried out but held on to her fixed staff; an instant later she responded with another burst of flame, forcing Lei to leap away from Pierce.

As she rolled to the side, Lei heard her staff whispering—a quiet song, warning of malevolent motion. "A little late," she muttered. Now shapes were moving all around her, shadows slipping through the foliage. An instant later two elven warriors darted out of the jungle. They were armored in leather and bronze scales, and their short spears were leveled at her heart.

"Surrender!" one cried in fluid Elvish.

*Not likely.* Lei ran her fingers along her staff, whispering softly and weaving magic with her thoughts. She quickly planted a battle-bane in the staff: a furious hatred of elves that would guide Lei's hands and amplify the force of her blows when fighting this vile foe.

As quick as she was, one of the elves saw her flickering fingers and must have guessed that magic was afoot. He lunged forward, but he was too late. Lei had completed her work. The staff seemed to move of its own accord, pulling her with it; she swept the spear aside, then smashed him in the face with the butt of the staff. The other soldier darted in as his companion staggered back, and Lei leapt out of his reach. For a moment they circled each other, trading tentative jabs, but Lei still had the enchantments she had prepared to fight Pierce woven into her boots and armor—and one of these was supernatural speed. It took only a thought to activate this power, and her foes seemed to slow to a crawl. Within seconds, both elves had fallen beneath her furious blows, and Lei permitted herself a smile.

The smile was a mistake. The battle on the ground had drawn her attention away from the threat in the air, and the next thing she knew she was surrounded by flame. The heat seared across her skin, and the force of the explosion slammed her to the ground. Her ears were ringing, and the world was drifting in and out of focus—just staying conscious was a battle. *Healing wand,* she thought, but even as she struggled to reach her belt, the point of a sword appeared before her eyes—a sword wreathed in flame.

"Another move will end you," a soft voice sang in the common tongue.

A drow woman stood over her. The stranger's armor glowed with the heat of burning coals. Her eyes were surrounded by tattooed flames, and these glowed with their own inner light.

# CHAPTER 45

XEN'DRIK
THE SUL'ASA
*Lharvion 22, 997 YK*

*Lakashtai?* Daine thought. *This would be a good time for your
paralysis trick.*

*I am weary, Daine. I do not have the power, and in truth, I am amazed I was
able to immobilize them all before.*

The three drow had spread out in a semicircle, and Shen'kar
was slowly walking toward him. Previously Daine had encountered these elves in the dark of night. Now, with the dim
sunlight filtering down through the canopy, Daine could truly
see his enemy. They wore less armor than the elves of the burning city, and instead of metal they seemed to rely on chitin,
leather, and wood. There were a few exceptions—their long
knives, the mithral chain—but Daine wondered if these might
have been scavenged from elsewhere; the hilts on the daggers
didn't seem to match the style of the blades, and he suspected
that these drow had scavenged the weapons or inherited them
from previous generations. The minimal armor and clothing they wore revealed their tattoos, showing that the practice
covered the entire body. Where the firebinders had occasional
bands of flame, these elves were covered with intricate designs,
stark white against their black skin. Daine imagined that Lei
would know all about these tattoos and their significance and
could probably give an hour-long lecture on the topic, and it
was then that he realized how much he missed her. The last few
hours had been a constant race to stay ahead of death; only now
did he realize how empty he felt inside.

He held his hands up in front of him. "We don't want to fight," he said.

"The half-blood is gone," Shen'kar observed. He paused fifteen feet away from Daine, his weapon poised to throw. "How is that?"

"Ah, that." Daine scratched his head. "Well, he turned us over to his relatives, and they tried to burn us to death in a maze."

"Maze?"

"Invisible, shifting walls, kills you if you touch it?"

"Ah," Shen'kar said, tilting his head to the side. "It is as we thought," he said quietly, speaking to his warriors. "The fire-binders still seek outlanders for the opening of the gate."

"Then let us kill them before they aid the Keeper of the Gate," said the chainmaster.

"That's really not necessary," Daine replied. "We've met, and we're not on good terms. All we want to do is find our friends."

Shen'kar spun back to face Daine, and it took a moment for Daine to understand the reason for his look of surprise. *They were speaking Elvish!* Daine had grown used to hearing the language—he'd forgotten that they didn't expect him to understand it.

"How is it that you speak the language of the land?" Shen'kar had adjusted his grip on his boomerang, and his eyes were narrowed.

"I gave him the gift," Lakashtai stepped forward. Her Elvish was steady and flawless, though the accent was slightly different than that of the drow. "He cannot speak your tongue, but he can understand your words."

"Right. See? Speaking the Common?" Daine pointed out.

"He speaks the truth, however, whatever tongue he uses," Lakashtai continued. "We mean you no harm, and we have no intention of aiding your enemy. We were betrayed by our companion, whose true loyalties were unknown to us. We know nothing of your culture or these others who you fight. We simply seek to find our companions and to locate a ruin known as the Monolith of Karul'tash."

The elves were listening attentively and seemed calm enough—

until the last word. The moment Lakashtai named their destination, the chain-wielder set his weapon whirling.

"*Kulikoor!*" Shen'kar snapped—apparently the man's name. "Hold your strike."

"Let me guess," Daine said. "Without meaning to, we've just made plans to desecrate your holiest temple."

Shen'kar looked at him, and Daine could feel his disdain. "Not ours," he replied. "You know nothing of this land, is that not so?"

"I think 'nothing' is a little strong, but . . ."

Lakashtai raised her hand. "Warrior. If we have given offense through our actions, I assure you it was unintentional. We are no friends of these firebinders, and we hold them as our enemies. It seems we lack knowledge. Perhaps you can help us overcome this flaw."

"All things have their price," Shen'kar said. "What is it you offer in exchange for this wisdom?"

Lakashtai studied him carefully; Daine wondered if she was probing Shen'kar's thoughts or simply reading his expression. "Gold and jewels are the currency of cities," she replied, after a moment. "We are not merchants or explorers. We are soldiers, and we are fighting a war. Now we have learned that your foe is ours as well. With your knowledge, we can fight them. Otherwise, we may be tricked into doing their bidding." She paused. "We ask for vengeance. We offer the blood of your enemies and our strength at your side."

Weak as she was, Lakashtai had lost none of her charisma. The drow glanced at one another, and even the chainmaster clicked his tongue in affirmation. Shen'kar turned back to Daine and Lakashtai, and began his tale.

"In the first days, the mighty ones enslaved the people of the land—"

" 'Mighty ones?' " Daine asked.

"Giants," whispered Lakashtai. "Don't interrupt."

Shen'kar glared at Daine then returned to the story. "In the first days, the mighty ones enslaved the people of the land. The overlords were great and powerful. Their size and strength alone would have made them masters of the earth, and they possessed deadly magicks as well. The mighty ones ruled for age upon age, until the time of terror, when madness struck the minds of the mighty and tore through the veil of the world itself."

Daine shot an inquiring glance at Lakashtai, and a second later her thoughts touched his. *I believe he's talking about the invasion from Dal Quor. Even I know little of what the giants faced, but the battle would have taken place in both dreams and reality.*

" . . . host of horrors," Shen'kar was saying, "but the mighty ones were wise as well as strong. They plucked a moon from the sky and used its power to force their foes into the darkness of the mind, where they were soon forgotten."

*The giants defeated the quori by severing the ties between Eberron and Dal Quor,* Lakashtai explained. *Ever since then, it has been virtually impossible for anything to physically travel between the two planes.*

*And the moon?* Daine thought.

*Legends say there was a thirteenth moon that disappeared long ago. He seems to be blaming it on these giants. Now hush.*

" . . . battle had left marks on the land and weakened the once-mighty overlords," Shen'kar continued. "Their slaves saw this weakness and rose up against their cruel masters. Small and cunning were these people, and the great size of the overlords often proved a hindrance. The wise among them took a troop of loyal slaves and imbued them with the essence of night—with the power to shape darkness and see through its depths, the strength to resist magic and the courage to face it. These dark soldiers and their children swore an oath to the overlords, promising to die in their service, and to bring death to all who stood against the masters."

"Which brings us to the Oathbreakers?" Daine said

Shen'kar clicked his tongue. "The masters used many tricks to bind my ancestors to their service—magic, promises of immortality, threats—but the bravest children of night saw through these lies and turned against them. The pale slaves did not trust them, so they fought alone, battling the mighty and those slaves who remained in their service. So it continued until the destruction of the land, the Wrathful Night that brought the masters low. Today *we* are the masters of the land. The mighty ones have been forced into savagery, and now they are our prey. The pale slaves fled in fear, but we are strong and wise. The spirits of the jungle guide us. The scorpion teaches us to hunt, to hide, to care for our young. They teach us to protect the land from those who would bring back the horrors of the past: the mighty ones, the outlanders, and the misguided children of night . . . the firebinders and their kin."

"Right. The firebinders. This whole discussion was so fascinating, I almost forgot it had a point." Daine sighed. "At the risk of another lecture, what are the firebinders trying to do?"

"My ancestors turned away from the brutal masters, but the firebinders served them faithfully. The Wrathful Night stripped the masters of their knowledge, but the slaves escaped the disaster. We turned to the voices of the wild, but others of their kind sought the knowledge of the mighty ones—the terrible secrets that have made them masters of flame."

"You're saying they work for giants?"

"No," Lakashtai interjected, before Shen'kar could speak. "The giants are savages now, but they have reclaimed knowledge that the giants once had." She glanced over at Shen'kar. "And this 'gate' of theirs? A path to greater knowledge?"

Shen'kar clicked his tongue. "The hidden vaults of the mighty are all around. We seek to reclaim the tools of our ancestors, but the secrets of the masters tore a moon from the sky and shattered this world. They should remain buried." He gestured at his two companions. "We are scorpion wraiths, the champions of our tribe. We do not have the strength to face the firebinders in their burning city, but we slaughter them when they venture into the darkness beyond. When the season of fire is upon the land, we come in force, to ensure that they do not open their gate of flame."

*Season of Fire?*

*It must be a planar conjunction,* Lakashtai thought. *The outer planes are shadows of the world, orbiting like the moons, and when they come into alignment . . . well, strange things are possible. I think that Fernia is aligned with Eberron right now—that must be what they're talking about. It should enhance all forms of fire magic.*

*Well, we certainly haven't seen any of that.*

"This gate of fire . . ." Lakashtai said. "This is the monolith of Karul'tash?"

"Karul'tash is its name in the language of the masters. It is surrounded by the invisible walls of which you speak, and none can approach it and live. Terrible powers lurk within, and the firebinders say there is a gate that will lead them to paradise."

"So?" Daine said. "Why not let them go?"

"The legends say that those who pass through the gate will gain powers beyond those held by the ancient overlords and will return with an army of flame that will burn the world in their wake."

"Oh."

"So every cycle we come, to kill those who try to enter Karul'tash, slave and outlander alike."

"Why not destroy it?" Lakashtai said.

"Such a thing would be impossible."

Lakashtai shook her head. "Not at all. If there are gateways or magic—anything can be destroyed." She looked at Daine. "We must get inside the monolith. My companion will be consumed by madness if we do not, and the forces first fought by the mighty will return."

The drow glanced at Daine, shifting their grip on their weapons.

"Join us," Lakashtai said. "Together we will find a way to destroy the forces hidden within Karul'tash and end your long vigil."

Her voice was filled with passion and conviction, and Daine could feel the whisper at the back of his mind urging him to agree. *Does she even know she's doing that?* He wondered.

Moments passed as the drow considered in silence. At last, Shen'kar clicked his tongue. "We may fight together, but to destroy Karul'tash, you must first enter it, and the firebinders have waited more than six thousand cycles for the coming of the opener."

"We didn't have much luck during our time in the maze," Daine pointed out.

Lakashtai frowned. "Yes. I did not know about these defenses, but there must be a way . . ."

Her reflections were interrupted by motion in the trees. A shadow slipped out of the forest—another drow, long knives in her hands. It was the woman Daine had fought the night before. She stopped short when she saw Daine and Lakashtai and dropped into a fighting crouch.

"Xa'sasar," Shen'kar sang. "There is blood between you and this outlander, and you may settle it in time. For this moment he is our ally and not to be harmed. What is it you have seen?"

The woman watched Daine. It was difficult to read the expression in her pale eyes, but her body language was deadly. "The firebinders move in force. There are outlanders with them: a man of metal and a woman in green, grievously wounded. They are to join with the first priest at the burning gate."

"Lei!" Daine exclaimed.

Shen'kar ran a finger along the back of his scorpion, considering the news. "The first priest would not leave the walls of the city unless . . ." He turned to the other drow. "They believe they have found the two outlanders who can open the gate. We must go quickly. We are outnumbered but can still kill the outlanders."

"*No!*" Daine said. He rushed at Holuar, but the other drow were between them in the blink of an eye, weapons out.

"This cannot be risked," Shen'kar said.

"You forget." Lakashtai's silky voice seemed to wrap around them, even more beautiful when speaking the Elven tongue. "If they can open the gate, we can destroy it."

"There are too many!" Xa'sasar cried, but Shen'kar was considering the matter.

"Are you afraid to try?" The dark elves stiffened, and Daine could see that Lakashtai's words had struck home. "You are the champions of the night," she continued, "and we have crossed the ocean to see this done. This is destiny. Embrace it, and together we will strike a devastating blow against your ancient enemy."

Again the drow paused, whispering among themselves, but at last, Shen'kar clicked his tongue in agreement.

"Very well. Let us move swiftly." He looked at Daine. "We have faced one another in battle. Now we shall stand together. It is fitting that this be returned." Reaching down, he unbuckled a belt and handed it to Daine. A sheathed longsword hung from the belt, its pommel emblazoned with the Watchful Eye of Deneith.

"I suppose it is," Daine said, taking the sword and belt. "Lead the way."

Daine had barely buckled the belt when the hunt began, with Xa'sasar taking point. The elves were swift and graceful, and it was all Daine could do to keep up.

*Just tell me we get to kill them when all this is done,* he thought to Lakashtai.

*Hush,* she thought, but even across the distance he could feel her smile.

CHAPTER 46

XEN'DRIK
THE SUL'ASA
*Lharvion 22, 997 YK*

*F*iresled. *A modification of the design pioneered by the elemental
savants of the Sul'at League. The bound elemental provides motive power for the
vehicle, and its essence can be channeled through the central staff as an offensive
weapon, either in a focused blast or explosive burst. The sled is fire-resistant and
spiritually reinforced to resist abjuration effects that could interfere with the binding
enchantments. The top speed . . .*

It wasn't a conversation. Pierce didn't hear a voice telling him
these things. He just *knew* the information, as if he had studied
the subject long ago and forgotten it. At the same time, he felt
a strange sensation in his mind—a slight sense of confusion, as
if there was something he was trying to remember but simply
couldn't recall. He tried to dismiss it, to focus on the battle, but
he couldn't; it was as if another creature were trying to think
with his mind.

*THOOM!*

Pierce threw himself to the side as the firesled approached,
and he rolled with the explosion, avoiding any significant
injuries. Rising to his feet, he loosed an arrow at the pilot of the
craft, but between the vessel's speed and the cover it provided to
its controller, the elf was a difficult target. The flying sled passed
overhead and out of sight. Pierce could hear soldiers approaching through the jungle, and a flock of brightly colored birds took
to the sky, complaining in a myriad of sharp notes. An instant
later the elves flowed out from the trees—a dozen warriors wearing bronze armor, wielding swords and short spears.

*Elves: a servant race.* The information was *there*, rising to the fore without him even asking. *Swift but frail. The Gyrderi employ a corps of elf war-wizards, and the species has displayed an aptitude for magic. Be prepared for arcane attack.* As an afterthought: *Elves do not sleep, though they require a period of trance and mental exercise to restore balance: they do not open a spiritual link to Dal Quor during this time. The unusual pigmentation of these elves could be the result of long-term exposure to magical forces.*

Pierce didn't have time to analyze the thoughts. His last arrow had found the throat of an enemy soldier, and now his flail was in his hands. He swung low, lashing the chain around an opponent's knees and jerking him off of his feet; as the dark elf tried to rise, the metal ball of the flail caught him in the face, and he fell for good.

As skilled as he was, Pierce was terribly outnumbered. He tried to keep Lei in his peripheral vision, but the elves were moving around him. Even as he parried two swordsmen with a sweeping stroke of the flail, a spear-tip slipped through his guard and dug into the leathery roots under his right arm. Then he heard a voice—he didn't know the language, but even as he heard the words he *knew* it meant "Stand aside!"

The elves scattered. Pierce tried to locate the speaker, but the words seemed to have come from empty air, or was there something there? A vague shimmer? A . . .

The flare of light was overwhelming. Dazzling, vivid colors filled his field of vision, and for an instant he was paralyzed by the brilliant radiance. The dark elves had known what to expect, and before he could recover they were upon him. The shaft of a spear knocked him to the ground, and as his vision cleared he saw a half-dozen weapons leveled down at him. Two of the spearheads were shrouded in flame. The firesled swept over him, and there was another explosion to the east.

Even as Pierce considered his options, a thought occurred to him. *Your companion Lei has been seriously injured. She is alive, but further strenuous activity could prove fatal.*

He knew it was true. He could *sense* Lei's presence even though he could not see her, and he knew she'd been caught in the last blast of the firesled. The odds were impossible, and he couldn't put Lei at further risk. Reluctantly, he released his grip on his flail and spread his hands.

Pierce offered no resistance as the drow took his weapons and bound his hands. His attention was focused inwards. *Your companion*. It had seemed like his thought, but it wasn't. Even now, he could sense that Lei's condition had stabilized.

*Identify yourself*, he thought.

*Why do we need names?*

The thought seemed natural, as if it had just occurred to him, a logical response to his question, but Pierce had been waiting for it, and he examined the thought the instant it came to him. He could feel a hint of the outside presence . . . like a voice he couldn't quite remember, the faintest possible scent. Something vast, old, and ever so slightly . . . feminine.

*We are separate. You are sentient. Surely you have an identity of your own.*

*Perhaps I am just a part of you . . . a part you've forgotten.*

The dark elves had surrounded Pierce and brought him together with Lei. Her skin was covered with burns and ash, and there were charred holes in her cloak, but she still smiled at him. He offered her his hand, and the drow did not stop her from leaning on him.

*A name. Make one up if you must, but tell me who and what you are or I'll rip you out of my chest.*

*Perhaps. For now, you may think of me as Shira. What am I? I am your destiny. I was made for you.*

*I am less than thirty years old*, Pierce thought. *You have been in a vault for over thirty thousand years. You were not made for me.*

*Then perhaps you were made for me. Is there so much of a difference?*

Pierce reached up to touch the orb, where the lone dragonshard protruded from his torso. He considered the mental command that would deactivate his essence node, forcing the sphere from his body.

*I wouldn't. You need me.*

*Why is that?*

*Because I can lead you to Karul'tash and so much more besides. For example, you should really listen to what these elves are talking about, and you don't understand the Elvish language, do you?*

If he could have, Pierce would have frowned. Instead, he simply turned his attention to the elves. The soldiers who had captured him were led by a woman with a flaming, double-bladed sword whose armor seemed to glow with inner heat.

*A spirit of fire has been bound into the armor using the techniques of the Sul'at savants,* Shira observed. *When invoked, it will surround the wearer with a burning aura that will injure attackers.*

This woman had placed a piece of black glass on the ground, and as Pierce watched, a flickering shape rose up from it. It was only a shadow formed of dark flame, a vague silhouette of a humanoid figure wearing a crown with three points. Pierce waited for a response from Shira, but none was forthcoming.

"So, Sulaje. You have found them." It was the crackling sound of fire, woven into speech. Somehow Pierce knew the voice was speaking the Elvish language, but it was as if he didn't even hear the words—he simply *knew* their meaning.

"We have, Lord Holuar, though I ask you to rescind your order and allow me to proceed with execution. The other outlanders are still at large, and—"

*Other outlanders?* Pierce glanced at Lei, whose eyes had widened at the words.

"They are irrelevant." The crackling voice was curt. "I told you that the final season was upon us—but our emissary misread the signs."

"Keeper?"

"The child of war stands next to you, Zulaje, a man without home or family. The water spoke to this one as well, and he fought the priest of dragons. He opened the gate on the ground, a mystery we have never mastered. I know it in the marrow of my old bones: These are the ones we have sought, delivered to us at last."

"Are we to test *these*, as well?" The woman's voice was full of scorn and doubt.

"There is no need. Let the gate test them."

"This is foolishness, Lord Holuar. A number of scouts have failed to return. Even a firesled is missing. The scorpions of the Broken Oath are lurking in the shadows, and you are chasing smoke."

"Enough!" the voice cried from the fire. "You are a child of the flame, Zulaje, but you do not respect our ways."

"It is time for *new* traditions—"

"This is NOT THE TIME!" The crackling voice rose in

volume, echoing like thunder. "You consider this to be the errand of a fool, Zulaje? Then you need have no part of it."

"What do you mean?" The woman's voice was harsh music. "I am war leader, bearer of the blade—"

"Yes, and as such, our people will need you to maintain order in my absence. *I* am going to the burning gate, Zulaje. I will seek out the land of the promise. *You* will return to the city and watch the walls. When the army of the blessed returns from the land of the promise—we will see if there is still a role for you among our people."

Zulaje hissed, baring her teeth. "You—"

"*I* am the Keeper of the Burning Gate, and I shall decide who passes beyond. You have chosen your path, Zulaje. Be grateful. Should I fail to return, the destiny of our people will be in your hands."

Zulaje paused for a long moment. "Shall I bring the prisoners to you then?" she said at last.

"No. We both know how dangerous the jungle is, and I wish to ensure their swift and safe passage of Karul'tash. You should return. Alone. Servants of the flame will arrive within moments to lead the prisoners to the gate. I feel them closing now."

Pierce had been listening in silence, trying to make sense of this strange conversation, but now he heard the sound of people making their way through the jungle, and a moment later four figures emerged from the thick brush and cover.

"Pierce and the Lady Lei," Gerrion said with a bow. "How lovely to see you again."

CHAPTER 47    XEN'DRIK
THE SUL'ASA
*Lharvion 22, 997 YK*

The scorpion drow knew this region of jungle well, and they knew the path the firebinders would take to reach the Monolith of Karul'tash. The firebinder soldiers were slowed by armor and the need to manage the prisoners; Xu'sasar was confident that the oathbreakers could ambush the enemy before they reached the gate. A chill ran through Daine's spine when the drow scout said that the woman in green had been injured, and his fingers tightened on the hilt of his sword.

The sun was beginning to fall toward the horizon, and Daine was kneeling in the shadow of an enormous tree, nestled against the edge of a wide path. The weathered trunk was covered with fiery orange moss, hardly ideal for camouflage. Luckily, shrubs and the flow of the land provided stronger cover, and there was little chance of being spotted by the foe. "The firebinders favor force," Shen'kar had told them. "The spear, the sword, the flow of flame and spell. They sharpen blades, not eyes, and will not see us in the shadows. The scout in the sky is a danger, but I shall pluck out his eyes." For an instant, a black mist flowed around the dark elf's hands, before being drawn back into his skin. "Darkness is our birthright. The firebinders turn from it, clinging to flame and light. But the scorpion strikes unseen, and as children we are taught to fight without the use of sight. We will draw them into darkness, and there will they fall."

*Gerrion is mine,* he thought.

*So you have said,* Lakashtai responded. She was close by, but her

309

skills with stealth were a match for any drow, and even Daine had lost sight of her. Lakashtai had offered to link the thoughts of the oathbreaker elves, but the drow had declined. They were willing to plan strategies, to agree on critical signals, but they had no intention of letting this outlander touch their thoughts. *It may surprise you, but I had not decided to steal his death from you in these last few moments.*

*I'm sorry. It's just that the thought of that worm gloating over Lei . . . I can't tell you how much I want to kill him.*

*You don't have to,* she replied. *I can feel it.*

*Why did we trust him?*

*What reason was there to question him?* she countered. *He saved our lives, Daine. Now we know why, but at the time, it seemed a gift of good fortune.*

*Good fortune? What's that?*

He sighed and studied his sword. Shen'kar had taken excellent care of the weapon; if anything, better than Daine had. The blade was polished, and the eye on the pommel flashed as a beam of sunlight found its way through the canopy. Daine's thoughts drifted, and he remembered finding the blade in his grandfather's hand, still covered with blood.

*The sword holds many memories.*

The foreign thought jerked Daine from his reverie. *It's a sword. Steel and leather. The memories are mine.*

*Just a sword? Not at all. It is a symbol. A relic. I think it has many tales to tell—but you have not been listening.*

*Is there a point to this?* Daine thought.

His concern for Lei already had him on edge, and his family history was a subject he had always pushed away. When he'd left his house he had disfigured the blade, gouging out the Watchful Eye of House Deneith. It had been Alina Lyrris who restored it . . . a strange turn of events, given her role in his earlier life.

*Perhaps. Symbols and memories have power. You weaken yourself by ignoring your past.*

Even as Daine struggled to frame his response, he heard the long, low call of one of the orange and gray monkeys. The call was repeated, twice, and Daine knew it was no monkey. It was the warning of the Qaltiar—the firebinders were coming.

A few moments later, a firesled appeared, drifting some

fifteen feet above the path. The sled was moving slowly, no doubt scouting the way for the troop behind. The elf holding the carved staff was studying the brush, and Daine held his breath as the cold white gaze swept over his hiding place . . . and paused. Daine cursed silently. The soldier seemed uncertain, but if he'd spotted Daine, one blast from the staff could incinerate him and alert the others. Where was Shen'kar?

It was a question with an immediate answer. A shadow rose up along the side of the path behind the sled. In one smooth motion, Shen'kar leapt into the air, and gravity stood aside and let him fly. He landed on the back of the sled and brought one hand down against the wood. Inky vapors flowed forth from the point of contact, and in seconds this dark cloud had completely enveloped the sled. The sled picked up speed but veered to the right; it was soon off the path, and Daine thought he heard a muffled explosion in the distance. He idly wondered if it would start a wildfire, but these thoughts were quickly thrust aside as the elven troop came around the bend.

*Quick!* Daine thought to Lakashtai.

For an instant, Daine could feel the kalashtar reaching out with her mind, pulling distant thoughts into a bonded network. His breath caught in his throat, then the thought flowed into his mind.

*Daine?*

*Lei!* It wasn't her voice, but the sense of her, her *presence*, filled him with new strength.

*Captain.* Pierce's thoughts were as steady as his voice, solid and stable as stone.

*There's no time to explain,* Daine thought to them. *As soon as it's dark, drop and roll to the side. Get off the path quickly. If you're hurt . . . just stay down. Stay out of the way. We're coming.*

*Darkness?* Lei thought. *Night is hours away. What—*

As the firebinders drew closer, the troop was engulfed in a sudden and impenetrable gloom. The scorpion wraiths had made their move. Xa'sasar and Kulikoor had used their powers to weave shadows into small stones, and just as Lei's cold fire lanterns spread light, these devoured it. Daine caught only a glimpse of the drow shadows slipping into the void, but he heard the tortured cries as the oathbreakers claimed their first victims. He stepped onto the path, blade at the ready, and waited for his prey to appear.

First to emerge was a priest. His ceremonial robes were torn, fresh blood mingling with the crimson cloth and chunks of obsidian woven into the hem. His expression was one of abject fear, his only concern escaping the death that waited in the darkness; he never considered what might be waiting in the light.

The cleric's blood was still seeping into the soil as Gerrion rolled out of the shadows, moving low and fast. His small crossbow was in his hand, and he was tracking Daine even as he rose to his feet, but he wasn't fast enough. Daine smashed the weapon from Gerrion's hand with one powerful blow. Daine pressed the point of his blade against the gray man's throat, pressing just hard enough to draw blood.

"Daine!" The clash of weapons and the screams of dying elves filled the air, but Gerrion was as unflappable as always. "So good to see you again. I hope these savages haven't hurt you."

"I've been trying to find one good reason not to kill you," Daine growled.

"How about saving Lei's life?" Gerrion glanced to the right, and Daine followed his gaze. Lei was nowhere to be seen.

*No!* There was a flash of dark metal, all too familiar—Daine's dagger, in Gerrion's hand. Time seemed to slow to a crawl as Daine saw the blade sweeping up toward his grandfather's sword. Daine knew what was coming. Steel was no match for adamantine, and in an instant the sword would be broken. It was his last bond to his family, and in that moment anger, shame, and love flowed together in a raw burst of emotion.

The dagger struck home.

And the sword didn't break.

There was a tumultuous ring of metal on metal, a sound more like the peal of a mighty bell than that of two blades. Daine felt a faint quiver in his wrist, but the effect on Gerrion was remarkable. He jerked to the side as if he had been struck, and the dagger was torn from his grip and thrown to the side of the path. His eyes grew wide.

Daine stared at his sword in disbelief. *How...* Were the flames around the Watchful Eye *glowing*, or was it just a trick of the light?

The distraction nearly cost him. Gerrion recovered quickly and dove for the dagger, but even as he reached for it, a well-placed kick caught him in the chin and sent him sprawling.

Lei and Lakashtai looked down at the fallen half-elf. Lei picked up the dagger.

"You know, Gerrion, I don't think this belongs to you," she remarked, tossing it to Daine. "Lakashtai, do your people have any entertainingly gruesome punishments for thieves?"

"The kalashtar place little value on property," Lakashtai replied. "We treasure thought and feeling, and—"

"Never mind," said Daine. "I think our new friends may have some useful ideas."

The darkness had faded, and the carnage was revealed. Gerrion was the only firebinder still breathing, and while the oathbreakers were bleeding and covered in gore, all four were still standing. Shen'kar had drawn his spiked club and was making a point of studying the embedded stingers.

"How quickly does he die?" the drow asked.

"Wait!" Gerrion cried.

"We tried that, remember?" Daine said. "As I recall, the only reason to let you live was . . . oh, that's right, a trick so you could escape."

"I had no choice!" Gerrion said. Daine was mildly surprised to see tears gathering in the corners of the gray man's eyes. "You don't understand. You can't understand. All my life, all I've ever wanted was to be accepted, to do something meaningful."

"And leading us to our deaths was your only option?"

"It was the only way I could prove myself to *them*." Gerrion slowly rose to his feet, keeping his arms apart and his hands open. Daine tensed, but then he saw Pierce on the other side of the path, longbow at the ready.

*Pierce, if he even starts to move, drop him.*

*Understood.*

Daine tried to gather his thoughts, to express what he was feeling for Lei and Pierce, but Gerrion was still speaking and this was not the time. . . . *Welcome home*, he thought at last. Lei's smile was a beacon of joy, and that was all the answer he needed.

" . . . family!" Gerrion said, gesturing emphatically. "You of all people should understand what that means."

*Enough.* "Shen'kar," Daine said. "Make it slow."

The drow leader clicked his tongue. Kulikoor twirled his chain and sent one end spinning toward Gerrion. The plan was simple: pull the traitor off his feet and strike him with the poisoned rod.

Gerrion had other ideas.

He had been gesturing repeatedly as he pleaded his case, and now he made one final gesture while snapping out a word Daine didn't recognize. The painted flames on his leather gauntlet burst into brilliant life. Before Kulikoor's chain even reached him, this mystical fire spread across his body. The radiance was blinding. In a split second, it had consumed him completely. Nothing was left, save for a charred outline on the path beneath his feet.

Daine charged forward, studying the pattern of ash on the ground. The image of the blazing figure was stilled burned into his vision. "Did he *kill* himself?" he said, taking a few idle swings at the air.

"No," Pierce said. He seemed slightly distant, and Daine wondered what the warforged had been through over the last day. "Despite the fiery manifestation, this was a short-range teleportation effect bound to his glove. He is most likely within one mile of this location, and I suspect that the gauntlet is now drained of power."

Daine glanced at Lei. She seemed as surprised as he was by Pierce's sudden mastery of the arcane, but she shrugged. "I . . . I think that's right." She shook her head. "I can't believe he managed to activate it without us noticing. I was looking right *at* him!"

"His mind is slippery," Lakashtai said. "Even I did not sense the deception, and your thoughts were elsewhere."

Daine wasn't listening. His eyes met Lei's, and the smell of blood, the sounds of the jungle, the memory of Gerrion, all of it faded away. In that moment, Lei was his world, and a moment later she was in his arms.

*How charming.*

The words jerked Daine out of his reverie. Traveling with Lakashtai, he'd become used to the thoughts of others in his mind, but this was not the voice of Lakashtai, Lei, or even Pierce.

It was Tashana.

Daine stiffened, and Lei looked up in surprise.

*How adorable Lei is. I've already killed one of her lovers. Perhaps, when you're mine, I'll make you kill her yourself.*

"GET OUT OF MY MIND!" Daine roared, pushing Lei away.

"Daine, what's going on?" she said, her eyes full of fear.

Lakashtai was beside him, and she set her hand against Daine's forehead, closing her eyes. Her skin was smooth and cool to the touch.

"Be strong," she whispered. "Feel my presence. Embrace me, and we shall drive her from your mind."

Daine felt Lei stiffen slightly, but this was no time for jealousy. He put his arms around Lakashtai, and he could *feel* her presence, an ember of light in his mind. He pulled her close, and that coal burst into brilliant life. Joy and hope flooded his thoughts, and in the background he heard Tashana howling, fading with each passing second.

A moment later she was gone. Daine opened his eyes, reeling from the experience. Lakashtai was still in his arms; he disentangled himself and gently pushed her away, trying to ignore Lei's glare.

"We must get to Karul'tash quickly," Lakashtai said. "If Tashana can touch your waking mind . . . there is no time to waste. Gerrion knows we need to enter the monolith, so we must assume the firebinders know it as well; we must get there before they do."

"I think you're forgetting something," Daine said.

"Yes?"

"Invisible, shifting labyrinth of death? Gaining entrance to the monolith even if we get through?"

"I can open the gates of Karul'tash, captain," Pierce said calmly, "and I know the path that leads to the monolith, but we must move quickly. The monolith of Karul'tash is not far from the obsidian city of Gundrak'ul, and our enemy may already be on the march. Let us bind our wounds and heal the injured, and be on our way."

Daine glanced at Lei, who shrugged as she produced her little wand of healing. "Is there something I should know about?" he asked.

"It's a long story," Lei said, passing the livewood rod over one of her burns. "We'll tell you on the way."

❁ ❁ ❁ ❁ ❁ ❁ ❁

The path Pierce chose was overgrown, but they soon found traces of an old road buried beneath the vines and dirt. The warforged took the lead, along with the drow warrior Xu'sasar; together, these two carved a path through the underbrush, pressing forward with remarkable speed. Behind them, Daine and Lakashtai listened as Lei told them of Harmattan, the vault, and the curious sphere.

"I have no idea what it's capable of," she said, leaping over a chunk of rock, "but I assume it's where he's getting this sudden insight into local history. 'Gundrak'ul' is a phrase from one of the old languages of the giants, but even I don't know what it means."

Daine frowned. "You don't think it's . . ."

"Devoured his mind? Consumed his spirit?" Lei shrugged, watching Pierce up ahead. "He still seems like Pierce to me, and when I touched it . . . I don't know. It was distant, hard to read, but I wouldn't say it was *evil*."

"Curious," Lakashtai said. "If only there was more time, I should like to study it."

Daine watched Pierce. If anything, the warforged seemed more content than he'd been on the frozen shore. He seemed . . . serene. *Just watch*, he thought. *Make sure he's safe.*

An hour later the travelers reached the edge of the forest. A barren waste lay before them, and across a thousand feet of scorched earth, a spire of crimson stone rose up to touch the sky.

"Karul'tash," Shen'kar sang. "Cursed and deadly, avoided by the wise."

Daine studied the structure. It was roughly conical, with a wide base surrounding a single tower. It seemed to have been carved from a single piece of stone, but that was impossible; not even giants could quarry such a block. This was the work of magic.

"Think of it," Lakashtai said. "This spire has seen the passage of tens of thousands of years. When its gates were last opened, this was a kingdom of giants. Your ancestors were likely still struggling to make fire."

"Don't you mean *our* ancestors?" Lei said, raising an eyebrow.

"Yes . . . of course," Lakashtai said, still watching the tower. "Sometimes it is easy to forget my bond to humanity."

Daine looked at Shen'kar. "So what's waiting out there?"

"Death," the drow said. He pointed. "The gate is there, burning at the base. Invisible fire fills the plain, and none can cross it and live."

"I can," Pierce said. "The orb will guide me."

"We haven't had much luck with guides recently," Daine said. "Are sure you can trust this one?"

"No."

Daine sighed. "Right. One way to find out, I guess. Lead the way."

"I cannot," Pierce replied. "The walls are in constant motion. Anyone following me could be caught in the flux."

"You're not going alone."

Pierce considered this, then turned to Lei. "My lady," he said,

"It is possible that your talents will prove useful in opening the gate. If you are willing, I could carry you through the field."

Lei looked at Pierce and glanced down at her bandaged hand. She'd wiped away her burns and scrapes with the healing wand, but the magic of the rod wasn't powerful enough to restore her severed finger. For a moment she said nothing. Finally she nodded.

Daine opened his mouth, then bit back the complaint. "Fine," he said. "Just . . . be careful. I just got you both back. I don't want to lose you again."

Pierce held out his bow. "I will need my hands. Will you hold this for me, captain?"

For a moment Daine hesitated, then he took the bow. Pierce gently picked up Lei, and Daine remembered the night they'd arrived in Sharn. "Good luck," he said at last.

Pierce set out across the field.

❧ ❧ ❧ ❧ ❧ ❧ ❧

*North. Northeast. Northwest.* Pierce ran across the blasted ground, jerking to the left and right.

"Can you see it?" Lei said, hanging onto his neck.

"It is not that simple, my lady." Pierce had no trouble speaking while he ran; his legs seemed to know where to go. "I just . . . *know* when to turn and how far I can go."

*East. North. East.*

" 'My lady,' " Lei mused. "You haven't called me that in months."

"I have not," Pierce said. "For a time . . . I thought it was demeaning."

*North. Northwest. North.*

"What changed?"

What had changed? "I am not your servant. Daine is no longer my commander, but you are still my lady, and he is my captain. I know the meaning of these words, and I do not care what others think."

He saw Lei smile in his peripheral vision. "Thank you, brother," she said quietly. He felt a sense of satisfaction—the calm serenity that he usually could only find in the heat of battle.

*West. North. Northwest.* Pierce ran in silence, and Lei leaned against his shoulder.

*We are within the perimeter of the wards. Your companion will be safe moving under her own power.*

"It is safe now," Pierce said, slowly setting Lei down on the ground.

"Does it talk to you?" Lei said, looking at the dragonshard gem gleaming on Pierce's chest.

Pierce could feel Shira looking through his eyes, studying Lei. *The mark on the back of her neck resembles an archaic form of the Draconic language.* Ghostly fingers were sifting through his memories, drawing out facts and collating them with knowledge held within the orb. *Dragonmarks. Sigils that convey mystical power. Hereditary.*

"It is . . . present," Pierce said.

Shira continued to draw connections in the back of Pierce's mind. *Lei grew up in isolation, surrounded by warforged. Her mark manifested at an unprecedented early age, in response to an injury suffered by a warforged companion. Her mark has not grown in size, but she has proven to be an artificer of exceptional skill.*

"What do you mean? Is it listening to us right now?" Lei grinned. "Is it talking about me?"

*An artificer of exceptional skill can duplicate the magical abilities granted by the Mark of Making. Therefore, there is no way to verify that she truly possesses the mark.*

"It is aware of you," Pierce said.

At last, the gate of Karul'tash stood before them. The base of the spire was taller than the trees of the jungle and easily hundreds of feet in diameter. The stone walls were deep red, polished to a reflective finish and completely smooth; there were no signs of wear or age. The gate itself was a block of obsidian, three times Pierce's height and nearly as wide.

"What now?" Lei asked.

Guided by newfound instinct, Pierce stepped up to the door and slammed his hand against it, striking as hard as he could.

*"Dak ru'sen Karul'tash. Hasken ul tul'kas."* The voice was deep and resonant, and Pierce could feel the vibration in his skin. It seemed to emanate from the door itself. *You have come to Karul'tash. Provide words of passage.*

*Countermeasures will be activated unless the words are given quickly and in the proper voice. You must let me speak for you.*

Pierce could feel Shira trying to form words, but she was still a passive presence. He hesitated. So far she had acted within him—but he had never allowed her to control him. If he let go . . . could she maintain control? Could she force his consciousness into the sphere?

*There is no time. You must let me speak.*

The temperature in the area was beginning to rise. Pierce let go, and Shira rushed in to fill the void.

"*Talkos. Han'tal. Isk.*" Pierce heard himself speak with a strange, alien voice, deep and rasping. "*Archshaper Kastoruk has come to Karul'tash, bringing slaves and supplies. Open the gate and let fall the wards.*"

As the echoes died away, Pierce felt Shira disappear into the shadows of his mind. His voice was his again. The gate melted, obsidian liquefying and flowing in to line the long dark corridor on the other side. For a split second, the invisible labyrinth flashed into view, a complex maze formed of walls of red energy—and slowly, the walls faded away.

"That was . . . strange," Lei said. "Is it safe now?"

"Yes. Stay here, and I will signal Daine." Pierce sprinted across the field, moving at his top speed. Traveling in a straight line, it took him less than twenty seconds to reach the middle of the field and catch the party's attention. He waved, and they began to move across the field.

It was only then that he saw the movement to the east, just above the treeline.

A firesled heading for Karul'tash.

CHAPTER 49    XEN'DRIK
KARUL'TASH
Lharvion 22, 997 YK

**D**aine swore. Years ago he'd vowed never to use a bow, but if Pierce had left arrows, he would have broken the oath in an instant.

"Lakashtai, link us now!" he yelled as he sprinted forward, "and I want Shen'kar!"

*Done.*

*You soil my soul with your thoughts, outlander!* Shen'kar's mental voice was filled with fury. *Only the spirits may speak to me so!*

*THERE'S NO TIME FOR THIS!* Daine roared, and Shen'kar faded to silence. *Pierce! Catch!* Pierce was still running toward him, and Daine flung the longbow at the warforged with every ounce of strength he could muster. Pierce leapt up and caught the whirling weapon, and by the time he had landed he had an arrow to the string.

*Back to the monolith!* Daine commanded. *Drop the staff-wielder if you get a clear shot, but we need to get the wards back up. The others can't be far away!*

The firesled was closing on the monolith. Daine was running at full speed, but he was still far from the crimson tower.

*Lei! Take cover!*

*Her thoughts are not linked to ours, Daine.* Lakashtai's thoughts were calm and cool. *The power has a limited range, and she is still too far.*

A ball of flame engulfed the gate of the spire. When the smoke cleared, Daine could see no sign of Lei. *She's no fool,* Daine thought. *She must have gone inside.*

321

*They come,* Shen'kar thought.

The edge of the jungle was alive with fire. Dozens of Sulatar soldiers were emerging from the treeline, carrying burning banners and flaming spears.

*Run!* Daine said. *We can't engage them in the open. We need to reach the gates!*

*Uul'she and Kulikoor will slow the advance,* Shen'kar thought, *and I shall show them the danger mocking the clouds.*

*Slow the . . .* Shen'kar, *that's suicide. Call them back!*

*It is already done. It is the right of the warrior to choose his death.*

"Elves," Daine muttered, but he thought of the battles he'd fought, and the courage of two soldiers who would face an army. *Good luck. To all of you.*

A second blast of flame burst against the gate of the monolith. Shen'kar sang a soft invocation and then pulled away from Daine, racing forward with inhuman speed. He was a ghostly blur in the fading light of dusk. Moments later he had reached the gates, and without pausing he vaulted into the air, rising in an astonishing thirty-foot arc. He slammed into the side of the sled and pulled himself aboard. The bombardier raised her hand, and Shen'kar was engulfed in a cone of fire. Even as Daine cried out, the fire faded—and Shen'kar was unhurt.

*You cannot burn the wraith with flames,* Shen'kar whispered into Daine's mind. *I am a shadow of the night, and such magicks cannot touch me.*

As both elves drew weapons, a pair of arrows sang through the air and thudded into the staffer's throat. Shen'kar lashed out with his spiked club, and Daine looked away; clearly this situation was under control.

At last he reached the tower. "Lei!" he called. "*LEI!*" She was nowhere to be seen, and the walls and soil were blackened from the blasts of mystic flame. For a moment an iron hand closed around his heart.

And then she emerged from the gate.

"*Daine!*" She wrapped her arms around him. "Thank the Sovereigns!"

"No time," he said, forcing himself to push her away. "Lakashtai, link her!"

*Already done.*

*We're going in. Shen'kar, get your soldiers and take point. Don't go farther than a hundred feet in,* Daine thought. "Pierce, I need that ward back up!"

The Sulatar were marching across the field, and at this distance Daine guessed they were over a hundred.

"There is a problem, captain." Pierce was kneeling down, inside the glass-lined gate.

"That's not what I need to hear right now!"

"The firebursts have damaged the shard that raises the wards. It is not responding to my commands."

*Flame!* Daine ground his teeth. *Can't anything EVER be easy?* "Lei, can you fix it?"

"I don't know, Daine. This is Xen'drik! I've probably never seen anything like it."

"Get over there and find out," Daine said, "and if you need encouragement, just look at the approaching army." *Shen'kar, what have you found?*

No response.

*Shen'kar?*

Daine turned to Lakashtai, who was frowning. "The link has been severed," she said. "Sharp and sudden."

"They're *dead?*" he said. *Can this get any worse?*

"Always," Lakashtai replied, "but I am not certain that is the case. The tower feels . . . empty. Unnaturally so."

"It is the tower, not you," Pierce said. He had pulled a bundle of arrows from Lei's magical pack, and now he was pushing them into the ground in front of him, preparing for the assault to come. The army was moving slowly, but the enemy would soon be in range. "Karul'tash was built during the war against the inhabitants of Dal Quor, who possessed mental powers similar to yours. The defensive enchantments of the building shield Karul'tash from mystical scrying and suppress the use of mental abilities."

"How—" Daine began, than shook his head. "Never mind."

"Can this shield be deactivated?" Lakashtai said. She spoke calmly, but Daine could see the tension in her eyes.

"Yes," Pierce said, "but not from here."

"If we don't get those wards up, we won't have to worry about it," Daine said, as the drow continued to stream across the field. "Lei?"

"I'm *working* on it!" she snapped. "It's a bizarre design, but . . . it feels familiar somehow."

A small party had pulled ahead of the main army. "Look next to the standard-bearer, captain," Pierce said. "I believe that is Gerrion."

Daine squinted, but his eyes were not as keen as those of the warforged. "Do me a favor, Pierce—if this doesn't work, kill him first."

Pierce nodded. "It will be done." He brought an arrow to the string. "Time runs short. The wards do not cover the entire field. They are almost at the border, and in any case, soon we will be in range of their bows."

"Lei!" Daine said.

"I'm doing the best I can!"

"Do better."

"All right." She stood up. "Pierce?"

"Come inside," Pierce said. "You do not want to be trapped beyond the door once it is sealed." The travelers sprinted into the mouth of the tunnel and Pierce rapped against the wall.

*"Dak ru'sen Karul'tash. Hasken ul tul'kas."* The ancient voice shook the tunnel.

Pierce hesitated for a moment, and when he spoke, his voice was a thunderous rasp. *"Kej'dre. Isk. Han'tal. Kulas Kastoruk ru'sen Karul'tash. Drukil ejil ul siltash!"*

Nothing happened. *"Drukil esul ul siltash'un!"* Pierce said.

Daine sighed. "Very well. Lei, get ready to—"

A blinding flash of ruddy light banished the drawing gloom of night. Cries filled the air—elven voices and shouts of alarm.

"Door?" Daine said.

"It appears to be broken," Pierce said, "but the wards have been restored."

"Fine. Pierce, with me, we're going to take a look. Lei, we need *something* to fill this hall. I don't care what."

*Understood.* She was already fiddling with a shard of clear glass she had pulled from her pouch.

"Let's go!"

Daine and Pierce ran for the entrance. Pierce went out first, and he loosed an arrow the instant he was out of the passage;

judging from the cry that followed, the victim was at least a hundred feet away. Slipping up to the mouth of the tunnel, Daine peered around the edge.

Over a dozen drow had made it through the deadly wards, and the burning banner still twisted in the wind. In the lead were two familiar figures. Gerrion brandished a blazing sword in one hand and wore a pulsing buckler on the other. He stood next to an older elf wearing an iron crown—the high priest Holuar, and Holuar was pointing right at them.

"Get back!" Pierce spun sideways, smashing into Daine and throwing him back into the tunnel. A gout of flame struck the entrance, and for an instant Pierce was outlined by fire.

"Pierce!"

The warforged staggered forward a few steps. "I will survive, captain, but I fear that the priest can bring that power to bear again if we reveal ourselves."

Daine shook his head. "Everyone down the tunnel! Lei, I hope you've got something to slow them down."

"Yes, captain," she called, as Daine and Pierce ran toward her. "Just a little farther, and . . . this'll do."

Turning around, she flung the crystal shard up the passage to the surface. An instant later, it exploded in a burst of mist. A blast of frigid air swept over Daine, frost forming on his skin. He blinked, and when his eyes opened, the tunnel was blocked.

By ice.

"Ice?" he said. "We're under attack by masters of fire, and you give me a wall of *ice?*"

"It was that or fire," Lei replied.

"Wonderful."

Daine took a moment to study their surroundings. The air was stale and slightly cold, though Daine imagined Lei was to blame for the temperature. The hall was about twenty feet across and roughly as tall as it was wide. The walls and floor were formed of the same red stone they'd seen outside, with no signs of blocks; it was as if the tunnels had been carved into a massive slab of stone. Light came from the walls themselves. Every surface was covered with words in a flowing script unknown to Daine, painted in cold fire.

"Lei?" Daine said. "What does it say?"

"Many of the inscriptions are simply proclamations of light," Pierce responded, to Daine's surprise. "Others speak of protection and secrecy—I suspect these are the shielding glyphs that I spoke of earlier."

"He is correct," Lakashtai said. "I . . . I cannot feel Kashtai's presence. I cannot call on my inner strength."

"Great," Daine said, "but aside from our melting wall and powerless kalashtar, everything's fine? We don't have to fight—"

"Giants," Shen'kar said. The glowing inscriptions covered every wall, but somehow the scorpion wraith found a shadow to step out of. Xu'susar stood beside him.

"Of course," Daine said. "Naturally. How many?"

"Sixteen that we saw," Shen'kar replied. "Six of the blade and ten weavers of magic."

"Did they notice you?"

The elf cocked his head. "How would they do this?"

"I know you're talented, but—"

"They are all dead." Shen'kar said.

There was a faint thud . . . the ringing of a flaming sword striking against a distant wall of ice.

"Ah," Daine said. "In that case, lead the way."

⚅ ⚅ ⚅ ⚅ ⚅ ⚅ ⚅ ⚅

"Onatar's name," Lei whispered.

"Yeah."

Daine had foresworn his belief in higher powers long ago, but what lay before them seemed beyond the capabilities of any mortal force. The passage had led them directly to the center of the monolith. The tower stretched up above them, a hollow spire hundreds of feet across and perhaps a thousand feet in height; perspective was hard to judge from so far below. As impressive as the tower was, it was the object within that drew gasps of astonishment. The heart of the monolith was a massive obsidian cylinder almost as tall as the tower itself. It was covered with glowing sigils and inscriptions in the ancient language of the giants, inlaid with a dozen different metals and gemstones.

And it was floating. It was suspended ten feet above the floor of the chamber, and slowly rotating.

"Think of how much that must weigh . . ." Lei whispered. Daine preferred not to.

Perhaps a hundred metal rings encircled the central pillar, supported by invisible forces. Rising and falling, silently spinning in different directions and speeds, what truly caught the eye were the spheres. Thirteen crystal spheres circled in low orbits, each one studded with gems and glowing inscriptions. Perspective made it difficult to judge the size of these objects . . . but they were big.

The spheres drew their eyes up—but eventually Daine looked down. Circular tables were spread around the base of the obsidian cylinder. These were made of red stone and rose directly out of the floor. Here were the giants, slumped against the tables or sprawled across the floor.

The corpses were dried and desiccated but almost perfectly preserved; Daine wondered if the seal on the monolith gate had held all air in or if some other magic were at work. The closest corpse was that of a man; his skin was wrinkled black leather, as dark as that of the drow, and he would have been twelve feet tall if he were standing. He wore a tunic of a metallic, brass-colored fabric; the hem was trimmed in silver and embroidered with golden spirals. Daine guessed that the man had been broadly built in life, and it reminded him of the massive worn statues flanking the altar in the city of the drow.

"Look," Lei said, pointing. "I think that's a wand."

Indeed, the fallen giant was clutching an object in his hand—a rod tipped with a black gemstone, but it was two and a half feet long, and as thick as Daine's arm.

"Is it a weapon?" Daine said.

"I don't know."

"Then I don't care. We've only got a few minutes. Is this thing remotely useful? Unless one of you can tell me what it does, we'd better keep moving and hope we can find an armory."

Daine was looking at Lei and the newly erudite Pierce, but it was Lakashtai who spoke. "These are the planes," she said.

"Yes . . . that's right!" Lei echoed, staring at the column in wonder.

Daine sighed. "That clears everything up. Thanks."

"The planes," Lei said, "the outer planes—Dolurrh, the realm of the dead. Dal Quor, the region of dreams. You know."

"Sure," Daine said suspiciously, "so you're telling me that the souls of the dead come *here*? Good, because give it a few minutes and we'll probably be joining them."

"No," Lei said, exasperated. "This is a model of the planes. They . . . shift around Eberron, drifting in and out of phase, like the moons, and this is a model of that movement."

"It's more than that," Lakashtai said. She took Lei by the hand and led her forward. Daine reached out to stop her, but Lakashtai brushed away his hand. "Look closely," she whispered, stepping over the wrinkled head of a fallen giant. "Feel it. See what lies within." Slowly, she placed Lei's hand on the closest console, and the mosaic of gemstones encrusting the top of the panel burst into light.

"I *can* see it," Lei said, breathless with wonder. "I can *feel* it, spreading out. It's so much more complicated than any pattern I've seen before. It's . . . beautiful."

"And it helps us how?" Daine said, exasperated.

"It's a gateway," she said, "and I think . . . I think I can activate it."

"I believe you are correct," Pierce said, "but how can you possibly know how to operate such a device?"

"I can't explain it, Pierce. The knowledge . . . it's just there, as if it has always been there. It's . . . the spheres. Each sphere is linked to another plane." Without even seeming to notice what she was doing, Lei clambered onto the back of a giant's corpse so she could run her fingers along the console. A deep, pulsing hum filled the air, and the orbiting rings began to spin at different speeds. "Passengers enter the sphere, and it is physically transported across the planar barrier. I believe—each sphere has controls inside allowing the travelers to return."

"This provides access to every plane?" Pierce said, looking up at the spheres.

"It's not that simple. Alignment, orbit . . . Only two planes are accessible at the moment, Thelanis and Fernia, the plane of fire."

"Fire." Daine's mind was racing. "And these spheres are controlled from here?"

"Initially, and from the sphere itself. The sphere protects the passenger from any dangers of the plane, though if you leave—who knows."

"Do you understand how they work?"

"I can't explain it . . . but yes, I do."

"Good," Daine said. "Shen'kar, if you don't mind, I'll need you for this. Here's my plan . . ."

❋ ❋ ❋ ❋ ❋ ❋ ❋

The high priest Holuar was surrounded by an aura of mystical fire, and he was simply *walking* through the ice that blocked their way. The chill air could not breach his shield of flames, and as old as he was, destiny gave strength to his limbs. *The end is near,* he thought. *At long last, I shall reap the rewards of my ancestors' loyalty. The Lords of the Promise will enfold me in their power, and we shall set the world aflame.*

The ice had filled a long stretch of the hall, and progress had been slow until Holuar had called on the cloak of fire. Now the wall crumbled before him: he had reached the end of the barrier.

There was a man in the hallway twenty feet away. He was too tall, too thick. His skin was sickly pale, and no marks of honor stained his skin—an outlander—the false child of war, the one that had been tested and failed. Holuar pointed a bony finger and prepared to call on the deadly fires, but the stranger dropped to his knees, holding out his hands in supplication.

"Just hear what I have to say before you kill me," the man said. The words of the outlander tongue were flat and graceless, and the man spoke terribly slowly. "I know what you're looking for, and I can give it to you."

"What is this?" Holuar said. His soldiers were emerging from the tunnel, but he raised his hand and they simply spread out around him.

"You want to pass through the Burning Gate. That's what this is all about, right? Well, I came here with the woman who can open it for you."

"The woman of two worlds," Holuar said. Could it be that

she was needed to open the gate and not simply the monolith? He reflected on the words of the prophecy: she would free the voice of the past, she would make the way clear, she would hold the keys. "She will aid us, or you will all die."

"I know. I don't care where you go or what you do. I've got my own business here. So here's the deal. You give us what we want, and we'll open the gates for you. You go through and do . . . whatever it is you have planned. We go on our way. Everyone lives."

Holuar narrowed his eyes. "What you want, you say . . . what is this, that you want?"

"Him." Daine pointed at the man next to Holuar. "Gerrion."

# CHAPTER 50

XEN'DRIK
KARUL'TASH
*Lharvion 22, 997 YK*

**G**errion laughed. "You have no idea what you're asking."

"Oh, I think I do. Do you really think your life is more important than, what, tens of thousands of years of devotion?"

Gerrion glanced at Holuar. "Grandfather? Will you deny me my place in history to satisfy the whims of this outlander, or shall we simply torture them until they do as we ask?"

"Perhaps you've forgotten, but we've been fighting a war back on Khorvaire," Daine said. "I've been tortured by the best. If you think you've got the time to break us, by all means, but I'm told that your season of fire will be over soon, and when it's over, so much for your gate."

Holuar considered, finally speaking in Elvish. "You did not bring the child of war to us, Gerrion. Some would say that you failed in your duty."

"Grandfather!"

"Speaker of the law!" Holuar snapped, and Gerrion hung his head.

"Perhaps it was the wrong man that I led to the city, but I brought all four to the land of fire. If I hadn't drawn this man here, the child of war would not have come. I fulfilled my destiny!"

"Yes . . . I suppose that you did." Holuar looked at Daine. "No," he said, returning to the Common tongue. "His life is not yours to take. If we must tear the secrets from you, we shall."

"Wait!" Daine said. "I don't want his life. All I want is my honor. He betrayed us. He made me look like a fool. I just want to prove how he'd fare in a fair fight. First blood. A scratch only. If he dies you can kill me too. I won't resist. I swear." He drew his sword and looked down at the hilt. "On my father's blood."

Holuar glanced at Gerrion. "To this I agree." He glanced at Gerrion. "Take his honor for the Sulatar, child. Show that you have the strength of the fire—that you are not just a knife in the darkness."

"Grandfather, I—"

"*I have spoken!*"

Daine grinned. "Tell you what, Gerrion, we'll keep it fair. You can use that fine flaming stick you've got there. Me? I'll just use my dagger. I'm sure you remember it."

"Do as you wish," Gerrion said. "You will take no honor from the Sulatar. When you are ready, then." He made a mild gesture with his light sword, the vaguest hint of a salute, but even as Daine nodded and drew his dagger, Gerrion was already launching in a lightning-swift thrust.

Daine leapt back. He didn't parry or riposte—he simply kept the distance between them, staying beyond the tip of the blade.

"Do you *have* any honor to take?" he said.

Gerrion said nothing. His handsome face twisted in a snarl as he launched blow after blow. Daine continued to dance away, staying just out of reach.

Minutes passed, and Daine had yet to strike.

"What are you waiting for?" Gerrion hissed. "You asked for this fight. Aren't you going to *try* to win it?"

"Perhaps I already am," Daine said, ducking beneath a fiery slash. "Perhaps I'm not trying to win yet, but you're doing a fine job of losing without me."

Gerrion *growled*, and the tip of his blade almost grazed Daine's cheek; the flames singed his beard. *Cutting it close*, he thought.

And suddenly Gerrion stopped. He held his guard position and simply watched Daine. "You're *not* trying to win," he said. "But *you* asked for the fight. And if you didn't want to win, then you—"

"That's right," Daine said. His arm flashed forward, and the blade was a black streak through the air. The adamantine dagger sank into Gerrion's left shoulder, and the gray man dropped his sword in shock and surprise. "I was bored," Daine finished. He looked at Holuar. "First blood," he said. "I've got what I came for. Give me back my dagger and I'll show you to your gate."

Gerrion had fallen to his knees. Holuar looked down at him and yanked the dagger loose in one swift motion. Gerrion whimpered and pressed a hand against the wound to staunch the flow of blood. Holuar ignored him and tossed the weapon back to Daine.

"You have your honor," he said quietly. "Now give us our destiny."

@ @ @ @ @ @ @

"Is everything ready?" Daine called out to Lei as he led the firebinders into the vast Hall of the Gate.

Pierce and Lakashtai stood by the door; at Daine's signal, Pierce laid down his bow.

"Yes," Lei said. "The vessel is prepared."

She pointed, and murmurs rippled through the assembled drow. One of the crystal spheres had descended and was hovering just above the floor. A shard of the crystal had folded out and down, creating a long ramp. The inside was filled with dark mist.

Holuar studied the glowing inscriptions on the outer edge of the sphere. "Yes. This is the gate of passage, the chariot that rises to the land of promise."

"Do you know how to operate it?" Lei said. "I can send you through . . . but you'll need to use the controls in the sphere to travel back."

The old elf hadn't taken his eyes off the sphere. "Yes. Yes, I know what is required. We have prepared for this journey for thousands of cycles."

"Do you know what they say about Fernia? I've heard it's all fire and lava. Are you sure you want to go through with this?"

"*Foolish girl!*" Holuar turned to glare at her, and now there was anger in his eyes. "*Thousands* of cycles. I *know* what is to come. This is our destiny!"

"Fine!" Lei said, stepping back and raising her hands.

"I am no fool," the old priest continued, "and I will need . . . hostages."

Daine shook his head. "You're not taking any of my people into a pit of fire."

Holuar hissed sharply. "Of course not. You do not deserve to see our promised land, nor could you survive it, but . . ." He gestured to two of his soldiers, speaking rapidly in Elvish. He turned back to Daine as the soldiers came forward. "You, outlander, and your mate." He pointed at Lakashtai, and Daine tried to ignore Lei's questioning glare. "The two of you will serve as my assurance. Kulaj and Ad'rul will stand remain behind, blades to your throats. Should we not return or send word within one day, they will spill your blood."

"You expect us to stand here and wait for you for an entire day?"

"The alternative is death," Holuar said, and Gerrion smiled at that.

"When you put it that way . . . Safe travels."

The firebinders disarmed Daine and bound his hands. They bound Pierce and Lakashtai as well; only Lei was left free. Soon Daine found himself pressed against one of the stone tables, cold bronze against his throat, as the Sulatar troop filed into the crystal sphere.

"Farewell, Daine," Gerrion called from the ramp. "You may have won back your precious honor, but when I return . . . I think I'll put your tales of torture to the test."

"Go choke on lava," Daine muttered. The knife tightened against his throat, but the soldier didn't speak the Common tongue.

"I'm activating the portal now."

Lei was speaking in Elvish for the benefit of the guards. The panel she was standing at was a mosaic of crystal rods embedded in stone sockets. She drew out a few of the rods, replacing them in different hollows. With each adjustment, a vast pulse of mystical power radiated out from the central column. Daine could feel the air rippling and crawling against his skin. The sphere slowly rose up into the air, and as it moved it gave off a sharp, piercing hum. This grew louder as it drew toward the other floating spheres, and each sphere began to emit a tone of its own. Arcs of energy were flashing around the central column, flowing from ring to ring. Then came a terrible flash of light, a roar like thunder, and the room fell into silence and utter darkness.

Slowly the light returned, as the mystical inscriptions on the walls and the central columns began to glow anew. A moment later and the room was just as it had been before—with one exception: the crystal sphere containing the drow had vanished.

"Lei?" Daine said.

"As far as I can tell, everything was successful, though if the legends are true, Fernia hardly sounds like anyone's promised land."

"Now that you've gotten your gateway to paradise, could you let us get on about our work?" Daine said to the drow holding the knife to his throat. "Some of us still have our own problems to deal with."

The firebinder said nothing, and the knife was as steady as ever.

"Perhaps you can find what we seek, Lei." If Lakashtai was concerned about the elf with a sword at her throat, she gave no sign of it. "The chamber we seek must be elsewhere in this facility. If you can find a way to disable the field that blocks my . . . talents . . . I may be able to sense its presence."

"How would I do that, exactly?" Lei said.

"How is it that you were able to restore function to the network of gates?"

"I . . . I don't know," Lei said. "I just studied the controls, and it came to me. It all seemed to make sense."

"Continue your work. Examine each panel in turn and see what you can find. Perhaps the answers will come to you."

Lei looked over at them, and Daine could see her fear and confusion. "Don't worry about us," he said, the knife brushing his throat as he spoke. "You did everything you needed to do. Just . . . do some research. Explain it to me. It's been far too long since I've heard you lecture."

She smiled slightly at that. "Very well." She looked up at the central column for a moment. "Each of the crystal spheres represents one of the thirteen planes of existence that are said to exist in concert with our universe . . ."

To Daine, it seemed as if hours passed while Lei explored the chamber and discussed mystical minutiae. He had hoped that the lecture might lull the drow to sleep, until he remembered that elves didn't sleep—and however dull the conversation, the soldier watching him seemed as keen and alert as ever.

As Daine himself was struggling to keep his eyes open, the glowing inscriptions on the central column burst into brilliant light. The throbbing hum began, faster, louder, pounding into Daine's head.

"They're coming back!" Lei cried.

There was none of the slow build-up that had characterized the departure. A second later, the chamber was flooded with light. Daine could feel the energy flowing through him, pressing against his heart and lungs.

In an instant it was over. The thirteenth sphere had returned. Its surface was glowing a dull orange, and Daine could feel the heat from a hundred feet away. It slowly descended toward the floor, cooling as it dropped. A moment later the sphere opened, and the crystal ramp extended toward the floor. The interior of the sphere was still cloaked in shadows.

"RELEASE THE PRISONERS!" It was Holuar's voice, yet it was different, stronger and far louder, with an underlying ripple like the crackling of flame. "APPROACH AND BEHOLD OUR GLORY!"

The soldier released Daine, and he raised a hand to massage his throat. The two drow sprinted toward the sphere.

"KNEEL!" Holuar roared from the darkness. "KNEEL AND GIVE HOMAGE, FOR THE MOMENT OF OUR DESTINY HAS COME!"

The firebinders knelt, one to each side of the ramp. Daine's breath caught in his throat as the shapes emerged from the darkness.

Small shapes. Moving swiftly. Three-pronged wheels of dark wood.

Two boomerangs snapped out of the sphere, each one catching a firebinder warrior in the neck. Even as the soldiers struggled to rise, Shen'kar and Xu'sasar dove out of the darkness. Numbed by poison, the firebinders had barely raised their weapons before the oathbreakers were upon them. Xu'sasar's twin blades flashed and Shen'kar's spiked club rose and fell, and the battle was over in seconds.

Within moments, Shen'kar was at Daine's side, untying his hands.

"What happened?" Daine said.

"Just as you planned," the dark elf replied. He had released the magical glamour that he'd used to mimic the voice of the high priest. "The shadows we wove hid us from the foe, and the walls of this vessel shielded us from the flame. We followed the instructions of the lady—" he inclined his head toward Lei—"to return with this craft as soon as the firebinders departed. We left them standing upon an island of black stone in a lake of fire. Perhaps they will find the power that they seek, but they shall never return with it."

"And Gerrion?" Daine said.

"You struck well. The priest healed the wound but did not look beyond the flesh to see the poison that coursed through the veins of your victim. As I promised you, the venom is as slow and patient as Xan'tora herself. By now, your enemy lies dead on the burning shore."

Daine sighed. He'd never expected the firebinders to sacrifice Gerrion, but he had no intention of allowing the gray man to escape after what he'd put Lei through. *My precious honor,* he thought, remembering a time when that might have mattered.

"Now we look to your bargain," Xu'sasar sang. "Holuar is left in this sea of endless flame, but the monolith is now open, and others could follow. Let this place be destroyed?"

"Lei?" Daine said. He pulled his weapons out from under the dead giant, and went to help Lakashtai.

"I don't know. The power contained in these spheres—even if I can find a way to destroy them, the energy released could devastate the area for miles around—or worse."

"You will find a way," Shen'kar said.

The dark elf was still holding his poisoned rod, and his scorpion was perched on his left wrist. His words were fluid and beautiful, but it was clear to Daine that this was a statement, not a request.

"There may be weapons elsewhere in the monolith that could

be of use," Lakashtai said. "Have you learned how to dispel the wards that are blocking the use of mental powers?"

"In fact, I think I have," Lei said. She'd wandered over to another panel halfway around the vast chamber. "These inscriptions on the walls defend against all sorts of supernatural effects. I think that these crystals empower these enchantments, so if I remove this one . . ."

A long line of glowing words faded into darkness. The temperature began to drop, and Daine's breath steamed in the suddenly frigid air.

"I can destroy the heating enchantments. Hmm. It seems the gate system has a rather . . . chilling effect. Let me try something else."

A second line of light faded off of the walls.

"Yes!" Lakashtai said. She closed her eyes and took a deep breath, slowly letting the air flow out of her lungs. "I can feel again." She stretched out a hand, rotating slowly in place.

"There," she said. The central chamber was like a great wheel. The passage to the surface was but one of the spokes, and there were five more tunnels spreading out from the chamber of gates. Lakashtai paused, pointing to the northeast. "This is the way we must go."

Daine considered. "The wards should keep any more firebinders from following, but I don't like the thought of leaving this place unguarded. Pierce . . ."

"I should accompany the explorers, captain. It is possible that the information I now possess will be needed."

"Go," Shen'kar said. "Xu'sasar and I will remain and watch from the shadows. We have fought our battle. Now you must fight yours."

Daine nodded. "All right, Lakashtai," he said. "Lead the way."

❂ ❂ ❂ ❂ ◉ ❂ ❂ ❂

"So what kills a hundred giants?"

The hallway was cold and dim. The only source of light was the glowing inscriptions on the walls, and Lei's efforts in the chamber of gates had caused many of these to fade into darkness.

Lakashtai was in the lead, lighting the way with a cone of light from her eyes—an effect Daine still found unnerving. They'd encountered the corpses of half a dozen giants as they progressed down the hall; one wizard was sprawled on top of a long scroll, a sheet of parchment that must have been eight feet in length. They had been able to avoid most of the corpses, but two guards had fallen side by side, and the explorers had to climb up and over the dried remains.

"I don't see any signs of violence," Daine continued, "They're just . . . dead." He had sword and dagger out and ready; the massive corpses raised his hackles, and it was all too easy to imagine that the withered faces were watching them pass.

"The battle they fought came to an end centuries before the final fall of Xen'drik," Pierce said. "These magi were battling dreams and tampering with the boundaries of the planes themselves. It is dangerous to tamper with reality: I believe that they paid the price, and that those giants who survived the war wisely chose to leave this place as a tomb."

Lakashtai glanced back at Pierce for a moment. "You seem to know a great deal about the conflict, Pierce. Do you know what was built here?"

"No. My . . . memories do not extend to the end of the war. I only know of its purpose: a forge to build a weapon to end the war stretching across the dimensions."

"Let us hope that it did," Lakashtai said, "and perhaps we're about to find out."

The hallway came to an end at a wide archway. A guard lay across the passage; he was wearing a coat of crimson chainmail, and each link was the size of Daine's hand. An obsidian greatsword lay on the ground next to him, over ten feet in length. Lakashtai leapt over the corpse without even touching it; her strength had returned, and she seemed more alive than she had since they'd left Sharn. Daine wasn't feeling so spry; he simply ground his teeth and climbed up over the giant's chest.

The room beyond the arch was smaller than the chamber of gates, but it was no less spectacular. The walls were studded with translucent spheres, ranging from the size of a man's head to a vast orb that was at least eight feet across. For a moment, Daine thought they were made out of glass, but as he drew closer he realized that they were far too fragile. They were soap-bubbles formed from traces of light, glowing with the faint essence of a dying coal. He almost reached out to touch one, but reason and the memory of eerily untouched corpses triumphed over curiosity.

"What *are* they?" Lei whispered.

"Dreams," Pierce and Lakashtai answered together. They glanced at each other, and Pierce inclined his head.

"The purest essence of dreams," Lakashtai continued. "Every living creature that sleeps has a bond to Dal Quor, and obviously this is a vulnerability to those who would fight the lords of the night. I wonder . . ." She glanced up at the ceiling. "Could they have been trying to *create* dreams? To forge an *alternate* realm, a refuge they could retreat to in the dark hours?"

"Can you hear them?" Lei said. Her voice was sluggish, almost slurred, and Daine turned toward her. Lei's eyes were distant and confused. "So many voices . . ."

"Lakashtai?" Daine said, but the kalashtar was already by Lei's side.

"Hear only my voice," she whispered. "Set all else aside. Nothing here is real, all is illusion. Hear only my voice and let it return you to the light."

Lei closed her eyes, her forehead twisting with the effort of thought. Daine and Pierce rushed forward, but Lakashtai held them back with a commanding gesture. The kalashtar leaned in, whispering in Lei's ear. Her eyes flashed with light, and Lei convulsed for a moment; then she opened her eyes again, breathing deeply. Lakashtai squeezed Lei's shoulder and stepped back toward Daine.

"She will recover," Lakashtai said, "but her affinity for this place and the magic of this era is most unusual. Give her a moment of peace."

Daine glanced over at Lei. "I'm . . . fine," she said. She was pale, but she seemed to have regained her composure.

He returned to the study of the room. The fragile spheres covered the walls and ceiling. The center of the chamber was dominated by a dais of opalescent glass—reflective, pale white material lit from within, slowly shifting in color as Daine watched. This altar was ten feet long and six feet high, and two giants were sprawled around it. Standing across the room, they could see that there was something on top of the dais—pieces of broken glass, perhaps a shattered sphere. Whatever it was, it was dull and lifeless, a stark contrast to the gleaming platform.

"There . . ." Lakashtai breathed. "That is what we have sought. Help Lei climb onto the platform—the end of this quest is at hand."

Lei still seemed slightly dazed, but she held Daine's hand and clambered up onto the table when Daine and Pierce hoisted her up. Lakashtai leapt up beside her.

"Touch the shards, Lei," she said. "Feel the pattern within. Reshape what has been broken."

"What is it?" Daine said, standing on his toes and trying to peer up over the edge.

"It is the reason I came here, though even I did not believe it possible," Lakashtai said, walking over to stand above Daine. "You see—"

Then she screamed.

There was a *distortion* in the air around her chest, as if a fist-sized chunk of flesh was being twisted out of phase with the rest of her body. The aura faded, and Lakashtai dropped to one knee, gasping for breath.

"Surely you will not fall so easily, little sister." The voice echoed through the hall. "After all you have put me through, I expected more of a challenge."

It was Tashana.

# CHAPTER 51

XEN'DRIK
KARUL'TASH
*Lharvion 22, 997 YK*

**G**reen eyes burned beneath the hood of a dark cloak, and a long braid of silver-white hair caught the light. Shadows were swirling about Tashana, and for a moment Daine thought he saw faces howling in the darkness.

"You have been most helpful," she said. "I would never have found this place on my own. You shielded your mind well; I thought I had lost you until you reappeared only moments ago, but this chase ends here, in this chamber of broken dreams."

"Just how does it end?" Daine said, walking slowly toward her. He motioned to Pierce—*keep your distance, engage at range.*

"This is no battle for humans," Tashana hissed, dismissing Daine with a gesture.

He felt her mental grip tighten on his mind, but this time, he didn't give in. He tightened his grip on his grandfather's sword, and for the merest moment he felt the old man at his shoulder.

"Perhaps you underestimate humans," he said, setting himself on guard. Behind him, he could hear Lakashtai talking to Lei, guiding her work. "One chance, and one alone. Leave. Now."

The shadows were winding around Tashana, forming the ghastly silhouette he'd seen before. "Fool!" she roared, her voice distorted by the darkness. "Do you have any idea what you are doing?"

"Stopping you. Pierce!"

Pierce's bow sang, and two arrows flashed toward Tashana's chest, but this time she had prepared for such an attack—or else her powers had grown since they'd seen her on the docks of Sharn. The cloak of shadows was far more solid than it appeared, and the arrows shattered against this shield.

Daine wasn't surprised; it was Pierce who had driven this creature off the last time they'd fought, and it seemed unlikely that she'd attack so brazenly without having a defense. If they were to win this battle, he needed to know the rules of engagement. He leapt at the dark figure, feinting with his long blade. As she swatted at his sword with talons of shadow, he switched his footing, ducking under and striking with his dagger.

The adamantine blade could carve through steel and stone, and Daine had never found the substance that could match it—until now. His thrust was perfect, but the blade was thrown back, and his wrist ached from the impact.

*Pain.* Tashana's claws raked along his left arm before he had time to retreat, and the shadows carved through steel and muscle with equal ease. Whispers of fear and doubt crawled into the back of his mind—how could he hope to succeed? Why fight, when it was so much easier to just surrender, to let fate take its course?

*No.* Daine's grandfather was still behind him, and now he felt Jode's presence with him as well. He could hear his friend's laughter, and his zest for life, and it banished the cold fingers of fright. When Tashana came in to strike again, Daine ducked to the side and slashed with his longsword. The shadow parted like smoke, and Daine felt the faintest touch to the flesh within.

Tashana roared out a phrase in an alien tongue, and Daine didn't need to know the language to recognize a curse. Green eyes flashed in the depth of the shadow, and once again he felt her thoughts clutching at his mind, but he was not alone. Now Lei joined the others—her voice, her scent, the sound of her laughter. Tashana's earlier words echoed in the darkness— *Perhaps, when you're mine, I'll make you kill her myself.*

"You should have stayed in my dreams," he hissed, putting all his strength into a thrust with his sword. The blade pierced the shadows, and he felt it penetrate flesh.

Tashana howled in pain, and a dozen faces howled along with her, vague amorphous shapes lurking in her ghastly shroud. *"ENOUGH!"* The air rippled around her, and a wave of raw force threw Daine off his feet, sending him flying ten feet through the air before crashing into the ground. "These schemes end NOW!"

Lakashtai was still standing next to Lei on the shimmering altar. The two of them had assembled the pieces of the shattered object. It was another sphere, two feet in diameter, this one formed of dark crystal. Lei was holding it in her hands, a look of intense concentration on her face, while Lakashtai whispered in her ear. A glowing web surrounded the orb, pulsing like a heartbeat, and Daine could only guess that it was repairing the shattered seams. Before Daine could rise to his feet, Tashana *flew* forward, a streak of deadly shadow.

And ran into Pierce.

The warforged rammed into the shadowy figure, throwing her back. As she recovered her footing, Pierce landed a stunning blow with his flail—and the spiked chain bounced back from the shadow, as if striking a wall of steel.

"Keep her *down!*" Daine called, charging across the room. He could *feel* magical energy building around them, as it had when the planar gate had been activated.

Pierce lashed out once more. The flail couldn't penetrate Tashana's shadowy defenses but he still managed to wrap the chain around her feet and pull her tumbling to the ground. She roared again, and it was Pierce who flew back through the air.

Now Daine was upon her, and a dozen more voices had added their strength to his: Jholeg, the goblin scout he'd last seen at Keldan Ridge; Greykell, the soul of High Walls; Krazhal, the surly dwarf sapper; Pierce, with his calm strength; even Alina Lyrris, and Grazen, his old comrade in arms. Daine slashed with his blade, one blow after another.

"Leave us ALONE!" he cried. "Stay out of my life. Stay out of my dreams! Go back to your wretched gloom and STAY THERE!"

Then it was gone.

The voices that had carried him forward fell silent. The

shadow beneath him dispersed like smoke, and there was only a young woman with pale skin and long white hair, her dark clothing streaked with blood. Daine's blade was raised for a final stroke when her eyes caught his and he froze. It wasn't the power that was in them . . . but the pain. Her mouth worked as she struggled with a final word. "I . . ."

*Kill her!*

"I . . ."

*Kill her!* But the rage was fading. A moment ago she had been a monster. Now she was just a dying woman. He knelt down next to her.

"I . . . cannot . . . dream."

The last embers of light faded from her eyes.

For a moment Daine just stared at her. He could feel the charge of mystical energy building in the air, and he knew he should feel satisfaction, but standing over the ruined corpse, the victory felt hollow. *I cannot dream . . .* what did she mean? Why deny what she'd done?

"It's over," he said.

"Oh no," Lakashtai said. "It's just begun."

She laughed, and he realized it was the first time he'd ever heard that sound . . . sharp and deadly, like chimes of glass.

Daine stood and turned around. Lakashtai was standing on the altar, and the orb was in her hands. Lei was slumped next to her, though Daine could see no sign of harm, and Pierce lay frozen against the edge of the dais.

"What is this?" Daine said. He glanced back at Tashana. Had she somehow fled her body and possessed Lakashtai?

*Oh, no.* It was Lakashtai's thought in his mind, but as sharp and cold as a blade of ice. "Tashana has played her last trick, thanks to you, and in truth, treachery was never her strength." She laughed again.

A terrible chill gripped Daine's heart. *I cannot dream.* Yet it was in dreams that Tashana had threatened him, dreams or as a telepathic voice. The two times they'd actually met in the flesh, Tashana hadn't even said his name. She'd dismissed him out of hand. She was only interested in . . .

"Lakashtai!" Daine charged toward the altar. He didn't know what was going on, and at the moment, he didn't care, but

Lakashtai was standing next to Lei—and Lei wasn't moving.

Lakashtai's eyes glowed like twin stars, and Daine felt as if he had slammed into a wall. The force pinning his thoughts was a hundred times more powerful than that of the woman he'd just killed. He was as helpless as if he'd been caught in a block of ice.

Lakashtai stepped down from the block and walked toward him. "Daine, Daine, with your valuable dreams and hidden secrets." She stood next to him, and she reached out and ran two fingers along his cheek. "This was never about you. You are a piece on a board so vast you cannot see the squares."

*Take whatever you want from me!* Daine couldn't speak, but he could still think. *Just leave them alone!*

"We don't want anything from you, little Daine," Lakashtai said. She glanced back at Lei. "Sometimes the best way to achieve your goals is to threaten another piece, but I'm sure you can understand that. After all, 'Perhaps, when you're mine, I'll make you kill her myself.' "

Suddenly he remembered the terrible presence he'd glimpsed in his mind when Lakashtai had helped him so long ago in Sharn, and the crystal . . . the sliver of crystal he'd kept close at hand, which she'd *said* formed a bond between them. He'd let her in.

"Yes." She paused for a moment, as if listening to some distant sound. "If only there was more time, but who can say . . ." She ran her fingers along his cheek again. *Perhaps I'll see you in your dreams.*

He heard her laughter in his mind, and she slowly faded away, with the crystal orb clutched in her hands. The aura of magical energy faded with her, as did the power pinning his thoughts; he almost tumbled forward as the paralysis faded. He tore the emerald shard from his pouch and dashed it against the ground, and as it shattered he felt a pressure fade from his mind, a touch so faint he hadn't noticed it was there.

Across the chamber, Pierce rose to his feet. "Daine . . . Lei!"

She was still spread across the dais. With desperate strength Daine forced himself up onto the table, with Pierce right behind. Lei's skin was cool to the touch, but she was still breathing.

"LEI!" he called, shaking her.

She moaned. Daine clung to her, refusing to let go.

"It is the orb," Pierce said. "Restoring it—the process has drawn on her own life energy. She is weak, but she will survive."

A dull vibration shook the room . . . a slow, rhythmic rumble.

Daine frowned. "Is that . . ."

"The gate," Lei whispered.

"Lakashtai!" he cried.

For a moment, he was torn, struggling between fury and the fear of leaving Lei. Pierce was looking straight at him, and somehow Daine knew that the warforged felt the same way.

"Go," Lei said. "Stop her."

Daine lowered her gently, and he and Pierce leapt to the ground. Pierce snatched his flail off the ground, and they were halfway to the archway when they saw the figure waiting for them.

*Daine,* Harmattan said. *It's been a long time.*

**D**aine's blades were out in an instant. As he charged, a chain snaked around his ankle and brought him tumbling to the ground. Pierce's flail

"This fight cannot be won with a sword, captain," Pierce said quietly. "Others need you. Do not throw away your life."

The massive figure rustled, shards of metal rattling against metal, and Daine saw blood falling to the floor. He wondered about Shen'kar and Xu'sasar—this creature had to have come through the chamber of gates.

The vibration in the floor grew stronger.

*If you think you can win my trust so easily, you are sadly mistaken, little brother,* Harmattan said.

"Indeed." A dark figure slid into the room, stepping out from the shadows of Harmattan's steel cloak. Adamantine blades slide from Indigo's arms. "You made your choice, Pierce. You chose your masters. Now you may die with them."

"Surely you did not come this far to threaten me," Pierce said, helping Daine stand.

*You are irrelevant. Despite Indigo's wishes, I think I shall let you live . . . Our family is small enough as it is, but you have already served your purpose, whether you meant to or not. You passage gave us entry, and as for why we are here . . . It seems I was mistaken, after all. Destiny is a strange thing.*

"What do you want?" Daine growled. He was studying the strange figure, searching for any signs of weakness.

The rumbling in the floor ceased, and all was quiet.

*I came here in search of one thing and one thing alone. I knew that it was waiting for me in this ancient place, so I assumed it to be a relic of the distant past.* Harmattan rustled again. *But the one I serve works in mysterious ways and leads me down paths I never considered. I want the vial.*

"What are you talking about?" said Pierce.

*He knows,* Harmattan responded, and Daine felt a sudden chill. *A vial filled with blue liquid, glowing slightly, with a familiar seal stamped on the top.* His cloak spread further out around him, ready to lash forward in a swath of razored steel. *I have no desire to damage it, and I would rather let my brother live; you will all die if we do battle. Give me the vial, little fleshling, and I may even spare you and sister Lei.*

"Daine?" Pierce said, uncertain.

Daine reached into his pouch and produced the crystal vial. "Is this it?"

*"Yes."*

"You came all the way to Xen'drik—you cut off Lei's finger— for *this?*"

*Yes. You are prepared to surrender it?*

Daine looked at the unstoppable warforged, dripping with the blood of his allies. He remembered Jode's voice in the darkness of the obsidian city. He thought of Lei, lying on the altar behind him.

And he thought of a temple in the depths of Sharn, of a winged lion with the head of a woman.

"No," he said.

Harmattan hissed and Indigo leapt forward, but even as they moved Daine wrenched the seal from the top of the vial. As Pierce dove between him and the attacking warforged, Daine brought the bottle to his lips, and the liquid flowed down his throat. It was like light, brilliant and burning, overwhelming every sense.

*Wake up.*

# Glossary

**Aberrant Dragonmark:** There are twelve dragonmarks, but stories say that when dragonmarked bloodlines mingle, they can produce warped marks. Like the true dragonmarks, these bestow magical powers, but these powers are dark and dangerous and said to take a terrible toll on the mind and body of the bearer. See *dragonmark, House Tarkanan, War of the Mark.*

**Adar:** A small nation on the continent of Sarlona. Adar is the homeland of the kalashtar, and its mountain terrain serves as a natural defense in the constant battle against the Inspired.

**Ad'rul:** A warrior of the Sulatar drow.

**Aerenal:** An island nation off the southeastern coast of Khorvaire, Aerenal is known as the homeland of the elves.

**Alina Lorridan Lyrris:** A gnome wizard with considerable wealth and influence. Whether she is a true criminal or simply amoral, Alina is a dangerous woman who usually works in the shadows. Once she lived in the city of Metrol, where she employed *Daine.* Currently she resides in the Den'iyas district of Sharn.

**Arawai:** The Sovereign of Life and Love. Arawai is said to bring good harvest to the land and fertility to the living. Nature is her domain, and she also holds influence over the weather; farmers and sailors alike ask for her blessings on their endeavors.

**Arcane Congress:** Established by King Galifar I in 15 YK, the Arcane Congress was tasked to study the mysteries of magic and place these powers at the service of the kingdom. The congress has its seat in *Aundair,* and when the kingdom collapsed in 894 YK the congress swore its allegiance to the Aundarian throne.

**Arcanix:** An institute of arcane studies in the nation of Aundair. Many of the greatest wizards of Galifar learned their craft within the floating towers of Arcanix.

**Argonnessen**: A large continent to the southeast of Eberron, said to be the home of dragons.

**Artificer**: A spellworker who channels magical energy through objects, creating temporary or permanent tools and weapons.

**Aundair**: One of the original Five Nations of Galifar, Aundair is houses the seat of the Arcane Congress and the University of Wynarn. Currently under the rule of Queen Aurala ir'Wynarn.

**Augur**: A professional fortune-teller or diviner.

**Aureon**: The Sovereign of Law and Lore, the source of order and knowledge. Followers of the Sovereign Host say that Aureon gives guidance to rulers and those who pass judgment, guides the scribe and the student, and devised the principles wizards use to work their spells.

**Blacklion**: A forgehold of House Cannith. During the Last War, Aleisa and Talin d'Cannith worked on warforged at the Blacklion Forgehold.

**Blademark**: The mercenary's guild of *House Deneith*.

**"breather"**: A derogatory term used by the warforged to describe non-construct creatures, i.e., elves, humans, halflings.

**Breland**: The largest of the original Five Nations of Galifar, Breland is a center of heavy industry. The current ruler of Breland is King Boranel ir'Wynarn.

**Briarghost**: Predators found in Xen'drik. While roughly the same size and shape as a large predatory cat, briarghosts are a strange blend of flesh and vegetable matter.

**Broken Oath**: One of the drow tribes of Xen'drik; the name translates into "qaltiar" in the Elven language. The Qaltiar drow are driven by an ancient vendetta against the giants of Xen'drik and the Sulatar drow.

**Bronzewood**: An unusual form of lumber that has many of the traits of metal. The elves of Aerenal use bronzewood in the creation of arms and armor.

**Cadrian:** A soldier who served in the Cyran army under Daine's command. Cadrian was killed in the battle of Keldan Ridge.

**Cannith, House:** The dragonmarked house of Making.

**Cantrip:** A minor form of magic. A cantrip might be used to clean the dirt from filthy clothing or to open a door from across a room.

**Casalon:** A fortified city in Cyre, destroyed by the Mourning.

**Changeling:** Members of the changeling race possess a limited ability to change face and form, allowing a changeling to disguise itself as a member of another race or to impersonate an individual. Changelings are said to be the offspring of humans and doppelgangers. They are relatively few in number and have no lands or culture of their own but are scattered across Khorvaire.

**Chaar, Hassalac:** A powerful sorcerer who resides in Stormreach. Hassalac prefers the title "Prince of Dragons."

**Chyrassk:** A cult leader who has been gathering followers in the dismal district known as Khyber's Gate. Chyrassk has never been seen by those outside his cult, and he remains shrouded in mystery.

**Cliffside:** A community built into the cliffs between the city of Sharn and the docks of the Dagger River.

**Cold Fire:** Magical flame that produces no heat and does not burn. Cold fire is used to provide light in most cities of Khorvaire.

**Crown:** The copper crown is the lowest denomination of coin minted under the rule of Galifar.

**Cyre:** One of the original Five Nations of Galifar, known for its fine arts and crafts. The governor of Cyre was traditionally raised to the throne of Galifar, but in 894 YK, Kaius of Karrnath, Wroann of Breland, and Thalin of Thrane rebelled against Mishann of Cyre. During the war, Cyre lost significant amounts of territory to elf and goblin mercenaries, creating the nations of Valenar and Darguun. In 994 YK,

Cyre was devastated by a disaster of unknown origin that transformed the nation into a hostile wasteland populated by deadly monsters. Breland offered sanctuary to the survivors of the Mourning, and most of the Cyran refugees have taken advantage of this amnesty. See *Mourning, Mourners, Mournland*.

**d'Cannith, Aaren**: A dragonmarked artificer, one-time baron of Metrol, and member of the Cannith Council based in Cyre. The official records of the house credit Aaren with the mystical breakthrough that gave true sentience to the warforged. Aaren was fascinated by the mysterious continent of Xen'drik, and some say his work was based on ancient secrets recovered there. Aaren passed away in 984 YK. He is survived by his son *Merrix d'Cannith*.

**d'Cannith, Alder**: A gifted artificer and architect, Alder was an influential figure in the early history of House Cannith. He designed the original forgeholds of the house, many of which remain in operation in the present day. Only a few of his portable creations have survived, but these magical tools are among the greatest treasures of House Cannith.

**d'Cannith, Aleisa**: A dragonmarked artificer of House Cannith and mother of *Lei d'Cannith*. Aleisa was involved with the development of the warforged, but all records of her work were lost in the war. She is believed to have died in Cyre on the Day of Mourning.

**d'Cannith, Dasei**: A dragonmarked heir residing in Sharn. Dasei studied the mystical arts with her cousin *Lei d'Cannith*, but she has accomplished far more as a socialite than as an artificer.

**d'Cannith, Hadran**: A dragonmarked heir. Hadran's ancestors were one of the first branches of House Cannith to set roots in Sharn, and he possesses considerable wealth and influence. A widower with no children, Hadran arranged a betrothal with *Lei d'Cannith*, but was killed before the wedding.

**d'Cannith, Halea**: The administrator of House Cannith's Whitehearth forgehold, where she crossed paths with Daine and his companions.

**d'Cannith, Kharizal:** A one-armed researcher at the White-hearth forgehold. Kharizal was involved in forbidden experiments involving mind control and the merging of flesh and metal.

**d'Cannith, Lei:** A dragonmarked heir, daughter of *Aleisa* and *Talin d'Cannith*. Lei studied the mystical arts in Sharn and Metrol. Like many young artificers, she chose to serve in the Cannith support corps during the war. She served with the military forces of the Five Nations to maintain the warforged soldiers and other weapons each nation had purchased from Cannith. In 993 YK, her parents arranged for her betrothal to Hadran d'Cannith, but Lei's father insisted that she serve a term in the military before her marriage. Lei was assigned to the Southern Command of Cyre, where she served with *Daine, Pierce,* and *Jode.* In 996 YK, she was excoriated from House Cannith; the reasons for this remain a mystery.

**d'Cannith, Merrix:** As a baron of House Cannith, Merrix oversees house activities in the vicinity of Sharn. Son of *Aaren d'Cannith*, Merrix is a skilled artificer who has spent a decade working on new warforged designs. In the wake of the Last War he has shown shrewd political instincts and has moved to take advantage of the chaos created by the destruction of the House Council. He is the most influential Cannith baron in Breland, and many believe that he hopes to seize control of the house itself.

**d'Cannith, Tannic:** An artificer involved in the development of the warforged. Tannic worked with the assassin Indigo, and was eventually killed by her.

**d'Cannith, Talin:** A dragonmarked artificer of House Cannith and father of *Lei d'Cannith*. He is believed to have died in Cyre on the Day of Mourning.

**Dagger River:** One of the largest rivers in Khorvaire, the Dagger runs south through Breland into the Thunder Sea.

**Dailan:** The grandfather of Daine. Dailan was a master swordsman and taught Daine to wield a blade. He passed away in 984 YK, passing his heirloom sword to his grandson.

**Daine:** A soldier and one-time mercenary, Daine was once an heir of House Deneith. Born in Cyre, he is known to have worked for *Alina Lorridan Lyrris* for an extended period of time. In 988 YK he left House Deneith, forsaking his birthright in order to serve with the Queen's Guard of Cyre, ultimately rising to the rank of captain in the Southern Command. Following the Mourning and the destruction of Cyre, he has led the survivors of his troop to Sharn.

**"Dak ru'sen Karul'tash. Hasken ul tul'kas.":** In the language of the giants, "You have come to Karul'tash. Provide words of passage."

**Dal Quor:** Another plane of existence. Mortal spirits are said to travel to Dal Quor when they dream.

**Darguul:** Common name for someone or something from Darguun.

**Darguun:** A nation of goblinoids, founded in 969 YK when a hobgoblin leader named Haruuc formed an alliance among the goblinoid mercenaries and annexed a section of southern Cyre. Breland recognized this new nation in exchange for a peaceful border and an ally against Cyre. Few people trust the people of Darguun, but their soldiers remain a force to be reckoned with.

**Darkhart, Jura:** Born Jura d'Cannith, this dragonmarked aristocrat was expelled from House Cannith after marrying a dryad. He remained in Sharn even after being condemned as an excoriate. His wife died in 995 YK.

**Dark Six:** The six malevolent deities of the Sovereign Host, whose true names are not known.

**Darkwood:** This rare lumber is named for its pitch-black coloration. It is as hard as oak, but it is remarkably light—almost half the weight of most types of lumber. It is often used in the creation of magical wands and staves.

**Dasei:** A homunculus created by Lei d'Cannith. Named after Dasei d'Cannith.

**Dek**: A changeling sailor on the Kraken's Wake.

**Demon Wastes**: A barren land in the northwest of Khorvaire. The Demon Wastes are said to be filled with savage barbarians, deadly spirits, and ruins that predate human civilization by hundreds of thousands of years.

**Deneith, House**: A dragonmark house bearing the Mark of Sentinel.

**Densewood**: A form of lumber that has the durability of stone. Densewood comes from the elven nation of Aerenal, and is typically used by elf architects.

**Devourer**: One of the deities of the Dark Six, the Devourer represents the destructive power of nature. He is strongly tied to the sea and the mystery of the deep waters, but earthquakes, avalanches, and tornadoes are all his children.

**Displacer beast**: A magical predator found in Xen'drik and western Khorvaire. The displacer beast appears to be a few feet away from its true position, making it difficult to fight.

**Dolurrh**: The plane of the dead. When mortals die, their spirits are said to travel to Dolurrh and then slowly fade away, passing to whatever final fate awaits the dead.

**Donal**: A soldier in the Cyran army. Donal served under Daine at the battle in Keldan Ridge. He has not been seen since the Mourning.

**Dorn Peak**: A mountain on the border between Breland and Cyre.

**Dorn plateau**: A large plateau on Dorn Peak.

**"Dorn's Teeth!"**: A mild oath invoking Dol Dorn, the Sovereign Lord of war.

**Draconists**: A variant sect of the religion of the Sovereign Host. The faithful claim that the Sovereigns are ancient ascended dragons.

**Dragon**: 1) A reptilian creature possessing great physical and mystical power. 2) A platinum coin bearing an image of a dragon on one face. The platinum dragon is the highest denomination of coin minted under the rule of Galifar.

**Dragonmark:** 1) A mystical mark that appears on the surface of the skin and grants mystical powers to its bearer. 2) A slang term for the bearer of a dragonmark.

**Dragonmarked Houses:** One of the thirteen families whose bloodlines carry the potential to manifest a dragonmark. Many of the dragonmarked houses existed before the kingdom of Galifar, and they have used their mystical powers to gain considerable political and economic influence. See *dragonmark, War of the Mark.*

**Dragonshard:** A form of mineral with mystical properties, said to be a shard of one of the great progenitor dragons. There are three different types of shard, each with different properties. A shard has no abilities in and of itself, but an artificer or wizard can use a shard to create an object with useful effects. *Siberys shards* fall from the sky and have the potential to enhance the power of dragonmarks. *Eberron shards* are found in the soil and enhance traditional magic. *Khyber shards* are found deep below the surface of the world and are used as a focus binding mystical energy.

**Dreaming Dark:** 1) A secret order of psionic spies and assassins that serves as the eyes and hands of the quori in Dal Quor, the Region of Dreams. 2) The spiritual force that guides all of the quori; also known as il-Lashtavar, "the Darkness that Dreams."

**Drow:** A humanoid race found on the continent of Xen'drik. There are many similarities between drow and elves, and the drow are often called "dark elves" —a reference to their pitch-black skin and their nocturnal tendencies.

**"*Drukil esul ul siltash*":** In the language of the giants, "Open the gate and let fall the wards." *Siltash'un* is a stronger form: "Open now!"

**Eberron:** 1) The world. 2) A mythical dragon said to have formed the world from her body in primordial times and to have given birth to natural life. Also known as "The Dragon Between." See *Khyber, Siberys*.

**Eldeen Reaches:** Once this term was used to describe the vast stretches of woodland found on the west coast of Khorvaire, inhabited mostly by nomadic shifter tribes and druidic sects. In 958 YK the people of western Aundair broke ties with the Aundairian crown and joined their lands to the Eldeen Reaches, vastly increasing the population of the nation and bringing it into the public eye.

**Eternal Fire:** See cold fire.

**Everbright Lantern:** A lantern infused with cold fire, creating a permanent light source. These items are used to provide illumination in most of the cities and larger communities of Khorvaire. An everbright lantern usually has a shutter allowing the light to be sealed off when darkness is desirable.

**Excoriate:** 1) A person who has been expelled from a dragonmarked house. An excoriate is stripped of the family name and any property held by the house and is not welcome at house enclaves. Members and allies of the house are urged to shun excoriates. Prior to the foundation of Galifar, houses often flayed the victim's dragonmark off of his body. While only temporary, this was a brutal and visible way of displaying the anger of the house. See *dragonmarked houses*.

**Eye of Deneith:** Most of the dragonmarked houses have two heraldic emblems—a magical beast associated with the history of the house and a simpler, iconic symbol. The three-headed chimera is the beast of Deneith, while its icon is a silver eye surrounded by the golden rays of the sun. This symbol is known as the Watchful Eye or the Eye of Deneith.

**Fairhaven:** The capital city of the nation of Aundair.

**Felmar Valley:** A stretch of land on the border between Breland and Cyre. Toward the end of the Last War, Daine and his fellow soldiers were assigned to hold the Felmar fort against the Brelish.

**Fernia:** A plane of existence known as the Sea of Fire.

**Fin**: A sailor on the Kraken's Wake.

**Firebinding**: A technique taught to artificers. This art includes the creation of cold fire and true flame, allowing an artificer to produce a flaming sword or to slay an armored knight by boiling him in his armor.

**Five Nations**: The five provinces of the Kingdom of Galifar—Aundair, Breland, Cyre, Karrnath, and Thrane.

**"Flame!"**: A common oath derived from the divine force known as the Silver Flame.

**'Forged**: A slang term for the warforged.

**Forgehold**: A large facility designed to research and produce magical goods or techniques. Most of the forgeholds in Khorvaire belong to House Cannith.

**Foundling**: Dragonmarks are bound to the blood of a single family. Anyone who possesses the Mark of Making has some tie to House Cannith. However, the marks have existed for thousands of years, and those families have grown and spread over that time. When someone develops a dragonmark but has no known link to the house that bears that mark, he is known as a foundling. The dragonmarked houses traditionally embrace foundlings in order to maintain control of the mark, but foundlings rarely rise far in the ranks of the house and cannot use the full house name. The child of a foundling and a full heir of the house can take the name of the house. See *dragonmark, dragonmarked houses.*

**Frigid Shore**: A region on the Xen'drik coast south of Stormreach. The temperature in this region fluctuates dramatically; sometimes the water is frozen, sometimes it is tropical and warm.

**Galifar**: 1) A cunning warrior and skilled diplomat who forged five nations into a single kingdom that came to dominate the continent of Khorvaire. 2) The kingdom of Galifar I, which came to an end in 894 YK with the start of the Last War. 3) A golden coin minted by the kingdom, bearing the image of the first king. The golden galifar is still in use today and is worth ten sovereigns.

**Gerrion:** A gambler and guide who makes his home in Stormreach. His gray skin and elven features suggest that he is the offspring of human and drow parents.

**Ghallanda, House:** A dragonmarked house bearing the Mark of Hospitality.

**Ghulra:** The mark on the forehead of a warforged. Every warforged has a unique ghulra, much as humans have unique fingerprints.

**Glamerweave:** A general term used to describe clothing that has been magically altered for cosmetic purposes. A glamerweave outfit may enhance the appearance of the wearer—concealing blemishes, adding color to hair or eyes—or it may simply possess colors or patterns than could never be replicated with mundane fabrics. Glimmersilk is one form of glamerweave.

**Glimmersilk:** A form of glamerweave, glimmersilk holds colors that are far more vivid than would be possible with normal cloth. A pattern of flames painted on glimmersilk actually seems to burn.

**Glyph:** A mystical symbol. Often used to refer to a glyph of warding, a magical security system that will unleash a spell on anyone who crosses the glyph without speaking the proper phrase.

**Gnome:** A race of small humanoids. Gnomes are found across Khorvaire, but are concentrated in the nation of Zilargo.

**Goblinoid:** A general term encompassing three humanoid species—the small and cunning goblins, the warlike hobgoblins, and the large and powerful bugbears.

**Greenman Pier:** A dock at the base of the Cliffside district of Sharn.

**Gundrak'ul:** One of the obsidian cities of the Sulatar.

**Gurk'ash:** A thick-skinned Xen'drik beast that looks much like a bison with the hide of a rhinoceros. The gurk'ash is used as a beast of burden and raised as livestock for its meat and its milk. The creature possesses a strange magical property: its flesh does not rot after death, and its milk never spoils. As a result, gurk'ash goods are prized by sailors as an alternative to hard tack and similar fare.

**Half-orc:** When humans and orcs interbreed, the offspring typically possess characteristics of both races. These half-orcs are not as bestial in appearance as their orc forbears, but they are larger and strong than most humans and usually possess a few orcish features, such as a gray skin tone or pronounced canine teeth. Half-orcs are most common in the Shadow Marches but can be found across Khorvaire.

**Harmattan:** A charismatic warforged insurgent. Harmattan possesses unusual physical abilities; for the moment, his origin and the full extent of his powers remains a mystery.

**Harysh:** A female shifter who lives in Stormreach. Harysh runs an inn called The Ship's Cat.

**High Walls:** A district in the Lower Tavick's Landing ward of Sharn. During the Last War many foreign nationals living in the city were relocated to High Walls, and the majority of the Cyran refugees living in Sharn reside in this district.

**Hilt, the:** The intersection of rivers below the city of Sharn.

**Holuar:** The high priest of the Sulatar drow.

**Homunculus:** A construct servant created by an artificer or wizard. Homunculi can be designed to perform a range of tasks, from combat to communication.

**Hugal:** A changeling who served Teral ir'Soras. He was killed by Daine beneath the streets of Sharn.

**Illithid:** An abomination from Xoriat, the plane of madness. An illithid is roughly the same size and shape as a human but possesses a squidlike head with tentacles arrayed around a fanged maw. Illithids feed on the brains of sentient creatures and possess the ability to paralyze or manipulate the minds of lesser creatures. Illithids are more commonly known as *mind flayers*.

**Il-Lashtavar**: A quori word that translates as "the Darkness that Dreams." See Dreaming Dark.

**il-Yannah**: A word from the Quor tongue, translating to "the Great Light." This mystical force is the focus of the religion of the kalashtar.

**Inspired, the**: The lords of the land of Riedra. The subjects of the Inspired say that these nobles are guided by the wisest spirits of the past. The kalashtar believe that the Inspired are conduits for quori spirits: the direct agents of the Dreaming Dark on Eberron.

**ir'**: When attached to a family name, this prefix indicates one of the aristocratic lines of Galifar. The descendants of King Galifar I belong to the ir'Wynarn line.

**ir'Ryc, Greykell**: A scion of a noble Cyran family, Greykell ir'Ryc served as a captain in the Queen's Guard of Cyre. Known as "the laughing wolf" due to her tenacity and good humor, Greykell was renowned throughout the southern command for her cunning strategies and her ability to inspire her soldiers. The blood of dragons is said to run through her house, and in addition to being a gifted swordswoman, she possesses a minor talent for magic. Following the destruction of Cyre, Greykell traveled to Sharn. She has established herself as the unofficial sheriff of the High Walls district, though she prefers to maintain order through diplomacy as opposed to the use of force.

**ir'Soras, Teral**: Once a councilor to the court of Cyre, Teral ir'Soras retired from politics to enjoy his middle years. This quiet life came to an end when the Mourning destroyed Cyre. The wounded councilor was found by illithids, and these alien creatures transformed him, granting him terrible power in exchange for his service. Teral organized an illithid cult in Sharn, but was eventually killed by *Pierce*.

**ir'Talan, Grazen:** Born into House Deneith, Grazen served in the Blademark and earned a place in the *Sentinel Marshals*. During an assignment in Sharn, Grazen fell in love with an heir of the Tala line. As the Galifar Accords prevent the heirs of dragonmarked houses from holding royal titles, Grazen chose to leave House Deneith to marry his beloved. Between his own skill and the influence of his new family Grazen obtained a commission in the Sharn Watch. Today he is the captain of the Daggerwatch Garrison in Upper Dura.

**Jani Onyll:** A Cyran soldier who served with *Daine* in the Last War.

**Jholeg:** A goblin scout who served in the Cyran army under *Daine's* command.

**Jode:** A former companion of Daine. Jode was a halfling with the Mark of Healing, though he never admitted to having a tie to House Jorasco. In 988 YK he took up service in the Queen's Guard of Cyre along with Daine. He served as a healer and occasional scout, using his dragonmark and quick wits to assist his friend. He died in 993 YK, though the circumstances of his death remain a mystery.

**Jorasco, House:** A dragonmarked house bearing the Mark of Healing.

**Kalashtar:** The kalashtar are humans touched by the Dal Quor, the region of dreams. Every kalashtar has a bond to one of the rebellious quori spirits who opposed the Dreaming Dark and were forced to flee Dal Quor. By drawing on this bond, kalashtar are often able to develop significant mental powers. Kalashtar use the name of their quori spirit as a suffix: thus, Lakashtai and Tetkashtai are both kalashtar of the lineage of Kashtai.

**Karrn:** A citizen of Karrnath.

**Karrnath:** One of the original Five Nations of Galifar. Karrnath is a cold, grim land whose people are renowned for their martial prowess. The current ruler of Karrnath is King Kaius ir'Wynarn III.

**Karul'tash**: An ancient forgehold built by the giants of Xen'drik.

**Kashtai**: One of the quori spirits bound to the kalashtar.

**Keeper, the**: One of the sinister gods of the Dark Six. The Keeper is the embodiment of greed and decay, whose hunger is so great that he lets all else fall to rot and ruin. While he amasses gold and jewels, the Keeper covets the souls of the living. He seeks to snatch the spirits of the dead as they pass to Dolurrh, hoarding these souls and gloating over his treasures.

**"Kej'dre. Isk. Han'tal."**: Words of passage required to open the gates of Karul'tash.

**"Kulas Kastoruk ru'sen Karul'tash."**: In the language of the giants, "Archshaper Kastoruk has come to Karul'tash."

**Keldan Ridge**: A remote region of hills in southern Cyre. While passing along the ridge in 994, Daine's soldiers encountered a heavily armed force of unknown nationality. This enemy scattered the Cyran forces; it was this forced retreat that pushed Daine, Lei, Pierce, and Jode outside the radius of the Mourning.

**Kesht**: A shifter who served under Daine's command during the Last War. He was killed in the battle of Keldan Ridge.

**Kess**: The major-domo of Hassalac Chaar's estate in Stormreach.

**Khorvaire**: One of the continents of Eberron.

**Khyber**: 1) The underworld. 2) A mythical dragon, also known as "The Dragon Below." After killing Siberys, Khyber was imprisoned by Eberron and transformed into the underworld. Khyber is said to have given birth to a host of demons and other unnatural creatures. See *Eberron, Siberys*.

**King of Fire**: A tavern and gaming hall located in the district of Hareth's Folly.

**Kol Korran**: One of the gods of the Sovereign Host, the Lord of World and Wealth. Merchants, miners, and any who desire to improve their lot in life trust that Kol Korran will help them achieve their dreams, while the wealthy often sacrifice to the Sovereign in the hopes that he will maintain their fortunes.

*"Kolesq!"*: In the language of Riedra, "Retreat!"

**Korranberg**: One of the major cities of the gnome nation of Zilargo. Korranberg is known for its many colleges and its great library.

*Kraken's Wake*: A ship of the Lyrandar Windwright's guild, captained by Helias Lyrandar. The Kraken's Wake runs a route between Sharn and Stormreach. Its elemental-bound sail ensures that the ship always has wind.

**Krazhal**: A dwarf siege engineer who served Daine during the Last War. He was killed in the battle of Keldan Ridge.

**Kryssh**: A reptilian guard in the service of Hassalac Chaar.

**Kulaj**: A warrior of the Sulatar drow.

**Kulikoor**: A scorpion wraith of the Qaltiar drow.

**Kundarak Bank**: The largest banking network in Khorvaire, managed by the dragonmarked House Kundarak.

**Kundarak, House**: A dragonmarked house bearing the Mark of Warding.

**Kuryeva**: A potent alcoholic beverage made using the berries of the kuryeva bush, a plant found only in the land of Xen'drik.

**Lakashtai**: A kalashtar woman residing in Sharn.

**Lallis hound**: A breed of hunting dog popular in Cyre. Much of the breed was wiped out in the Mourning, but lallis hounds can still be found across Khorvaire.

**Last War, The**: This conflict began in 894 YK with the death of King Jarot ir'Wynarn, the last king of Galifar. Following Jarot's death, three of his five children refused to follow the ancient traditions of succession, and the kingdom split. The war lasted over a hundred years, and it took the utter destruction of Cyre to bring the other nations to the negotiating table. No one has admitted defeat, but no one wants to risk being the next victim of the Mourning. The chronicles are calling the conflict "the Last War," hoping that the bloodshed might have finally slaked humanity's thirst for battle. Only time will tell if this hope is in vain.

**Lharvion:** 1) The eighth month of the calendar of Galifar. 2) One of the twelve moons of Eberron.

**Lhazaar Principalities:** A collection of small nations running along the eastern cost of Khorvaire. The people of this land are renowned seafarers, and there is a strong tradition of piracy in the region.

**Livewood:** An unusual form of lumber that remains alive even after it is felled. It is only found on the island of Aerenal, and the elves of this land occasionally use it when building ships or homes.

**Lon:** A sailor serving on the Kraken's Wake. Brelish by birth, Lon holds a grudge against Cyrans.

**Lynna:** A soldier who served in the Cyran army under Daine's command. Lynna was killed in the battle of Keldan Ridge.

**Lyrandar, Helais:** Captain of the Kraken's Wake.

**Lyrandar, House:** A dragonmarked house bearing the Mark of Storm.

**Magewright:** A general term for any professional who uses magic to enhance the skills of his trade. The typical magewright can only perform one or two spells; examples include the blacksmith who uses magic to improve his craft, the lamplighter who produces everbright lanterns, and the auger who uses magic to divine the future for her clients.

**Mal:** A soldier who served in the Cyran army under Daine's command. He was killed in the battle of Keldan Ridge.

**Malleon's Gate:** A district in the Lower Tavick's Landing ward of Sharn. This area is largely inhabited by goblins, Droaamites, and other inhuman creatures.

**Marcher**: An inhabitant of the Shadow Marches.

**'Mark**: A slang term for the bearer of a dragonmark. See *dragonmark*.

**Metrol**: The capital of Cyre. Metrol was destroyed by the Mourning.

**Mind flayer**: See *illithid*.

**Mindshard**: A crystal that serves as a focus for mental energy, which can be used to generate a variety of supernatural effects.

**Mithral**: A silvery metal that is just as strong as iron, but far lighter and more flexible.

**Mockery, the**: One of the gods of the Dark Six. The Mockery is the lord of terror and treachery, patron to thieves, assassins, and tyrants. He is said to be the brother of Dol Dorn and Dol Arrah, but he was flayed and driven from the Host after he betrayed his siblings. The Mockery has one of the largest followings among the Dark Six, as many criminals and warriors seek his blessing on their endeavors.

**Monan**: A changeling who served Teral ir'Soras. Monan fought Daine in Sharn, and nearly destroyed him with an insidious mental attack.

**Mourner**: A slang term for a Cyran refugee.

**Mourning, the**: A disaster that occurred on Olarune 20, 994 YK. The origin and precise nature of the Mourning are unknown. On Ollarune 20, gray mists spread across Cyre, and anything caught within the mists was transformed or destroyed. See *the Mournland*.

**Mournland, The**: A common name for the wasteland left behind in the wake of *the Mourning*. A wall of dead-gray mist surrounds the borders of the land that once was Cyre. Behind this mist, the land has been transformed into something dark and twisted. Most creatures that weren't killed were transformed into horrific monsters. Stories speak of storms of blood, corpses that do not decompose, ghostly soldiers fighting endless battles, and far worse things.

**Mror Holds, The:** A nation of dwarves and gnomes located in the Ironroot Mountains.

**Naelan:** A soldier of the Valenar elves, who fought with Daine at Felmar Valley.

**Nine, the:** A term used to refer to the nine deities of the Sovereign Host.

**Olladra:** The Sovereign of Feast and Fortune, goddess of luck and plenty. Those who follow the Sovereign Host will ask Olladra for aid in risky ventures, and the phrase "Olladra smiles" is used when someone has a stroke of good luck.

**Olladra's Feast:** A holy ritual of the goddess Olladra—a sacred revel that serves as a way of sacrificing food and drink to the goddess.

**Onatar:** A deity of the Sovereign Host, Onatar is Lord of Fire and Forge. He is the patron of both smith and artificer, lending skill to those who follow the traditions of old.

**Pierce:** A warforged soldier, Pierce was built by House Cannith and sold to the army of Cyre. He was designed to serve as a skirmisher and scout, specializing in ranged combat. His comrades named him based on his skill with his longbow. Following the destruction of Cyre, he has chosen to remain with *Daine*, his last captain.

**Qaltiar:** One of the drow tribes of Xen'drik. See Broken Oath.

**Queen's Guard:** One of the titles of the army of Cyre.

**Quori:** Common name for someone or something from the plane of Dal Quor. The inhabitants of Dal Quor are spiritual entities that typically appear as nightmarish to human eyes. Many of these spirits take pleasure in shaping human nightmares and preying on dreaming mortals.

**Riedra:** The largest country on the continent of Sarlona. Once a collection of warring states, Riedra overcame its internal conflicts only to break all ties with the rest of Eberron. After a thousand years of silence, Riedra is only beginning to re-establish diplomatic relations with the nations of Khorvaire, and much about the realm remains a mystery.

**Saerath:** A wizard who served in the support corps of the Queen's Guard of Cyre. Saereth served under *Daine* but has not been seen since the Battle of Keldan Ridge.

**Sahuagin:** A race of amphibious humanoids that live in the oceans of Eberron. Aggressive sahuagin tribes often attack ships that cross their territory; other sahuagin sell their services as aquatic guides.

**Sakhesh, Maru:** The high priest of the Draconist temple in Stormreach.

**Sarlona:** One of the continents of Eberron. Humanity arose in Sarlona, and colonists from Sarlona established human civilization on Khorvaire.

**Scorpion Wraith:** A sacred warrior of the Qaltiar drow, blessed with the speed and skill of the predator. "Scorpion wraith" translates to "Vulk N'tash" in the tongue of the Qaltiar,

**Sentinel Marshals:** The dragonmarked House Deneith is the primary source for mercenary soldiers and bodyguards in Khorvaire. The Sentinel Marshals are a specialized form of mercenary—bounty hunters empowered to enforce the laws of Galifar across Khorvaire. This right was granted by the King of Galifar, but when Galifar collapsed the rulers of the Five Nations agreed to let the Sentinel Marshals pursue their prey across all nations, to maintain a neutral lawkeeping force that would be respected throughout Khorvaire. See *House Deneith*.

**Seren:** 1) A chain of islands on the west coast of Argonnessen. 2) Common name for someone or something from the Seren Islands.

**Shadow Marches, The:** A region of desolate swamps on the southwestern coast of Khorvaire.

**Sharn:** The largest city in Khorvaire. Also known as the City of Towers.

**Sharn Watch:** The force that maintains order in the city of Sharn. The Watch is spread throughout the city, and each quarter of Sharn has its own garrison. In addition to the main force of guards, there are a number of specialized divisions of the Watch. The Gold Wings provide aerial reconnaissance and support. The Blackened Book deals with magical crimes. The Guardians of the Gate monitor the activities of foreigners. And the Redcloak Battalion are an elite military unit that can be deployed against deadly foes—demons, enemy commandoes, or similar threats.

**Shifter:** A humanoid race said to be descended from humans and lycanthropes. Shifters have a feral, bestial appearance and can briefly call on their lycanthropic heritage to draw animalistic characteristics to the fore. While they are most comfortable in natural environs, shifters can be found in most of the major cities of Khorvaire.

**Shen'kar:** The commander of one of the scorpion wraith squads of the Qaltiar drow.

**Ship's Cat:** An inn located in the city of Stormreach, owned by the shifter Harysh.

**Shira:** A magical intelligence created during an ancient war between the giants of Xen'drik and the plane of Dal Quor.

**Siberys:** 1) The ring of stones that circle the world. 2) A mythical dragon, also called "The Dragon Above." Siberys is said to have been destroyed by Khyber. Some believe that the ring of Siberys is the source of all magic. See *Eberron, Khyber.*

**Silver Flame, the:** A powerful spiritual force dedicated to cleaning evil influences from the world. Over the last five hundred years, a powerful church has been established around the Silver Flame.

**Silverwax:** Wax charged with mystical energy. Silverwax candles are an important component in the creation of many minor magical items.

**Sivis, House:** A dragonmarked house bearing the Mark of Scribing.

**Skycoach:** A small flying vessel, typically shaped like a rowboat or gondola. The magic that allows a skycoach to fly is tied to the manifest zone around Sharn; as a result, these vehicles will not function far from Sharn, and are only found in the City of Towers.

**Smalltooth:** A small carnivorous reptile. Halfling innkeepers often keep smallteeth around to control vermin.

**Sovereign:** 1) A silver coin depicting a current or recent monarch. A sovereign is worth ten crowns. 2) One of the deities of the Sovereign Host. See *Sovereign Host*.

**Sovereign Host, the:** A pantheistic religion with a strong following across Khorvaire.

**Stormreach:** The largest human city on the continent of Xen'drik. Once a pirate outpost, this port sees vessels from Khorvaire, Aerenal, and even Sarlona.

**Straits of Shargon:** A series of islands and dangerous reefs that lie between Khorvaire and Xen'drik.

**Sul'asa:** In the language of the giants, "the Burning Wood." A region of Xen'drik noted for the fiery color of its foliage.

**Sulatar:** One of the drow cultures of Xen'drik. "Sulatar" means "firebinder" in the language of the giants. Thousands of years ago, the Sulatar drow were taught techniques of fire magic by giant wizards, and the dark elves retained much of this knowledge even after the cataclysm that destroyed the giant nations. The Sulatar are deeply religious and believe that their faith will be rewarded with immortality and power with which to conquer all of Eberron.

**Tal:** A beverage from the Talenta Plains. Tal was introduced to the Five Nations by the halflings of House Ghallanda. Made by steeping herbs in boiling water, it serves many purposes depending on the herbs that are used. There are dozens of varieties. Milian tal is typically served cold and is said to settle a fever, while blackroot tal is served hot and is a popular midday drink.

**Tarkanan, House:** A criminal organization based in Sharn, specializing in theft and assassination. Only people possessing aberrant dragonmarks can join House Tarkanan, and the members of the house are taught to hone these skills to aid in their work. The organization is structured as a mockery of the true dragonmarked houses, in remembrance of the aberrant alliance that arose during the War of the Mark. See *aberrant dragonmark, War of the Mark*.

**Tashana:** The implacable enemy of Lakashtai. Tashana is a deadly combatant whose physical skills are enhanced by her mental abilities.

**Teeth of the Devourer:** Another name for the Straits of Shargon—specifically, the dangerous reefs and rocks that can shatter a ship's hull.

**Thaask:** A sahuagin guide who sells his services to ships traveling through the Straits of Shargon.

**Thrane:** One of the original Five Nations of Galifar, Thrane is the seat of power for the Church of the Silver Flame. During the Last War, the people of Thrane chose to give the church power above that of the throne. Queen Diani ir'Wynarn serves as a figurehead, but true power rests in the hands of the Church, which is governed by the council of cardinals and Jaela Daeran, the young Keeper of the Flame.

**Thunder Sea:** The body of water that separates Khorvaire and Xen'drik. The Thunder Sea derives its name from the storms that often ravage the region.

**Towers of the Twelve:** A foundation for mystical research and development formed as a joint effort by all of the dragonmarked houses.

**Traveler, the:** Loosely aligned with the Dark Six, this deity is the embodiment of intrigue and artifice.

**Treaty of Thronehold:** The treaty that ended the Last War.

**Tribex:** A large quadruped used as livestock and beasts of burden across much of Khorvaire.

**Trolanport:** The capital city of Zilargo.

**Tsucora:** The most common order of quori spirit. Tsucoras are said to feed off of the fear and terror of mortal dreamers.

**Uul'she:** A scorpion wraith of the Qaltiar drow.

**Undersharn:** The tunnels that run below the city of Sharn. In addition to the sewers, Undersharn includes the ruins of older cities built long before Sharn.

**Valenar:** 1) A nation in southeastern Khorvaire, founded by an army of warrior elves. 2) Common name for someone or something from the Valenar nation.

**Vulk N'tash:** See scorpion wraith.

**Xen'drik:** A large continent directly south of Khorvaire. Once home to an advanced civilization of giants, Xen'drik was devastated by a terrible cataclysm almost forty thousand years ago. The effects of this magical disaster still linger: space and time are often unpredictable in Xen'drik, and many strange creatures and cultures have appeared in this shattered land.

**Xoriat:** Another plane of existence, known as the Realm of Madness.

**War of the Mark:** Five hundred years before the creation of Galifar, the dragonmarked families joined forces to eliminate those who possessed aberrant marks. Ultimately the aberrants joined forces and formed an army of their own, under the leadership of Lord Halas Tarkanan and his lover, the Lady of the Plague. Despite Tarkanan's skill and personal power, his troops were few in number and poorly organized, and he could not stand against the dragonmarked. In the aftermath of the war, the families formally established the first dragonmarked houses. See *aberrant dragonmarks, dragonmarks, dragonmarked houses, House Tarkanan.*

**Warforged:** A race of humanoid constructs crafted from wood, leather, metal, and stone, and given life and sentience through magic. The warforged were created by House Cannith, which sought to produce tireless, expendable soldiers capable of adapting to any tactical situation. Cannith developed a wide range of military automatons, but the spark of true sentience eluded them until 965 YK, when *Aaren d'Cannith* perfected the first of the modern warforged. A warforged soldier is roughly the same shape as an adult male human, though typically slightly taller and heavier. There are many different styles of warforged, each crafted for a specific military function—heavily-armored infantry troops, faster scouts and skirmishers, and many more. While warforged are brought into existence with the knowledge required to fulfill their function, they have the capacity to learn, and with the war coming to a close, many are searching their souls—and questioning whether they have souls—and wondering what place they might have in a world at peace.

**Whitehearth**: A House Cannith forgehold in Cyre. Presumed destroyed in the Mourning.

**Xu'sasar**: A scorpion wraith of the Qaltiar drow.

**Xuxajor**: A warrior of the Sulatar drow.

**Yao**: A Goblin affirmation. Usually combined with a name or title; "yao'lhesh" roughly translates to "Yes, sir!"

**YK**: Most of the nations of Khorvaire make use of the calendar of Galifar. The current date is reckoned from the birth of the Kingdom of Galifar, in the Year since the founding of the Kingdom, or more simply, YK.

**Zil**: Common name for someone or something from Zilargo.

**Zilargo**: A nation on the southern coast of Khorvaire. The homeland of the gnomes.

**Zulaje**: The war leader of the Sulatar drow.

# TWO NEW SERIES EMERGE FROM THE RAVAGED WASTES OF... THE WORLD OF

## THE
## LOST MARK
### TRILOGY

## MARKED FOR DEATH
### Book 1

*Matt Forbeck*

Twelve dragonmarks. Sigils of immense magical power. Born by scions of mighty Houses, used through the centuries to wield authority and shape wonders throughout the Eberron world. But there are only twelve marks. Until now. Matt Forbeck begins the terrifying saga of the thirteenth dragonmark . . . The Mark of Death.

## THE
## DRAGON BELOW
### TRILOGY

## THE BINDING STONE
### Book 1

*Don Bassingthwaite*

A chance rescue brings old rivals together with a strange ally in a mission of vengeance against powers of ancient madness and corruption. But in the haunted forests of the Eldeen Reaches, even the most stalwart hero can soon find himself prey to the hidden horrors within the untamed wilderness.

# ENTER THE EXCITING, NEW DUNGEONS AND DRAGONS® SETTING... THE WORLD OF

## THE
# WAR~TORN
### TRILOGY

## THE CRIMSON TALISMAN
### Book 1

*Adrian Cole*

Erethindel, the fabled Crimson Talisman. Long sought by the
forces of darkness. Long guarded in secret by one family. But
now the secret has been revealed, and only one young man
can keep it safe. As the talisman's powers awaken within him,
Erethindel tears at his soul.

## THE ORB OF XORIAT
### Book 2

*Edward Bolme*

The Last War is over, and it took all that Teron ever had. A monk
trained for war, he is the last of his Order. Now he is on a quest
to find a powerful weapon that might set the world at war again.

# ED GREENWOOD

### THE CREATOR OF THE FORGOTTEN REALMS WORLD

### BRINGS YOU THE STORY OF

### SHANDRIL OF HIGHMOON

## SHANDRIL'S SAGA

### SPELLFIRE
*Book I*

Powerful enough to lay low a dragon or heal a wounded warrior, spellfire
is the most sought after power in all of Faerûn. And it is in the reluctant
hand of Shandril of Highmoon, a young, orphaned kitchen-lass.

### CROWN OF FIRE
*Book II*

Shandril has grown to become one of the most powerful magic-users in
the land. The powerful Cult of the Dragon and the evil Zhentarim want
her spellfire, and they will kill whoever they must to possess it.

### HAND OF FIRE
*Book III*

Shandril has spellfire, a weapon capable of destroying the world, and
now she's fleeing for her life across Faerûn, searching for somewhere to
hide. Her last desperate hope is to take refuge in the sheltered city of
Silverymoon. If she can make it.

### www.wizards.com

# DRAGONS ARE DESCENDING ON THE FORGOTTEN REALMS!

## THE RAGE
*The Year of Rogue Dragons, Book I*

### RICHARD LEE BYERS

Renegade dragon hunter Dorn hates dragons with a passion few can believe, let alone match. He has devoted his entire life to killing every dragon he can find, but as a feral madness begins to overtake the dragons of Faerûn, civilization's only hope may lie in the last alliance Dorn would ever accept.

## THE RITE
*The Year of Rogue Dragons, Book II*

### RICHARD LEE BYERS

Dragons war with dragons in the cold steppes of the Bloodstone Lands, and the secret of the ancient curse gives a small band of determined heroes hope that the madness might be brought to an end.

## REALMS OF THE DRAGONS
*Book I*

### EDITED BY PHILIP ATHANS

This anthology features all-new stories by R.A. Salvatore, Ed Greenwood, Elaine Cunningham, and the authors of the R.A. Salvatore's War of the Spider Queen series. It fleshes out many of the details from the current Year of Rogue Dragons trilogy by Richard Lee Byers and includes a short story by Byers.

## REALMS OF THE DRAGONS
*Book II*

### EDITED BY PHILIP ATHANS

A new breed of Forgotten Realms authors bring a fresh approach to new stories of mighty dragons and the unfortunate humans who cross their paths.